CRUEL AS THE GRAVE

CRUEL AS THE GRAVE

Cynthia Harrod-Eagles

This first world edition published 2020
in Great Britain and 2021 in the USA by
SEVERN HOUSE PUBLISHERS LTD of
Eardley House, 4 Uxbridge Street, London W8 7SY.
Trade paperback edition first published
in Great Britain and the USA 2021 by
SEVERN HOUSE PUBLISHERS LTD.

British Library Cataloguing in Publication Data
A CIP catalogue record for this title is available from the British Library.

ISBN-13: 978-0-7278-9085-6 (cased)
ISBN-13: 978-1-78029-743-9 (trade paper)
ISBN-13: 978-1-4483-0471-4 (e-book)

This is a work of fiction. Names, characters, places and incidents are either the
product of the author's imagination or are used fictitiously. Except where actual
historical events and characters are being described for the storyline of this novel,
all situations in this publication are fictitious and any resemblance to actual
persons, living or dead, business establishments, events or locales is purely
coincidental.

All Severn House titles are printed on acid-free paper.

Severn House Publishers support the Forest Stewardship Council™ [FSC™],
the leading international forest certification organisation.
All our titles that are printed on FSC certified paper carry the FSC logo.

Typeset by Palimpsest Book Production Ltd.,
Falkirk, Stirlingshire, Scotland.
Printed and bound in Great Britain by
TJ Books Limited, Padstow, Cornwall.

ONE

Another Day, Another Douleur

Atherton was singing, in his Dean Martin voice. 'When you're down by the sea, and an eel bites your knee, that's a moray.'

'For God's sake!' Slider muttered.

'I thought you liked my singing.'

'I'm cursing the traffic. I love your singing. Your singing fills me with transcendent delight.'

'Well, if you're going to be like that about it, I shall sit here in wounded silence.'

It was a warm day for November, but a glum one, under a sky like wet dishrags. There were roadworks in Holland Road, with a coned-off lane and contraflow, turning the normally heavy traffic to automotive molasses. Behind the cones, eight men in hard hats and hi-vis jackets stood with their hands in their pockets staring at the tarmac. Well, it was a rotten job, but somebody had to do it.

And why did everyone these days choose grey cars, Slider wondered. The only bit of colour anywhere was the big red bus he was crawling behind.

Now a motorcyclist was trying to overtake him, despite the fact that there was no possibility of getting past the bus. 'There's no hope for mankind, is there?' Slider said.

'No, there is no hope,' said Atherton. 'But don't let it get you down. Next on the right.'

Russell Close was a short side turning, now taped off to traffic and full of the various police vehicles generated by a murder shout. Its right boundary was the high blank end-wall of the terrace of houses on Holland Road. Its left was a parade of four shops: a laundry and dry cleaners; the Kwik-Fix Heel and Key Bar; a rather dusty-looking shop called K D Electronics, its window obscured by venetian blinds; and a newsagent-tobacconist. At the end of the close was a newish block of flats.

Atherton, Slider's bagman and friend, gestured towards them. 'That's it. Russell Court.'

'There used to be a pub there,' said Slider.

'I remember. Called The Russell. Big Victorian place.'

'They did live jazz at weekends. I went there once with Joanna because a trumpeter friend of hers was playing. Shame it's gone.'

Pubs were closing everywhere. More and more, people didn't want to go out and mingle with live human beings, preferring to stay at home with their screens. Slider wondered where it would end. Already teachers were reporting that children were starting school almost unable to talk; and there were teenagers with such poor communication skills they had trouble ordering food in restaurants, or buying ket from their local dealer.

Where The Russell had stood there was a square, three-storey block of nine 'luxury' flats, in yellow brick, with blank, surprised-looking windows. Anti-glare glass gave them the blankness, but why, Slider wondered, the surprise? Then he realized it was because each embrasure had an arc of decorative end-on bricks over it: supercilia. Well, at least the architect had made the effort. It was marginally less ugly than most new buildings.

They got out, and Atherton stretched, catlike. Tall, elegant, sartor's plaything, he was as out of place at a dreary crime scene as an orchid in a vegetable patch.

He consulted the note. 'Flat six, it says here. Deceased is Erik Lingoss. With a k. *Why?*'

'Perhaps we shall never know,' Slider said tersely. It was too early in the day for questions that could not be answered, especially a day that began with a murder and wretched traffic, plus heartburn from last night's pizza. Joanna was heavily pregnant and hadn't felt like cooking, and Dad, who lived in the granny flat with his new wife and could usually be relied upon to don the white cap, had been out at a Scrabble tournament. Slider had promised Jo to bring something home and had planned on fish and chips, but had forgotten that their local chipper was closed on a Tuesday. By that time he had been too tired to look further afield than the convenience store on the corner, where the only immediately edible thing available was a heat-it-yourself pepperoni pizza. Slider had never liked pizza. Now he hated it.

The street door was wedged open. The unfortunately-named PC

Organ was keeping the log, and marked them in. The entry hall still smelled faintly of plaster, and the exhibition-grade beige carpeting was not yet filthy: the block was only a couple of years old.

Another uniform, the handsome and agreeable PC D'Arblay, filled them in as they trod up the stairs.

'Cause of death is several heavy blows to the head. The girl-friend called it in at about a quarter to eight this morning. She's a Kelly-Ann Hayes, age nineteen. She says she found him like that when she arrived this morning, but there was blood on her clothes and her hands and face, and no signs of break-in and no apparent robbery.' His exposition ended on a hopeful uptone. It was good to have an obvious suspect.

Slider merely grunted. Crimes of passion were often easy to solve, especially when the perpetrator was found standing over the body with a bloodied poker saying 'he was asking for it'; on the other hand, they could be the most harrowing.

'Forensics have nearly finished, sir, and Doc Cameron's here.'

'And the suspect?'

'She was hysterical and we couldn't get any sense out of her, so Lawrence has taken her back to the station to get swabbed, bagged and checked over by the doctor.'

The flat's door was also wedged open, and all the lights were on. A small army in ghostly white coveralls was padding about inside performing their mysterious rituals, and it wasn't a big flat to start with ('luxury' in developer-language meant there was a street door that locked and a lift: size didn't come into it). Bob Bailey, the Scenes of Crime Manager, confronted them prohibitively in the doorway. 'We've nearly finished,' he said loftily, 'then you can come in.' SOC Manager was a civilian post, so not under police discipline, more was the pity. Bailey waved a transparent evidence bag temptingly before Slider's nose. 'Deceased's in the bedroom. We've got the murder weapon. Nice bloody fingermarks on it, and they look good for the girl, so you shouldn't have any trouble with this one.' They carried a field kit for the preliminary matching of fingerprints: of course, more detailed analysis would be needed for a court case, but often it gave a useful early indication.

'Nice of you to do our job for us,' Atherton said with delicate irony. After all those American CSI shows where a man in sunglasses with his hands on his hips solved the crime through science alone without bothering the detectives, it was hard to be gracious to the forensic bods.

The object in the bag was a three-kilogram neoprene barbell, with obvious blood and matter on the hexagonal head. The weight was helpfully embossed on the end.

'Deceased was obviously a fitness nut,' Bailey went on. 'He's got all the kit in there. And we've got his laptop, but no mobile.'

'That's odd,' Slider said. What young person these days didn't have a mobile? They practically popped out of the womb welded to them.

'Maybe the girl's got it on her,' Bailey said indifferently. 'Oh, the doc wants you.' His men were drifting out of the bedroom. 'Yes, all right, you can go in now,' he concluded grudgingly.

The bed was a super-king-sized mattress on a frame which was all-of-a-piece with the headboard and cabinets – what looked like a custom job in light oak with a built-in overhead shelf and reading lights. The wall to the right, as you lay in bed, was covered with a mirror-doored fitted wardrobe. The wall opposite the end of the bed was also completely mirrored, and in front of it the wooden floor was laid with rubber gym mats, on which stood a weights bench, a weights rack of dumb-bells, and a complicated resistance machine, all chrome and black leather, for working the arms and legs. The overhead lighting was from sunken halogen lamps. Something struck Slider as odd, and it took a moment to realize that there was no window in the room. From the position of the flat, it must have been behind the mirrored wall. Obviously having the mirror to work in had been more important to the occupant than daylight: reflection trumping refraction.

Freddie Cameron, the forensic pathologist, greeted him. 'Bill! I hoped it would be you. Long time no see. How's Joanna? She must be due any moment.'

'Another three weeks,' Slider said. 'End of the month.'

'But all's well this time?'

'Yes, thanks. She seems blooming.'

Cameron gave him a canny look. Slider was in any case a

worrier, and Joanna had had a miscarriage last time. 'Well, nearly over now,' he said. 'Then you can relax.'

Slider almost laughed. 'Yes, relax with a newborn in the house! Tell me about deceased.'

'Seems to be in his early thirties, extremely fit-looking, probably about five foot ten. Appears healthy and well-nourished, no apparent drug use, no apparent injuries apart from the blows to the head.'

The body was lying prone beside the bed, wearing only a pair of grey sweatpants that even Slider could see were expensive and well-fitting. The naked upper body was well-muscled and unblemished, the bare feet were clean and the nails unusually well-kept, suggesting he had visited a pedicurist. Few people could cut their own toenails that well.

'This was the first blow, you see,' Cameron said, 'to the left temple. It would have felled him, may have caused him to lose consciousness, but it didn't kill him, to judge from the quantity of blood. Scalp wounds do give rise to a lot of passive leakage even after death, but the spread suggests more active bleeding.' There was a considerable pool under the head. 'Then there was a second attack with several blows to the back of the head, probably four, given with extreme violence. They would have been fatal.'

They had been powerful blows, Slider noted. The skull had been smashed and grey matter as well as blood clotted the hair.

'In my estimation,' Cameron went on, 'there was a gap of a few minutes between the first blow and the second attack, otherwise the bleeding would not have been so extensive.'

'She must have thought she'd killed him first off.' This was Bailey, looking over their shoulders. 'Then he started to move, and she had to finish him off.' *Simple*, said his look. *I could do your job, easy.*

Cameron's assistants had now turned the body over, so Slider could see the face. It was firm-featured, with a straight nose and attractive mouth; so far as any face could be when dead and devoid of animation, you'd have called it unusually handsome. The hair was dark brown, springy, expensively cut and highlighted; the hands were professionally groomed. The skin was smooth and lightly tanned. There was no jewellery, no tattoos. A man who took care of his body and his appearance.

'Primed and ready for love,' Atherton commented.

'Until she killed him,' said Slider.

Freddie nodded. 'He probably loved not wisely but too many. Looks the sort. The "frenzied attack" of phrase and fable so often stems from plain old jealousy.'

'But she said she found him like this,' Slider mused.

'Well, she would say that, wouldn't she?' said Bailey impatiently.

Slider ignored him and looked at Cameron. 'I didn't ask – what about time of death?'

Freddie nodded to his men to start bagging the body. 'From the condition of the blood, the temperature, and the lividity and rigor, I'd say six to twelve hours – probably closer to twelve. You're looking at late yesterday evening.'

'Not this morning?' Atherton said, the disappointment apparent in his voice.

'Define "this morning",' Freddie said, with a shrug. 'But if you mean just before she phoned it in, then no. Most likely, it was between ten and twelve last night.'

With the forensic team pulling out, they could look round the rest of the flat. The kitchen had new-looking expensive fittings, and everything was sparkling clean. If anyone had eaten here recently, they must have washed up and put away the dishes. In the fridge were bottles of water, cartons of energy drink, an unopened tub of cottage cheese and one of natural yoghurt, a carton of oat milk, a bottle of probiotic drink, a box of eggs, and a lonely pack of tofu. The vegetable drawer was full of salad and vegetables; in the freezer were several steaks, chicken fillets and portions of fish.

In the first cupboard there were boxes of cruelly fibrous cereal, energy bars, tubs of protein powder, packets of brown rice, quinoa, oats and spelt, and instant couscous mix. Opening a second, Atherton ducked as something fell out on him. The cupboard was packed with vitamin and mineral supplements. Atherton looked at the little plastic tub he had caught on the rebound from his bonce. 'High strength omega 3,' he read.

'Are you hurt?'

'Super fish oil injuries. The man's a health nut.'

'The body is a temple,' Slider reminded him.

'Up to a point. Let he who is without sin bore the pants off everybody else.'

The living room was smaller than the bedroom: obviously he had chosen the larger room for his bedroom so as to accommodate the gym equipment. It was very spare and modern, with a bare wood floor, everything done in shades of grey, cream and beige. There was an enormous fawn leather sofa, two punishingly avant-garde canvas and chrome armchairs and a glass-topped coffee table. Opposite the sofa was an enormous TV. In one corner was a small round table with two upright chairs, and a sort of low sideboard on which stood several framed photographs – the only sign of personality in the room. Everything was inhumanly clean and tidy, as if the developers had just left and no one lived here yet.

The photographs turned out to be of deceased himself. One was a moodily-lit black and white sports shot, a close-up of him lifting a weight, muscles bulging, and looking sidelong and sultry into the camera. One showed him in dinner jacket on a stage of some kind receiving a scroll from a well-kept older man with bouffant white hair and a Hollywood tan. Deceased was beaming with film star teeth and the bouffant one looked as if he'd been taxidermied. The third showed him in chinos and a sweater over a checked shirt, sleeves rolled up, sitting on a country gate, feet up on a lower rung, smile casually charming, hair slightly windblown – why was it, Slider wondered, that one felt the wind had co-operated in the shot? It looked like an illustration from a men's fashion catalogue. The fourth was a studio portrait, in a close-fitting, V-necked jumper, looking slightly away from camera, the lighting throwing his cheekbones into relief, making him appear lean, serious, and uncommonly handsome.

'Somebody likes himself,' Atherton commented sourly.

Slider was fighting down his own feeling of irritation with the man. 'Notice there are no women in the shots. No trophy hanging on the arm.'

'Likewise no dear old mum,' Atherton added. 'No family shot. No jolly group of pals. He was the star of his own show, all right.'

There were two more frames, larger, and they were not photographs, but certificates fancily done, with an embossed scrolled heading and elaborate colophon, issued by David Gillespie Fitness and Leisure Clubs Ltd: awards for Personal Trainer of the Year for each of the past two years, with the name Erik Lingoss, with a k, inscribed in heavy black italic inkwork.

The Gillespie clubs were a countrywide franchise, so it was probably praise worth having. It also nailed down his job, and the reason for his fitness.

One of Slider's own came up behind him: his other sergeant, Hart, still in coveralls, but with the mobcap and mask removed now forensics had finished. Her hair was plaited today in thin rows from front to back, the plaits gathered together in a figure-eight chignon at the back, like a sleeping nest of black snakes. She looked neat, elegant and dangerous – the latter would probably have been her preferred epithet.

'Interesting,' she said. 'There's a Gillespie's in Lime Grove, boss.'

'I know. Where the old swimming baths used to be.'

Hart looked blank. She was too young to remember the swimming baths. 'Anyway, that's the nearest,' she said. 'Maybe he worked there.' She sniffed. 'Who would bother framing a poxy certificate from their employer?'

'It must have meant something to him,' Slider said. 'There's nothing else on display.' He glanced around. 'It's not what you'd call a cosy nest, is it? No books, not even a magazine, no entertainment apart from the TV – not even any music.'

Hart looked at him kindly. 'iPod in the bedroom, guv. And who reads books?'

Slider felt mulish. 'Did you find any paperwork? Letters, bills, bank statements, credit card statements.'

She looked even kinder. 'All done online these days, guv. Nobody has paperwork hanging around any more. But,' she went on quickly, 'we did find a couple of Moleskines, a notebook and a diary. We've bagged them up. And his laptop was on the coffee table.'

'So I heard. I suppose we have to be thankful for small mercies. Can we move on – all this pastel blandness is giving me an ice-cream headache.'

'I was just going to get the canvass organized, boss, if you've finished with me here,' Hart said.

'All right. Carry on. I'll finish looking round, get a feeling for the place.'

The bathroom was spotless, and contained a huge variety of grooming aids: hair products, skin unguents, toners, creams and serums, bath oils, shower gels, colognes and after-shaves, nose-clippers, tweezers, *two* magnifying mirrors, electric hair tongs, and in a cupboard in the corner the largest collection of fluffy towels of different sizes that Slider had ever seen.

Atherton marvelled over it all. 'And I thought *I* was fussy.'

'It's his profession,' said Slider. 'With you it's only a hobby.'

Atherton investigated a leather toilet bag on the windowsill. 'Is this make-up?'

'Must be the girlfriend's.'

'No, this one says foundation for men.' He pulled out various sticks and bottles. 'It's all for men. Stone the crows, it's a bag of butch slap.'

'Or it's a pigment of your imagination,' Slider offered.

'Pinch me. Nope. It's real all right. And, by the way, no girlie stuff, you notice. It's looking as though the girlfriend didn't spend much time here. Didn't live here, anyway.'

And so back to the bedroom, now minus the body. Only a ghastly stain showed where it had been. 'Sic transit,' said Slider.

'Inglorious Tuesday,' Atherton replied.

On one of the bedside cabinets there was a leather-covered box, which proved to contain six wristwatches. They fitted into purpose-built slots, so the box was evidently meant to contain them. 'It's a watch caddy,' Atherton informed him, keeping a straight face. 'What man can manage without one?'

'Six?' Slider queried with a pained expression.

'To go with different outfits,' said Atherton. 'They're good ones,' he noted. 'He must have been making a good screw.'

'But they're still here, so no robbery motive.' Slider opened the bedside drawers. 'Condoms in both of them. An unopened twelve pack of thin-feel in this one, plus two loose ones, and an opened forty-eight variety pack in the other.'

Atherton gave a soundless whistle. 'That's a lot of action. Any little stimulants to hand?'

Slider shook his head. 'Nothing pharmaceutical except a pack of ibuprofen. No sign of drugs at all. This was a clean-living boy.'

'And – did you notice? – no alcohol anywhere. Not so much as a can of beer. That's unnatural.'

'I'm beginning to suspect narcissism was his drug of choice.'

The mirrored wardrobe contained a large collection of fine clothes, all clean, carefully hung and impressively organized. Suits were hung together, jackets and coats together, trousers in another place, leisure clothes in another, shirts arranged by colour. Some sweaters were hung up on padded hangers, others – the pure wool ones – were folded in a range of cedar drawers inside one end of the wardrobe. Other drawers held T-shirts and underwear. Shoes and trainers – a multiplicity of them – were neatly racked. There were two pairs of shoes in boxes that appeared never to have been worn.

'The man's inhuman!' Atherton complained. 'Look, look at this tag – he had his jeans dry-cleaned! Who does that?'

'And it looks as though his underpants have been ironed,' Slider said, similarly bemused.

'If he made the girlfriend do it,' said Atherton, 'that may be why she slugged him. I know I would.'

'Speaking of the girlfriend – there are no women's clothes here.'

'It's definite, then, she *wasn't* living here,' Atherton said.

On the narrow top shelf of the wardrobe – the sort of make-up space left by fitting the wardrobes floor to ceiling, the place where you put things you didn't use often, because they were inconveniently high up – there were two expensive tennis racquets in leather covers, and a box containing a pair of black inline fitness skates. That seemed to be all, until Atherton, with his extra reach, felt all the way back, and pulled out another shoe box. 'What was wrong with this pair?' he said.

But inside were bundles of notes, fifties and twenties, held together by rubber bands. Atherton did a quick count. 'Fifties are twenty to a bundle – that's one, two, three . . . nine, ten. No, eleven. Eleven thousand pounds. And twenties – also twenty to a bundle, how annoying of him – four hundred pounds each, five of them, another two thousand. Thirteen thousand pounds. Well, well. I wonder what he was up to.'

'Need he have been up to anything?'

'Normal people don't keep large amounts of cash in the wardrobe.'

'He might just have been suspicious of banks,' Slider said.

'Oh, I do hope not,' said Atherton. 'I've taken a dislike to Mr Clean Living. No one's that spotless. I want him to be bad.'

'Well, at least it's more evidence of no robbery.' He stood still and looked around, frowning. 'She said she found him like that this morning. And he was killed earlier.'

'It's not necessarily a setback,' Atherton reasoned. 'She had a row with him last night and slugged him. Ran off in a panic. Then this morning returned to the scene of the crime like a dog to its vomit—'

'Thank you for that image.'

'And realized properly what she'd done. Cue weeping, hysteria—'

'And calling the police.'

'To make herself look less guilty. "Wasn't me, guv – it was me what called you in."'

'Well, it could have been that way, I suppose,' Slider allowed. You couldn't expect the ordinary members of public to act rationally. And it was surprising how often people did return to the scene of the crime, particularly when the crime had been committed on impulse, in a violent passion. A mixture of curiosity and disbelief compelled them to have another look. Did I really do that? Wow, I really *did* do that.

'And she was all over blood,' Atherton added reassuringly.

Finally, back to the bed. It had been made – in the sense that the duvet had been pulled up and smoothed and the pillows were undented. If it weren't for the evidence of the blood, they might have concluded that it had not been slept in. Slider lifted the pillows to look underneath them. 'Hello!' he said. 'What have we here?'

It was a folded bundle of banknotes – twenties. Slider counted them. 'Seven hundred pounds. Now what's that all about?'

'A test, like the princess and the pea?' Atherton suggested. 'If she could feel the money through the pillow, she was of the true blood royal.'

'It suggests payment for sex,' Slider said, with a frown. 'Otherwise, why under the pillow?'

'But who was paying whom?' Atherton asked.

As they came out of the flat's door, Slider noted that the door to number five, opposite, was open a crack. Someone was watching through the gap. Slider looked across enquiringly. The door opened revealing a tiny old lady, who beckoned, importantly but nervously. She looked ancient, but was smartly dressed in a tweed skirt, twinset and pearls, and shiny court shoes. Her white hair was permed and carefully arranged, her face fully made up. She looked benign and attractive, but more importantly, her bright blue eyes were intelligent and direct.

'Are you the chief officer?' she asked. 'The "boss"?' It was clear from her tone that there were inverted commas round the colloquialism.

'I'm Detective Chief Inspector Slider, ma'am, and I'll be heading this investigation. This is Detective Sergeant Atherton.'

She ignored Atherton. It was the top dog she wanted. Slider knew the type. Always complain straight to the manager. Don't waste your time with anyone lower down. And he'd have bet she'd always got what she wanted.

'I'm Mrs Gershovitz,' she told him. 'Ida Gershovitz. That poor young man is dead, isn't he? I saw them carry him out in a bag. And the girl – I saw them take her away, crying most dreadfully. Was it a burglary? There are some bad people about these days. You aren't safe in your own home.'

He felt he ought to reassure her, without giving too much away. 'It wasn't a burglary,' he said. 'Did you know him?'

'Only to speak to. But he always said hello and gave me a smile when we passed in the hall. Nice manners. Not like some I could mention. I was glad to have somebody quiet and pleasant opposite – you just never know these days, do you? And obliging. When I had to get a heavy box down once from the wardrobe, I came across and knocked, and asked him to help me, and he couldn't have been nicer. "Call me Eric," he said. I had an uncle Eric, my father's younger brother. It's a nice name – unusual these days. So he came across and lifted the box down for me with no trouble, just as if it was a feather! I said to him, "My, you're very strong, aren't you?" And he said, "It's my job. I'm a fitness trainer." We had quite a little chat about it. He told me he worked at the gym in Lime Grove, teaching people how to stay fit. Even told me some little exercises I could do.' She smiled to show how absurd that was. '"Never too late to keep yourself fit," he said. "You'll live longer that way." And now he's dead. What a terrible waste!

Just a young man, his whole life ahead of him. I'm ninety-one, do you believe that? Ninety-one, and I'm still here, and he's gone. What a world! Was it an accident? Or heart, maybe? Those very fit ones, they can sometimes be damaging their hearts with all that exertion.'

'Did you hear a disturbance last night?' Slider asked.

'A disturbance? No, I can't say I did. But these flats are well built, well insulated. You don't hear your neighbours much.' She shook her head, thinking, then lifted her eyes to his. 'But they did have a quarrel yesterday, Eric and that young woman.'

'A quarrel? What time was that?'

'It was about half past six. I'd just come back from the social club. My bridge afternoon. It finishes at six, but I'd stopped to talk to Geraldine Beekman. Her husband died just a month ago. The club isn't far, but I get a taxi, because I find the buses difficult – they will start off before you're properly sitting down. My friend Rhona was thrown off her feet that way and broke her hip. And I'd let myself in and come up in the lift, because I can't manage the stairs any more, not easily, and as I got out of the lift, there she was, the young woman, standing at the door arguing with him.'

'What about?'

'Well, I couldn't hear what they were saying, but it looked as if she was asking him for something, pleading with him, and he was refusing. He had his arms folded across his chest, like this, standing in the doorway as if he wasn't going to let her in. And then he saw me, I suppose, because he stepped back and slammed the door, and she rushed past me in tears, and ran down the stairs. I was quite upset about it, because I didn't like to think of him being unkind to her. But of course, one doesn't know what had been going on between them before that. She might have been quite unreasonable, for all one knows.'

Lingoss was obviously her pet, and she didn't want to think badly of him.

'Did you hear anything more that evening, or this morning?' Slider asked.

'No,' she said with genuine regret. 'Nothing. But I was watching television all evening, so I wouldn't, really. And this morning after I got up I didn't hear anything, or know anything about it until I was looking out of the kitchen window and saw the police car arrive down below, and the police come to the door. So naturally I came to my door to see what was going on and who they were coming for.' She shook her head sadly. 'That poor young man.'

'Would you be willing to make a statement about the quarrel yesterday, if it turns out to be important?' Slider asked.

She beamed. 'Certainly. It would be my duty.'

Clearly it would also be her pleasure. Slider thanked her, and they turned away.

'Back to the factory, I think,' said Slider. 'Have a word with the chief suspect.'

'It's annoying that he was killed in the evening,' Atherton said. 'I mean, if the old girl's right, and the girlfriend left him obviously alive, she must have come back.'

'We know she came back,' said Slider impatiently. 'She was there this morning.'

'No, I mean came back in between times to kill him. But it's a lot of to-ing and fro-ing. Makes it look untidy.'

'Relationships are untidy. And why the money under the pillow?'

'That could have been there for a while. Maybe he just hadn't put it away yet.'

'That's no answer,' said Slider.

TWO
Text and the Single Girl

K elly-Ann Hayes had a snubbily pretty face, though at the moment it was swollen and blotchy with weeping. Her eyes were puffed almost closed; and there was also a little crop of fresh spots below the right corner of her mouth. She looked very young, and very pathetic, hunched like a bird in the rain over her misery.

Slider had taken Gascoyne in with him, as having a kinder face than Atherton, who could be intimidating. Swilley was still there for the female cover. She was tall, blonde and babelicious in a Venice Beach sort of way, but there was nothing soft about her. She was the best shot in the firm, and the best at martial arts, and she suffered fools less than gladly. Many a new arrival at the factory started by having a casual crack at her and ended regretting it.

'She's negative for drugs and alcohol,' Swilley reported before they went in, 'and no bruises or scratches, nothing to indicate a struggle. She had blood on the knees of her jeans, her cuffs, and smears on her hands, forehead and cheek.'

'As though she'd brushed her hair back?' he suggested.

'Consistent with that. I haven't managed to get anything out of her yet. Any mention of deceased just starts her crying again.'

'She might respond to a new face,' Slider said. So it proved – though it might be simply that she was responding to his maleness. He had long contended that many, if not most, upset females would prefer to unburden themselves to a fatherly man than to a woman, even a motherly one, which Swilley wasn't. Women expected judgement from other women, while men were there to be manipulated. Atherton said this proved him a world-weary cynic – which was something, coming from Atherton.

But certainly Kelly-Ann looked up as he came in, and her eyes remained on him as he sat down, made a show of making himself comfortable, and asked her if she wanted another cup of tea. She shook her head.

'Now then,' Slider said cosily, 'let's start with you. How old are you, Kelly-Ann?'

'Nineteen,' she answered easily.

'And what do you do?'

'I'm a beauty therapist,' she said with a touch of pride. Slider nodded, and she added, 'At Harmonies.'

'Harmonies? Where's that?'

'At Gillespie's. It's the health and beauty centre there. Gillespie's in Lime Grove.'

Swilley rolled her eyes at Gascoyne; in ten seconds he'd got more out of her than Swilley had in hours. Gascoyne shrugged, not knowing what she was rolling about.

'That must be nice,' Slider said, and Kelly-Ann nodded. Her shoulders were beginning to unhunch. 'What sort of therapies do they do there?'

'Oh, we do everything – hair, nails, waxing, electrolysis. And stuff like massage and reflexology, but you have to have special training for those. But I'm going to do a course on seaweed wraps after Christmas, when it's quieter. It's our busy time now so I can't be spared.'

How easily she had been distracted, Slider thought. Casually he said, not as if it was a question, 'Erik worked there as well, didn't he? Is that where you first met him?'

She put her hands between her thighs and squeezed in, her shoulders going up again. But she said, 'Yeah,' on an outward sigh; and then, as Slider continued to look interested, she went on. 'My first day, he came up for a mud facial. He has one every month, to keep his skin nice, because he says shaving is terrible for men's skin. He gets it on the house, because his appearance is important, to attract clients. It wasn't me that did it, though. Jerrika always did them, and went over his face with tweezers. Ingrown hairs can ruin your skin. They can go septic, like. He's got lovely skin. Soft – but not like a woman's soft. His is firm as well.'

'So how long have you been going out with him?' Slider slipped it in.

'Seven and a half weeks,' she said proudly, which told Slider everything. The affair was so important to her, she still counted half weeks. She was humbled and grateful for the attention of such a god-like creature. Probably besotted by him. But besottedness could easily turn – especially in an intellectually unregulated person – to rage.

'Really!' he said in an impressed way, and then added, with a little concerned-for-you frown, 'But you had a fight last night.'

'No,' she protested – not alarmed yet, but not wanting to admit to a rift in the lute.

'A quarrel, then. You were heard having words with him at the door of the flat.'

Her mouth turned down and her eyes filled alarmingly quickly with tears. How did she do it? She ought to have been all out of them by now.

Slider glanced at Gascoyne, thinking a new distraction was needed. He had a boyish, favourite-nephew look about him that was as far as possible from intimidating. He took his cue, leaned forward slightly, and said gently, 'What did you quarrel about? Was he being mean to you?'

She nodded, then said in a burst, 'So mean! I couldn't believe it! I thought we were . . . you know . . . all right. I was happy. We were happy. And then he said . . . he said . . . he was breaking up with me.'

'And you had no idea?'

She gave a sob, and mashed the tears away angrily with one hand. 'Not a clue. I was supposed to be going over there last night, when he got back from work, about half-six. Then he texted me to say not to come, he didn't want to see me any more. And when I texted back he didn't answer. So I go over anyway, when I was supposed to, and he doesn't even let me in. Just stands at the door and says it's not working for him and he's finished with me.'

'That *is* mean,' Gascoyne said. 'No wonder you were upset.' She nodded gratefully. 'So what did you do?' A shrug.

Slider took it back. 'You ran off when he slammed the door on you. Where did you go?'

'I went home,' she said simply.

'Where's that?'

'Lena Gardens. I share a flat with Jerrika – you know, from Harmonies.'

'Was she there when you got home?'

'No, she came in later. She wasn't very nice to me. She said she could've told me how it would end up. As if I wasn't good enough for Erik! And then she went out again.'

'And what did you do? Did you go out again?'

'No, I stopped in. I was crying – like, a *lot*,' she said defensively. 'I couldn't believe he'd, like, *do* that to me! I loved him so much! And I thought he loved me! And then – just like that, he dumps me. Who *does* that?'

'So you sat and cried,' Slider said temptingly. 'All evening?'

'I watched a movie. *Sleepless in Seattle*. It's like my favourite.'

The bathos almost made him smile. 'And what time did Jerrika come back home?'

'I don't know. I was in my bedroom.'

'You've got a TV in your room?'

She looked blank for a moment, then understood the question. 'I was watching on Netflix. On my phone. It made me cry some more and then I must have fallen asleep because it was morning and I was lying on top of my bed.'

This was not what Slider wanted to hear – an alibi that was no alibi. He wanted it settled one way or the other. 'So when did you go back to the flat?' he asked carefully.

Now she looked shifty for the first time. 'I—' she began, and broke off, as if she was about to say, 'I didn't,' and then realized that was not a tenable position. 'I . . . I went back—'

'I know you did. What time?'

'I dunno. It was in the morning. When I woke up. I thought if I saw him, talked to him, he'd realize it was a mistake and it'd be all right. I . . . I never had a chance to talk to him last night, it was all so quick. I thought . . .'

'So you went back to plead with him.' She looked down at her hands, and said nothing. 'What time was that?'

'It was about seven-ish, I think. I knew he'd be at home – he never left till half-eightish. I thought if I went round . . .' Her eyes slid away from Slider, and sought out Gascoyne. Away from Dad and towards nice cousin Phil. 'See – Erik, he liked to have sex first thing. He always said morning sex was the best. So I thought – well, he'd let me in, and we'd do it, and he'd realize he really did – love me . . .'

Her voice trailed off.

'How did you get in?' Slider asked quietly. If her story was that he buzzed her in, he had her. By any calculation, Lingoss was dead by that hour.

'With my keys.'

'He gave you keys? Surely he'd ask for them back when he broke up with you.'

'He didn't know I had them. He didn't want me to have a key. He was a very private person. I wanted us to live together – I thought it was time – but he said he had to have his space, and maybe one day, but for now . . .'

'So how did you get the keys?'

She turned her eyes away. 'It was – like, one day, he was having a new mattress delivered, and he couldn't wait in for it, so I said I'd do it. He dropped me off a set of keys in the morning and I was to give them back when I saw him in the evening. But after they'd delivered it, I . . .' She actually blushed. 'I nipped across and had them copied at the Kwik-Fix across the road.'

'Now why would you do that?' Slider asked.

She met his eyes, still red, but wordless. He understood – she just wanted a bit of control, to feel she had some hold on the slippery demi-god who held all the power. 'I never used them,' she said defiantly. 'Not till this morning. But I thought – I thought if I rang the bell he mightn't let me in. I thought, if I could just *see* him, if I could just *talk* to him . . .'

He remembered suddenly, from history lessons, that Catherine Howard had run through the corridors of the palace, trying to get to King Henry VIII, convinced if she could only speak to him he wouldn't have the heart to have her beheaded.

It was a depressing image, and rang unfortunately true. He passed it back to Gascoyne while he thought.

'Tell me exactly what you did,' Gascoyne said, 'when you got to the flats. It's important, Kelly-Ann. Everything you did.'

She looked impressed. 'I let myself in downstairs,' she said carefully. 'I went up to the flat. I couldn't decide at first whether to knock or not – I thought he might be angry when he found out I had keys, but then I thought once we'd made love he'd forget about it. And if I knocked he might not let me in. So I let myself in. I called out, "It's only me," but he didn't answer. I hoped he was still in bed, then I could just get in with him. So I went to the bedroom, and – and there he was.' She stopped with a shudder.

'I'm sorry,' Gascoyne said. 'Tell me exactly what you saw.'

'He was laying there. I could see blood on his face and on the floor. And his head was all . . . all bashed in. I didn't believe it at first. I didn't think it was real.'

'Not real?'

'You know, like people have those Halloween masks with all, like, horrible big wounds and eyeballs falling out and everything, and they're, like, so realistic. I thought he was, like, playing a trick. I thought he'd jump up and scare me. So I said, "Erik, stop messing around," but he never moved. And then I went up and touched him and it was—' She stopped. Then she added, in a low voice like a moan, 'I could smell the blood. It was horrible.'

'Is that when you knelt down beside him?' Gascoyne asked.

'You what?' She sounded bewildered.

Swilley spoke, a little impatiently. 'You had blood on the knees of your jeans.'

'I suppose – I must have knelt in it,' she said vaguely. 'I touched – where it was all bashed in. I thought it wasn't real. But it was.'

'And where was the dumb-bell?' Gascoyne asked.

'What dumb-bell?'

'You know what dumb-bell,' Swilley said relentlessly.

Her eyes dilated a little as she looked at Swilley. Perhaps she was beginning to realize she was in trouble. 'It was laying just there, beside him. I–I must've picked it up. I couldn't work out – I thought it wasn't real. But I saw there was all like blood and . . . and . . . brain stuff on it, and I like threw it away from me.' Unconsciously she wiped her hands on her knees as if reliving the feeling. 'Then I knew he was really dead and I didn't know what to do. So I rung nine-nine-nine.'

She stopped, and looked from Swilley to Gascoyne and finally, pleadingly, at Slider. 'I did the right thing, didn't I? I called the police. I didn't know what else to do.'

Det Sup Porson, Slider's immediate boss, was surging restlessly around his office like a storm in a teacup. He rarely sat down; and indeed, stillness in Porson could be a phenomenon to alarm. Either he was sick, or you were in very deep trouble.

'Clear-up rates? Have you done the figures?' he barked as Slider appeared.

'I was going to start them today,' Slider said mildly. 'Until this came up.'

'Right. Right.' Porson nodded his massive head. Outside the window the grey day had sunk into twilight, and under the cruel strip lighting he looked old and bumpy. His tie had the tight and greasy look about the knot that comes from taking it off over your head every evening rather than untying it. He had lived alone since his dear wife had died. She would never have allowed that. 'What have you got so far?'

Slider summarized the facts. 'We've got a team out doing the canvass,' he concluded. 'We've got his laptop but no mobile phone. No sign of break-in or theft.'

'And the girlfriend was standing over the body covered in blood?' Porson always knew things before he was told. 'So what's the problem?'

'No mobile phone, for one thing. I thought maybe the girlfriend had pocketed it, but no. He must have had one, so why didn't we find it?'

'He could have left it somewhere – at work maybe – or lost it.'

'I know. It's just odd – and I don't like odd.'

Porson nodded without agreement. 'What else?'

'Seven hundred pounds under the pillow. That's a mystery. And then there's the girl – she's only nineteen.'

'So you don't want it to be her,' Porson said impatiently. 'Let's keep feelings out of it.'

'It was a violent attack, sir. Would a young girl like that—'

Porson shoved his hands down on his desk and leaned on them, the better to present his stern face for Slider's education. 'It's not a matter of young. At nineteen they don't think about conse-quences. And they all think they're starring in some film. None of it's really real.' He straightened up and paced again. 'What's her family?'

'We haven't got it out of her yet. She's refusing to say.'

'Doesn't want her parents to know,' Porson conjectured. 'That's good. If she was innocent she'd be calling for her mum. Right. Keep it up. Be nice if you could sort it out before Friday.'

'It would indeed, sir,' Slider said, and trudged away.

In the CID room, most of the team were back. When Slider entered, Swilley was saying, 'She's got the motive, the keys, the bloodstains, and no alibi.'

'We haven't looked into alibi,' Gascoyne pointed out.

Swilley snorted like an impatient horse. 'If she had anything like an alibi she'd have trotted it out. Her fingerprints are on the murder weapon. That's material.'

'All right, that's the pros. Any cons?' Slider asked.

'Well, she did call nine-nine-nine,' said LaSalle. Tall and skinny, with stiff ginger hair, he looked like an upturned yard brush. 'That looks like innocence. She could have just run away.'

'She knew she'd left too many traces of herself,' said Swilley. 'She had to have a covering story.'

'Would she think of that?' Slider asked.

'They all watch the cop shows on TV,' said Swilley. 'They know all the forensic stuff.'

That was true. 'Still,' said Slider, 'she didn't strike me as being very bright. Could somebody a bit thick work out a plan, and act so convincingly?'

'An intelligent person can act thick,' said Lœssop. 'A thick person can't act intelligent.'

Swilley looked at him impatiently. 'So what does that mean? She's thick or she isn't?'

He wasn't committing. 'Just saying.'

'Look, we know he wasn't killed in the morning,' Swilley said. 'And we know she ran off at half-sixish. So, she comes back later, maybe around eleven or midnight, when it's all quiet. She lets herself in – or maybe she rang and he buzzed her in. He had no reason to fear her. She asks him to think again, take her back.'

'What are they doing in the bedroom?' LaSalle asked.

'Why would he even bother talking to her?' Lœssop objected. 'He could get another girlfriend. He wouldn't want another row. *I* wouldn't.'

'He lets her in so she doesn't make a racket out in the street,'

Swilley said. 'And maybe he thinks he might as well have one last shag since she's there, and invites her into the bedroom.'

'Ouch,' said Hart. 'That's cold, girl.'

'Narcissism *is* cold,' Atherton said.

'Who says he's a narcissist?'

'You haven't seen his toiletries. A show pony at Wembley gets less grooming.'

'*When* you've quite finished,' said Swilley. Atherton made a 'carry on' gesture with his hands. 'She finally cottons on that he's just using her, loses her temper, grabs the dumb-bell and whacks him. Then she runs away – immediate reaction. Back home she's churning it over the rest of the night, and realizes she's left traces of herself all over the scene. So she goes back. Maybe she was meaning to clean up, but when she sees it, she realizes she'll never manage it, so she concocts the story that she came in and found him like that, and got the blood on her from touching him, and rings the police to make herself look innocent.'

'All that sobbing looked genuine,' Hart objected.

'It *was* genuine,' said Swilley. 'She was in love with him. And she was scared shitless. Plenty of reasons for tears.'

Gascoyne nodded slowly. 'That holds together. It all makes sense, guv,' he added to Slider.

'Yes,' said Slider, 'I know it does. I wish it didn't.'

'Why, just out of interest?' said Atherton.

'Because there are bits of the story that I think it would take a brighter girl than her to invent. Thinking it was a Halloween rubber wound on the back of his head, for instance. That rang horribly true.'

'In a dopey sort of way,' LaSalle agreed reluctantly.

'Also she's – what? – five foot five?' Slider went on.

'Five-six,' said Swilley.

'And he was five-ten. Could she really hit him on the side of the head, hard enough to knock him down. Could she even reach?'

'If she was angry enough, she'd hit him hard enough,' said Swilley.

McLaren swallowed a mouthful of the Ginsters beef and onion slice that had been keeping him out of the conversation. 'Remember that old lady last month, Mrs Cobbold? Pasted her old man with a poker. She was five-foot nothing and made of spit and cobwebs.'

'He was sitting down, though, wasn't he?' said LaSalle.

'Maybe Lingoss was sitting down,' said McLaren. 'Sat on the bed to take his kecks off.'

'He'd have seen her coming in the mirror,' Atherton objected.

'Not if he was sitting on the side of the bed facing the door,' said Lœssop.

'But she'd have had to go past him to pick up the weight. Wouldn't he have wondered what she was doing?'

'Yeah, but even if he saw her pick it up, there's no reason he'd be scared of her, not until she actually whacked him. Who would expect that?'

'True, I suppose,' said Atherton. 'What about the seven hundred pounds?'

'I don't believe Kelly-Ann's ever had seven hundred pounds at one time,' said Swilley. 'It's probably nothing to do with her.'

'It suggests there was someone else there,' said Slider.

'But not necessarily at that time,' said Swilley. 'He had cash in the box in the wardrobe. Maybe he was heading to put it in and the phone rang or something, and he shoved it under the pillow while he answered it and then forgot about it.'

'That's dopey,' Atherton said.

'We don't know that he wasn't,' Swilley pointed out.

'Well, the case against Kelly-Ann Hayes looks plausible, and we've got nothing else. Let's start getting it together. Nothing from the canvass, I suppose?'

'No, guv. Three wise monkeys,' said Hart.

He nodded. 'We'll need more background on Hayes and Lingoss. Find out who their next of kin are. We'll need a proper timeline – some evidence of her journeys to and from the flat. Check any security cameras en route for that. Search her room.'

'I'll do that,' Swilley volunteered. 'I'm on late tonight.'

'All right. And speak to her flatmate while you're about it. She might at least be able to confirm the absence of an alibi.'

'Got you,' said Swilley.

THREE
Kelly-Ann of Green Fables

Lena Gardens, off Shepherd's Bush Road, was lined either side with terraces of Victorian three-storey houses that might have been designed for the very purpose of being divided into flats. They were solid, yellow-brick buildings with white coping stones and a bay window on the ground and first floor. Kelly-Ann lived in a ground-floor flat, and her flatmate Jerrika Chamberlain met Swilley at the door. She was a tall, lean, mixed-race woman in her late twenties, with her afro combed up onto the top of her head and tied into a huge puffball. She was wearing black leggings and a baggy T-shirt, her feet were bare, and her finger and toenails were painted in matching burgundy glitter polish. Her black eyeliner gave her eyes an upward slant, which, with her rangey movements, gave her a cat-like air. She looked . . . prowly, Swilley decided. If that wasn't a word, it ought to be.

Swilley introduced herself, and Jilly Lawrence, who she had brought with her – one of the uniforms assigned to the investigation. It was often useful to have the visible sign of the law at one's side on these occasions.

Jerrika looked at them sharply, took the trouble to examine their warrant cards, then stepped back to let them in. 'I suppose it's about Kelly-Ann and Erik? It's terrible. We heard at the gym – well, someone said he'd been murdered. Is that right?'

She had a quick, impatient way of talking that seemed like a mannerism. Certainly there was nothing nervous about her – she seemed supremely self-assured.

'How did you hear?' Swilley wanted to know. 'Who told you?'

'The manager, Deedee, knows someone who lives just round the corner from Erik in Holland Road. She got it from one of the reporters, and she knew Erik worked at Gillespie's so she rang Deedee. And Deedee came up and told me.'

'Because she knew Kelly-Ann shares a flat with you?'

Jerrika gave a snorting laugh. 'She rents a room in *my* flat,' she corrected. 'It pisses me off when she calls herself my flatmate. She's my lodger, that's all. Do you want to sit down?'

She had led them into a kitchen-cum-living-room, tidy and clean, but small, and not luxurious. The fitments were old, the furniture flatpack-cheap, and the paint job looked home done. There was a sofa and a TV in the sitting part, and the kitchen end had a breakfast bar and two high stools.

'Do you want coffee or anything?' Jerrika asked.

'No, thanks,' Swilley said.

She and Lawrence sat on the sofa, and after a moment's hesitation, Jerrika pushed magazines and a box of tissues off the coffee table facing them and perched on that, as if she might get up any minute and – yes, prowl.

'How long has Kelly-Ann been your lodger?'

'Two months. Since she started at Harmonies. Deedee knew from the interview that she needed a room to take the job, and she knew my previous lodger had left.' She shrugged. 'I'd sooner not have a lodger, but I can't afford the mortgage without. This place is small, but prices round here are monster. There's only this room and the two bedrooms. And the bathroom, of course. My previous lodger, Alex, was a research student at the Charing Cross and he worked in a bar in the evenings, so we hardly ever saw each other, which was perfect. It hasn't been so good, I have to tell you, with Kelly-Ann, especially working in the same place as well. I can't get away from her.'

'She's a beauty therapist at Harmonies, I understand,' Swilley said.

The snort again. 'No, *I'm* a beauty therapist. Kelly-Ann's a manicurist. She paints nails, in other words. But that's what she always does – talks herself up. So suddenly she's my flatmate and suddenly she's a therapist!'

'It's natural, I suppose, to want to present yourself in a good light,' said Swilley. 'Maybe there's a little hero worship of you there as well?' She thought a bit of flattery might oil the wheels.

'Oh yes, she'd like to be me,' Jerrika said impatiently. 'But it takes years to learn all the techniques and get qualified. Her sort just want the glamour without the hard work.'

'You don't like her?' Swilley suggested.

Jerrika made a restless movement of her shoulders. 'Oh, she's all right, I suppose. I don't *dis*like her. It's just that she's a clinger, and a fantasist. And a spouter – oh my God!' She rolled her eyes. 'She never stops talking. Every detail of her boring little life, all her girlish hopes and dreams. She's a bit pathetic, if you want to know the truth. But I'm not her mum – I shouldn't have to look after her.'

'Speaking of her mum, so you know where her parents are?'

'Her dad's dead. Her mum – you see, this is what she does,' she interrupted herself with an exasperated look. 'She told me her parents owned this big farm in Hertfordshire, made it sound like Downton Abbey, and it turns out her mum lives in a house near Barnet and keeps chickens in the back garden.'

Lawrence asked for the address and after an impatient search in several drawers Jerrika provided it.

'Tell me about her relationship with Erik Lingoss,' Swilley said.

'Relationship! Well, I suppose *she* thought it was one. She'd only been seeing him a few weeks.'

'Was it a sexual relationship?'

'I don't think Erik has any other sort. He came mooching upstairs to Harmonies as soon as he heard there was a new girl, and Kelly-Ann was so green she just fell into his arms. He always had to have any new girl that started.'

'Did he try it on with you?'

'Yeah, when I first joined, but he didn't get anywhere. I *had* a boyfriend, thank you very much. Still have. I told him I wasn't interested and that was that.'

'But Kelly-Ann fell in love with him.'

'Well, he *is* gorgeous-looking. And a terrific body. I mean, what was not to like? But he was just using her for sex, if you want my opinion.'

'Why do you say that?'

'Because he never took her out anywhere, not after the first date. He just sent for her to his flat when he wanted sex. But she was all starry-eyed about him so she didn't see it.'

'I suppose she told you all about it?'

Jerrika rolled her eyes. 'Oh my God! Spouter, remember? I got sick of the sound of it – Erik this and Erik that. Every bloody word he said to her, every smile, every touch. I had to stop her giving me a blow-by-blow account of how they made love.' Now she did get up and pace. 'She was going to move in with him, and then they were going to get married. Talk about fantasy land! They were going to open their own gym and beauty club. Erik was saving up for it. She'd do the beauty and he'd do the fitness. She had their whole lives mapped out. Every detail. Three kids and roses round the door. I had to make a rule that when I was in my room with the door shut, she wasn't to disturb me, otherwise she'd have been rabbiting on all night.'

'So tell me about yesterday. What time did you get home?'

She came back for that and sat down again. 'I suppose I got here about seven or a bit before. She was sitting at the breakfast bar with her head on her arms sobbing.'

'Was she at work yesterday?'

'Yeah, but she was on her half day. She finished one o'clock. She told me she was seeing Erik in the evening, and she was spending the afternoon tarting herself up for him. She said she was going to ask him about moving in with him. I said good luck with that! Anyway, I get home and there she is in floods because he's dumped her – by text. I mean, who does that? Then she's gone over there – to plead with him, I s'pose – and he wouldn't even speak to her.'

'That was cruel, wasn't it?'

She shrugged. 'Yeah, well, it's what you get if you make yourself a doormat. I told her he wasn't worth it, told her to pull herself together. She was sobbing about going back and pleading with him some more. I told her if she did that she could find herself somewhere else to live, I wasn't going to live under the same roof with someone who had no self-respect.'

'Did that help?'

Jerrika shrugged. 'Just made her cry more. But someone had to say it. Anyway, I had a date, so I had to get myself ready. I went out about eight, met my boyfriend and some mates at Roxies in Hammersmith.'

'And where was she then?'

'She'd gone into her room and closed the door. I shouted out goodbye, but she didn't answer.'

'And what time did you get home?'

'About half past eleven, I suppose.'

'Did you see Kelly-Ann, or speak to her?'

'No, her door was closed. The light was on, and I could hear her watching something from inside, that was all.'

'You didn't think to see if she was all right?'

She gave them a defiant look. 'The rule works both ways. No bothering each other if the door's shut. If I broke it, she'd think she could as well and I'd never get away from her.'

'So you don't actually know for sure where she was all evening.'

Jerrika looked surprised. 'Where else would she be? She was crying her eyes out in her room.' Swilley looked at her steadily, and her eyes opened wide. '*No-o!*' she said in a shocked and excited husk. 'You don't mean . . .?' She stared from Swilley to Lawrence and back. She was thinking. Then she shook her head. 'No,' she said, almost regretfully. 'Not Kelly-Ann. She wouldn't have the balls. In any case, she was in love with him.'

'Love and hate are very close.'

But she shook her head again. 'No. Look, Erik's tall, and just about the fittest bloke I know. I've massaged him a couple of times, and he's got muscles like you wouldn't believe. He'd have nothing to fear from her. She's got arms like spaghetti. She doesn't exercise. Even if she tried to hit him, he could hold her off with one hand and eat Chinese with chopsticks with the other. In any case, I know she just wouldn't. She's the wettest, wussiest girl in London.'

'Well,' said Swilley, getting up, 'thank you for your input. I'd just like to have a look at her room, if that's all right.'

Jerrika shrugged. 'Help yourself.'

'Have you been in there since yesterday?'

'No, why would I?'

Jerrika had the larger, front room with the bay window. The kitchen-living room was the back addition room, overlooking the garden, and in between was what would have been a child's bedroom, so it was very small, about ten feet square. It contained a queen-sized bed, a Lloyd Loom chair, a wardrobe and a tall chest of drawers. The furniture was all old brown stuff that had been painted in pale yellow to make it look more modern. The bed was unmade, and half hidden under a drift of screwed-up tissues. There were clothes everywhere, bulging out of the wardrobe and drawers, on the chair, on the floor. On the top of the chest of drawers pots and tubes of make-up and other beauty products sprawled capless with more smeary tissues and cotton-wool pads. Swilley noted that some of the bottles were Harmonies branded, presumably either free samples or purloined from work. And amongst the room's detritus were empty tumblers, coffee mugs, and crumby plates. A troupe of mice could live happily in here for months – and, given all the scope for hiding, might already be doing so.

On the bed the two pillows had been dragged together in the centre for viewing comfort, and in the space where one of them had been there was an empty half-litre carton of Ben and Jerry's Chocolate Fudge Brownie with a spoon sticking out of it. Beside it was a plate that from the look and smell had contained buttered toast.

Swilley nudged Lawrence and gestured to them. From her long experience in the Job, she knew that when crossed in love, men turned for comfort to drink and women to food, typically ice cream, bread, cake and chocolate. A girl whose boyfriend has just dumped her might well go home to cry her eyes out, and sit up in bed watching *Sleepless in Seattle* while ingesting large quantities of ice cream and toast. But would a not-very-bright girl concocting an alibi think of that, and fabricate the evidence?

Swilley didn't think so.

They came out of the room, closing the door behind them, and Jerrika accosted them restlessly.

'What happens now?' she demanded. 'I mean, do I have to get a new lodger, is what I'm asking, because I can't make the mortgage alone, and it takes time to find someone. And what about her stuff? If she's going to jail or something – do you think she did it? I s'pose you can't tell me, but do you think she's coming back?'

'Oh yes,' Swilley said. 'I think she will be.'

She couldn't tell whether Jerrika looked relieved or disappointed. It's like that with cats.

'There was no laptop or tablet, and no diary or anything like that, so whatever she's got it's on her mobile,' Swilley told Slider. 'We've got that so we can go through it. But honestly, I'm starting to think she's telling the truth.'

Slider nodded. He trusted Swilley's instincts. 'The fact remains she was on the spot, she has the motive, and she has no alibi. And as far as we know she's the only one with keys. We'll be under pressure to keep going with her. We've got to find another suspect.'

'Yes, boss. Well, we've hardly started yet. Seems as though he was a good-looking guy and a womanizer, so he must have had enemies.'

'Yes, and there's the question of that cash. There may be a simple reason, but I'd like to know where it came from. And where his mobile went to. Plenty to look into.'

'What'll you do with Kelly-Ann?'

'Oh, I think we'll let her go on bail. Start finding out who Lingoss's friends and acquaintances were. There was no break-in, so it must have been someone he knew.'

'Yes, boss. The canvass might still turn something up. Pity the flats had no security cameras, but there are the shops opposite. We need to know who was coming and going. And we can look into his finances.'

'We'll do all those things, but not tonight. Go home, Norma.'

'You too, sir,' she grinned.

The damp, foggy night let him through reluctantly, halation running the street lamps together and smearing the traffic lights against the darkness like sticky sweets. When he let himself into the house, Jumper reached him first, gave him the furry figure-eight around the legs and then posed, tail vertical and back lightly arched for his caress. Joanna was not far behind, but arrived third, after the baby-to-be. He had to embrace her at arms' length.

'How are you feeling?' he asked.

'Large,' she said wearily. Her hair smelled of outdoors, and her face was cold.

'You've only just got in,' he deduced. 'You look tired.'

She stepped back. 'I am. It's natural after a day's work. Aren't you tired?'

He managed not to say, *I'm not pregnant.* He hadn't wanted her to take the sessions at Denham – music for the new *Star Wars* film – so close to her due date. He had half expected the fixer to send her home when he saw the size of her. But they paid very well, and there would be royalties later, too; and apart from the money, she loved playing. She especially loved doing session work: meeting old friends, being with her peers, and the whole professional atmosphere of it. He understood. He loved his work, though it distressed him on occasions, and wore him down on others. When he had remonstrated with her – as tactfully as he could – about working up to the wire, she had said, with an air of curbing impatience, 'If you're worried I'll go into labour, I could hardly do it anywhere safer. Surrounded by ninety intelligent people, under bright lights, and no more than five miles from the nearest hospital. It might be embarrassing, but it wouldn't be dangerous.' And when he'd opened his mouth to argue further, she'd said impatiently, 'What if I'm here at home, alone, and I slip on the garden path or fall down the stairs?' So he'd been forced to shut up.

He said, 'Yes, I'm tired. Can I ask you just once, and then I promise I won't go on about it – you're not overdoing it, are you? You don't have to do these sessions.'

'If you take on the work, you don't let people down.'

'I know, but they can get another violinist. I can't get another you. No music is worth risking your health for.'

'It's John Williams!' she said with mock indignation. 'Proper music, musicians' music.' He gave her a steady look, and she sighed. 'If I admit that there is a lot of scrubbing involved, and that I *am* tired, and a little bit of me wishes I didn't have to go in tomorrow, will you let it drop?'

He drew her to him again, and let her prop her big belly on him. He kissed the top of her head and said, 'Just promise me you won't take any chances. If you get a pain don't go heroically toughing through it.'

'I promise. Anything like a pain and I'm out of there like a scalded chihuahua. I won't even play to the end of the bar.'

'Is there anything to eat?' he asked, to show he was keeping his word. 'Or shall I go out for something?'

'There's a portion of your dad's stew in the freezer. I can heat that up and nuke a jacket potato.'

'I'll do it,' he said. 'You sit down.'

She laughed. It made her tired face light up. 'What makes you think that sitting down is a treat? You try it with a watermelon stuffed in your trousers. *I'll* do the supper – you go up and change and see your boy.'

'He'll be asleep.'

'I bet he isn't. He always wants you to say goodnight.'

When he came downstairs again, he could smell the stew.

'Nearly ready,' she said.

He laid the table and poured water. 'George just told me that the three wise men brought gifts of gold, frankypants and moo. I suppose it was the association in his mind with the ox and the ass; and not knowing what myrrh is.'

'There's that line in "Away in a Manger": – "The cattle are lowing",' she said. 'His friend Luca at pre-school calls milk moo-moo.'

'Why is he talking about Christmas already?' Slider complained.

'It's the other pre-schoolers opening his eyes to the commercial possibilities,' she said, bringing plates to the table. 'They're all such little Alan Sugars. You notice that the aspect of Christmas that's uppermost in his thoughts is the gifts.'

'I saw the first Christmas lights on my way home. As soon as Remembrance Day's over . . .'

'You don't go into shops much, do you, my darling? The supermarkets have had Christmas stuff on display since the beginning of October.'

'We're robbing children of their childhood,' he grumbled. 'Kelly-Ann Hayes is only nineteen. She should be having crushes on pop stars, not full-blown sexual relationships.'

'Where have you been for the past fifty years? Christine Keeler was only nineteen.'

'Yes, and how well did that work for her?'

'Who's Kelly-Ann Hayes?'

He told her.

'Well, all is explained,' she said. 'So that's why you're tired. You don't like suspecting her.'

'I'm not sure I do any more, but I didn't like that I did, or that I had to.'

'It takes a wife to understand that sentence. But I know what you mean. She looks like the obvious suspect. But wouldn't it take someone with enormous self-confidence to rely on a set-up like that for an alibi?'

'And she seems like a bear of little brain. And yet . . .' He frowned.

'Yes?'

'It doesn't do to ignore the obvious. Or to underestimate people's stupidity. She could have killed him in the evening, and gone back in the morning for absolutely no reason whatever. People do that sort of thing all the time. Trouble is, when you present a case in court, the jury like a motive they can understand. You can't just shrug and say, well, that's how it was.'

'It's early days,' she comforted him. 'I'm sure there are lots of juicy suspects out there just waiting for you to stumble over them. Big meaty men you can enjoy taking down.'

'Hmm. It doesn't change the fact that this girl, not even out of her teens, was being used for sex by a complete—'

'Bounder? Darling, she's over eighteen – she can do as she likes.'

'And that makes it better? Eighteen is still a child, no matter what the law says.'

She knew what was troubling him. Kate, his daughter from his first marriage, was fourteen. It wouldn't be long before she was sixteen and could legally have sex. She said, 'The fathers of girls always have a hard time letting go. They never want to think of their daughters having sex.'

He gave her a reluctant smile. 'If that's a girl,' he said, nodding towards her bulge, 'you'll find out. It's not all princess dresses and unicorns, you know.'

'No daughter of mine is going to wear princess dresses. And no unicorns! She'll be getting her first socket wrench at four.'

'And the trombone lessons?'

'Squeezed in between bricklaying and heavy engineering.'

'That's good. It'll keep her busy, because she's never leaving the house until she's thirty-five,' Slider said genially. 'Is there any pud?'

FOUR

Do You Know the Crumpet Man?

'Did you know,' said Atherton, as they turned into Lime Grove, 'that *A Tale of Two Cities* was first serialized in two English regional newspapers?'

'Really? Which ones?'

'It was the *Bicester Times*, it was the *Worcester Times*.'

Slider looked at him. 'When is Emily coming back?'

'Sunday. Why?'

'You need someone to take the edge off you.'

'You don't understand what it's like, having curatorship of a magnificent brain,' Atherton complained.

'Oh, thank you,' said Slider. 'This is it.'

Gillespie's had kept the Edwardian façade of the old Hammersmith Baths, but nothing else; behind, it was all modern and brash: bare floors and walls, harsh lighting, and thumping work-out music so loud it'd make your ears bleed. Slider enquired after the manager, while Atherton sloped cautiously up to the Harmonies centre like a cat entering a roomful of toddlers and finger paint. He looked as if he feared forcible beautification.

Diedre Donnelly ("Call me Deedee – everybody does,") had an office which, although it had one largely glass wall, was insulated from the music. It still came up through the floor in a disconcerting pulse, but at least conversation was possible. She was a short, stocky woman in her forties with the look of impatiently hidden muscles; a black skirt suit over a white shirt signally failed to make her look civil servant material. Despite full make-up and hair pinned back in a French pleat, there was something indefinably untidy about her, as though she had only recently been abducted by the style police. You could imagine her ripping off the outfit with a magnificent two-handed gesture and emerging in a body suit and cape, ready to fight crime and injustice.

Her office was also untidy, cheaply-furnished in Corporate

Stingy style, and overflowing on all sides with documents, folders, brochures and dead house plants. The Gillespie's logo – an outline man and woman embraced by a curly capital G, as though by a giant snake (one small logo for the company, one giant meal for a boa constrictor) – covered one wall and appeared on many objects, including a circular badge on Deedee's lapel, just above her plastic name-tag.

She greeted Slider in a friendly but distracted manner. 'Please, sit down – sorry about the mess. Just put that lot on the floor – here, I'll do it.' She cleared a chair for him and went behind her desk for the only other sitting-place, then was up again instantly. 'Oh, would you like a coffee?'

'No, thanks,' Slider said. He hated the expression 'a coffee' with irrational fervour, and suspected the beverage provided by someone who used it would be undrinkable. 'I'd like to talk to you about Erik Lingoss.'

'Erik with a k,' she said, wrinkling her nose in a reaction that interested Slider. 'That was how he always introduced himself. As if it mattered. Actually, his HMRC records have it as Eric with a c. I think he just wanted to make himself more interesting.'

'You didn't like him?' Slider suggested.

She put her hands to her cheeks. 'Oh God, I forgot for a moment. He's really dead? He was actually murdered? That's terrible. Forget what I just said. Wait, you're a police officer – you can't, can you? Sorry!' Her very slight Dublin accent and rapid delivery had a slightly soothing effect that Slider tried to resist.

'Tell me why you didn't like him,' Slider said, smiling to show it was not a hostile question.

'Oh well, he was a brilliant trainer, don't get me wrong. He'd the way of motivating people – of either sex – and getting the best out of them.'

'Trainer of the year?'

She gave a little shrug. 'But, you know, it's countrywide – there are fifty-six Gillespie's, and the trainer of the year contest is national, so it's worth having on your CV. Plus there's a thousand pound prize, not to be sneezed at. I'd not refuse it, I can tell you. Erik was in with a chance to win again this year, if he'd not gone part-time. So that tells you how good he was.'

'Why did he go part-time?'

'Just my impression, you know? But I think the award went to his head a bit. It was just after he got it the second time, he said he wanted to branch out and make more of himself. Set up on his own.'

'Open his own gym?' Slider queried.

'Oh, there's a lot of them have that dream,' she said. 'Well, I did myself once upon a time, but it's just bubbles. You'd need a heck of a lot of capital – these days people expect all the machinery, plus the luxury stuff, spas and restaurants and so on. It's not just a matter of a coupla mats and a weights bench any more. And it's a crowded field – there's chains all over the place. Oh yes, I heard Erik talking about it, but it was just if-I-win-the-lottery talk, if you get me? No, I think he wanted to take on private clients, rather than go through a club. There's good money to be made that way if you can get the client list together. And he was popular with the punters.'

'They liked him?'

'He was very charming when he wanted to be. And Janey, that boy was ripped! Handsome, too. And he got results. I was sorry to lose him – otherwise I wouldn't have kept him on. It's not really a Gillespie's thing to take part-timers – they're big on corporate loyalty – but I argued the case with them rather than lose him altogether.'

'When did all this happen?'

'A year back. Well, the award is in October, and it was just after he won the second time he came to me and asked to go part-time – two days a week. And that's how it's been ever since.'

'So why didn't you like him?' Slider asked again.

She paused for a moment, as if wondering whether or not to be frank. Then she took a deep breath and said, 'He was a nuisance with the female staff here – every new girl who arrived he had to have. And he treated them like shit – all over them to get them into bed, then just using them until he got bored and dropped them. I mean, they can date the punters if they want – I can't stop them – as long as they do it outside working hours. I won't have any messing about on the premises. And you can't stop the staff seeing each other in their private time, though I'd discourage it. But with Erik it was trouble. Most of these Harmonies girls are very young, some of them trainees, school-leavers, and they didn't know what hit them. He went through them like a combine harvester. There was Emma last year, and Lisa, and Adrienne and Tina before that – I forget them all now. Broken hearts all over the kip. Floods of tears, and girls coming to me as if I was Mother Superior. "Why won't he answer my texts, Deedee? Why is he treating me like this, Deedee?" Because you're an eejit, girl, I'd be thinking, but you can't say that. No, if he hadn't been so good for business, I'd have found a way to be shot of him, because I was tired of cleaning up his messes.'

'Like Kelly-Ann?'

She made a face. 'Last in a long line.' Then she put her hands to her cheeks again. 'Janey, I was forgetting again. It really is the last, isn't it? He's gone. You don't think Kelly-Ann did it, sure you don't?'

'Don't you think her capable of it?'

'She hasn't got the gumption. She's as wet as a week in Limerick. From what I heard, he was bashed on the head, is that right? I don't think she'd even have the strength. She's just a Harmonies girl, and she doesn't train. Some of them do – they get concessionary rates for using the club – but she's never asked for a card. Mind you, she's only been here a short time. There's a big turn-over in Harmonies. A lot of these girls use Gillespie's as a training-ground, then go on to more exclusive places where they can earn more.'

Slider nodded, digesting all this, then said, 'You have some personal data on Lingoss, I assume?'

'Yes, I got his personnel file out yesterday, when I heard, just to have a look at it. Didn't know if I'd be required to do anything. I've never had a staff member die before. Had a geezer drop dead on the treadmill once, a client. That was bad enough. Where's that file? It's here somewhere.' She rummaged messily amongst the paperdrifts, and eventually came up with a manila folder. She leafed through it. 'I don't know what you want to know – there's not much here. Age thirty-six. He didn't look it,' she added in parenthesis. 'Joined Gillespie's four years ago. Before that he was at Riverside in Chiswick, and before that he was staff physio with Intersys London – the big data company in Brentford – you know? God knows what he did there. Executive neck massages for all I know. He'd an FHT diploma for massage, did I say? And an IHS diploma in Diet, Nutrition and Lifestyle Coaching. References. Employment record with Gillespie's. Awards. Next of kin – he left that blank.' She looked up at him. 'I called him in over it, and he said he didn't have anyone. Said his parents divorced when he was eighteen and both remarried and he never sees either of them. Said he didn't even know where they were. No brothers or sisters. When I pressed him – because we're supposed to have a name, in case of accidents – he said why didn't I put my name down for it? He smiled when he said it, and d'you know, I near as dammit agreed. I could feel me hand twitch! That's the power of him. I'd only known him five minutes, but that *smile* . . .' She shuddered. Then read Slider's face. 'If he hadn't been an employee, I could've gone for it, I swear to God.'

'He sounds like quite a player. Can you tell me anything about who his friends are? Where he's working when he's not here? Anything about his private life?'

She shook her head. 'I've not had anything to do with him personally, only dealt with some of his discarded girls. But I tell you who probably could help you. You should speak to Ivanka. She's one of the trainers here, and she and Erik were quite pally. They were an item once upon a time, but they'd stayed friends, for a wonder. Still hung out once in a while.'

'He didn't break her heart?'

Deedee grinned. 'You haven't met Ivanka. Not one to be messing with. Try to break her heart, she'll break your arm.'

Atherton shook his head. 'Nothing useful. Ten minutes of how badly he treated Kelly-Ann, but nothing about what he did or where he went or who he hung about with.'

Slider made a show of peering closely at his face. 'Are you looking unusually toned and plucked, or is it my imagination?'

Atherton shied his head away. 'I just had a neck massage and a manicure while we were talking.'

'Really?'

'What do you take me for? Of course not. But those girls are seriously bored, I can tell you. No wonder a handsome bounder found them easy pickings.'

'To be clear, this is Lingoss we're talking about, not you?'

'Two of them have had the Erik treatment – both when they

first joined. Thought he was the bee's knees, got diddled then
dropped after a couple of weeks. I heard more than I wanted to
about how fabulous he was in bed, but I detected a certain wistful-
ness as well as wrath.'

'Resentment of Kelly-Ann?'

'No, I didn't get that. They seemed to be going for feminine
solidarity. Though sympathy for Kelly-Ann was mixed with a
certain worldly-wise superiority. Mostly they seemed to be enjoying
their indignation against Lingoss. It certainly hasn't occurred to
any of them that Kelly-Ann might have clubbed him to death –
though they couldn't offer any suggestions as to who might have.'

'Fortunately,' Slider said, 'I've got an Ivanka up my sleeve.'

'I thought you were walking oddly. What's an Ivanka?'

'We're just going to find out.'

Ivanka was in the main hall, running on a treadmill with appalling
ease. She was tall, slim, beautifully muscled, dressed in three-
quarter leggings and a matching cropped top in shiny purple Lycra
that left everything to be desired. Her long streaky blonde hair
was tied back in a horse tail that swished back and forth mesmeric-
ally as she ran. Because of the cortex-bashing music, they had to
go round in front of her to catch her attention. Her face was
smooth and had the taught, shiny look of someone with very little
body fat; she had beautiful smoky eyes, but any claim to beauty
was marred by a beaky nose and thin lips. She had evidently gone
into a running trance, because her face and the eyes were blank,
and it was a noticeable moment before she registered their presence, clicked off the machine and ran to a standstill. When she
understood what they wanted, she beckoned them away. 'I have
client in half an hour. We talk until then. Not here – too noisy.'

Amen to that, Slider thought fervently. In one corner a man in
Lycra, presumably a trainer, was bellowing at a man lifting weights,
'Come ON! Come ON! Five more! Don't fade on me now! Fight
through the burn! Four more! Squeeze it! Pump it! Burn it! Three
more! You can do it! You've *got* it!' The man with the weights
made a sort of animal groan, as if what he'd got was the suspicion
of a hernia. The trainer sounded demented. Slider contemplated
the weights in the sufferer's hands and just then it seemed only
too natural for someone to use one of them for other purposes.

Ivanka led the way to the cafeteria, the horribly-named GLicious Cafebar. 'What?' Atherton appealed sub voce.

'G as in Gillespie's, I suppose – and also maybe as in "Gee, what delicious food!"?'

'Cafebar, all one word?'

'Settle down. I'm supposed to be the sensitive one.'

The décor was probably meant to be cool and modern, but came across more as spartan – Ikea with a hint of airport terminal – but at least it was quiet. Ivanka loped like a large lioness across to a corner table and sat down, looking at them expectantly. Slider felt obliged to offer her refreshment, but she asked only for a bottle of water. She looked so fit and pure, with her limpid skin, he thought she'd probably found a way to dispense with food altogether. Maybe you could buy ichor at Ottolenghi's these days.

Slider had got some basic details from Deedee and knew that her name was Ivana Anosov; she was thirty-two, unmarried, originally from Ukraine, had been in England ten years, and joined Gillespie's about the same time as Lingoss.

'Ms Anosov,' Slider began.

But she tapped the plastic name-badge on her front. 'Ivanka,' she said. 'Important to have a sexy name, one the clients can remember. So I am Ivanka, always. That was why Erik changed to a k. People remember it.' She made a contemptuous sound with her lips. 'Eric with a c is a nothing name! I told him to change. It made him.'

'You've been friends with him for a long time?'

'Tell me first – he is really dead? Somebody really killed him?'

'I'm afraid so.'

She nodded, and looked introspective for a moment; sad perhaps, but not heartbroken. 'So,' she said at last, 'what you want to know?'

'When did you last see him?'

She thought about it. 'Three weeks, maybe.'

'What was your relationship with him? You were lovers once, weren't you?'

'Long time ago. Now just friends, I guess.'

'Friends with benefits?' Atherton put in.

She knew what that meant. 'I see him here twice a week, pass in the hallway, "Good morning, how are you". Nothing more. But now and then we meet after work. It would be weeks, then he would ring and say, "Ivanka, come for drink with me," and we'd meet a few times, then it would go quiet again, see at work only. I think he called me when he'd finished with someone. Just to make sure I was still around.'

'But on those occasions, did you have sex with him?' Atherton asked.

She didn't seem to resent the bluntness. She turned her amazing eyes on him, examined him, and said, with a shrug in her voice, 'Of course. We were good together. I enjoyed him. But there was nothing . . .' She lifted her hands and clasped them together, then let them drop. 'We were not a couple.'

'Were you before?' Atherton asked.

She thought about that. 'Not really,' she said at last. 'At the very beginning it was intense, we spent lot of time together, every moment we could, so people think we were a couple. But it was always not love, just sex. You understand, Erik, he likes to break hearts, but he could not break mine. We stayed friends. I don't think,' she added contemplatively, 'he had many friends.'

'Why is that?' Slider asked.

'He is very competitive. You cannot be friends with someone you are trying to beat, and he wished to beat everyone. Only me, he could not beat, so we were friends. Friends must be equals . . . hmm?'

Slider didn't answer that. He said, 'He tried to beat everyone? Even the women he went out with?'

'Of course,' she said. 'They must be completely under his spell, they must worship him, then when he knows they are his slaves, he throws them away. Because he can.'

'That's not very nice.'

She shrugged. 'Women are stupid. Anyone could see what Erik was, but they all think, "Me he will love, I am different, I am special". They think they can tame him. *Duraki!*'

She reached behind and freed her hair from its tail, and for a moment it fell round her face like a wild lion's mane, before she gathered it up again in both hands, dragged it back and confined it. On the surface she was just making herself tidy again, but Slider thought it an impressive, even aggressive gesture: even if only subconsciously, she was demonstrating her power.

'You sound almost as if you didn't like him,' he said.

She shrugged. 'I liked him all right. He was good company. He was good sex. He had beautiful body. Have you seen his flat? His bedroom? All those mirrors. He liked to watch while we were making love. I liked it too. We looked good together. We would turn this way and that way – good! I had what I want from him. What he did with other girls – not my business.'

'Speaking of business,' Slider said, 'he was only working here two days a week. Do you know what he was doing the rest of the time?'

'He talked to me about it. He wanted more private clients. Take them in the daytime as well as evenings. If you do the right things, they pay well.'

'What would be the right things?'

'Personal training. Very personal – tailored to them. Diet advice. Sports massage.' She paused.

Atherton said wryly, 'Sex?'

'If they want it, afterwards, maybe. Why not? He is good looking, has perfect body. They pay extra – a lot. And he wanted to make a lot of money quick, while he could.'

'While he could?' Slider queried.

She looked at him pityingly. 'You cannot do this job for ever. What do you think? The body does not last. Erik and me, we are both over thirty. When you get to forty – pff! All finished. Then you have to find other job. Bad job, maybe, stupid job. Erik, he wanted enough money so he did not have to do bad, stupid job. Money, money, money – then get out. So – private clients. Rich people.'

'And where would he get these private clients?'

'Not here,' she said, with a contemptuous look round. 'No rich people here. Shapes, in Kensington – rich people go there.'

'That's a gym, like this?'

'Fitness club – all luxury, not like this. You choose your own hours, all self-employed, charge what you like. Make lots of money.'

'Why didn't you go there, then?'

'Because here I get paid holiday, sickness, pension. Security. Maybe management job when I get too old.' She shrugged again. 'Maybe I not ambitious enough. Erik, he would fight hard for what

he wanted. Fierce. Aggressive. He will succeed. It's not for me. I
am stuck here, I know it. Good luck to him.'

She looked at them for a moment, clear-eyed, and then her
composure wavered. 'I forgot. He's dead. My God, who did this
to him? Do you know?'

'We'll find out,' Slider said.

Outside, it had turned colder, and the seamless grey cloud cover
was lower. Tiny random fragments of snow were coming down,
widely scattered and at present harmless. It was as if the sky had
dandruff.

Atherton said, 'If he left a trail of broken hearts behind him,
there'll be plenty of women with a motive to kill him. Not to
mention their boyfriends-stroke-fathers-stroke-brothers. The field
is opening up.'

'What did you think of Ivanka?'

'She seemed pretty laid back about it all. Had the measure of
the happy chappy all right. I can't see her getting so worked up
about the latest Kelly-Ann that she'd whack him.'

Slider remembered that sleek, feral movement of freeing and
retying her hair. The hard body, taut face and impassive eyes of
a powerful person. Suppose Lingoss had promised something – a
partnership of some kind – and then reneged on it, would she have
taken it lying down? He shook himself. That was pure off-grid
speculation, and they didn't have time for that.

'Still,' he said, 'we'd better check up on her, see if she has an
alibi, at least.'

Freddie Cameron was in Slider's room when he got back, sitting
in Slider's chair and contemplating the continental drift of papers
covering the desk. Freed of the coverall chrysalis of that morning,
he had emerged in full splendour, his suit a grey whisper of perfection, his bow tie an exquisite confection of golden-yellow silk with
cranberry spots. Atherton was elegant, but a scientific expert earned
a great deal more than a lowly detective sergeant, and Cameron
was wealthy enough to indulge his sartorial bent. Rumour had it
that he even had his pocket fluff handmade in Savile Row.

He raised his head as Slider came in. 'I don't think I've ever
seen the surface of your desk,' he said.

'Come to that, neither have I,' said Slider.

'Some of that stuff must be pretty old. I'm wondering if Shakespeare's *Cardenio* might be down at the bottom.'

'I thought I heard voices coming from under there the other day, but it might have been my imagination. Did you have something in particular to say, or are you just having fun at my expense?'

Freddie got up and came out from behind the desk. 'My dear boy, where are my manners? Hogging your seat. I was passing the shop, so I thought I'd call in with my preliminary report, rather than phoning you.' He went to put the document down on the desk, hesitated, and placed it in Slider's hand instead.

The bit of by-play was not lost on Slider. 'Anything untoward in it?'

'No, it's pretty much as we saw at the scene. Deceased was exceptionally fit. Excellent muscle tone, very low body fat – and unusually smooth, supple skin, if that means anything.'

'He had a lot of expensive bathroom products,' Slider said.

'Hmm. Well, he obviously took care of himself. No signs of any drug use, no alcohol in his system. There was no food in his stomach, in case that helps you to pinpoint the time of death – he hadn't eaten anything in around four hours. I would say he had very recently bathed or showered – he was not only clean but smelled of soap or a similar product. He was circumcised. No scars, blemishes, bruises or tattoos. He's about the healthiest specimen I've ever examined. And the most perfect. I suspect, judging by all those mirrors in his bedroom, that he knew it, too.'

'All those fitness fanatics are narcissists, aren't they? We're just back from the gym, and they're all watching themselves lifting weights and flexing their muscles.'

'Ballet dancers watch themselves while they work,' Freddie pointed out. 'It's the pursuit of perfection.'

'Only a narcissist would think perfection was within their grasp,' Slider said.

'You're tired and cranky,' Cameron said kindly. 'I prescribe one hundred and fifty millilitres of tea, taken internally.'

'Thanks, I'll get that filled right away. What about the blows? Is the murder weapon the murder weapon?'

'As certainly as anything is in this imperfect life. The first blow, to the left side of the forehead, has a slight upward trajectory, as you'd expect from someone picking up the barbell, or already holding it at the ready, lifting and swinging it at the victim's head, probably two-handed, like this.' He demonstrated. 'Rather like a tennis shot.'

'So the murderer would have to have been standing in front of him?'

'Or just to the side. Given that he fell forward, I would judge the latter slightly more likely. The blow would have incapacitated him – possibly he lost consciousness – so he probably crumpled from the knees rather than falling straight like a tree from the force of the blow. There was considerable bleeding from the gash. The other blows were delivered from directly above, with great force and determination – bone fragments were driven into the brain. I would judge from the amount of bleeding that they were delivered two or three minutes later.'

'So the killer hit him, went off to do something – search for something perhaps – then came back to finish him off.'

'Supposition's your department, not mine,' Freddie said. 'Happily, I deal with scientific facts.'

'Could he have been regaining consciousness? The killer thought he'd killed him the first time, then heard him groan or saw him move?'

'That is possible.'

'And the force of the blows? The killer would have had to be strong? And around the same height?'

'I can't tell you that definitively. The four-foot-ten little old lady is probably in the clear, but there could be a discrepancy in height of a few inches. And moderate strength would be needed, but it needn't be another fitness fanatic. You know yourself that passion creates energy.'

Slider nodded. 'That's very unhelpful, thank you.'

'We aim to confuse. Well, I must be off. Give my love to Joanna. When she's out of purdah, you must come over and have dinner. It's been ages.'

FIVE

An Inspector Calls

Shapes was a very different prospect from Gillespie's: it shrieked exclusivity. It occupied a large corner plot in Kensington High Street, itself something of a premier shopping venue. And the full name, elegantly inscribed across the façade in grey and cream, was Elite Shapes of Kensington.

'This used to be a bank, didn't it?' Slider mused as they parked down the side road.

'Certainly looks like it,' said Atherton. It had the tall windows and massive wooden door with brass furniture. The reception area had a bank's high ceiling, and the walls were panelled floor to ceiling in alternate four-foot widths of mirror glass and polished black granite with gold flecks in it. To one side there were two leather sofas, one black, one white, and a glass coffee table of magazines. The high reception desk to the other side was curved, presumably because it could be, and was topped with the same granite. The floor was oak, but an inset runway of black carpet led from the entrance to a pair of further doors with small square mirror-glass panes, which presumably led to the inner sanctum. Inevitably, there were single orchids in pots on the desk and the coffee table. The finishing proof of luxury was that there was no piped music.

Two exquisite young women were behind the desk, in smart black suits, with nothing so vulgar as a name-badge or corporate logo to sully their perfection. In the atmosphere of hush, they almost whispered their enquiry as to whether they could help. The manager, they informed Slider, was Mrs Lane-Adams, and they would ask if she could spare them a few minutes.

Stephanie Lane-Adams seemed to be about fifty, but was so beautifully made-up and coiffed that at a quick glance she could have been thirty-five. She had large hair, a lot of costume jewellery, and a smile of radiant insincerity, with teeth so big and white you

could have tiled a swimming pool with them. She came in person
to collect them from reception, and led them through the mirrored
doors into a corridor of twinkling downlighters above and heavy
wooden doors to either side.

'Treatment rooms,' she explained to their enquiring glances.
Slider continued to look interested, and she said with an air of
resignation, 'Would you like to see around?'

'Yes, please,' said Slider.

At the end of the corridor was a cross passage with, straight
ahead, the double doors into the main gym. It was smaller than
Gillespie's, and though there was work-out music, the volume was
tolerable. It had mirrored walls on two sides, the usual machines,
and there were about a dozen people working away quietly on
their bodies, half of them with a trainer in attendance.

Coming out of the gym, she gestured to the left and said, 'Down
there is the swimming pool and the sauna,' but she turned them
to the right. More closed doors, numbered in black on nice old-
fashioned white oval enamel plates. 'Exercise rooms, where clients
can work with their trainers in privacy,' said Mrs Lane-Adams.
She did not offer to show them inside one. At the end of the
passage were stairs which led up to: 'Our Serenity Lounge', a
quiet place for clients to relax after exercise. It featured soft
lighting, leather sofas and reclining chairs grouped around low
tables, and tall kentia palms in pots. A woman and a man were
occupying one sofa, sitting forward with their heads close together,
talking in low voices. 'We do not allow mobile phones or laptops
in this area,' the manager explained with a touch of pride. 'They
are not conducive to serenity.'

Through more double doors into: 'Our Wellness Refectory'.
This was brightly lit, with a food service counter along one side,
and square wooden tables and chairs with upholstered seats.
Everything had a solid look about it, more John Lewis than Ikea,
the sort of place that would never describe itself as GLicious. A
dozen or so people were sitting at the tables, scrolling or tapping
serenely on mobile phones – except for the young man in the
corner, alone with an open laptop and the manic expression of a
City trader finding himself in the wrong place at the wrong time.

Beyond that was: 'Our Concord Bar', very low-lit, a leather-
fronted bar with tall stools, thick carpet, and a few small round

tables and tub chairs lurking unoccupied in the gloom. Serenity, Wellness and Concord – it was a stiff ask, Slider thought, of the ordinary human being. But perhaps their clients weren't: almost by definition, anyone who could afford the sort of membership fee needed to pay for this lot was not going to class themselves as ordinary.

At the far side of Concord a heavy wooden door was labelled Private, and Mrs Lane-Adams led them through, saying, 'The administration suite is through here.'

Her office was all dark wood and plush carpet, windows onto the High Street covered with white voile daylight blinds, and the hushed air of a library. She gestured them to handsome upholstered chairs, took herself behind the desk, and asked them how she could help.

Slider took a moment to assemble his thoughts. It was so far from the noise and brashness of Gillespie's that he wondered how Lingoss had managed to adapt. He remembered the manic trainer bellowing like a rutting elephant seal. How did they motivate clients here in this cloistral hush? Beat them lightly with scented orchids?

'I'd like to ask you for everything you know about Erik Lingoss.'

The manager frowned – interesting first reaction. 'He's one of the personal trainers. What has he done?'

She was appropriately surprised to hear he was dead by violence – after all, even in the modern urban setting it's not a part of everyday life – but she did not seem moved by his loss. She looked thoughtful, as if she was wondering what paperwork the situation was going to generate. Slider had a certain sympathy for that reaction.

'He hasn't been with us very long,' she said. 'About a year, I think. But he is popular – particularly with our more mature ladies. He has the right manner with them to get results. Our members are demanding and discerning – training methods must be tailored to the individual.'

'I understand the trainers are not directly employed by you,' Slider said.

'No, they're all free-lances. We find the members prefer it that way.'

Yes, Slider thought, and you can avoid National Insurance and other bothersome extras. 'So how does that work?'

'The members make their own arrangements, and pay them direct. The trainers pay a premium to us for insurance, and we charge them to rent the private rooms for their sessions.'

Just enough to make them definitely self-employed and not employees.

'Your members are all wealthy people, I take it?'

She inclined her head rather than voice assent to such a coarse supposition. 'We are an exclusive club. Our facilities are superior. And our members are assured of discretion.'

'You're not worried, then,' Atherton asked, 'that you might be introducing them to predators.'

She raised a frosty eyebrow. 'Of course, we do background checks and take up references before we allow a trainer to use our facilities. We are very particular. But access to top trainers is a facility our members expect.'

'What did you think of Erik Lingoss?' Slider asked.

She pursed her lips in thought. 'He had good qualifications and references, he was well-spoken, personable, obviously very fit, and knew what he was doing. I had no doubts about him. As I said, he was popular.'

'Was his popularity with the "more mature ladies",' Atherton said, putting audible quotation marks round it, 'in any way due to his sexual attractiveness? Did he offer them more than just a training regime?'

She coloured slightly with annoyance. 'There is nothing of that sort going on here! Good God, do you think we're running a brothel?'

'Indeed not, but don't the trainers do home visits as well?' Atherton asked smoothly. 'It was suggested to us that Mr Lingoss did.'

'What they do outside these premises is their business, theirs and the members'.'

'So you wouldn't know if he had any, shall we say, special clients?'

'I would not be so impertinent as to ask,' she said angrily.

Slider intervened. 'Did he have any particular friends here, among the staff or other trainers? Someone we could talk to, who knew him personally?'

'I really couldn't say,' she said, turning her head away.

'Was he involved in any incidents – any trouble while he was here?'

'I have never had any complaints about him from the members.'

'Or the staff?'

'My staff are all top professionals in their field,' she said woodenly.

It was obvious she wasn't going to be co-operative – and of course, it might be that she really didn't know anything. Slider flicked a glance at Atherton and stood up. 'I'd like a list of your members, if you wouldn't mind,' he said.

She stood too. 'I most certainly would mind! My members rely on our absolute discretion – some of them are very eminent people. I will not supply any personal data about them without a direct court order. I'm sorry, but I'm afraid I can't help you.' She pressed a button on her desk as she said it. Slider was half expecting a Mr Burns-type trapdoor to open under his feet, but all that happened was that a young woman came in from the door in the corner and looked enquiringly. 'Show these gentlemen out, please, Jessica.'

Jessica crossed the room to open the other door, holding it for them to pass through. In the corridor she turned the other way from the bar; at the far end here was another staircase, marked as the fire escape. As soon as they were a few paces from the manager's door, she turned to them and said in a low voice, 'I heard what you were talking about. It's terrible about Erik, isn't it? She was only pretending not to know. It's all over social media. I told her about it myself this morning. But she pretends all that sort of thing's beneath her.'

'What sort of thing?' Atherton asked.

'Oh, what people do, ordinary people, like us and the trainers. Everybody in the world, really, apart from the members. She's all about the members.'

'Isn't that her job?'

'Yes, but she fawns over them. It's sickening. Just because they're rolling in money doesn't make them more important, does it?'

It was meant to be a rhetorical question, but Atherton answered it. 'Well, yes, it sort of does – to someone providing a service for them.'

She had pushed through the fire door onto the staircase, and there stopped and turned to face them. 'Yes, but she thinks they're better, too. Like, *better* better. I happen to think everybody's the same and we should all be treated the same.' She presented this novel view with all the pride of the innovative thinker.

Slider diverted her gently. 'Did you know Erik Lingoss?'

'Only to know who he was. To say hello to.' She blushed suddenly. 'He wouldn't be interested in somebody like me.'

'Like—?' Slider began, puzzled.

She went on quickly, avoiding his eyes. 'I'm nothing to look at. He could have anyone he wanted.'

Oh dear, Slider thought. Her perfect make-up gave her the impression of beauty, but underneath, if you analysed her features, she was rather plain, with an over-large, oddly shaped nose and insufficient chin. But of course, most people didn't go round analysing other people's features; and attractiveness didn't lie in any particular configuration of nose, eyes and mouth. She would have been perfectly attractive if only she'd thought she was.

'Were you interested in him?' he asked.

'Everybody was,' she said. 'He was *gorgeous*. But he only went with really smart, beautiful girls.'

The ones who'd look good on his arm and enhance his appearance. Like an expensive watch other men would envy. He wasn't dating, he was accessorizing.

'So can you tell us anyone in particular who would know more about him? Someone he was close to? Did he have any friends here, people he spent time with?'

'Well,' she said, 'there's my friend Lucy. She works at Heneage's, the antique shop on the corner of Phillimore Walk. She went out with him for a bit. Her brother, Jack, he and Erik are friends – at least, they *were* friends once, but I think they'd fallen out recently, I don't know what about.'

'Surname?' Atherton asked.

'Gallo. She's Lucia really, and he's Giacomo, but they call themselves Lucy and Jack. They're Italian,' she added helpfully. 'Only they've been over here since they were children, so you wouldn't know.'

'And what does Jack do?'

'He's a personal trainer as well. He has his own gym now – not like this, but more like a muscle factory, for men mostly. He used to work here before he opened his own place.' She paused, and then, looking at Atherton, lowered her voice. 'What you were saying in there' – she nodded in the general direction of the manager's office – 'asking if he had sex with the clients. Well, I bet he did. A lot of the members, they're very rich women with nothing to do, no job or anything, and they get bored, and the trainers get paid a lot extra for giving them a sorting-out.' She blushed again, and added, 'I don't *know* anything for certain, but that's what everybody says.'

'Thank you, that's very helpful,' Atherton said, giving her a smile that deepened her blush to critical point. 'How did you hear what we were saying?'

It steadied her. 'Oh, she forgets to turn off her intercom. She's always doing it. I don't tell her, because I often hear interesting things,' she explained without shame. 'She isn't as clever as she thinks she is,' she added with bracing contempt.

Outside, the grey blanket of cloud seemed to be thinning, as though the sun might come through at some point. To counterbalance that, a niggling cold wind had got up. 'We ought to get back,' Slider said, 'but given that Phillimore Walk is only just over there . . .'

'And we haven't got any useful information so far,' Atherton agreed.

The antique shop was called Heneage and Seagram, and was one of those ultra-high-end places that mostly seemed to be full of expensive emptiness. Inside, one or two exquisite pieces of furniture lounged elegantly around an expanse of moss-green carpet as if they had no intention of doing anything as vulgar as being sold. Those with flat surfaces further sported some desirable *objet* – a Carolean clock, a silver epergne, a Sèvres vase – picked out by an artful spotlight. You had to ring the bell and be buzzed in to gain access – and, frankly, if they weren't expecting you, you might as well not bother. It didn't say 'by appointment only' on the door, but you'd have to be a bit of a thick not to know it was implied.

At the far end a young woman was using as a desk a gilt-inlaid console table that would have made a *Roadshow* presenter unseemly with excitement. She looked up when Slider pressed the bell, but did not immediately hasten to admit them. Nothing good could be expected of walk-ins. Slider pressed his warrant card against the glass of the door, and she rose in a leisurely manner and came to the door to look at it. She frowned at them enquiringly and they saw her lips form the question 'Police?' and when Slider nodded and mouthed 'Can we speak to you?' she pressed a latch and opened the door.

She still seemed slightly wary, so Atherton offered his brief as well, and said, 'We're investigating the death of Erik Lingoss. May we come in and ask you a few questions?'

Slider liked his use of 'may' rather than 'can', and either that or something about their appearance reassured her. She relaxed and let them in, saying, 'Anything I can do to help.'

'Are you Lucy Gallo?' Atherton asked.

'Yes, that's me. About Erik – they're saying on the internet he was murdered. Is that true?'

For some reason, Slider had been expecting a small, slight girl, but Lucy Gallo was tall, and slim but of athletic rather than twig-like build. She seemed to be in her early twenties, but had the air of confidence that probably – to judge from her accent and lustrous skin – came from a private education. She seemed to be what he would class as a sparky girl, with bright eyes and a wide, ready smile, though at the moment it was suppressed by funereal thoughts.

'I'm afraid so,' Slider said. 'Can I ask, what was the nature of your relationship with him?'

She led them back to the console table, and drew out for them two bow-legged, gilt chairs that didn't look as if they ought to be sat on, while she perched on the edge of the table and folded her arms across her chest. She was wearing beige pleat-fronted trousers and a sage-coloured silk shirt, and her glossy dark hair hung down behind, held back by a matching green hairband. She was the perfect example of what Slider had been thinking in relation to Jessica: apart from unusual gold-brown eyes, her features were in no way remarkable, but she was a beautiful girl because she thought she was. Or, more likely, she never gave it a thought either way, which worked just as well.

'Erik was friends with my brother Jack,' she said. 'They were both trainers at Elite Shapes – the club across the road?'

'Yes, we know it. How long has your brother known Erik?'

'Oh, quite a few years. They met when they did a diploma course together in fitness psychology and it went on from there.'

'Were they good friends?'

'Oh yes. Well . . .' She hesitated a fraction of a second, then went on. 'Yes, they were, though they weren't able to meet all that often, until Erik started working at Elite Shapes. Jack got him onto that, you know. He'd been telling him for ages that he ought to go for a better class of client, where he could make more money. He wanted to start his own business – Erik did – but you need money, or backing, or both. So Jack got him an interview at Elite Shapes and he got taken on.'

'And your relationship with Erik was only that of his friend's sister?'

A faint blush coloured her cheeks, but she held Slider's gaze. 'I suppose you know it wasn't, or you wouldn't be here.'

'You went out with him?'

'Yes, but only recently, and not for very long,' she said. 'I'd known *of* him as Jack's friend for a long time, but I'd only met him in passing, really. But after Jack got him on at Elite Shapes, he was seeing more of him, and I started to meet him more often. Then Jack invited him to a party of some friends of ours, and we really got talking. There was a spark between us. And he asked me out.'

Now she was avoiding his eyes. Slider let Atherton take over.

'You dated?' Atherton said. 'When did that start?'

'Oh, about three months ago. It was in the summer – July, I think. Maybe June. I know it was the summer because it was at a roof garden party in Phillimore Place.'

'And when did your relationship end?'

'What makes you think it ended?' she said. She was going for insouciant, but her eyes were too bright.

'Because you don't seem terribly upset about his death.'

'Of course I'm upset,' she said. Her voice wavered, but she quickly regained control. 'But you're right, we had broken up. I was – I was mad about him, at first. Jack didn't approve. But he's always been overprotective of me. He's the eldest and I'm the youngest, and since our parents died he's always felt he had to look out for me. He didn't want me to go out with Erik. I thought he was just being, you know, the usual "no one's good enough for my little sister". He's never really liked anyone I dated. So when he told me things about Erik, I wouldn't listen.'

'What sort of things?'

'That I shouldn't trust him. That he wasn't good to women. I was mad about him and I thought he felt the same. He really seemed to . . .' She bit her lip, then shook herself. 'But it seems Jack was right and I was wrong. A month ago he suddenly broke up with me, and I haven't seen him since.' She raised her eyes defiantly to Atherton's face. 'I did all my crying then. So I'm not going to cry now. It was all over between us. I'm sorry he's dead – of course I am. And terribly shocked. But I won't cry for him.'

'What did Jack think about it?' Atherton asked.

'He said it was Erik's way, to use people as stepping stones. When someone more useful came along, he moved on. But . . .' She stopped, looking down at her knees. She didn't seem to be going to continue.

Slider prompted. 'Yes?'

She looked up at him, seemed to be searching his face for sympathy – as if she thought he might ridicule her. She looked very young. He tried to project fatherly at her – something Atherton would struggle with.

'I don't think that was true. It didn't feel like that at the time,' she said at last, in a low, uncertain voice, so different from her original polished self-confidence. 'It felt real between us. I really thought he cared for me.' She gave herself a little shake and went on more briskly. 'I suppose if someone's a con artist, that's what they do. I mean, they wouldn't be successful if they weren't good at making you believe them, would they?'

Slider reflected that he had certainly been seeing at least one other person: there was an overlap between Lucy and Kelly-Ann. Probably he had been seeing Ivanka as well, which made it likely there were others too.

'Was your relationship sexual?' he asked, a blunt question to distract her from her feelings.

It did seem to brace her. She didn't look in any way embarrassed. She just said, 'Yes.'

'Did you ever go to his flat?' He didn't like to think of her being performed with between those mirrored walls.

'No,' she said. 'I've got my own flat in Aubrey Walk. We went there.'

'Did you ever meet any of his other friends?'

'No,' she said. 'I only saw him with Jack's crowd, or alone.' A slight frown flitted across her brows. 'He never talked about any other friends. When we were together, we only talked about us.' It seemed to be striking her, perhaps for the first time, as odd. But, as human beings do, she quickly rationalized it. 'He was very driven. He was all about his profession, and his ambition for his future. I don't suppose he had time for much socializing.'

Except with a number of other sexual partners, Slider thought, but he didn't say it aloud.

SIX

It's Gym Life, but Not as We Know It

'I don't understand,' Slider said. 'What did an oaf like Lingoss have to attract a gem like her?'

Atherton shrugged. 'Having a posh accent doesn't make you clever. It just makes you *sound* clever.'

'But she's been left alone in charge of the shop, so she must have something.'

'Then perhaps Lingoss wasn't an oaf.'

'He must have had a superficial charm to attract so many women,' Slider admitted.

'Superficial?' Atherton said in a pained voice. 'I don't think you realize how much intense effort and thorough preparation goes into being irresistible. The life of a hound is one of constant toil and responsibility.'

'Stop, I may weep.' The promised sun had broken through in a watery I-may-not-stay-long way. Still, it was an improvement. And Ken High Street was seething with well-dressed, bright-looking people going about their business and not bothering anyone. It was a scene to warm a copper's gnarled old heart. 'At least we've got a lead to someone who might have known him,' Slider said. 'Someone other than a sexual partner, that is.'

Atherton was working away on his mobile. 'Here we are. Jack Gallo. He's got quite a presence on the internet. Big following on Twitter. And here's his gym. Pex Muscle Gym, Notting Hill Gate. Rave reviews from happy customers. "Not the usual pussy gym," says someone called Ironhead. "Serious worx," spelled with an x, says Big Lifter. "Perfect place for a good sweat," says Megapump. Well, I don't know about you, but I'm sold.'

'Good thing too, because you're going there. I have to get back to the factory.'

'*Me?* In these trousers?'

'You need to see how the other half lives,' said Slider.

McLaren had been eating a Jumbo Cornish Pastie. The flakes of pastry on his lips looked like advanced dermatitis.

'The laundromat and the heel bar don't have any security cameras,' he said. 'The newsagents have got one, but it's facing the counter, so there's no view of the street. The other place is still closed, so I can't find out if they've got anything.'

'If an electronics shop can't have a camera, who can?' Slider said.

'Yeah, guv, but it might be pointing inwards, like in the newsy. Protect the stock, sort of thing.'

'And why is it closed?'

'Dunno, guv. I asked Kadan in the heel bar, and he said he's hardly ever seen it open.'

'A front, do you think?'

'More likely one of these techie hobby places, run by some geek so he can talk bollocks to other geeks all day.'

'Hardly all day if it's not open.'

'Well, he could be off sick or on holiday. And I wouldn't trust Kadan to know, anyway. He's inside working all day. With those venetian blinds on the window, you can't tell if it's open unless you try the door.'

'Well, shelve that for now. You'd better start looking at street cameras in Holland Road – something might cover the end of Russell Close. And if not, it may have to be bus cameras.'

McLaren did not look thrilled. 'We don't know what time we're looking at,' he pointed out.

'Wouldn't be the first time,' said Slider. 'Start with ten until midnight. That seems the most likely time. If necessary, we can extend it later.'

'There's four buses go down Holland Road. That's a lot of buses in two hours.'

Slider was impressed he knew. 'You've checked already?'

He shrugged. 'I know buses, that's all. And three night buses: they all start after midnight, but if we have to look at later—'

'Let's see how we get on. It's a weekday, so there may not be that many people around after ten. Or all that many cars turning into Russell Close. Get the indexes, and see if anything comes

back to anyone connected with Lingoss. And get Fathom on
checking taxis and minicabs – anyone dropped off at the flats or
in the road.'

Hart passed him in the doorway. 'Still nothing on the canvass,'
she reported. 'Nobody heard any disturbance. We've talked to all
but two of the flats, and they all agree with the old lady – that
building's got good insulation. Couple of 'em knew Lingoss by
sight, but that's all. But there's one woman' – she checked her
notes – 'Aditi Prasanna. She lives in flat nine on the top floor.
Single, twenty-six, data analyst. She says she met him in the hall
one morning a couple of months back when she was going to
work and they walked out together. Says he started talking to her
about some kids charity he was involved in, she thinks it was
called Fit and Fun, or Fitness Fun, something like that. Helps
disadvantaged kids. Supposedly if they get fit it gives 'em confidence and gets 'em off crime and drugs and so on. Though it
seems to me,' she added in parenthesis, 'that all you'd get is fitter
burglars, but what do I know?'

'Interesting,' Slider said. 'Getting involved in a charity doesn't
tally with what we know about him so far.'

'Yeah, boss,' said Hart. 'She said she thought he was trying to
get her involved, like help with a campaign or cough up some
dosh or something. But thinking about it afterwards, she reckoned
he was just trying to get off with her. She's quite a good-looking
babe. She reckoned it was just a pickup line. All events, he never
followed up on it.'

'Would a man that attractive need a line?'

'You're asking me?'

'Humour me. My dating days are long behind me.'

'Well, it never hurts. Women like men to have a sensitive side, as
well as looks. Like you, boss,' she added with a cheeky grin. 'You
care about people. That's really hot. Caring is the new macho, right?'

Slider gave her a discouraging look. 'He seems to have got on
all right just treating women badly.'

'What, Kelly-Ann and her lot? Well, there are always dumb
females just asking for it. Maybe he was trading up, going for a
better class of date. Or maybe he always did both.'

'Yes, probably that. A man of voracious appetite would have
to spread his net wide. He might not have a "type".'

Hart grinned. 'There's some blokes whose "type" is horizontal but still breathing.'

'Needlessly cynical, sergeant,' Slider said sternly.

She was unabashed. 'Ask Jim Atherton.'

'I'm still waiting for the bank and the credit card companies to send copies of his statements,' Swilley said. She had recently had a very short haircut, which entirely failed to make her look boyish. Slider had always had a thing for short hair on women, anyway – it made them look somehow vulnerable, which made him want to protect them. *Hot damn, I'm so sensitive!* he thought. At the very least, with the current fad for long straggling locks it made a woman stand out like a rock in a kelp bed.

'He banked online,' she went on, ignorant of how her shorn poll was affecting him – *or was she?* – 'but without the pass-words it's easier to wait for the bank. I've got a good contact there, so it shouldn't be long. Meanwhile, I've had a look at the rest of his online history. He doesn't have much of a presence – no website or Facebook, didn't seem interested in Twitter. He posted a lot of pictures of himself on Instagram – muscle poses.' She gave an eye-roll. 'Nothing untoward in his emails so far. I just wish we had his mobile, so we knew who was contacting him at the end.'

'That's why the murderer swiped it, obvs,' said Lœssop, pausing in passing. 'We know it had to be someone he knew, because there was no break-in, and the fact that it happened in the bedroom.'

'Not necessarily. They might have been talking in the living room, he went into the bedroom to get something and the killer followed him in,' Swilley said.

'But then, what about the mirrors?' said Lœssop. 'He'd see them coming in the reflection. And they'd have to go past him to get to the weights rack. He'd have asked what they were doing, he'd have been on his guard, there'd at least have been a struggle or some defence wounds.'

'So you think it must have been a woman? Someone he was having sex with?' Slider asked.

'The seven hundred pounds under the pillow,' said Swilley. 'If he was being paid to have sex, that makes him a prostitute.'

'Not necessarily sex. His mats and equipment were all in the bedroom. It might have been someone he was giving a home training session to. That could have been what he charged for private training. And then the killer would have every reason to pick up one of the barbells.'

'True,' said Slider.

Lœssop liked the encouragement. 'My idea is that someone wanted him made away with, arranged a private training session at the flat – probably rang him up to arrange it, which is why the murderer had to take the phone away.'

'But we can get phone records from the providers,' Swilley objected.

'Yes, but not everyone knows that. So if we find somebody who had a grievance against him—'

'Or if it was a sex partner, it could have been a spur-of-the-moment thing,' Swilley said. 'A sudden row.' She looked at Slider, who nodded. Among people who were emotionally volatile and not very bright, a quarrel could easily lead to violence. They had seen it again and again. 'They go into the bedroom to do the nasty, words are spoken, offence is taken, she grabs one of the weights and lets him have it. And he doesn't defend himself because he's taken by surprise. He doesn't expect that from her. Maybe he's even laughing at her while she's threatening him. And that tips her over the edge.'

'And what about the seven hundred?' Lœssop put in.

'That could have been there from earlier. We don't know it's anything to do with the killer.'

'Well, either way, we have to find out who came to his flat, which means finding out who his friends and enemies were,' Slider said. 'The usual grind.'

'I'll make a list of his contacts from his laptop,' Swilley said.

'Atherton's following up one of them right now,' Slider said, and told them about Pex Muscle Gym.

Swilley looked horrified. 'You sent Jim to an iron-pumping club?'

'He can handle himself,' said Slider.

'It's other people handling him I'm worried about,' she muttered.

Atherton hadn't thought you could get louder music than at Gillespie's. In a way, he was right. The music at Pex was so deafening it had passed beyond normal aural ranges into a realm of harmonics where the distinction between the different senses was eroded, where sound became feeling and, as your eyeballs bounced to the beat in their bony sockets, sight too.

Smell was otherwise fully engaged and hadn't attention to spare for the pounding music. Smell was already having to deal with rubber mats, machine oil, rubbing liniment, various ultra-manly colognes and deodorants, feet – a biggie, that one – and sweat. Lots and lots of sweat. Atherton wasn't at all sure that testosterone wasn't also nasally detectable. One sniff inside the gym, and the hair in his nostrils took on a growth spurt.

Everything was black and chrome and so stern and manly it made the Imperial War Museum look like a princess tea party. And despite being a weekday and in normal working hours, every infernal machine was occupied, and everywhere slippery bodies were heaving and groaning and straining like the damned in a tenth circle of Hell. Atherton stared in bemusement. He was obliged as a policeman to maintain a certain level of fitness, and for his own vanity he didn't want to be fat and flabby, but this! Well, it was more like some very, very obscure form of sexual perversion.

He was brought back to earth by the realization that as he stared at them, one or two were starting to stare back at him with equal bemusement. He was quite glad when a man who detached himself from the torment and came to ask if he wanted anything turned out to be very short – though extremely wide at the shoulders – and friendly.

'Is he expecting you?' asked the short one when Atherton asked for Jack Gallo.

'Probably not, but it's a friendly visit – just looking for some information,' Atherton said, showing his warrant card.

'Righty-oh, he's in his office. It's this way.' He led the way, rolling a little in his walk because his leg muscles were so hugely developed, his inner thighs were no longer within touching distance of each other. He was so muscled and so short, he looked like a cube of flesh. Atherton was still wondering why anyone would do that to themselves when he was shown into Gallo's office.

It was an office fit for a man of action – small, scruffy, undusted, with the cheapest of furnishings, and nary a pot plant in sight. And at the first sight of Jack Gallo, Atherton ceased to wonder why anyone 'worked out'. He was taller than Atherton by an inch, but much bigger in mass, and not one ounce of that volume was fat. And it was not the ludicrous, overblown, veiny balloons of the Mr Universe contest, but beautiful, proportionate, usable muscles. He was wearing a clinging cutaway training vest and black Lycra trunks, so it was all on display, and it was impressive. His man-breasts looked like two turkey crown roasts, nicely browned. This was a powerful man. Even his chin had muscles. He looked as though he could do press-ups with his tongue.

It didn't hurt, either, that he had thick, glossy, near-black hair, the smooth natural tan of the Mediterranean type, and gold-brown eyes so arresting you didn't immediately notice the rest of his features. Atherton saw a resemblance to Lucy of the antique shop. He began with: 'I've just been talking to your sister.'

'About Erik?' Gallo said. 'Yeah, that's a bummer. D'you wanna sit down?' He said it as an afterthought – sitting down probably didn't feature much in his life. Atherton declined in favour of leaning against the wall, figuring that Gallo was more comfortable standing. He chose the wall by the window where the light would fall on his subject.

'Tell me about Erik,' he said. 'You two were friends for a long time.'

'Yeah, I don't know how long. Years, anyway.'

'What was he like?'

'He was all right.' Real men didn't go into details about their friendships, but Atherton just nodded and waited, knowing that most people feel impelled to fill in a silence. Eventually, Gallo went on. 'We hung out, you know? Had a few laughs. He was OK company. I mean . . .' He ran out of steam.

'You got him the job at Shapes,' Atherton said to wind him up again.

'Yeah. Well, it's not a job, like a *job*. It's all freelance. But it gets you contacts.' Atherton waited, and Gallo shifted his weight and splurged. 'You see, he'd been doing all right where he was, but it wasn't enough. He's good, Erik – a really good trainer. He knows how to get the best out of people. He's better at that sort of stuff than me. I'm good at power lifting, weight training, strength development, that sort of thing. I like working with men. I haven't got the patience for all that feel-good business, all that motivation and empathy and stuff you have to do with women. Like, we both did a psychology course, and Erik totally aced it, but it was . . .' He passed his hand over his head, four inches above it. 'You got to know where your strengths lie, right? Erik, he can do all that "I feel your pain" bollocks. He can do sincerity till the cows come home. And the women love him – I mean, *love* him. He can get work out of them that . . . Well!'

He'd stalled himself again. Atherton said, 'So why did he need the job at Shapes?'

'He wanted to build up his private work. The pay at a gym's all right, but that's it, right? If you take on private clients, the sky's the limit. Especially rich people, and Shapes' clients are some of the richest in London.' Atherton nodded receptively, and he went on. 'He was ambitious, Erik. He wanted to be the best, he wanted to be famous, he wanted to be the name when people asked who they should go to. Like, Gillespie's, it was started by a trainer, David Gillespie, and now it's a chain, it's a name everybody knows. Erik wanted that.'

'And money?'

Gallo gave a goes-without-saying shrug. 'I mean, he needed money to start up his own gym, lots of it. I started up Pex, and I think he was jealous of that. Not in a bad way – but he wanted the same, only better. I got backing for my start-up, and my backers own half the business, but he didn't want that, he wanted it all. So he'd need a lotta money – I told him that. But it wasn't only for the business. He loves the lifestyle money gives you. I mean, you'd want to see his clothes.' He puffed his lips and rolled his eyes. 'Suits, shoes – I mean, I don't care about that stuff. You're clean, you're smart, that's enough, right? But he had to have the best. He wanted everyone to see he had money – even when he didn't. He just . . . loved money.'

'And sex?'

Gallo gave a short laugh. 'Yeah, that too. I mean, we all like it when we can get it, am I right?' Atherton declined to comment. 'But Erik was like, a sex addict. He had to have it all the time. I swear, if he didn't get his rocks away every couple of hours, he'd get antsy.'

'Did he have sex with his clients?'

Gallo hesitated, as if being asked to break a confidence. Atherton folded his arms and nodded to convey that he was here for the long haul and all avenues were to be explored. Some more encouragement was obviously needed, so he said, 'The clients he met at Shapes, for instance?'

He yielded. 'Well, that was part of it, part of why he wanted to get in there. You see' – he looked keenly at Atherton to see if he *did* see – 'it's an expensive place, Shapes – exclusive. People who want personal, tailored attention, and they got the money to pay for it.'

'Attention including sex?'

He looked away for a moment. 'You got to understand, there's all these rich women. Some of them are young birds married to rich old guys who maybe can't get it up any more, or not often enough. Or it might be an older woman, she's bored, got nothing to do but go shopping, husband's always away a lot on business. They get attention from a personal trainer, one-on-one attention, it makes 'em feel good, feel wanted. And if they get a massage as well . . . You do a good, strong training session, then you get a massage to relax you afterwards, from this good-looking guy who seems to like you, and – well . . .'

'One thing leads to another?' Atherton offered.

He shrugged. 'What's the harm? No one gets hurt. The husband never knows. The trainer's not going to break up the marriage, all right?'

'So do a lot of trainers do that?'

'Not all. Quite a few.'

'You?'

He looked embarrassed. 'Once or twice, in the early days. Not now. Like I said, I work with men mostly. I'm not in that area any more.'

'But Erik was.'

'He did massages, he was good at it. And he liked sex.' He gave Atherton a frank look. 'I tell you this, I don't think you could do that – service clients – if you didn't enjoy it. I've known some rent boys in my time – they come to trainers to improve their bodies – and the successful ones are the ones who don't have to pretend. It'd break your spirit, otherwise.'

'OK,' said Atherton. 'And there's money in it – the extra services? The trainers take money for sex?'

'Yeah, why not?' There was a touch of defiance in the tone, but only a touch. 'You're giving the client what they want, they're loaded, why wouldn't they give you a little present, a bonus, whatever you want to call it?'

'How little is a little present?' He shrugged. 'How much did Erik get, for instance? For having sex with a client?'

'I don't know, all right?' He tried to sound indignant. Then, yielding, he added, 'It'd vary, wouldn't it, depending on the client.'

'Give me an idea. He must have found it worthwhile.'

He shrugged again. 'Maybe five hundred? On top of the normal fee. That'd be an average. Some of them would give more, depending on how much they liked the guy. Could be a thousand. Maybe for a special occasion. Or it might be a present, like a nice watch. Look, these women have got money to burn, so much they don't know what to do with it. A thou to them's like a tenner to us. They'd barely notice it.'

'And it would be cash, would it?'

'Of course. Out of their pocket money. Not a cheque their husband might find out about.'

'So Erik was getting the contacts at Shapes, to do private training sessions, plus extras – in *their* homes? Or his?'

'Oh, theirs,' Gallo said with a short laugh. 'They wouldn't want to go slumming. Or be seen going into another guy's pad. These are not women looking for a divorce, you get me?'

'I get you. He does private training sessions with rich women, gives them a massage, and boffs them, and gets a nice fat bonus on top of the fee. He must have been making a lot, then?'

'I suppose so. Like I said, he was saving to set up his own place.'

'He must have been grateful to you, then, for getting him in in the first place.'

Gallo's face darkened. 'You'd think so, wouldn't you?'

'Shouldn't I? You knew he wanted the chance to have sex with rich women in return for presents. He wasn't springing any surprises, was he?'

'He can have sex with every woman in the country for all I care. He can have sex till his dick drops off. But when he messes with my little sister!' He stopped abruptly, reddening.

'It's all right,' Atherton said. 'Lucy told me. You're not giving anything away.'

He stared broodingly at his hands, which were clenching and unclenching. 'What makes me so fucking mad is that I introduced him to her in the first place. She was just a kid, he was her big brother's friend, that's how she saw him. That's how he treated her. But then when she gets old enough to be interesting, that dirty dog goes and – he goes and . . .' He didn't want to say the words.

'How old is Lucy?'

'She's only twenty now,' Gallo said, and sounded almost tearful. 'I know that's supposed to be adult, but it's not, not when it's your little sister. See, when our parents died, I had to look after them all, I was the oldest. Lucy was the baby. I'm thirteen years older than her. She was fifteen, sixteen when I met Erik. He met all my family. He knew them. I thought I could trust him, but then he goes and messes with Lucy, sleeps with her, breaks her heart. It's not on. It's not bloody on.'

The words were mild but the tone and the expression weren't. This was a big man, Atherton reflected. Bashing Erik Lingoss's head in wouldn't make him break a sweat. And yes, someone who wanted him dead would go back and finish him off when he realized the first blow hadn't done it.

Quietly, he said, 'If it's any consolation, she didn't seem heart-broken when I spoke to her just now.'

He had been staring broodingly at his hands again, but now he looked up. 'You don't know her. And she doesn't know you – she wouldn't let on to you. And you didn't know Erik. He could charm the birds off the trees when he wanted. She thought he really loved her – it was serious for her. Her first love. And then he dumps her, just like that. That's the sort of bastard he was.'

'Where were you on Tuesday night?' Atherton asked.

He went still. After a measurable pause, he said, 'What time?'

'Start with when you left work.'

'We're open six till ten, Monday to Friday,' he said. His voice was careful, his eyes steady as though determined to be accurate. 'I split the lates with my manager, Gerry – that was him that brought you in here. And I have two other guys, Andy and Dez, who cover Saturdays and Sundays. And fill in for Gerry and me if we need time off.'

Atherton nodded attentively. 'So what time did you leave on Tuesday?'

Another pause. 'Gerry did the late. I finished about six.'

'And what did you do then?'

'Showered, changed. Went for a pint.'

'Where?'

'The Britannia in Allen Street.'

'I know it. Then what?'

'Went home,' he said, closing his lips tight as if that were the end of that.

'What time did you get home?'

'About half-eight.'

'And then what?'

'Nothing. I stayed home. Had something to eat. Watched some sport. Went to bed.'

'You live alone?' Nod. 'Can anyone verify that you were at home on Tuesday evening?'

A flicker of fire in the eyes. 'No,' he said. 'And if you're trying to make out I killed Erik bloody Lingoss, you're on a loser. You've got nothing against me. So back off, all right? Back off, or I'll—'

He stopped himself, but his fists were clenched. 'You'll what?' Atherton asked, at his most smooth and annoying. He wanted to see what Gallo would do if provoked.

But Gallo backed off. 'Nothing,' he said moodily. 'You've got nothing against me, that's all I'm saying.'

And you've got no alibi, Atherton thought.

SEVEN

He Stooped to Conk Her

Porson's eyebrows were drawn together like two sumo wrestlers in a clinch.

'Where are those figures?' he bellowed. Slider drew breath to answer but Porson powered on. 'Tell me at least you're working on them.'

'I've got a homicide case,' Slider gave the obvious answer.

Porson growled. 'Haven't you sorted that out yet? Hammersmith've got a load of piddly cases they want to pawn off onto us, and I need some ammunition. And don't forget,' he added, reeling into his usual back and forth prowl, 'there's that climate change march next week. The commissioner'll be pulling every warm body he can to cover it, and that'll include your little bunnies.'

'Surely they won't cut down a murder squad for that?'

'Priorise a live march in central London over a dead weightlifter? What d'you think they see when they look out of their windows in Whitehall? Lingoss's old mum demanding justice for her baby boy, or ten thousand crusties followed by the media?'

'That's ridiculous,' Slider protested feebly.

The rikishi strained harder against each other. 'Ninety-nine times out of ten these decisions are political, you know that. The PM leans on the home secretary, he leans on the commissioner, and PR triumphs again.' He fetched up against the filing cabinet, breathed for a moment, then pushed off again like a swimmer doing lengths. 'It's time they brought in some legislation about these marches.'

'The right to protest is a vital element of free speech,' Slider said mildly. The Old Man seemed unusually bitter this afternoon. Hammersmith had a bad effect on his bile duct.

'Yerss,' Porson said darkly. 'They'll shut down London for eight hours because that's free speech. But if anyone calls them names they want 'em arrested for hate crime.' He sighed and relaxed to his normal state of muted – as opposed to overt – frenzy. 'Where have you got with Lingoss?'

Slider told him about Jack Gallo.

He brightened. 'That's more like it. A bloke with muscles and a good grudge. Better than the jilted girlfriend.'

'We're checking his story, though it doesn't cover the important hours, so it's not an alibi. But if he becomes a suspect, we'll have to show we've been thorough.'

'And it might give you a direction to look in. Say he's said something to somebody in the pub or whatever.' He rubbed his big dry hands together with a sound like someone wrapping rocks for Christmas. 'You can see it – has a few pints, brooding over his wrongs, gets fuelled up and goes to have it out with laughing boy.'

'It's a possibility,' Slider said. But without direct evidence, it was only a story. Porson knew that as well as he did. It was evidence of his frustration that he even voiced it. 'I wish we had enough to search his flat, but at the moment . . .'

'Well what are you standing there for? Go and get something,' Porson snapped.

Joanna was back when he got home. She was in the kitchen, sitting on one chair and contemplating her feet, which rested on another.

'I used to have nice feet,' she said by way of greeting. 'Now I look as if I'm on a stand.'

He bent to kiss her. 'Good day?'

Her eyes lit. 'Yes, very good. They had a lot of extra brass in today to do the loud bits.'

'Woah, woah, you're losing me with all the technical terms. Loud bits?'

'Funn-ee. And one of the trumpets was my old pal Peter White.'

'Oh yes.' Slider had often heard about him. 'Did you have a nice natter?'

'Yes, in the break. We were swapping old tour stories. Fun! Like the time in Hong Kong he was sharing a room with Jimmy Ruddles. Jimmy used to sleep walk, but generally Peter woke up when he heard him bumping about and herded him back to bed. But on this particular night drink had been taken, and Peter was out like a light. So Jimmy got out of the room, went down in the lift to the reception area. He woke up just as the lift doors opened and he stepped out into the foyer at the same time as a party of elderly Chinese tourists came in from a late flight.' She grinned. 'It should be mentioned that Jimmy always slept in the buff. It was a toss-up who was more surprised, him or the tourists.'

'What happened?'

'A quick-thinking receptionist dashed over with a waste-paper basket to cover his shame. A-a-ah!' she sighed. 'The good old days. How was yours?'

'We've got a new suspect – well, not even really a suspect at this stage, but a person of interest.' He told her.

'So your deceased took money for sex? No wonder massage has got such a bad name.'

'No law was broken. I'm relaxed about it.'

'And you think this Gallo might have killed him in a row over his sister?'

'It's nothing more than a possibility at the moment. And I'm sure others will arise. In the absence of any material evidence, we'll have to check up on all Lingoss's contacts, which will be a long process. Unless we can trace the mobile phone.'

'Which one?'

'The victim's, which is missing. He might have lost it, or left it somewhere, but it might have been taken away by the murderer. If we can find it, it might give us a lead. Of course, if the murderer did take it, he probably smashed it or dumped it, or at the very least turned it off. We'll see. Meanwhile, we just keep doing the hard yards.'

'Poor old thing! Well, help me up and I'll get some supper on.'

'I'll do it. You sit there and be comfortable.'

'Make up your mind. At this stage of pregnancy, I can do one or the other. By the way, after supper we ought to look over the baby things and see what we need, so we can get them this weekend. I've still got George's wee outfits, but some of the equipment might have deteriorated.'

'You kept George's baby clothes?' he said, pleased. 'When we weren't planning to have another?'

'Couldn't bring myself to part with them,' she said, heaving herself up. 'There, you made me admit it. I'm as soppy as the next woman.'

'There is no next woman for me,' he said, engulfing her and kissing the end of her nose. 'You're all the woman I can handle.'

'Oh Rhett, you say such pretty things,' she purred. Then, back in practical mode: 'At the very least, we'll need a couple of gross of Pampers. I know it's ecologically indefensible . . .'

'There's a climate change march in Westminster next week,' he mentioned. 'They wouldn't approve.'

'*I* don't approve,' she said. 'But I'm not going to wash terry nappies at my age, and that's just an uncomfortable fact.'

'Mr Porson was saying we might get pulled off this case to help with policing the march,' he remembered.

'Maybe you could ask if any of them would like to come and wash nappies for me,' she said. 'Save the world one dimpled bottom at a time.'

LaSalle had done the early run to Mike's coffee stall, and brought in Slider's bacon sarnie with a mug of tea, from which he had forgotten to remove the teabag. Its string hung sadly down the outside like the tail of a suicidal mouse.

'I got something of interest, guv,' he said.

'Not the dead mouse, I hope,' Slider said, hooking a pencil under the string and lifting. It was only a teabag after all. He cupped his hand under it to stop it dripping on his papers as he conveyed it to the bin, then didn't know what to do with his wet hand.

LaSalle didn't understand the mouse reference, but they often didn't understand the guv's obscure comments, so it didn't bother him. 'There's a paper napkin inside the sandwich bag,' he offered helpfully.

'What have you got, that's of interest?' Slider prompted, mopping up.

'Oh! Yes – I was checking Lingoss on the PNC, and he hasn't got a criminal record, but he did pop up in relation to an incident at a nightclub called Deans.'

'In Dean Street? Yes, I know it. When was this?'

'A month ago. He got in a fight with Jack Gallo. It started off with an argument and raised voices, then there was a bit of shoving, and then punches were thrown. Someone called the police but by the time they arrived the club's bouncers'd got the two men up

into the street, so they were just given a warning and told to push
off.'

'Does the report say who started it? Or what it was about?'

'No, guv. But with what Gallo told Jim yesterday and the timing,
it could be about the sister, couldn't it? She said she broke up
with Lingoss a month ago.'

'Gallo didn't mention a fight with Lingoss,' Slider observed.

LaSalle smiled hopefully. 'Well, he wouldn't, would he?'

'All right, go and see what you can find out – find who was on
duty and interview them. I'd like to get enough on Gallo to turn
over his pad. And ask Atherton to come in.'

There are few places sadder than a nightclub in daytime. Cleaners
have to clean and bar staff have to bottle up, so the lights have to
be fully on, revealing what was never meant to be seen – at least,
not clearly and by the sober. The scratches on the black-painted
walls, the stains on the floor, the damp patches on the ceiling, the
cheapness of the furniture and its battered state, the trashiness of
the backdrop to the tiny stage, the smell of stale beer and the gale
of bleach from the toilets that didn't quite drown the whiff of
urine. LaSalle could feel his moustache wilting.

A woman behind the bar was making a great deal of busy clatter
with bottles. She looked up and said, 'We're closed.'

LaSalle showed his brief. 'I want to talk to someone about an
incident back in October.'

She gave a bark of laughter. 'You got here quick! Worth every
penny of our taxes.'

LaSalle had a good line in stolid. 'The person who called the
police at the time was a Jay Pheeney,' he said in best plod mode.
'I think he's the manager?'

'She is, and she's me,' the woman said, coming out from behind
the bar, wiping her hands on a tea towel. She examined his face.
'Ooh, a lady manager! Whatever next?' she parodied. She had a
robust Dublin accent and jet black hair that was obviously out of
a bottle. She was probably nearer sixty than fifty, but in the dim
night-time lights, behind the bar and with a full face of slap would
probably pass for younger. She was shortish, and solid, with
formidable barmaid's arms, and a flat, doughy face with the deroga-
tory eyes of a cat. She looked as if she'd seen it all and didn't

think much of any of it, especially the portion of it that emanated from the male of the species.

LaSalle reminded her of the fight between Gallo and Lingoss, and showed her photos of the two to refresh her memory. She gave them a sharp look and said, 'Yes, I remember the two o' them. What's it all about then, dear? You don't come bothering about a bit o' fisticuffs in the usual way.'

'I'm afraid Erik Lingoss – this one – has been killed, so we're looking for anyone who had a grudge against him.'

'A grudge, is it? Well, I'll tellya what I know, but it was the queerest bar fight I've ever seen, which is why I remember it. See, this one . . .' She tapped a photo.

'Jack Gallo,' LaSalle supplied.

'Him,' she agreed. 'Glorious big feller, with muscles on him like a panther, all sleek and rippling. We get that type in here sometimes, the weightlifters and bodybuilders, and they're usually no trouble – they're more interested in themselves than anyone else. The muscles are all for show. They're for fillin' out their T-shirts, not for lampin' anybody. Your man here' – she tapped Lingoss's picture – 'he was more the pretty type. Fit as the butcher's dog, but not your usual iron-pumper. More like an athlete.' She pronounced it 'athalete'. 'He was a bit of a Bob, if you want to know,' she added approvingly. 'He could get the ride off me any time!' And she gave a cackle of lascivious laughter.

LaSalle stuck to plod in self-defence. 'Did they come in together?'

'Now that I can't tell ya. There was a crowd in that night, which was why I was helping out serving. I saw them at the bar, is all, gassing away. I only noticed when it started getting a bit intense, and me radar went off' – she tapped her nose – 'because you want to get to fights before they start in this business.'

'Do you know what they were arguing about?'

She rolled her eyes. 'With the rock band playing? It was The Mighty Mouse – you couldn't hear a mammoth fart when they get going. But, I'll tell ya, it was like the big one was telling the ridey one off. He was leaning in and poking him in the chest, like he was giving out shite to your man.' She demonstrated on the air.

'And how was the . . . Lingoss taking it?'

'Taking his medicine at first, so it looked. A bit glum in the mouth but puttin' up with it. But then he starts getting annoyed, and he pushes your man. Like it might be, "stop pokin' me like that" and "who d'you think you're talking to?" Next thing I know, this one . . .'

'Gallo.'

'The same, he's thrown a punch – but, now, here's the thing. Nine times out of ten in a bar fight, th'eejit'll go for the chin, and hurt his knuckles as much as he hurts the other feller. Then it's all over except the cursing. But your man here – it looks as if at the last second he pulls the punch, and ends up kind of hittin' him on the shoulder. Then the ridey one hits him in the gut, and they grab each other and start wrestling about like pigs in an alley. See' – she lifted her eyes to LaSalle's face to check that he was taking it in – 'it's like this one couldn't damage th'other one's beauty. Not hit him in the face. As a professional, he just couldn't do it.'

LaSalle nodded. 'Yeah, I think I know what you mean. So what happened then?'

'Well, notice was starting to be taken, so I come out round the bar to break it up. I shove a bar stool between them, which is what I usually do to part them, but the big one, it musta caught him off balance and he sorta slings his arm out and pucks me on the head.' She demonstrated again. 'I don't think he meant it, but he's bloody strong, and it gets me rile up. So back behind the bar I go, ring for me boys, and call the peelers. The boys – my doormen, Lennie and Omar – they escort them out. Well, they'd stopped fighting and were looking a bit sheepish by then. But later Lennie comes and tells me that when they get up in the fresh air they start at it again, and him and Omar had to hold 'em apart until the gards arrived. And Lennie says it was all about some girl.'

'What were they saying? Did they say a name?'

'Lennie never said. I don't think he was paying that much attention. Anyway, that's it and all about it. I wouldn't have thought twice about it, except for that pulled punch, and the way the ridey one was puttin' up with being given out to, as if he deserved it. It looked as if the two of them were grand friends before that.'

'So you think the big one – Gallo – he wasn't really angry, deep down?'

She frowned, remembering. 'No, I'd say he was pure mad. But

the other one, his face was his fortune, and when it came to it, he couldn't hit him there.'

At his second visit, Atherton didn't see either Gallo or the short one in the main gym, but after a moment a tall West Indian, with glossy muscles barely confined by purple training shorts and stringer vest, came over. His hair was dyed acid blonde and he wore it in mad spikes above his head like Lady Liberty. Fortunately, since he topped Atherton by a good three inches, he was also wearing a friendly expression. 'Help you?'

'I'm looking for Jack Gallo,' Atherton said.

'He's not here. I'm Dez, I'm the manager. Is it about training sessions?' He gave Atherton a rapid, professional look over. 'I see you keep yourself fit, man, but a bit more can't hurt, am I right? You got the face, you might as well have the body to go with it. A couple of sessions a week after work, you'll soon gain a bit more definition. You got nice freads, bro, you'll be surprised how much better they look when you've done a bit of work, toned up just that bit extra.'

'Thanks,' Atherton said when he could get a word in, 'but it wasn't that. I—'

'You don't wanna be shy, man. First timer, right? But you're never too old. We get guys come in in their fifties, sixties, never worked out in their lives. I guarantee after ten minutes you'll love it. You'll wonder how you lived without it – it's the endorphins, see? Better than speed, man, the endorphins. Big, big high. And you'll see the difference in your body. Great mood, great looks, it's win-win! Whaddaya say?'

For a perilous moment Atherton was almost persuaded. He almost bought it. His hand made a definite twitch towards his wallet, and it was lucky he could divert it to his warrant card or a lifetime of exquisite and practised indolence might have gone out of the window.

Dez must have been endorphined right up to the brow ridge, because he led Atherton to the office to be interviewed with a serene and helpful smile, and offered him his choice between a bottle of water and a bottle of chilled Lucozade.

'Have you known Jack long?' Atherton began, accepting the water.

'Oh, years, man. Way before he opened this place. Him and me worked together at The Muscle Factory in Islington, gotta be ten years ago. We kept in touch when we went our ways, and when he started up Pex he asked if I'd like to come in wiv him. Well, I didn't have no capital to invest, but he give me a job right off, and made me a manager. I gotta lotta respec' for Jack. He's got brains, man, brains an' drive.'

'Did you also know Erik Lingoss?'

'Yeah, bro, like me and Jack and Erik all started off together at the Factory. We were tight. The Free Musketeers, we called ourselves.' He smiled happily as though this were a novel soubriquet. 'We used to get up to stuff – they was wild days!'

'What sort of wild? Drink, drugs, women?'

He looked serious for a moment. 'You can't do drugs if you want to look like this,' he said with a modest gesture towards his body. 'The body's a temple, man. No drugs – never! And not too much booze.'

'But women? That was OK?'

'Oh, man!' he said with a happy reminiscent smile, like a child remembering the best ice cream sundae ever. 'We used to go out a Friday night, give the wimmin five minutes' start, then go round 'em up! We shared a flat in Liverpool Road, Jack and me – Erik had his own place in Haggerston – and most nights the free of us ended up at the flat wiv half a dozen wimmin. Great days, man, glory days.'

'I knew Erik was a bit of a hound,' Atherton said in a conversational, all-boys-together tone, 'but I didn't know Jack was, too.'

'Kiddin' me? He was a maniac. I couldn't keep up! It was like a contest wiv 'em. "Erik," he'd say, "I'm over the limit, man, gotta throw one back," and Jack'd say, "There *is* no limit, man. Net 'em all!" He was a wild man.'

'And was Erik a wild man too?'

'Yeah, at the beginning, but he was always a bit more serious. Talked about career and stuff. Then he started doing these courses – wanted to better himself. So sometimes he'd be studying at night and wouldn't come out. Then he got this job with some tech company, house physio, and he was all like, nice suits and yuppie haircuts. I mean, he still come out wiv us, but not so often.'

'He wasn't interested in women any more?'

Dez rolled his eyes. 'Oh, man! Erik and sex? I mean, me and Jack calmed down as we got older. I'm married now – got a little girl – and Jack, he's been going steady for – what – over a year. But Erik can't help himself. It's not like he's wild, like the old days, but he's – like – *relentless*.' He found the word after a moment's thought, and seemed so surprised at himself he repeated it. 'Relentless. The relentless hunter. I don't know how many women he's got on the go at once. I don't suppose he knows. I mean, you can only stand back and admire. It's like . . . a professional sport, y'know what I mean?'

'You have to keep in practice?' Atherton offered.

Dez looked relieved to be understood. 'Yeah, and does *he* frickin' practise!' he breathed reverently.

'So do the three of you still go out together?'

Now Dez's face drew down into stern lines. 'What you playing at, man? Erik's dead, innee? You tryna trap me or somefing?'

'Not at all. I meant, were you all still friends before this happened.'

'Yeah, we see each other now and then. We got different priorities now, but we was still friends. Except . . .' He hesitated.

'Yes?'

'Well, Erik, he crossed a line, man, messing wiv Jack's sister. Jack's, like, Italian, and it's all about family wiv them. Same as wiv us, West Indians. Family's everything. I mean, if Erik'd had a go at my wife, I'd've killed him. You don't do that, man – mess wiv family.'

'What did Jack do to Erik when he found out?'

He looked uneasy. 'I dunno, man.'

'Was he angry?'

'He was mad as fire. I never seen him so mad. He went on the Hatton heavy bag and beat shit out of it. Hit it so hard he split it. Took it out that way.' He looked at Atherton, frowning seriously. 'He'd never hit Erik. He'd never hit anyone. It's his life, man, power training and weights and this place. He's a professional. He'd never betray that. It's like a religion: you don't use your power to hurt anyone, ever. We teach that, along with the weights. It's Jack's, like, mantra. He couldn't kill anyone. Couldn't do it.'

It was a lot of words. Atherton was thinking, *hit it so hard he split it.* 'Do you know Lucy?' he asked.

Dez's face lightened. 'Yeah, she's a great kid. I met all of Jack's family over the years but she's the best. Cute as hell.'

'She's the one Jack loves best,' Atherton suggested.

'I dunno. Maybe. She's the youngest,' he offered.

'Were you angry with Erik for messing with her?'

'Yeah, bro, he, like, crossed a line. But . . .'

'Yes?'

'Lucy, I don't think she was, like, heartbroken about Erik. She struck me as more angry. I mean, yeah, she was stuck on him at the beginning, when he first asked her out. But she's a smart girl. I reckon she'd already got the measure of him before he dumped her. I saw her a week, ten days ago, and she was fine. I reckon it was hurt pride, mostly. Nobody likes bein' dumped. But I don't fink she was cryin' in her pillow over him.'

'Did Jack tell you about the incident at a nightclub about a month ago, when he got in a fight with Erik?'

'What, at Dean's? Yeah, no, he never said they had a fight. He told Erik to meet him there. See, Erik told Lucy he was seeing someone else.' He shrugged. 'I said, it's Erik, man, what d'you expect? He's never kept to one woman in his life. But Jack says, nobody two-times my little sister, and he makes like to have it out with Erik. But there was no fight, man. Jack doesn't fight.'

'After that, were they still friends?'

'I dunno. I dunno if he's seen him again since then. But we didn't see each other all that often anyway, these days.'

'How has Jack been lately? What's his mood been like?'

'I dunno. No different. He's Jack, you know?' As if that answered the question.

'Can you tell me what you were doing on Tuesday night?'

Dez was about to answer, then drew back and looked indignant. 'Hey, what you at, man? I answered all your questions. I been nice. You tryna put something on me?'

'Not at all,' Atherton said soothingly. 'This is purely routine. We ask everyone who was associated with the victim the same question, just so that we can eliminate them. There's nothing to get upset about.'

Dez didn't look entirely convinced. He said, 'I was on early. I left here at four and went home, all right? And that's it. I was at home all night.'

'With your wife and your little girl?'

He hesitated just a feather of a moment. 'Yeah.'

'You didn't go out again later?'

'I was home all night, like I said. And now I gotta get back to work.' He stood up, like a basalt column thrusting up through the earth. Atherton stood hastily so as not to be overtopped, thanked him, and left.

There was definitely a lot of hero-worship there, he thought as he made his way out into the declining afternoon. And loyalty. Saint Jack had given him this job, made him a manager, shown him the True Path. And there was family feeling. Jack was family. Lucy was family. Would someone who worshipped Jack, but knew he would never kill the sleaze hound, feel compelled to do the deed for him? 'At home with the wife and child' was a good alibi – but there had been that slight hesitation. It made you wonder.

EIGHT
Awful Wedded Wife

Hart had brought a box of doughnuts in to the meeting – including a plain one for Slider, who thought putting things on top of doughnuts should be a hanging offence. 'It's a funny thing, boss,' she said, 'but that charity turned out to be real. The one Lingoss talked to that neighbour about, the Prasanna female.'

'Yes, she thought it was just a pick-up line,' Slider remembered, rescuing his virginal ring from the iced and sprinkled mob. It would be safe where he was going to put it.

'Well, it could still've been a line as well,' she said, passing the box on. 'It took a bit of finding, because there's about a million organizations with Fit, Fun and Kids in their names. In various combinations. I tell you, there shouldn't be a slobby kid with a bad attitude left in London. But I tracked it down in the end. It's called—'

'FitFunKidz. All one word. With capitals. And a "z" at the end,' Swilley anticipated. Hart gave her a look that could have lasered off blemishes. Swilley raised her eyebrows. 'What? I've got his bank statement now. He made donations.'

'You could've told me.'

'I didn't know until just now.'

'He made *donations*? To *charity*?' Lœssop said disbelievingly.

Hart was diverted. 'Yeah, but not only that, he gave his time. This charity's based in St Mark's Road, and it does schools in North Kensington, Willesden and Harlesden. Sends in a team to teach deprived kids about fitness, diet and well-being. Lingoss only did about one a month, but then he was a busy boy. And doing even one a month – for kids, for no money . . .' She left it hang, with a shrug.

'The tart with the heart of gold,' Atherton said wryly.

'So he did one good thing. Three cheers,' Fathom said grumpily. 'I don't see how that changes anything, from our point of view.'

'I never said it did,' Hart retorted. 'I just said it was funny.'

'Unless he was fiddling with the kids,' McLaren said indistinctly through a custard-filled doughnut. He had put the whole thing in his mouth in the hope of getting another before they were all gone.

'For God's sake, you're spraying crumbs and yellow gloop everywhere,' Atherton complained, moving further away. 'You're like an exploding boil.'

'Well, naturally they did the DBS check on him,' Hart said loudly over him, 'and we know he's got no form. And the female I talked to said he was very well thought of and there'd never been any complaints. It's all done in a big group, anyway, in the school hall or wherever, with three or four trainers in the team, and there's teachers present the whole time, so there's no chance of anyone being alone with a kid or anything like that. They don't even go into the changing rooms.'

'I think you're all being cynical,' said Gascoyne the Gentle. 'Why shouldn't he do something good? We've no evidence that he was a bad man.'

'Except for treating women like shit,' Hart said.

Swilley looked at Atherton. 'There's a lot of that about.'

Slider intervened. 'What else have you gleaned from his bank statement?' he asked Swilley.

'It's all very orderly,' she said with faint approval. 'He's obviously got a tidy mind. His mortgage, utilities, credit cards all paid for by direct debits. Never been overdrawn. Regular salary from Gillespie's, plus money paid in irregularly – from the private clients, I suppose. The only unusual thing is that he never draws out any cash.'

'That's not so unusual any more,' Atherton objected. 'Haven't you heard of the cashless society? You can even buy your Mars bar with contactless.'

'He wouldn't eat a Mars bar,' Fathom objected. 'He was a fitness freak.'

McLaren, who was sitting on his own desk, looked thoughtful and reached behind him to rummage in his top drawer.

'Energy bar, then,' said Atherton. 'Kale smoothie. Bottle of Lucozade. Illegal steroids.'

'Everybody still needs *some* cash,' Swilley countered. 'To pay the cleaner, the window cleaner, taxis – not every taxi has a card reader for those of us who don't use Uber.'

'What about all that cash in his bedroom?' LaSalle put in.

'That's what I was coming to,' said Swilley. 'The seven hundred under his pillow. Whoever drew that out of a bank, it wasn't Lingoss.'

'If he was getting bonus payments for the extra manly attentions,' Atherton said, 'they could well have been in cash. Hence the shoebox full – though why he didn't put it into a savings account . . .'

'At half a per cent interest, what'd be the point?' Swilley said. '*Taxable* interest. It was no worse off in the shoebox, and he had it to hand if he needed it. But my point is that the seven hundred is different. It was under his pillow, not in the shoebox or his wallet. He didn't draw it out, and he hadn't put it away.'

'We've already said it could be a payment from a client,' said Gascoyne.

'And one who had been there recently,' said Swilley. 'Maybe that very evening.'

'But it needn't have been the client who killed him,' LaSalle said. 'They could have come and gone, and the killer arrived before he had time to put the seven hundred away.'

'Fine. But if we could find out who the client was – they might have passed somebody on the stairs. Or Lingoss might have mentioned someone was coming.'

'Well, the only person we know who had a good grudge against him was Jack Gallo,' LaSalle said. 'Who also had a fight with him at a nightclub.'

'You know what Gallo means?' said Atherton. 'Cock. Rather appropriate, given what his pal Dez said about him. Dez of the mighty muscles and fierce loyalty. To Gallo and Lucy.'

'You're suggesting he killed Lingoss?' Swilley said impatiently.

'I'm not suggesting anything. Just observing. But both Gallo and Dez were old friends, whom Lingoss'd be likely to let in if they came calling.'

'Alibis,' said Slider.

'Haven't checked them yet,' said Atherton. 'Will do, though.'

'My worry about either of them is that the dumping of Lucy

and the fight were a month ago,' Slider said. 'It's not a very immediate grudge.'

'Could be the sort that festers,' Atherton said. 'You can be friends on the surface, but then something is said or done that triggers the old wound and out it all comes.'

'The trouble is,' Slider said, 'the killing looks both impulsive: the first blow – and calculated: the finishing off.'

'I'd say it was all calculated,' said Swilley. 'The first blow was meant to kill him, and when it didn't, chummy went back for seconds.'

'I'd say it was all impulsive – the serial actions of the enraged,' said Atherton. '"Die, you swine, die!"'

'Anything on cameras yet?' Slider asked McLaren, who was finishing the Mars bar.

'There's a lot of footage,' McLaren said by way of negative.

'I'll try and get you some more uniforms to help. We need proper evidence of someone going in there. At the moment, there's nothing to say anybody was at the flat at all.'

'Maybe he did it himself,' Atherton said. 'Clubbed himself, passed out, came round a moment later and thought, "Blast, I'm not dead" and did it again.'

'You're not helping,' said Slider.

It was after five when a call from downstairs told Slider he had a visitor. He went and met her at the lift and walked her back to his room. 'What are you doing here?'

Exasperated was the default expression of Kate, his daughter from his first marriage, but today it was toned down a notch, evidence to the trained mind that she was going to be asking for a favour. 'Didn't Mum tell you? School trip. Science museum.'

'Does she know you're coming here?'

He was glad that the fashion for looking like a downtrodden prostitute had passed. Although she was still wearing a microskirt, it was paired with thick black tights and clunky, thick-heeled footwear somewhere between shoes and ankle boots, which took the edge off any erotic allure. Her hair was bundled up into a knitted cap like a beanie, and her only obvious make-up was a bit of eyeliner. Exposed by the lack of the straggling locks that usually half-obscured it, her face was sharply pretty in a way that reminded him painfully of her mother. Irene had always been neat, dainty, and ladylike, with neat, dainty, ladylike ways of doing everything. Even of having sex and giving birth. Even of getting rid of him – she had left him for her bridge partner, Ernie, who was wealthy, predictable and dull, everything Slider was not. Well, Joanna didn't think he was dull. And Joanna was dynamite.

'I said I might. I mean, it's on the way,' Kate said, offhand; and then, to his insistent look, returned an eye-roll. 'I'll ring her in a bit, all right? Duh, Dad, way to make me feel welcome!'

'Of course you're welcome. I'm very glad to see you. If I'd known you were coming, I could have made arrangements to take you out for something to eat.'

Her eyes brightened. 'I'm starving,' she mentioned. 'It's, like, hours since lunch. You got any biscuits or anything? I thought people in offices always had tins of biscuits lying about.'

'Wait there,' he said, and went through into the main office, returning to Kate with an individually-wrapped slice of Genoa.

'Magic,' she said, and he refrained from saying, no, just McLaren. She hitched herself up on his desk. 'So, what you up to, anyway?' she asked through the first bite. 'Got anything good on?'

'Homicide case,' he said – that was the preferred nomenclature these days. The brass thought it sounded more official than murder, which was the sort of word anyone could use.

'Cool!' Kate said. 'I don't suppose it was anyone famous?'

'He was famous in his own circle,' Slider said apologetically. 'He was a fitness personal trainer.'

'Oh, right. But did he train anyone famous? Like TV presenters or actors or anyone?'

'He might have,' Slider said. 'We haven't assembled a list of his clients yet.'

'If it turns out he did, will you let me know, Dad? If it's anyone really famous?'

'What difference does it make?' Slider said, and got the eye-roll again. Of *course* it made a difference. Fame was the *only* thing that made a difference. It was what they all aspired to, not the reason for celebrity – not the extraordinary talent or activity or achievement – but the celebrity itself: a life of going to parties where you have to be famous to get an invitation, and where getting an invitation is the reason you're famous.

'I'll let you know,' he said hastily. 'If it turns out he did.' He waited until she had demolished the last of the cake, and said, 'Was there something you wanted to talk to me about?'

She smiled in a way that was almost affectionate. 'That's my dad!' she said. 'Always the detective!'

'It isn't hard to guess. I could count the times you've visited me here on the fingers of one foot.'

'You mean toes,' she said with her mother's literalness.

'Just spit it out.'

'OK. It's, like, I've got an offer to go to another school next year. There's a vacancy at North London College, and our head-teacher thinks I ought to go for it, because I'm not being stretched, she says. And it's, like, this really amazing school, and I *really* want to go, Dad.'

'Isn't it a highly academic school? Won't there be lots of pressure?'

The eye-roll again. 'You don't think I'm academic? You don't think I'd fit in with all those *really clever* girls?' Oooh, sarcasm.

'I didn't say that,' he said mildly. 'I'm just a bit surprised – I didn't think you were that dedicated to school work.'

'Well, you wouldn't know, would you?' she said, and a little hurt showed through. 'You don't know anything about what I like or don't like. And as it *happens*' – more sarcasm – 'I'm in the top five in my year in every subject, and I'm *the* top in maths and English.'

'Excellent. Well done. I'm very proud of you.' She was still a little pouty. 'Seriously. I am. And what did you want from me? If it's my approval, you've got it. I'm very pleased for you.' An alarming thought crossed his mind. 'Is it money?'

She looked scornful. 'No, it's not money. Ernie's paying for everything – school fees and everything. But the thing is, it's a day school. And it's, like, a long way to travel in every day. Mum's worried the journey'd be too much on top of everything, and I wouldn't get home till really late. So she thought – we thought – I could maybe stay at your house during term time. Just week-days, I mean. I'd still go home at weekends.'

She wouldn't look at him now, staring at the window with a bored expression and swinging her legs insouciantly. He was sufficiently up in Kate-language to understand that this was not indifference, that she was afraid he'd say no; and afraid not just because a refusal would throw a spaniel in the works, but because to be rejected by him would hurt her.

He ought to check with Joanna first, of course. In the split second it took to think this, she had heard a hesitation.

'It's not as if you haven't got room,' she said resentfully.

'Of course there's room,' he said. 'And it'd be lovely to have you there. Lovely to see more of you.'

'I can, like, help with the baby and everything,' she went on, still fighting the won battle.

'We'd love to have you,' he said, mentally crossing his fingers that Joanna would be delighted. After all, if it was the other way round, he'd be only too happy etc etc. What's mine is yours, including a fractious teenage daughter and all the responsibility thereof. 'I'd better arrange to have a talk with your mother about it, get all the details. Did she know you were coming here to ask me this?'

'I just said I might call in and see you. I didn't say I was going to ask. But it was, like, her idea for me to stay with you, so she must've, like, guessed, really.'

'OK, well let's give her a ring now, shall we?' She looked happy and relieved, and he wanted to hug her. 'But if you're going to this academic hothouse there is one thing – you'll have to stop saying "like" every other word.'

'Da-a-ad!' she said, the three-tone wail of protest. He'd gone and spoiled it now.

Joanna arrived after him, looking tired, so he didn't spring it on her at once. He let her tell some more orchestra tour stories she had been swapping with Peter White, like the time the co-principal trumpet, Sid Williams, went missing just before the concert, and was discovered backstage dead drunk and curled up asleep in the harp case. Luckily he'd had the presence of mind to change into his tails before passing out, so the rest of the section carried him out between them and propped him up in his chair. 'Instinct took over,' Joanna said, 'and he played the concert faultlessly, but afterwards he had no recollection of any of it.'

'Your brass friends seemed to have done a lot of drinking,' Slider mentioned.

'It's thirsty work,' she said, and cocked her head. 'What's on your mind? You're not entirely here, are you?'

She knew him as well as he knew her. So he told her about Kate.

She took it very well. 'Of course I don't mind having her here, and it'll be nice for you. But she's got to pull her weight.'

'She's already said she would help out with the baby.'

'Yes, I know she always liked playing with George, but it's not just the fun stuff, is it? She's got to keep her room clean, do her own washing, help with the rest of the house – be part of it all, not just sit around expecting to be waited on.'

'Of course,' he said.

'Yes, Bill, but it's not "of course", is it? She might throw herself into things or she might not, and if she doesn't, someone's got to police her. And it's not going to be me. You've got to be prepared to take a firm line with her if necessary. I know you won't want to—'

He took her by both elbows and looked straight into her eyes. 'I will take responsibility for her, I promise. You don't need to worry. And thank you, for saying she can come.'

'Of course she can. Family is family,' she said.

And at those words his mind went straight back to Jack and Lucy Gallo. She saw he'd gone, sighed slightly and detached herself gently from his grasp. 'I would so love a gin and tonic right now,' she said, heading for the kitchen.

'We've got the trace on Lingoss's mobile phone,' Hart said ebulliently as soon as he walked in.

The phone had left Lingoss's flat at nine fifty-nine on Tuesday evening and had not returned there.

'So it *was* the murderer who took it,' Hart said with satisfaction.

'*Somebody* took it,' Slider corrected her.

Atherton was on Hart's side. 'I think it's a working hypothesis – who but the murderer would want to take it?'

Slider let it go. 'And where did it travel to?'

'Not very far, boss,' Hart said. 'It went straight to Kensington, and stopped somewhere behind Ken High Street, where it remained stationary for half an hour. Then it was switched off, and it hasn't been transmitting since.'

'How closely have they triangulated it?' Slider asked.

'Within about two hundred metres, but there's a lot of buildings in that area. Come and look on the map.'

Someone had already drawn a line around the area. 'Somewhere between the High Street and Scarsdale Villas, going roughly north to south,' Atherton said, demonstrating with the end of a ballpoint, 'and Abingdon Road and Marloes Road west to east. So you've got all the shops along the High Street. Houses, flats – there's all those service flats on Allen Street, for instance, very densely populated. Offices in Wrights Lane, and more flats. A couple of hotels. There's the Armenian Embassy—'

'I don't even know where Armenia is,' Hart complained.

'Black Sea, isn't it?' Lœssop said vaguely. 'Sort of between Turkey and Russia?'

'How d'you know that?' Swilley wondered. She had never put him down as academic.

'Rugby,' he said, as if it was obvious. 'I follow the Lelos – Georgia rugby team. Georgia's in the same area.' She still looked blank. 'The country, not the American state.'

'Oh.'

'What's this?' Slider asked, leaning in. 'At the end of Adam and Eve Mews?'

'Army Reserve Centre, the Kensington Cadets.'

'Great, we got the bleedin' army involved now,' Hart muttered.

'But you know who lives in Marloes Road,' Atherton said in a pleased tone. 'Jack Gallo.'

Slider answered the implied question. 'Still not enough to shake him down. Get after those alibis, chop chop.'

From the mid-nineteenth century onwards, the western side of North Kensington had been home to innumerable railway depots, sidings, coal yards and small factories. In consequence, the streets and streets of Victorian terraced housing all around were designed for railway and factory workers. They were decent, solid, enduring brick-and-slate stock, but they were modest in scale, to say the least. Nevertheless, the modern housing shortage had seen most of them divided into two minuscule flats, and even *they* were pricey. The current occupants had done their best to upscale their tiny pride-and-joys with new front doors, brass knockers, lace curtains and window boxes, but still they wouldn't want to number cat-swinging among their hobbies.

Dez Wilson was safely at work and Hart had thought to find Dez's wife and child at home and vulnerable to a chat, but there was no answer to the doorbell. The curtain of the downstairs flat twitched, and Hart gave an inviting smile in that direction, which shortly brought an elderly woman to the door. She was shabby but neat, and had bothered to brush her hair and put on lipstick that morning, so Hart was confident of a chat. She allowed herself to be invited into the doll's house but refused a cup of tea. It was tidy, but smelled stale, and there was thick dust on the surfaces and stains on the cheap carpet. Mrs Eldridge wore large pink-framed glasses with thick lenses, so she probably couldn't see when she spilled her tea on the way to the armchair. And wouldn't see when residue was left after washing-up.

'They're ever such nice people, the Wilsons,' she confided. 'They're black, you know,' she added, looking carefully at Hart to see if she minded. Hart restrained herself from pointing out the obvious, that she was too. 'But not foreigners. They were both born here. Dez and Melanie – Mel. And their little girl Ayesha. I was a bit nervous of Dez when he first came here, because he's so big, but he's what they call a gentle giant. Ever so polite, and always willing to help with little things. He puts my bin out for me every Sunday night. I actually feel safer now, having him upstairs.'

'That's nice,' said Hart. She knew better than to hurry this sort along. 'And you get on with Mel all right, as well?'

'Oh yes. Well, I see more of her really, because Dez is at work all day.'

'And having a child living upstairs? That's not a problem? I mean, noise and such?'

'Well, there's a bit of noise,' she admitted. 'Footsteps, you know, and voices. These old houses weren't meant to be flats. Of course, when Ayesha was a baby there was the crying – that can get on your nerves. Mel was always apologizing – but I've raised two of my own, so I know. I said, you can't help it, dear. Babies will cry. She was ever so grateful to me for being understanding. Well, now she's older it's more the running around and shouting, but you can't keep a toddler quiet the whole time, it isn't natural.'

'So you hear them talking up there, do you?'

'Oh, not normal talking, only when there's raised voices.'

'When they have rows, you mean? Are there a lot of them?'

Mrs Eldridge pursed her lips and frowned judiciously. 'I wouldn't say a *lot*. I mean, all couples have their little ups and downs, don't they? And it's a small flat for three people, especially when one's a child. Sid and me found it cosy for two, but we'd been married forty years so we'd learned how to cope. And property's so expensive in London, isn't it?'

'So they had rows about the flat being too small, did they?' Hart eased her along. 'Mel wanted to move, I suppose.'

'It wasn't Dez's fault,' she defended. 'He's got a decent job and he works hard. They're saving up to get a better place, but a kiddie's expensive to bring up, and Mel hasn't felt up to going back to work, so it's just his wages. And a man has to have *some* little pleasures, doesn't he? A drink with a friend after work – it isn't as though he comes home roaring drunk.'

It was all there in a few phrases, a succinct précis of a marriage. Hart almost suspected Mrs Eldridge of doing it deliberately, but a glance at her placid, lined face did not reveal any Machiavellian intellect.

'Did he ever mention a friend to you, Jack Gallo?'

'Oh yes – well, I heard about him from Mel. Dez's best friend. And he got Dez his job so he's grateful to him as well. You couldn't have said a wrong word about Jack to Dez. Mel said he thought the sun shone out of his . . . well, you know, dear.'

'Mel doesn't like him?'

'Oh, I don't say that. But a wife likes her husband to come home to her in the evening, especially when she's been on her own all day with a small child. It's only natural.'

'She thinks Dez prefers Jack's company to hers?'

She looked away. 'A man has to have his man friend, it's human nature,' she said neutrally.

Hart smiled sympathetically. 'It must be hard, hearing such a lovely couple having rows, when you're so fond of both of them.'

She liked the attention. 'Well, it is,' she said, looking at Hart now. 'You can't interfere, but sometimes I want to say, just be grateful you have each other. Never let the sun go down on a quarrel, that's what my mother always said. And Sid and me never did. Always made a point of making up before bedtime.'

'This latest row they had,' Hart said temptingly.

She fell for it. 'Well, I couldn't help hearing, when they were shouting up there, and in the end Ayesha started crying, and I felt so sorry for the poor little mite, listening to her mummy and daddy fighting.'

'What was it about?'

'Well, I couldn't hear everything, of course, but I heard Jack's name, and another friend, Erik, so I thought it must be about him going out with them. She's complained to me about that once or twice. At any rate, she did shout something about how they could move out of this place if only he stopped wasting money, and saved it instead. And he said she could get a job herself and help, and she said what about Ayesha, and he said his mother'd offered to babysit, and she said she might as well go back and live with *her* mother because this wasn't what she'd expected when she married him.'

Evidently she could hear more than the occasional loud word, Hart thought. But none of this seemed to be leading up to killing Erik on Jack's behalf, so it wasn't helping her.

'Did he hit her?' she asked abruptly, hoping to surprise the answer out of her.

She hesitated a telling moment. Then she said, 'Oh no, I'm sure not. He's not the hitting sort. But,' she lowered her voice conspiratorially, 'he *throws* things. You can hear the crockery smash. And one time he punched the wall and made a big hole in it. Mel told me. I suppose he had to let off steam. But he adores her and the kiddie, he'd never hurt either of them.'

'And this row you're telling me about – when was that?'

'Monday night, dear. It ended with a big crash, but it was only a saucepan knocked off the kitchen counter. Mel told me Tuesday when she went out.' She looked grave. 'I tried to persuade her not to go, but she was in quite a state and she wouldn't listen.'

'Go where?'

'Back to her mother's. She had a suitcase and a bag with Ayesha's little things, and Ayesha was in her pushchair, looking all bewildered, poor little mite, not understanding what was going on. I gave her a barley sugar – I've always got some sweeties on hand, just in case – and that took her mind off. And I gave Mel twenty pounds for the taxi.' She looked at Hart defiantly. 'She said she'd pay me back, and she will. I wasn't worried. She said she'd left a note for Dez. I thought he might come down and ask me about it when he got home but he never did. I was a bit relieved. I didn't want to get in the middle of it.'

'I don't blame you,' Hart said. 'So this was Tuesday morning she went off to her mother's? And she's not been back?'

'No, I've not seen her since.'

'So Dez was all alone up there on Tuesday night?' So much for his alibi – at home with his wife and child. 'What time did he get home?'

'About five, I think it was. I heard him go up. I waited thinking he'd come knocking on my door, cos of the note, but he didn't. It was quiet as the grave up there. Then a bit later he went out again.'

'What time was that?'

'I don't know for sure, I think it might have been about six or seven. I wasn't really noticing,' she apologized.

'And what time did he come back in?'

'I don't know, dear. I didn't hear him come back. But I go to bed at half past ten, and once I take my hearing aids out I don't hear much, so he could come in and I wouldn't know.'

NINE
The Incredible Bulk

The Britannia in Allen Street was a tiny Victorian pub that had undergone the better sort of gentrification. The outside was painted in a Heritage grey-green shade with a simple pub sign in gold; the inside was cosy with a real fire, real ales and traditional pub food. LaSalle noted that Allen Street was also within the area where Lingoss's mobile had come to rest, but as the street was lined with blocks of flats and was thus home to hundreds of people, it was hardly what you'd call compelling evidence. And as Allen Street was only round two corners from Marloes Road, it was reasonable that Gallo should stop there for a drink on his way home.

A tall, lean New Zealander was keeping the bar, and looked at the mugshot LaSalle offered with intelligent eyes. 'Yeah, I've seen him in here. Really fit bloke. He comes in quite a bit.'

'He's a regular?'

'Sort of. I suppose so.'

'Ever any trouble?'

'God, no. It's not that sort of pub.' He fiddled with a tap. 'We get a lot of tourists in here. And people coming in for food. We're famous for our British grub – sausage and mash and that kind of tackle – but done posh, you know? And Kensington's a big place. You don't know your customers in this sort of pub, but you get to recognize one or two faces when they come in every week. And this bloke – you couldn't miss him, with the body on him.'

'He's a fitness trainer,' LaSalle offered.

'Yeah, well that makes sense. First time you see someone like that, you wonder are they going to be trouble. But I reckon a lot of these guys, they grow their bodies like prize marrows – not for using, just for display.'

'Can you remember if he was in on Tuesday night?'

He frowned in thought, and wiped a cloth over the bar top to help the process. 'Honestly? It's hard to remember one night from another. I mean, he could well have been. He's been in this week, I'm pretty sure, but whether it was Tuesday . . .'

'Who else was on on Tuesday?'

'Oh, right – Maeve was on. That's her, down there.'

Maeve finished serving a customer and came to a beckoning summons. Despite her name, she was no Irish colleen, but a fit, bronze student from California working her way round the world. She looked at the mugshot and said at once, 'Yeah, I know him. Not personally, just as a customer. Jack, that's his name. We've chatted once or twice. He owns his own gym somewhere – Notting Hill, I think. What's up, Pete?'

'Copper here wants to know was he in Tuesday,' said Pete.

'Yeah, Tuesday. He was here.'

'Are you sure it was Tuesday?' Pete said. 'I thought maybe it was Monday.'

'I wasn't in on Monday. Yeah, it was Tuesday. He was sitting at the bar. Then his buddy turned up – you remember, Pete – and they went and sat at a table.' She looked impatiently at her colleague. 'You must remember – his buddy was even bigger than he was. Big black guy, all muscles. We talked about it.'

'Oh yeah,' said Pete. 'I remember *him*. Muscles like bloody boa constrictors. That was Tuesday, was it?'

'Course it was,' Maeve said impatiently. She looked at LaSalle. 'Why you asking? Is he in trouble?'

'No, it's just routine,' he said automatically. 'Purposes of elimination, that's all. Do you remember what time he came in?'

'He was already sitting at the bar when I got here,' Maeve said. 'I came on at seven.'

'He hadn't been here long then,' Pete said. 'He was still on his first pint.'

'And the friend who joined him – was this him?' Hopefully he showed them a mugshot of Dez Wilson.

'Yeah – you can't mistake him, can you?' Pete said.

'Did it seem like an arrangement, that they were meeting?'

Pete scowled in thought. 'No, he looked surprised, this one – Jack. He said something like, "What are you doing here?"'

'That's right,' said Maeve, 'and this one said something to Jack and they went and sat at a table over there, in the corner. They had their heads together talking. I went over to see if they wanted to order any food, and it looked like serious talk.'

'What time did they leave?' LaSalle asked.

They looked at each other and slowly shook their heads. 'Hard to say,' said Maeve.

'You don't really notice the time,' said Pete.

'I guess they were talking for maybe an hour,' said Maeve, 'but don't quote me on it. Coulda been less, coulda been more.' Pete nodded in vague affirmation.

'Did they leave together?'

'No, the black guy left first. But only just. I went over to clear the table, and Jack finished his pint and got up and left just as I got there.'

'How did he seem?' She shrugged. 'Did he say goodbye to you?'

'No,' she said, 'but I didn't make anything of it. I mean, we weren't friends or anything. He was just a customer.'

Pete was studying LaSalle's face. 'Are you sure he's not in trouble? You're asking a lot of questions.'

'Like I said, we're just trying to eliminate him from an enquiry,' LaSalle said peaceably.

And not doing it, he thought.

Liverpool Road was a long one, lined on one side with tall Georgian terraced houses, and on the other with council flats. This being the London Borough of Islington, the road had vicious speed humps about every five yards, so that anyone being picked up by an ambulance would be jolted to death before they reached the hospital, thus saving the NHS the trouble of finding a bed.

Hart found a parking space in the courtyard, and climbed the stairs to Mel's mum's flat. There was a lift, but she had a healthy horror of using a lift where the person who had to answer the alarm bell was not actually on the premises but somewhere in an office in Aylesbury.

The lady who opened the door to her was unmistakeably a West Indian mum, and Hart felt immediately at home. Inside, the place was spotless. Everything that could be patterned was patterned, with jolly, cortex-curling results, and every surface was crowded with ornaments, keepsakes and framed photographs of the extended family. Mrs Hawkins was neat, trim and busy, with iron grey hair scraped back and held in place with savage-looking hair slides, and noticing eyes.

'I've told her she's got to go back,' she said. 'You don't run out on a marriage the first minute something goes wrong. But you young people today – you are spoiled. You won't put the work in. I said to Melanie, you fit enough to get a job now. If you want to get out of the flat, you got to do something about it, not wait for someone to rescue you. I'll look after Ayesha. I've always said that. Get a job and get your self-respect back.'

'Mu-u-um,' Mel protested sulkily. 'Don't go on.'

'So, what is all this about?' Mrs Hawkins demanded briskly. 'Is Desmond in trouble? Because I've a right to know if he is. Don't be keeping tings from me. I'm Ayesha's granny, and whatever he's done, she has to come first.'

'Cute kid,' Hart said. Ayesha, in a red polka-dot dress and a red cardigan that looked home-knitted, was staring at her with big eyes. Her hair was tortured into two little bunches on top like Mickey Mouse ears. They'd been pulled so tight it gave her a slightly surprised look. Hart remembered that age, and could imagine the wails. Her mum used to rap her hand with the back of the hairbrush to make her stay still. Childhood, the best days of your life. 'I'd just like to ask you a couple of questions,' she said, addressing Mel.

'What you say, you say in front of me,' said Mrs Hawkins. She folded her arms across her bosom in the way that said, end of argument. 'In my own house!' she added in an outraged undertone.

Hart shrugged inwardly. 'You left the flat with Ayesha on Tuesday morning, is that right? What time would that be?'

'I dunno,' Mel said indifferently. 'About half-nine, ten.'

'It was just after ten when she got here,' said Mrs Hawkins, with an air of waiting to be angry about something. 'In a taxi. With the cost of them these days!'

'And did you go home again?'

'No she did not!' said Mrs Hawkins.

Hart looked at her patiently but without much hope. 'Please let her answer herself. If you don't mind.'

Mel shrugged. 'No, I ain't been back. What's there to go for – a rat box like that? One bedroom! Ayesha has to sleep in the lounge. She ought to have a room of her own. I seen this lovely bed, with all Disney princesses painted all over it, and this mobile to match what you hang over it. And I picked out the wallpaper at Homebase. I mean,' her voice rose indignantly, 'that's a bachelor flat, Dez's. One bedroom!'

'Is that what you had a fight about, Monday night?'

'It wasn't a fight,' she retorted. 'I just told him. I said, I'm not putting up with it any more. We could've been out of there if he didn't waste so much money. I mean, all his stupid muscle magazines – and they're not cheap – and his supplements. And new workout kit all the time. He says he has to have it for his job, but when do I get new clothes, answer me that?'

'You had a new coat two weeks ago,' Mrs Hawkins mentioned.

'Mu-um! Don't interfere! And he goes out drinking with his precious mates. I'm sick of it. It's all he talks about – Jack this and Jack that. You think the sun shone out of his—' She stopped herself just in time as her mother's hand unfurled itself ready to slap. 'He's grateful to Jack for giving him the job, I get that, but he deserves it, and Jack knows that. He works his . . . socks off at that gym. It's him the punters come for. They love him. If it wasn't for Dez there'd *be* no Pex Gym, but still he talks like Jack's done him some big favour.'

Hart saw an opening. 'And does he feel he has to do Jack favours in return?'

She snorted. 'He's at his beck and bloody call!'

'Language!' Mrs Hawkins rebuked. 'Not in front of Ayesha.'

'Did Jack ask him for a favour recently?' Hart asked. 'Something in particular he wanted doing?' She watched Mel's face closely, and thought a slightly guarded look came over her.

'I dunno what you mean,' she said.

'You mentioned Jack – do you know another friend of Dez's, Erik?'

Mel gave another snort and an eye-roll, but Mrs Hawkins smiled. 'Oh, I like Erik. He's got lovely manners. Always makin' me laugh, that boy! And he's so good with Ayesha.'

'You've met him, then?' Hart turned to her.

'Couple of times, Desmond's brought him here when he's brought Melanie and the baby. But he talks about him a lot. They're all good friends, Desmond, Jack and Erik.'

'Wasn't there some trouble recently, between Jack and Erik?' Hart asked casually, dividing the question equally between them.

Mrs Hawkins looked blank, but Mel scowled. 'Yeah, about Jack's *lah-di-dah* bloody sister. Jack thought she was too good to go out with Erik, and Dez agreed with him, the stupid prat. He was all, "Oh, Lucy's so special, she's so delicate" like she's some, I dunno, some tropical flower. And I mean, I've seen her, and she's nothing to write home about, just some bog standard white girl! But he was all, Erik mustn't be allowed near her, and flexing his muscles, like he was some knight in shining armour and he was going to protect her. Went on and on about how wonderful she was and how poor Jack was *so-o-o* upset! Course, *they* mustn't be upset. Doesn't mind upsetting *me*, though, does he?'

'Is that what you were rowing about Monday night?' Hart asked. 'When the pots got thrown about?'

Mel was worked up now, and didn't question how Hart knew these things. 'I'd've cracked his stupid skull if it wasn't so thick! Concrete for brains! She was already over Erik, Lucy was, weeks ago. Ask me, it was never more than a casual fling. And she can take care of herself – hard as nails, that one. But Dez was still on about how wonderful she was. I was sick of the sound of her name, if you want to know. I told him he'd better sort out his bloody priorities, because I wasn't standing for it any more, and all he did was shout about friendship coming first. No, I said, your wife and kiddie come first, and *you'd* better bloody start acting like it! So I come home to Mum.'

'Does he ever get violent? Has he ever hit you?' Hart asked.

It was Mrs Hawkins who answered, arms well folded again. 'No he has not! I'd soon have someting to say about it if he lifted a hand to my daughter. He's a good boy, Desmond. Comes from a good family. I knew his mummy, you know – Mrs Wilson. She lived in the flats here as well. He grew up round here – that's how he met Melanie. And we would never have let her marry him, Daddy and me, if he hadn't been a good boy. Melanie's daddy was still alive then. We all look out for each other on this estate, we all know each other. Of course, Desmond wasn't good enough for Melanie: she has GCSEs, you know—'

'Mu-um!'

'Two GCSEs,' she went on stubbornly, 'but he's a good boy

from a good family. He may have his faults, he may have had his troubles in the past, but he works hard, and he'd never hit a woman or a child. There's wrong on both sides in any marriage. I love my children but I'm not blind to their little faults. Melanie had a hard time with little Ayesha, but she's over it now. But she likes to keep thinking she's not well. You a strong girl, Melanie, you can't keep wrapping yourself up in cotton wool. Go out and get yourself a job. It's no wonder Desmond gets impatient.'

Mel looked about to argue, and Hart felt they were straying from the useful line. 'So, can I just confirm, you were here Tuesday evening and Tuesday night? And you haven't been back to the flat since?'

'No – why? What's he done? Has he trashed it?'

'Have you seen Dez or heard from him since Tuesday morning?'

'No, she has not,' said Mrs Hawkins quickly. 'And why you asking all these questions? Has someting happened to him?'

Mel's eyes widened. 'Omigod, has he had an accident? Is that why you're here? He's dead, isn't he?'

Ayesha began to wail, and Mrs Hawkins stepped back and picked her up without ever taking her eyes from Hart's face. The movement was as automatic as if she was the mother, not the grandmother, of the child.

Hart felt it was time to come clean. 'No, there's been no accident. He's fine as far as I know,' she said. 'But I have to tell you that Erik Lingoss is dead.'

'Dead? What d'you mean, dead? He can't be.'

'He was killed on Tuesday night,' Hart said.

'*Killed?* You don't mean . . .' Melanie stared for a long moment, her brain obviously working. Then she said, 'You think Dez did it, you think *he* killed him?' She looked at her mother. 'That's why all these questions about Tuesday night.'

'No,' said Mrs Hawkins robustly. 'That's rubbish. My granddaughter's daddy is not a killer.'

'Of course it's rubbish, Mum,' Mel said. 'Dez wouldn't hurt a fly. Ask anyone. And him and Erik were friends.'

'I'm wondering, you see, why the subject of Lucy and Erik came up again on Monday night, when she'd broken off with him a month ago,' queried Hart.

'He was always talking about her,' Mel said bitterly. 'That wasn't nothing unusual. But if it's true what you say, and Erik was killed, you can forget about Dez. He had nothing to do with it.'

She said it with great certitude, but there had been that moment when she had thought about it, and what Hart had seen in her face then was that she believed he could have. And neither she nor her mother had asked any of the usual astonished questions people generally threw about when informed of something as outrageous as murder. They had closed ranks – around Dez, yes, but also against the police. They'd been indignant, but not indignant enough. Not nearly enough.

'So what it comes down to,' said Slider, 'is that neither Jack nor Dez has an alibi for the crucial time on Tuesday night.'

'And neither of them mentioned meeting the other at the pub,' Atherton mused. 'Strange, that. Almost as if they didn't want to draw attention to the fact.'

'But Dez actually lied about being at home with his wife and child,' LaSalle pointed out. 'That's worse. And it looks from what the barmaid said as if he sought Jack out.'

'"What are you doing here?" could mean anything,' said Hart. 'And the mobile phone ended up in Jack's neighbourhood, not Dez's.'

'Suppose they were both in on it?' said Atherton. 'They'd got it all planned out, then Dez turns up at the pub with last-minute doubts or questions. Jack's annoyed that he's getting them seen together on the critical night. "What are you doing here?" he says. They have a private, sotto voce conversation, Jack soothes him down and off he goes. Later they meet and do the deed, and Jack takes the phone away to destroy it.'

'If it was a planned thing, wouldn't they have arranged alibis for themselves?' Lœssop said.

'It's not that easy to do, set up a false alibi,' said Hart. 'Especially when you live alone. You've got to get someone to lie for you.'

'Dez didn't live alone,' said Lœssop. 'Surely if his wife was going to be his alibi, he wouldn't have had a row with her the night before and risked turning her against him.'

'You're assuming these people think things out rationally,' Hart said.

'Or at all,' said Atherton. 'I've met Dez Wilson. He's a big, goofy muscleman, so dumb he said he was at home with his wife when it was the easiest thing in the world to prove that he wasn't. That kind lives hand to mouth, moment to moment.'

'If they were in it together,' said LaSalle, 'they were probably expecting to be each other's alibis. Work something out afterwards.'

'What, and they forgot?' Lœssop said.

Gascoyne came in from the corridor. 'What are we talking about?'

'Dez Wilson's alibi's blown,' Hart said. 'Where've you been?'

'Computer room,' he said. 'I've been having a look into Jack Gallo and Dez Wilson. Can't find anything on Gallo, apart from that one fracarse outside Dean's. But Wilson had a bit of trouble as a juvenile. Shoplifting, fighting, a couple of run-ins with soft drugs.'

He had avoided getting a criminal record but was heading that way until he had been put in touch with a programme especially designed for troubled youngsters.

'So I've just given Tommy Rylance a bell – my dad's old pal?' said Gascoyne, looking round to gather their nods. Gascoyne's father had been in the Job before him and knew practically everyone in the area; Tommy Rylance had been a boxer, later turned promoter and manager, and had been a useful police liaison for a certain section of the population. 'He used to be involved with this scheme called Boxing Angels. They worked from a gym behind the Angel Islington. A bit like the thing Lingoss was in, FitFunKidz, but this was for troubled older boys and it was all about boxing – give them a healthy outlet for their aggression and teach them discipline and self-respect. Course, it's everywhere now, but it was a new idea in those days. Tommy says they had a lot of success with it. He remembered Dez Wilson, got interested in him because of his size and physique, thought he might have a career in the ring, but Dez just wasn't interested enough in boxing. But he liked the fitness side of it, so Tommy pointed him in the direction of The Muscle Factory – that's a power gym in Islington – helped him get a part-time job there, cleaning up and so on. Well, we know he went on to a proper job there later, training. And he's not been in trouble since.'

'The redemptive power of flexing your muscles,' said Atherton witheringly.

'Just because you've got no muscles,' Hart retorted.

'The brain is a muscle,' said Atherton, 'and mine is well-developed.'

'That must be why you've got such a big head,' she said.

'The point is,' Gascoyne said patiently, 'that he's been straight since then.'

'The point is,' LaSalle countered, 'that he *was* a bad lot. The violence is in him somewhere. And he lied about his alibi.'

'Him and Gallo both,' said Hart.

'And sadly we've got nothing else by way of a suspect,' said Slider. 'They're big, strong men and they knew the victim well enough to be let in by him.'

Atherton eyed him. 'But you don't like it.'

Slider stirred restlessly. 'I can see them killing him in hot blood, in a row or a fight, but a plot thought out beforehand? It doesn't sit right with me.'

'Well, maybe they went round *without* a plot or a plan, just to see him, and something was said, a row blew up, and hot blood got spilled,' Atherton offered.

'That's possible,' said Slider. 'I think if you're going to go that route we need to find some evidence of the movement of Gallo and Wilson between Lingoss's flat and wherever they ended up.' This was addressed to McLaren, who fielded it phlegmatically.

'Meanwhile, we must keep looking in other directions. If Lingoss was in the habit of having sexual relations with his clients, there's plenty of scope for resentments, jealousies, murderous feelings of all sorts. Let's see who else might have had it in for him.'

'I thought he had no trouble putting it in for himself,' Hart muttered as they dispersed.

TEN

The Impotence of Being Vermin

S lider was in his room, going over things with Atherton, when
Swilley came in.

'You wanted a list of Lingoss's clients, boss.'

'Did you find something on his laptop?' Slider asked.

'No,' said Swilley. 'It's those two black books we brought back
from the flat. One was a list of names and addresses and contact
details—'

'Usually known as an address book,' said Atherton.

She gave him a look that could have taken paint off a car. 'It
was an ordinary notebook and they weren't arranged alphabetically,
so I'll call it what I like.'

'You two have really got to learn to play nicely,' Slider sighed.
'Yes, Norma, what have you found?'

'It makes interesting reading,' she said. 'From the addresses
alone you can tell they're wealthy, and I've done a bit of background research, and a lot of them are influential people, or the
wives of influential people.'

'There are men as well?' Slider asked.

'The majority are women.'

'Surprise surprise,' said Atherton. 'He *was* a sexual predator.'

'The pot calling the kettle black.'

'Not at all. I'm a fully evolved homo sapiens. He was low life.'

'Yeah, well, he's dead, so being a predator didn't do him much
good, did it? Maybe you should watch your step.' She turned back
to Slider. 'But for instance, boss, there's Tim Tobias, the TV
presenter, and Anthony Bolger, who's a footballer.'

'He's the Gunners' top scorer,' Atherton said.

'How on earth do you know that?' Slider said. 'You don't like
football.'

'He was on the news last night. In the running for Sports
Personality of the Year.'

'Well, anyway, he must be mega rich,' Swilley went on. 'Footballers make millions. And there's a William Rutherford, who's some top cat at Goldman Sachs.'

'He spread his net widely, then,' said Slider. 'But God forbid we have to go and interview all of them. If they're rich and influential, it'll be a minefield.' He was still smarting from the fallout from the Kayleigh Adams case, when top bods from politics, business and even the Met had come under scrutiny. Top bods tend not to like attention from the Vogons. It puts them off their golf swing.

'We might not have to investigate them all,' Swilley said, 'because the other black book is a diary. He puts down appointments using initials – like "A.B. ten thirty", that sort of thing. And a quick look suggests the initials match people in the other book. I think this was his private clients diary, because there's nothing in it about sessions at Gillespie's, for instance, or social contacts like Kelly-Ann or Ivanka. He may have kept those sorts of dates on his phone – or just kept them in his head.'

'Well, don't keep us on tenterhooks,' Atherton said impatiently. 'What's he got written in for the last day?'

'There's only two on Tuesday,' said Swilley. 'There's M.A. at eleven a.m. and G.S. at nine thirty p.m. Nothing after that until Wednesday. There's an M.A. in the address book, Myrna Abrams, who lives in Bayswater – Moscow Road. I've checked the address and it comes back to a Gerald Abrams who's a musical agent – you know, books soloists for concerts and such. Classical music, not pop.'

'Yes, I know who Gerald Abrams is,' said Atherton.

'You may, but nobody else does.'

'I do,' said Slider meekly. 'I've heard of him, at any rate.'

'But you're married to a concert musician,' Swilley said kindly, as though forgiving him a slightly regrettable habit. 'Anyway, I suppose being an agent makes you rich?'

'Richer than their clients, anyway,' Atherton said. 'There's an old saying: "If you can, do; if you can't, be an agent and make a fortune."'

'And who was the nine thirty appointment?' Slider asked. 'That's the more important of the two. That could be our murderer. GS you said?'

'There are two GSs in the book,' Swilley said. 'One is Gavin Spalding. He's an actor. I looked him up, and he's been in some

TV soaps, like *Hollyoaks* and *Holby City*, and he's doing a West End play at the moment.'

LaSalle and Lœssop had appeared in the door behind Swilley.

'Gavin Spalding?' said LaSalle. 'He's that actor with the big nose.'

'Graphic,' Atherton murmured.

'You know him, Funky,' LaSalle insisted.

'No, I don't,' Lœssop replied. 'Who is he?'

'He's in lots of stuff. He was in *Line of Duty*. He played that copper that went out with that woman, that got mistaken for that other bloke. It looked for a bit as if he'd done it. But in the end he hadn't.'

Atherton rolled his eyes.

'What're you doing watching *Line of Duty*, anyway?' Lœssop wondered. 'I can't stand cop shows. They're total bollocks.'

'I don't mind if it's a good story,' LaSalle protested. 'You don't expect them to get the technical stuff right. I mean, it *is* fiction.'

Slider felt it was time to tug the reins. 'You said there were two GSs,' he said loudly to Swilley. 'Who was the other one?'

'Gilda Steenkamp,' she said.

'*The* Gilda Steenkamp?' Atherton said, eyebrows agog.

Swilley looked impatient. 'No, *a* Gilda Steenkamp. They come in a six-pack.'

'Who's—?' LaSalle began.

'Max Ridley,' Swilley said.

'Oh, that detective series on TV!' LaSalle was enlightened.

'I watched one, but I couldn't get into it,' said Lœssop. 'Was she in it?'

'They were books before they were TV,' Atherton said. 'Gilda Steenkamp wrote the books. And they're not detective stories, they're on the detective/thriller cusp. And she's a very fine writer.'

'What's a cusp?' Lœssop said innocently, but he was just trying to wind Atherton up.

'If they've been on TV,' said Slider, 'she must be pretty well off. Well, that gives us three new people to interview, including two possible suspects.'

'Bags me Gilda Steenkamp,' said Atherton quickly. 'She can't possibly have done it, but I know how to talk to writers.'

'You've had enough excitement for one day,' said Slider. 'Swilley, Myrna Abrams. Lœssop, you can take Gavin Spalding.'

'But guv, he'd never heard of him,' LaSalle complained.

'Exactly. You might go over the top with hero worship. I wouldn't want you to embarrass yourself,' said Slider. 'You can have another go at Jack Gallo, find out why he didn't mention meeting Dez Wilson on Tuesday night. Right, off you go. Time and tide gather no moss.'

Atherton unfurled himself reluctantly. 'So who gets Gilda Steenkamp?' he asked.

'Guess,' said Slider.

Joanna phoned. 'I suppose you'll be working late?'

'Saturday's a good day to catch people in,' Slider said apologetically.

'No, it's all right. Last session this evening and the brass section's invited me for a drink afterwards. Don't worry, I won't drink,' she added before he could speak, 'but I'd like to have a last natter before we all disperse. Who knows when I'll see any of them again.' It sounded melancholy.

'If you're asking me if I mind, of course I don't. Have fun.'

'Anything new to tell me?'

'We're going to interview the wife of Gerald Abrams.'

'What, Gerald Abrams the agent? He agented Nicky Adonis, the Famous Flautist.' It was what Atherton called him – he was always rather caustic about him because he said he wasn't that good, and had only been elevated to stardom because of his looks. Joanna, who had played in the same orchestra as him for many years before his transmutation, tended to agree with him. Actually, Atherton more often called him the Flatulent Flautist, but Joanna said that was needlessly reductive.

'So would Gerald Abrams be a rich man?' Slider asked.

'Well, Nicky Adonis is everywhere. Concerts, recordings, TV shows. He's never off Classic FM. And Gerald gets ten per cent of everything. Plus all his other super-successful clients. So I'd say, yes, he's doing all right. Why?'

'Our deceased liked to give private training sessions to rich women.'

'Oh yes, you said. And the little extras. Intriguing – Abrams' wife slumming with the help?'

'We don't know that she did, but she seems to have had an

appointment with him on his last day, so she may have something to tell us – something he mentioned about his plans for the rest of it, perhaps.'

'Oh well, good luck with that, then.'

'And have a nice time with your brass. Bring me back a story.'

She laughed. 'That's a given.'

LaSalle had been right about the nose, thought Lœssop. It met you halfway to the handshake. It was thin at the bridge and sharp all the way down. You could have used it to open letters.

Lœssop's nickname wasn't Funky for nothing. He wore his hair in shoulder-length dreads and affected a Jack Sparrow moustache and beard plaits (though without the beads – you had to draw a line somewhere) and with his general swarthiness and dark eyes he had a lot of Bohemian cred. The watchdog at the artists' entrance almost let him through unchallenged. Almost. The downside of not looking like a policeman was that his warrant card got a lot of close scrutiny before it opened doors.

'They've only just finished the matinée,' the doorman said, 'so he's probably still in his dressing room. He's not come past me, anyway. But he won't like being disturbed, with another show to do tonight. They don't get long to rest.'

'Police business,' Lœssop said. 'Can't wait. I'll try and keep it quick.'

'Go on, then,' said the doorman, and gave him convoluted directions.

Lœssop had been backstage of enough theatres not to be surprised at the lack of glamour. The walls were bare brick painted black to shoulder level and dingy pale green above. The lights hung down under dark green tin lampshades like coolie hats. Doors were painted industrial maroon, and fire extinguishers brooded in the shadows ready to catch your elbow as you passed.

There was a number on the door but no name. Lœssop knocked, and at the second assault a muffled voice inside said, 'Oh, come in if you must!' in martyred tones. The room was tiny, with a spotty mirror framed with light bulbs over a wide shelf that served as dressing table, with a wooden chair in front of it. A massive 1930s radiator occupied one wall; a forgotten wet cloth that had been dried on it had assumed jaunty planes and angles like a Frank Gehry installation. There was a tatty chaise longue against the opposite wall. Clothes hung everywhere on hooks on the walls and were piled on a basket-chair in the corner. A waste-paper basket overflowed with discarded newspapers and used tissues, and an old-fashioned enamel water jug held a bunch of long-dead roses. Other notable features were a stain the shape of the Isle of Wight on the ceiling, and a lurking red fire-bucket of sand waiting to trip you like a rake in the grass.

And then there was the nose.

Lœssop reflected that acting was about the only profession in which it could work as an asset. He tried not to stare at it. Gavin Spalding was tall for an actor, which meant he'd never be cast as the romantic lead. In showbiz only villains were tall. He was also thin, and with the help of the nose he looked almost gaunt, with dangerous cheekbones and a chin made for sinister stroking. He was wearing scruffy jeans and a blue Breton smock much stained at the neck with Max Factor (Lœssop wondered if it was part of his costume – he had no idea what the play was about) and his bony feet were bare. He looked tired, and stared at Lœssop as though his intrusion verged on the Last Straw.

'Who the hell are you?' he asked.

Lœssop introduced himself, showed his warrant card, and apologized for disturbing him.

'No, it's all right,' Spalding said resignedly. 'I suppose Marjie told you I was leaving for Hungary tomorrow so it has to be now or never.'

'Marjie?'

'Marjie Heinz. My agent. This piece of shit closes tonight. I've got two weeks filming for *Walking With The Dead IV*.' He said it with a hint of pride, and Lœssop realized he meant the movie franchise.

'I've seen the first three. They film it in Hungary?' he queried. 'I thought it was supposed to be England.'

'Hungary's cheaper,' Spalding said shortly. 'They get government subsidies. Is there something I can help you with? Only I'd like to have some grub and a nap before I have to go on again.' He gave a grimace instead of a smile. 'It's a glamorous profession, as you can see.'

Lœssop gave his best cheeky Johnny Depp grin. 'Yeah. Ours is, too.'

Spalding sat down on the chaise and waved him to the wooden chair. 'Has anyone ever told you you look like—'

'Yeah, it's deliberate. Gets me in to places a copper wouldn't be welcome.'

'I can see that. Well, what's this about? I can't remember having done anything illegal recently.'

'No, you're not in trouble. It's just that your name came up in reference to Erik Lingoss.'

'Really? I wonder why. What's he done?'

'He's dead,' said Lœssop.

Spalding's weary eyes opened wide. 'Dead? God, that's awful. He's quite young, isn't he? What happened?'

'Somebody killed him.'

'God, no! That's terrible. How did they do it?'

'I can't go into that, I'm afraid. But I would like to know the nature of your relationship with him.'

He looked put out. 'What are you talking about, relationship? I didn't have a relationship with him. What are you implying?'

'I'm not implying anything, I'm asking. I'll put it another way – how did you know him?'

'I did some fitness training with him, that's all. I needed to put on some muscle for a part, and Marjie found him for me. He was very good. But why on earth are you asking me? He must have had dozens of other clients since.'

'Well, you were one of the last people to see him. You had an appointment with him on Tuesday evening.'

Spalding tensed, but he looked worried rather than fearful. 'No, there's some mistake there. I haven't seen him for months. Why would you think I saw him on Tuesday?'

'It's in his diary – your initials and the time, nine thirty.'

He shook his head. 'Well, it wasn't me. It must be someone else with the same initials. Apart from anything else, I was here Tuesday night, like every other night except Sunday.' He gave a short laugh. 'About a thousand people saw me right here on stage. Evening performance, curtain goes up at seven thirty and the play's two hours fifteen. Work it out for yourself. I think that's a pretty convincing alibi, don't you?'

Yes, Lœssop thought, disappointedly, *it is*. Though skinny, Spalding looked fit enough and he had large hands; and temperamentally he thought an actor would be quite up to whacking someone who annoyed him.

He didn't want to slink away with nothing, so he said, 'Can you tell me when you last saw him?'

'Let me see – it would be in May, I think. I saw him twice weekly for about two months. Then the part finished and I didn't need him any more.'

'You didn't keep in touch with him?'

Another laugh. 'When would I have the time? I barely keep in touch with my mother! Look, he was a good trainer, and actually I liked him as well. He was good company. But that was all there was to it.'

He looked straight into Lœssop's eyes when he said that last bit – the liar's 'tell'. Yes, the alibi was about as close to cast iron as it was possible to get, but he was hiding something, that was for sure.

Lœssop tried another tack. 'Did you do your training sessions at his flat?'

'No, at mine. I've got a flat in Highgate, he came there. Oh, except once, when we met at a gym in Kensington. But I didn't want people seeing me working out. You know, videoing me on their phones and asking me for autographs. So I said it had to be my place. Look, have you done? Because I haven't got a lot of time.'

Lœssop ignored that. 'Was it just the fitness training? Because we've heard he was also good for some other services – little extras, you might say.'

The eyes brightened, and an angry flush came to his face. 'I don't know what you're talking about.'

'Oh, I think you do,' said Lœssop, going for steely – not a natural look for him, but it generally worked when there was a guilty conscience to hand. 'He provided something more, didn't he – not just the weights and the encouragement?'

Now the eyes moved away. 'Look,' he said, capitulating, 'it was nothing. Just a bit of charlie. One wrap. And it was just the once. I was out and he got it for me as a favour.'

'Cocaine,' Lœssop said evenly.

'Everyone takes it,' Spalding said defensively. 'If you're going to start cracking down on it, you'll have to arrest everyone in Ham and High, not to mention the whole of the House of Commons. It's a victimless crime, for God's sake!'

'He got you cocaine? Nothing else?'

'That's it, I swear.' He spoke firmly with the full eye contact again. He practically excreted sincerity. 'Are you going to arrest me? Because otherwise I'll have to ask you to go – I've got to prepare myself for the performance.'

'Was he still providing you with cocaine?'

'I told you, I haven't seen him since May. Or spoken to him. Or heard his name, come to that. It was a one-time thing, the training, and as far as I was concerned, it was over. I'm sorry he's dead, but it was nothing to do with me, all right?'

Lœssop stood up. 'Right,' he said. 'Thank you for being so frank. I won't take up any more of your time.'

He left, turned the wrong way and got lost, came up against a metal staircase with pierced treads and lit at what was surely a criminally low level, turned back, wandered a bit, and finally found a sign with a kitsch pointing finger that said EXIT. It was so grubby with the passage of bodies squeezing past each other in a confined space that he almost missed it, but moments later he was emerging into the daylight, such as it was. And he still thought Spalding was hiding something. The cocaine had been a diversion, good for taking the attention away: illegal but almost never prosecuted. Victimless crime indeed! It added another unwelcome little facet to Lingoss's character, though.

The Abrams lived in one of those red-and-white Edwardian blocks of mansion flats. Swilley didn't like old things. She preferred modern buildings and light, modern furniture, and when Myrna Abrams let her in and she saw how dark it was inside, she feared the worst. But everything was clean and polished and there was no damp or reasty smell – no smell at all, in fact, except for a faint hint of furniture polish. And as she was led through to the drawing-room, the impression she got was one of calm. It was a home designed first and foremost for being comfortable in.

The drawing-room was huge, with a high ceiling, a big fireplace, and shelves and panelled cupboards built into both alcoves, stacked with books above and old-fashioned vinyl LPs on the taller bottom shelf. The polished wooden floor was mostly covered with a beat-up Persian carpet. The bay window was occupied by a seven-foot grand piano, gleaming softly, the lid invitingly open, music ready on the rack. It was such a presence in the room, Swilley could almost hear it purring. The rest of the furniture looked slightly shabby, infinitely comfortable and definitely used. The fire was alight, and the flickering of the flames was comforting against the grey day outside, though she couldn't understand why anyone would bother when there was central heating.

Myrna Abrams must have been in her fifties, but she was a shining example of what HRT could do: she seemed bursting with health, with bright eyes, firm skin and glossy hair – Swilley bet she had a cold wet nose as well. The hair was very dark, arranged in giant-roller waves, and showed no thread of grey – helped, obviously. Her figure was trim and her movements lithe. We should all look so good after menopause, Swilley thought. She was smartly dressed in slacks and a cashmere sweater and made up to going-out standard.

Myrna Abrams was not surprised when Swilley introduced the topic of Lingoss. 'I had heard about it already,' she said. She had a brisk way of talking, and a faint South African accent. 'Gerald told me on – Wednesday, was it? It was all over the internet. He picked it up as soon as he got to the office and rang me so I shouldn't hear it some other way. It's a dreadful, dreadful thing. Poor Erik. Is that right, he was murdered? Who would do such a thing? It wasn't as if he mixed with bad lots – or did he?' she added, fixing Swilley with a sharp gaze. 'Of course, I didn't know everything he got up to, but he didn't strike me as the sort.'

'What sort would that be?'

'Well – Erik believed the body was a temple. He was always exquisitely clean and perfectly groomed and he didn't drink or take drugs, so I can't imagine he'd fit in with bad lots.' She smiled suddenly. 'Even after a workout he still smelled fresh. I used to say he sweated distilled water.'

'You saw him on Tuesday morning,' Swilley said, not making it a question.

'Yes, it was my usual weekly session. Oh dear!' She put her hands to her face. 'He was killed on Tuesday, wasn't he? That's what they're saying. It's a horrible thing to think of. All the time we were together he was living his last hours, and he didn't know it.'

'How did he seem?'

'No different from usual. I'm sure he had no idea of anything coming. We did our session, then we had a cup of tea together and chatted a bit, and then he went. I had no idea I'd never see him again. It's dreadful.'

'What did you chat about?'

'Goodness, I don't remember. It was just the usual, you know.' She frowned in thought. 'No, I honestly can't remember anything in particular we talked about. It was just chit-chat between old friends.'

'You have your sessions here?'

'Yes, always. I have the equipment set up in a spare bedroom – would you like to see it?'

'Perhaps later.'

'I use it every day – one must keep fit.' She looked Swilley over appraisingly. 'And Erik comes once a week to keep me up to scratch, keep me motivated. I've tried to get Gerald to take some lessons with him, because my God he needs it! It isn't good at his age to be so sedentary. I've told him, you're getting flabby. I refuse to be married to a flabby old man. But he won't do it. He hates the idea of exercise for its own sake. And he didn't entirely take to Erik, if I'm honest. Called him a poseur. He doesn't trust health fads, clean eating, veganism, any of those modern things. Calls it navel-gazing and narcissism. It's all I can do to get him to take a multivitamin every day.'

'Was there any other reason he might have objected to Erik?' Swilley tried.

The bright gaze sharpened. 'What do you mean?'

'I think you know what I mean. Your relationship with Erik Lingoss – did it go beyond fitness training?' Same bright look – she wasn't going to give it away that easily. Swilley went for broke. 'Did you sleep with him?' She half expected an indignant protest, but Myrna Abrams laughed.

'Fair question! Yes, I did sleep with him, but only a couple of times.'

'You mean twice?'

'Twice or three times. No more than that. Then I told him it must stop. He was good, he was very good, and it was all perfectly congenial – no pressure, no expectations. What is it they say in America? No harm, no foul. He used to massage me, you see, after the workout, and it's easy to slip into an amorous mood when you're relaxed and naked and a handsome young man has his hands all over you. And he was very good at massage – knew just where to dig in. You find yourself going all the way even when you had no intention beforehand. So I don't have the massage any more – too much temptation.'

'Why did you stop? Did your husband find out?'

'Gerald? You're imagining he walked in on us?' She laughed. 'Like a French farce! No, that never happened – though I wouldn't be surprised if he guessed. I was always in a euphoric state after Erik's visits. But he wouldn't have minded if he did know. We haven't had a physical relationship for years, not since the boys left home. We're very good friends, our marriage is solid, but there's nothing sexual between us any more.'

'Even so, men can be very territorial about their wives.'

'Oh, Gerald is a most civilized man. I'm sure he has his little poppets when he needs recreation. I don't mind in the least, and he wouldn't mind if I did the same.'

'So why did you break it off with Erik?' Swilley asked.

She wrinkled her nose. 'Break it off? It sounds like a teenage crush. Why did I stop sleeping with him, you mean?' Swilley nodded. 'Because I discovered he was sleeping with my sister, and I felt that was just a bit too – what shall I say – tacky. Too close to home. It didn't sit right with me, so I just said no more. Erik said he understood. We were both fine about it – there was no quarrel, if that's what you're thinking.' She laughed. 'I thought my sister needed it more than me. Definitely. So I let her have him.'

'Your sister is also a client of Erik's?'

'Yes, of course. That's what I'm saying.'

'And what is your sister's name?'

'Gilda Steenkamp,' she said.

ELEVEN

Sisters Do It for Themselves

'I thought you knew,' Myrna Abrams said.

'We have her name from Erik's client list,' Swilley said, 'but we didn't know she was your sister. Are you close?'

'Always have been. There's just the two of us, you see. Pappy died young and Mommy had to bring us up alone. He had two restaurants in Cape Town, and restaurants are hard work. He had good managers, but he would never leave it to them. Had to be hands-on. Control freak, you see. The restaurants killed him. He was only forty-six when he died. Pappy's best manager took over running the business, but Mommy still struggled. It was hard on all of us. In the end she married him, the manager. It was the only way she could cope. We didn't mind,' she added, as if Swilley had asked. 'Mervyn was all right. He was good to us girls. But the eighties wasn't a good time in South Africa, and Mommy wanted us out. So we came to England. I was twenty, and Gilda was eighteen.'

'Who looked after you?'

'Grandpa Gershon was already here – Mommy's father. We lived with him and Granny. Of course, the first thing he did was to get me married off to a nice respectable man. Gerald was the son of a friend of Grandpa's so he ticked all the boxes.'

Swilley picked up on the word 'off'. 'It was an arranged marriage?'

She frowned a little. 'Of course not. It wasn't like that. Marriage is an important life decision – why wouldn't you take the advice of someone older and wiser? Gerald's been a good husband and we've got along just fine. We had two boys, they've both done well. I've never wanted for anything. And Gerald and I are still friends, though we lead our separate lives. I've nothing to complain about. But Gilda, she was the wild child. She didn't want to do what was expected of her. She wanted to be different. Well, I was the eldest, so I had to toe the line, but the younger daughter can get away with murder.'

Interesting choice of word, Swilley thought. 'Like what?' she asked.

'Well, for a start she wanted to earn her own living. I've never had a job – it just wasn't done in those days. And then she married out. That put five thousand volts through the family. Oh, the ructions! Grandpa bellowed, Granny wrung her hands. Mommy wrote tear-stained letters from Cape Town, and when Gilda wouldn't change her mind she refused to come to the wedding. She died less than a year later, so of course everyone says she died of a broken heart and Gilda as good as killed her.' She made a rueful face at Swilley. 'Happy families!'

'But you were on her side?'

'Oh, Gerald and I aren't observant. We kept up appearances while the Olds were alive, and for the boys, to an extent, while they were at home. But neither of us cares about the religious stuff. I like the family side of it, and Gerald loves the networking – so useful in his game. But I can't take all the petty rules.' She puffed out her lips. 'I maintained Gilda had a right to her own life. Of course it didn't go down well, but I toughed it out. It upset Gilda much more than me, all the disapproval and tooth-sucking. And then when there were no children, of course they said it was God's judgement. Actually I don't think Gilda ever particularly wanted children. By the time it was clear there wouldn't be any, she had her books.'

'Has hers been a happy marriage?'

She hesitated for a telling second. 'Oh, as happy as any marriage is, I suppose. The rose-tinted glasses have to come off, don't they? And like with Gerald and me, there's an age difference, and that matters more as you get older.' She smiled at Swilley. 'Men pull out all the stops when they're courting you, but as soon as they've got the ring on your finger, they take off their corsets, figuratively speaking, and you see what you've really got.'

'What do they quarrel about?'

'I didn't say they quarrelled. There've been little frictions, but there are in any marriage.'

'Over the lack of children?'

'Possibly. Men find the old tribal business important, don't they?

Of course, *they* don't have to go through the actual child-bearing. Be different story if they did. And then there was Gilda's writing – it can't be easy for any man to see his wife more successful than him. Well, Brian always did all right, good enough for any normal couple, but when Gilda had a book made into TV, it moved her into a different league.' She stared at nothing for a moment, reflecting. 'I think that's the attraction for Erik. He loves money, that boy. But in a strangely pure way. Well, everything about him is strangely pure.' She seemed to have forgotten to use the past tense.

'What do you mean by that?'

'Oh, the body being a temple and all that sort of thing. I've never known such a clean man in all my life. I used to tease him about it sometimes – said he was going to turn into Howard Hughes. He didn't know who Howard Hughes was – that's another problem with the age difference. No shared references.'

'Erik was obsessive? OCD?'

'No, I was just joking. There was nothing wrong with him. No more than any of us, anyway. He came from a broken home . . .?' She looked to see if Swilley knew that.

'We knew both his parents had remarried and he didn't see them,' she said.

Myrna Abrams nodded. 'Poor kid. His parents hated each other, always rowing, and he was the only child so he didn't even have a sibling to huddle with. Breaks my heart to think how lonely he must have been. Then as soon as he was eighteen they got divorced – it was as if they'd just been waiting for his majority. And neither of them wanted him. He was thrown out into the big cold world, all alone. Had to fend for himself, and it was a struggle at first. Well, it's no wonder he's driven. He's found something he can do and make money at, and he's determined never to be poor again, or to have to depend on anyone else ever again. I get it, I absolutely get it. That's why I say his love of money is pure, in a funny sort of way. There's nothing dirty about money, for him.'

'Or about the ways of getting it?' Swilley suggested.

She shrugged. 'He didn't think so. I'm sure it didn't bother him, as long as it paid. But nobody got hurt, you know. It was all consensual.'

'Did you pay him for sex?'

'Oh, is that where you're heading? Well, why shouldn't I? It's a service, just as much as a massage. You get naked, someone gives you pleasure. What's wrong with that? If he didn't feel it was dirty, why should I?'

'You gave him money?' Swilley wanted it said plainly.

'I just added a bit to the basic fee. And when I told him we wouldn't be doing it any more, I gave him a present as well, to sweeten it.'

'What did you give him?'

'A very nice watch. I'd bought it for Gerald's birthday.' She raised an eyebrow at Swilley. 'Gerald didn't know about it, and I bought him another one. I just happened to have it in the house, is all. It was a Patek Philippe. I expect Erik sold it for cash as soon as he was out of the door, but that was his business. That boy loved cash.'

Swilley remembered the talk about the watch caddy on the bedside cabinet. 'I don't think he did sell it,' she said. 'Did you ever go to his place?'

'Never,' she said. 'That wouldn't be appropriate. I don't even know where he lived.'

'Tell me about your sister's relationship with him.'

'For that, you'll have to ask Gilda,' she said firmly. 'I can't tell you what there was between them. Erik didn't talk about her. He was always very discrete about his clients. He'd have to be, or he soon wouldn't have any.'

'So how did you know she was sleeping with him?'

'She told me herself. Big heart-to-heart one day and it all came out.'

'And did she know that you—?'

'No, I never told her I was.' She made a moue. 'Baby sister, you see – I got in the habit of looking out for her. So I didn't say anything, in case it upset her. Just resolved it wouldn't happen again. And it didn't. And I never told Erik I knew about him and her, either.'

So many secrets, Swilley thought. Outside, she rang Slider. 'Are you still in the office, boss?'

'I haven't moved from my desk yet.'

'So you haven't spoken to Gilda Steenkamp yet?'

'No – why?'

'I think you want to hear what Myrna Abrams told me before you do. I'm on my way back now.'

LaSalle found Jack Gallo easily – he was doing the late shift at Pex. The place was pulsing with sweating, grunting, bulging customers who made LaSalle feel like an underendowed beanstalk. If anyone asks, he thought, I'm telling them I'm a karate black belt and can kill a man with my thumbs. He tried to narrow his eyes in a dangerous manner, but as it meant he couldn't see where he was going it was more dangerous to him than potential attackers.

Nobody asked him, anyway. Gallo fielded him with a resigned air and led him to the office. 'Have you got anywhere yet?' he asked, offering a chair. 'I don't know that there's anything more I can tell you. I mean, I'd like to help, but . . .' He let it hang, and sat down on the edge of the desk in a weary manner, pushing paperwork back with his buttocks to make room. He looked, LaSalle thought, a bit frayed round the edges, which on the whole he took as a useful sign.

'We're interested, you see,' LaSalle said, not sitting – he didn't want to be looked down on by Gallo – 'that you don't have an alibi for Tuesday night.'

Gallo looked exasperated. 'Well, I don't see what I can do about that. Anyway, there must be hundreds of people in London who don't have alibis. Why pick on me?'

'They didn't all know Lingoss. And you lied to us.'

'What are you talking about? Tuesday night? I told the other detective I finished work, went for a drink, and went home. It's all true.'

'Maybe. But we checked up at The Britannia – oh yes, we check everything, mate, you should know that – and it seems you had a meeting with Dez Wilson there that night, which you didn't tell us about.'

Gallo coloured slightly, which could have been annoyance or guilt or both. He didn't actually say anything.

'Well?' LaSalle prompted. 'You met good old Dez in The Britannia – are you going to lie again?'

'I didn't lie,' Gallo said tautly. 'I didn't mention Dez, that's all. It's different.'

'Are you trying to pretend you forgot all about this important meeting?'

'You keep calling it a meeting,' Gallo said irritably. 'I didn't know he was going to come in. I wasn't expecting him. It wasn't arranged. I don't know why you're getting so fixated about it.'

'People usually have a very good reason for lying to the police. Or a very bad reason, I should say.'

'I didn't *lie*!'

'We're thinking, you see, that here are two big hefty lads with a grudge against Erik Lingoss, they meet on the evening he's killed, they don't have alibis, and they pretend the meeting never happened. So what was it all about? Working out the last details? Who was going to do what. Who was going to hold him down and who was going to whack him.'

'Oh, for God's sake!' Gallo surged to his feet, but he only stamped to the window and back. 'I didn't kill him! We were mates. I'd never kill anyone. It's crazy!'

'So why didn't you mention meeting Dez?'

A slight hesitation. 'I didn't . . .' Long pause. 'I didn't want to get him into trouble.'

'Trouble? Like being suspected of killing Erik Lingoss?'

Gallo spread his hands. 'Look, Dez was in a bit of trouble when he was a kid. I'm sure you know that by now – you'll have looked up his record. But he turned it round. The fitness training, the discipline, people believing in him – it showed him there was a better way, stopped him going to the bad. He's made a success of his life since then. He's done bloody wonders, if you want to know. He's a top bloke. But there's that record he can never shake off. And he's black. You people will always have a down on him. I wanted to protect him. So I just . . . didn't mention him. It was a spur of the moment thing. OK, it was stupid, but it didn't mean anything. Dez would no more hurt Erik than I would.'

'Why did you meet, then?'

'It wasn't arranged. Dez knew where I'd be, he came in to have a chat, that's all.'

'A very intense chat, according to the bar staff. Lowered voices and heads together.'

'Look, he'd had a barney with his wife, and he'd just come home and found she'd left him and taken Ayesha with her. Dez worships that kiddie. He was in a state, he didn't know what to do. That's what he came to talk about – not Erik.'

LaSalle shook his head. 'I can't see why you wouldn't tell us that. There's nothing about that to put him in the frame. Unless that's *not* all it was.' He waited to let Gallo speak, but he didn't. 'The barney with his wife, for instance – what was it about?' Gallo didn't answer, but LaSalle thought there was consciousness in the silence. 'It was about your sister, wasn't it? Mel was fed up with Dez being so concerned about Lucy, talking about her all the time. Yakking about how Erik done her wrong.'

Gallo looked up. 'If I'd said that, you'd have got the wrong idea. You'd have latched onto it – I know what you blokes are like.'

'You and Dez both, you both hated Erik for what he'd done to Lucy.'

'I didn't hate him. He was just – Erik. He was like that. You had to accept it. And Lucy had got over it.'

'But Dez hadn't.'

'It was all just talk. Dez would never hurt a fly.'

'Except that you think maybe he would.'

'Never!'

There was nothing more to be gained from the interview, without direct evidence. If only they had enough to search Gallo's pad and find the mobile. LaSalle nodded and stood up. 'We'll leave it for now,' he said. 'By the way, how did you find out that Erik was sleeping with someone else as well as your sister? Did he tell you?'

'Erik? No. He didn't talk about his clients – not by name. You've got to be discreet in this business. And I didn't "find out", as you put it. He told Lucy he couldn't see her any more because he was seeing someone else. And with Erik "seeing" meant "sleeping with".'

LaSalle pondered that a moment. 'From what you've said before, Erik didn't usually mind sleeping with more than one woman at a time. Wasn't it rather remarkable that he broke off with Lucy just for that reason?'

Gallo had to think about that. 'I suppose . . .'

'Yes?'

'I suppose he was . . . being more respectful of Lucy, really, by breaking it off. I hadn't thought of it like that before.' He seemed disturbed by the idea.

'Unless he had another reason. Unless he'd just got bored with Lucy. Maybe she didn't have much to keep him interested.'

Gallo's fists bunched. 'Don't you talk about my sister like that.'

'Take it easy, chap. I'm not a punch bag.'

'You're a bloody nuisance.'

'Interesting,' said Porson, staring out of the main office window at the traffic struggling along Uxbridge Road, both directions chokka, half the world trying to get home from work, the other half trying to go out for the evening. Slider reflected that there was no need for Porson to be there at that time of the day, or indeed at all on a Saturday, but since his dear wife died, he had nothing to go home for. The Job was all he had. Slider felt a surge of gratitude for Joanna and George, Dad and his wife Lydia. Family! He'd be in the going-home stream, no question. He'd never want to go out in the evening. And he had a moment of unwelcome pity for Lingoss, who'd had nothing and no one. The self-made man.

Porson turned. 'Gallo and Wilson is still the best bet. One or the other, or both acting in collision. Both'd be better. That would account for the two separate attacks. One clobbers him, the other goes back and finishes him off.'

'Sir, I can't help feeling that if they did it they'd have arranged an alibi,' said Swilley.

Porson snorted. 'We're not talking Brain of Britain here. Thinking things through is not your average criminal's fortress.'

'And the motive, sir – Lingoss and Lucy Gallo had broken up a month ago. Wouldn't they have done it while it was fresh, if that was the reason?'

'They could have had other motives as well,' Lœssop said.

'And Gallo admitted that Wilson was still sore about it,' said LaSalle.

'If they were in it together, they could have been each other's alibi,' said Hart. 'Said they were together at Gallo's flat, for instance. Why didn't they? Hard to disprove something like that.'

Slider wasn't sure if she was for the idea or against it. Apparently, neither was Porson, because he glared at her and said, 'They both lied, Wilson about his wife and Gallo about the meeting. There's no smoke without straw.' He looked at Slider. 'You've got nothing else, have you?'

'We haven't interviewed Gilda Steenkamp yet. She was apparently the last person to see him alive.'

'Well, I suppose you'd better get on and talk to her, but unless she was there when the killer or killers arrived . . . Nothing on any cameras? No witnesses come forward? Somebody must have seen them.'

'Nothing yet, sir,' Slider answered.

Porson shook his head disapprovingly. 'Well, you've got to pull all the stops out of the bag before Monday, because with this march coming up, I can see Lingoss being put on the back boiler, and there's nothing I like worse than a case hanging around like a bad smell. For Gawd's sake get something so we can search their gaffs at least.'

He stalked out, and Slider turned to McLaren. 'I know you'd have told me if you'd got anything, but I have to ask. Bus cameras?'

'It's a long time frame, guv,' McLaren said. 'Now we've got the nine thirty appointment I've had to widen it. And there's a lot of buses. I've got a few cars turning into Russell Close, but most of them you can't read the index, or its partial. I'm making a list, but it takes time to work through.'

'I know,' Slider said. 'And the electronics shop?'

McLaren shook his head. 'They've not turned up yet.'

'All right. Keep trying. I'd better get on and interview the famous Gilda Steenkamp, since we've nowhere else to go.'

'And by a huge stroke of luck, I'm free to go with you,' said Atherton. 'You need my niche expertise. You know I'm the only person in the firm who ever reads a book.'

'Take him, boss,' said Swilley. 'Then we won't have to listen to him using words like "niche".'

'Nothing wrong with niche,' said Atherton. 'Lovely sheashide town.'

'Oh God, take him away!' Swilley cried.

It was one of those massive white-stuccoed Victorian Campden Hill mansions that had been divided into two dwellings without in any way diminishing its luxury. The word 'flat' was pitifully inadequate. The ground floor was taken up with a splendid entrance hall and staircase. Gilda Steenkamp had the first floor, and the second and third floors were a separate maisonette. The conversion had been done back in Edwardian times, so the grandeur had been retained. This was no developer's cardboard-partition job. The door to her flat, for instance, was a nine-foot solid mahogany panelled beauty, glossily varnished and with brass door furniture that must have weighed pounds.

It was opened by a tall man in his sixties with a large head of beautifully-tended silver hair and a tasteful tan that suggested regular foreign travel. He was wearing a beautiful tweed suit; there were heavy plain gold cufflinks in his shirt, and his shoes were buffed to a gloss. Slider maintained you could tell a lot about a man from the way he kept his shoes and his hands. A quick glance proved this man's hands were perfectly manicured.

'Mr Steenkamp?' Slider enquired politely.

The mouth tightened. 'My wife writes under her maiden name,' he said. 'My name is Seagram.'

'I'm sorry,' said Slider. 'I suppose that must happen a lot. It must be annoying for you.'

'The husbands of writers have to get used to it,' he said, without exactly saying it was all right.

He examined their warrant cards seriously and let them into the hall, which was beautiful, with a high ceiling, magnificent mould-ings, a chandelier of Victorian authenticity, gleaming wood floor with a Turkish runner down the centre, and a Regency console by way of hall table with a vast gilded mirror on the wall above it, the frame finished at the top with a fat golden cupid tangled in ribbons and flowers. Even the lady's handbag on the console had the Chanel double C on it, which Slider knew meant it had cost thousands.

'I can't think why you want to bother my wife about this busi-ness,' said Seagram. 'But I suppose you have to do your duty. She's on the telephone at the moment, speaking to her agent in New York, but she'll talk to you when she's finished.'

He led them into a drawing room so full of exquisite antiques Slider didn't know where to look first, from the furniture to the porcelain to the paintings on the walls. It was a huge room, about thirty feet long, panelled up to the dado, and everything was elegantly arranged and perfectly polished. It looked like something from a National Trust property.

'You have some beautiful things,' he couldn't help saying.

'Thank you,' said Seagram minimally, as if he'd agreed a long time ago in a weak moment to say something and now felt he had to honour his commitment.

Atherton looked at Slider as the same thing clicked in his mind at the same moment. 'Excuse me,' Atherton said, 'but are you the Seagram of Heneage and Seagram? The antique dealers?'

'Yes,' Seagram said, like a horse whisking away a fly. 'I'll go and see if my wife is ready for you.'

He went out of the room, and Atherton said, 'Well that's interesting.'

'If you can't have nice antiques when you're an antique dealer, when can you?' said Slider.

'I meant, it's interesting that there's a link here. Lucy Gallo works for him.'

'Yes, I know that's what you meant. But I can't think what the significance of it is, so I thought I'd ignore it for now.'

'Fair enough,' said Atherton. Then: 'I'm going to meet Gilda Steenkamp. Oh-boy-oh-boy-oh-boy!'

'Settle down,' said Slider. 'Celebrities are never as exciting as you think they're going to be.'

TWELVE

Pie in the Sky with Diamonds

Seagram led them to 'my wife's study' which was at the back of the house, with a tall, gracious window – presumably looking over gardens, because Slider could see trees waving beyond. The room was large and warm and nest-like, deep with books and glowing dark wood, a worn red Turkish carpet on the floor, a faint smell of freesias from a bunch in a vase by the window. Flown in from the Channel Islands – expensive tastes! By the fireplace there was a big leather Chesterfield stuffed with cushions with a lamp invitingly placed for reading, and an enormous partner's desk with papers, books and a PC screen and keyboard on it.

And there was Gilda Steenkamp, standing in the middle of the room to receive them, like someone patiently waiting to do their duty, like the Queen about to present a long list of OBEs. She was tall and slim and wearing a garnet-red jersey wrap-around dress that outlined an athletic figure. Her dark hair was short and expensively cut, her face was strong-featured and handsome with a full-lipped mouth, and large dark eyes, with heavy lids like curved gardenia petals. But the eyes were blue-ringed, the mouth drooped at the corners; she looked drawn and pale. Some trouble, Slider thought, had come to her recently. She looked as though she'd been doing a lot of crying.

'Here are the police, dear,' Seagram said in gentle tones as if talking to an invalid.

She gave him, Slider thought, a scathing look.

Slider took over the introductions, and offered their warrant cards, which she waved away regally. There was a slightly awkward pause, which Steenkamp broke.

'Thank you, Brian,' she said firmly.

'Well, I'll leave you to it, then,' he said, and withdrew, closing the heavy door behind him. It made no sound as it closed, but it seemed to seal them in a velvety hush.

'You want to talk to me about Erik Lingoss,' she said. She took the armchair (French, late-eighteenth century) and waved them to the Chesterfield opposite. Her hands looked strong – a combination of typing and fitness training, Slider supposed – and perfectly manicured, with moderate-length nails lacquered dark red, and several rings whose large diamonds had the sparkle of authenticity. She was also wearing diamond stud earrings. This was, after all, he reminded himself, a very wealthy woman.

'I'm not sure there's anything useful I can tell you.' She sat like the Queen, too – back straight, knees together, feet crossed at the ankles, hands folded in her lap. Deportment lessons at school perhaps, Slider thought.

'You never know what might be useful,' he said. 'And it seems that you must have been the last person to see him alive.'

She flinched slightly at the words, but she said, 'I don't know why you think that.'

'You had an appointment with him at nine thirty on Tuesday evening.'

'No, I didn't,' she said, a flat denial.

'Ma'am,' Slider said, 'it was in his diary. Are you telling me you didn't keep it?'

'I'm telling you I never made it,' she said. She looked from him to Atherton. 'My regular session with him is on a Friday morning. I sometimes . . .' She hesitated. 'I sometimes see him on other days, if it happens to suit us both, if he has a vacancy and I feel I need more . . . more help.' She seemed to struggle to get her mouth under control.

'You're upset about his death,' Atherton said gently.

She caught a breath. 'Of course I am,' she said. 'A young man dying – killed – it's always shocking. And he was . . . I'd known him for quite a while. He was a good trainer.'

'And something more than that?' Slider suggested. 'Your relationship – how would you describe it?'

She looked at him coldly. 'I wouldn't.'

Atherton tried. 'You were more than trainer and client, weren't you?'

'I don't know what you're suggesting,' she said flatly, but she flicked a glance at the door as she said it.

So, hubby didn't know, Slider thought. But if ever a door was soundproof, it must be that one. 'I'm suggesting,' he said quietly, 'that you and Lingoss were lovers.'

She went red around the eyes – grief or anger? 'You've no right to say that. He was a good trainer, and I was fond of him, that's all,' she said. 'And I had no appointment with him on Tuesday. I would never make an appointment for nine thirty in the evening because that's during my writing time. Nine until midnight.'

'You have regular hours for writing?' Atherton said with unfeigned interest.

She looked at him with faint relief. 'When I'm actually in the process of writing, as opposed to researching or editing, yes. It's essential to be disciplined when you have a deadline to meet.' She seemed happier talking about her schedule, and relaxed slightly. 'Routine is important to writers. You have to control your physical environment to allow your imagination to run free. We all have our particular ways. I write the first draft longhand, for instance. I always have. I can't do it any other way. Then I input it later into the computer, at the polishing stage. And I've always preferred writing at night, when it's quiet. I find I concentrate better. I set aside those hours religiously.' She shrugged slightly. 'Occasionally some public appearance might intrude, but I never willingly make appointments of any sort during writing hours. I come in here at nine, close the door, and it's forbidden for anyone to disturb me.'

'What about your husband? Or telephone calls?'

'I disconnect the extension in here, and I turn my mobile off. And my husband above all would never disturb me. He understands the rule. We have dinner together, and then our ways part.'

'And you don't finish until midnight? Never?'

'Sometimes, if things are flowing, I work beyond midnight, into the small hours.'

'What about last Tuesday?'

She gave them both a straight look. 'I was in here writing from nine until midnight. I did not leave this room during that time.'

Slider left her a pause, but she didn't put anything into it. A strong-minded woman. He said, 'Well, that's very clear. Thank you,' and stood up.

Atherton followed suit. 'May I just say,' he said, 'that I enjoy your books very much. Especially the Max Ridleys. I have them on my bookshelf at home.'

'Thank you.' She looked worn to a thread, but for a moment her expression lightened. 'It's always nice to meet someone who actually *buys* books.'

And she voluntarily shook his hand.

'Nicely done,' Slider muttered to Atherton as they stepped out into the hall and she closed the door between them.

'You catch more flies with honey than with vinegar,' he replied.

'Is that even true?' Slider began, but further down the hall Seagram had stepped out from the drawing room with an enquiring look. 'Thank you, sir,' Slider accosted him. 'If I could just have a few words with you, then we'll get out of your hair.'

Back in the drawing room, Seagram remained standing, perhaps to signify that it had *better* be only a few. 'I hope you're not going to be coming here again, upsetting my wife. She's writing a book, you know. Nothing must be allowed to disrupt the creative process.'

'Has she been upset the last few days?' Slider asked.

'Well, of course she has,' he said with faint indignation. 'She writes about violence and death, but it's different when it intrudes into real life. When someone you actually *know* gets murdered, it's very upsetting. I'm upset myself and I didn't know the man.'

'But you have met him?'

'I know his name as my wife's trainer, I've never actually met him. But he *has* been in my house – that brings it rather too close for comfort.'

'On Tuesday evening, sir,' Slider said, feeling that a man with that sort of suit would like a bit of sir-ing. 'Where were you – just for the record?'

'I was here, at home,' he said.

'All evening?'

'Yes.'

'And your wife?'

'She was here, too.' He gave them a sharp look to divide between them. 'You can't possibly be suggesting that either of *us* had anything to do with this fellow's death?'

'Your wife was a client of his. I'm afraid we have to ask these questions.'

'Well she was at home with me all evening, so you can cross her off any ridiculous list you may have,' he said.

'Yes, that's just what we want to do,' Slider said soothingly. 'If you could just run through what you both did that evening?'

'We had dinner at seven thirty. That lasted until about eight thirty. We cleared the table, did some pottering about, then my wife went to her room to write at nine sharp. She was very disciplined about it.'

'And what did you do?'

'I went into my snug and spent the evening there. It's what I usually do if I'm at home when she's writing. Look, I'll show you.' He went to a corner of the room, where he lifted a pull-ring hidden under the dado and opened a concealed door. A big oblong of wall – panelling, dado, wallpaper and all – swung silently out.

'That's amazing,' Atherton said. 'You'd never know it was there.'

Seagram looked pleased. 'She has her private room, and I have mine.' He urged them, proudly, to look. It wasn't a large room, but it certainly was snug: book-lined, with a small antique desk and chair, and a modern leather recliner – the swivel sort with the separate footstool – facing a large flatscreen TV. Beside it was a small table bearing a tantalus and glasses. Apart from the fact that it had no window – which Slider would have found claustrophobic – it was very inviting. 'I have everything I need in here. I did some paperwork, then watched the cricket, which I had recorded, and then a film until I went to bed.'

'And did you see your wife at all during the evening?'

'No,' he said. 'She never comes out when she's working.'

'Did you go in to her?'

He looked shocked. 'I wouldn't do that. Absolutely no interruptions – that's the rule. That's what she needs – complete isolation.'

'What time did you go to bed?'

'Half past eleven, give or take.'

'Did you say goodnight to your wife?'

He scowled. 'How often do I have to say it – no interruptions! I went to bed, and went to sleep.'

'And what time did she come to bed?'

'We have separate bedrooms,' he said tersely.

'I see,' said Slider thoughtfully. 'You say you were at home with your wife all evening, but in fact you did not actually see her or speak to her between nine p.m. and – I suppose – the next morning?'

He looked angry, opened his mouth to speak, then shut it again. A thoughtfulness crossed his face swiftly like a cloud shadow on a breezy day. Then he smiled a sort of head-shaking, pitying smile. 'It's your job, I know. You have to ask these things. But I assure you if my wife had left the house – if that's what you're suggesting – I would have known. When you've lived with someone for twenty-five years, you have a feeling about them, you sense their presence. I don't need to see her to know that she's there. And now, without wishing to seem rude, I must ask you to leave, and I hope we will not be bothered by any more of your ridiculous questions. My wife had nothing to do with this man's death. She would never do anything so . . . unregulated.'

They backed out from the snug, he followed them and let the door swing shut, and showed them out.

'That's all very well,' Atherton said as they trudged back to the car. It was very cold, and the fine rain – almost a mist – that was falling was trying to turn into snow. 'But the fact remains that he doesn't know where she was on Tuesday evening at the relevant time.'

'Hmm,' said Slider with dissatisfaction.

'What? You don't want it to be her?'

'Do you?'

'Not if it stops her writing any more books.'

'Don't be facetious.'

'I wasn't. They're good. But there are some very violent passages in them. Yes, I know it's fiction, but isn't it possible that someone immersed so deeply in fictional violence might one day, if the circs were right, step across the line between that and reality?'

'Anyone can do that. Doesn't have to be a writer.'

'True. But not everyone had a hot relationship with deceased and looks like shit now he's dead.'

'She denies she had a relationship.'

'She denies it. Write that down.' He walked round to the

passenger side muttering, 'Important, unimportant – unimportant, important.'

Slider plipped the lock, then looked at him across the top of the car. 'One thing – did you notice that when he let go of the door to his snuggery, it swung shut all on its own?'

'Concealed doors do that,' said Atherton, 'otherwise they wouldn't stay concealed.'

'I know that. I'm just saying it makes it unlikely he was sitting in there with the door open. Two heavy doors between him and his wife. Plus the television. He wouldn't hear anything. And unless he left the room, he wouldn't see anything either – even with the snug door open, you can't see across the drawing room into the hall. I checked. So if she did want to leave the house without him knowing, she could do it.' They got in. 'And he knows that,' Slider went on as they buckled up.

'Yes, I saw it occur to him,' said Atherton. 'Hence all that new-agey bollocks about "feeling her presence".'

'But if she killed Lingoss,' Slider said, 'and we're a long way from even suspecting that she did, what was her motive?'

'Oh, we'll think of something,' Atherton said cheerfully. 'That's the least of our problems.'

'Unfortunately true,' said Slider.

'Another one without a proper alibi,' said Porson.

'Innocent people don't need alibis,' said Slider.

'Putting the cat before the horse, aren't you?' Porson said sharply.

'What I mean, sir, is that when you actually *find* someone with a cast-iron alibi—'

'You start wondering why, yes, I know, laddie.' He pulled his lower lip out into a shovel as he thought. 'But this is supposed to *look* like cast-iron, isn't it? Safe at home with hubby, and never out between nine and midnight. Which just happens to be the time we're interested in. Is that a bit too tidy?'

'Her husband confirmed that was her usual pattern,' said Slider.

'Do you think he's in on it?'

'No,' said Slider slowly. 'It sounded genuine – I mean, that that's where he thought she was. It shook him a bit when I made him see he didn't actually know for sure she was there.'

'Hmm,' said Porson. He pulled his lip out again, then let it snap back. 'Well, nothing more you can do now. Go home.' Slider drew breath to object. 'And don't come in tomorrow.'

'Sir, I feel we ought to be following things up as quickly as possible, not giving them time to cover their tracks.'

'Well, you've lost the elephant of surprise now, anyway, so another day won't make any difference. Let it mull over in the back of your mind, that's my advice. Wonderful thing, the subconscious. How's that lovely wife of yours?'

'Very well,' Slider said, surprised by the change of tack. 'She's finishing work today. Didn't want to, but it's getting close to the line.'

'I remember when my wife was at the same stage, she didn't want to stop. I think it's the nesting instinct. They've got this compunction to keep adding bits of straw till the last minute. You've just got to let them know best, is my view. Let them get on with it. Face it, none of us'll ever know what it's like. All we can do is fuss, and they don't like that.' He drew his brows down in mock menace, a sort of reverse smile. 'Now go home and spend some time with her!'

Slider thought of the Old Man going home alone to an empty house, and for one thrilling moment felt urged to invite him over. But the next moment he recollected how appalled Porson would be by a pity invitation, and swallowed it.

'Right, sir,' he said.

'Oh, this is nice,' Joanna said. With her big belly she had to lie on her side, so the only way he could cuddle her was from behind, spoon-wise, his arms wrapped round her. 'A lie-in.'

'It is nice,' he said. There was an unmistakeable soft thud as Jumper sprang up onto the bed, and a heavy purring sound as he located the back of Slider's knees, turned round three times and flopped into the perfectly cat-shaped space. Slider's hypersensitive nose caught a faint fishy whiff, proof that he'd been down for his first breakfast – the remains of last night's supper. He settled down to a thorough washing of paws and face, a steady soft jolting motion to accompany the purr.

Outside, the amateur snow was still blowing gently sideways but not managing to settle. Good! Or not. Slider had the countryman's hatred of snow, but he knew how thrilled George would be if there was proper snow, the sort you could do things with – make snowmen and snowballs with, fall into and get soaked with.

He wanted to slide back into a warm, fuggy doze, but his mind was waking and trying to ease back towards the Lingoss problem. No! Porson was right, it was best left to the subconscious for now. 'So you're glad you've finished work?' he said, really just for something to say.

'I'm glad *you've* finished work,' she said, muffled by his upper arm.

'My work is never finished,' he said, kissing the back of her neck. 'But it's nice not to have to get up early.'

'And your dad's doing lunch, so neither of us has a thing to worry about today.'

'You know what I was thinking about on my way home yesterday? My mother's curry.' She made an enquiring grunt. 'When I was a kid, in rural Essex, there were no curry houses. But Dad was sort of adventurous about food.'

'So that's where you get it from.'

'So Mum used to make him curry every now and then, with a tin of stewing steak, curry powder, and a handful of sultanas.'

She snorted with amusement. 'Omigod. Served on white rice with a side of sliced banana?'

'You know?'

'My dad adored Vesta Beef Curry with rice. Out of a packet. Just add water. Why were you thinking about it?'

'Having a craving. There's a certain sort of food that's so awful it's divine.'

'Yes, I know. Like battered saveloy and mushy peas from the chippy.'

'Don't. You're making me hungry.'

'Not a chance, buster. You're not getting me out of my warm bed before I've had my lie-in.'

'Daddy!' came a plaintive voice from the passage outside.

Joanna groaned. 'Nobody in!' she answered.

George appeared in the door, his pyjama trousers slipping so low he was in danger of tripping himself up. He was both tall for his age and skinny, which made getting bottoms to fit him difficult. If they were long enough, they were too big at the waist and fell down. 'Daddy, are you awake?'

'No,' Slider said.

George considered and discarded this. 'Why do you sleep in the same bed with Mummy?' he asked disapprovingly.

'Whose bed would you like me to sleep in?'

'Will I have to sleep in the same bed with the new baby?'

'No.'

'I don't want to sleep with anybody.'

'Keep it that way.'

A brief silence, and then the voice resumed, much closer. 'Daddy?'

'I'm asleep.'

George climbed up on the bed, and his breath, sweet as bubblegum, blew on Slider's cheek. 'You're not, I can tell.' He was settling in for the long haul. 'Daddy,' he said insistently, 'can you and Mummy get a divorce?'

Joanna made a sound which might have been a groan or suppressed laughter. Slider opened an eye. 'Why would you want that?'

'Jayden at school says his mum and dad are getting one, and he's getting a bicycle, and he's getting Minecraft, and he might be getting a puppy.'

Jayden was evidently George's financial advisor. 'You've got Jumper,' Slider reasoned. 'He wouldn't like a dog in the house.'

There was a pause while George located the cat and roughed it up lovingly. 'I like Jumper.'

'Good. Go away and draw a picture of him,' Slider suggested.

He seemed to be easing himself off the bed, but then he said, still from close proximity, 'So can you?'

'Can I what?'

'Get a divorce?'

'Do you know what divorce means?'

George nodded so vigorously Slider felt the draught. 'It means your dad spends every Saturday with you and takes you to cool places and buys you things.'

'There's a bit more to it than that,' Slider said. 'We'll talk about it later.'

'OK,' George said, and eased himself by inches out of the room, singing something under his breath.

'Ouch,' said Joanna. 'Your dad spends every Saturday with you?'

'I must try harder,' Slider said.

'At least he'll have you around for the paternity leave,' Joanna murmured. She was drifting back to sleep.

Slider was wide awake now, though. He waited a little while, until Joanna's breathing had slowed into sleep mode, then eased himself carefully out of bed. If he stayed here, he'd start thinking about the case. Better go and play with his boy, and show him it didn't take a divorce to get his father's attention.

Mr Slider – who would be coming up with Lydia from the granny flat for lunch – arrived bearing a roasting tin in which lay an enormous leg of lamb, studded with garlic and sprigs of rosemary, ready to go in the oven.

'It's huge,' Joanna said admiringly. 'You could feed an army.'

'Leftovers are no tragedy,' Mr Slider said serenely, smiling at her. He looked like a leaner, more lined and weathered version of her husband. His smile was the same, and the way his hair grew – though his was all grey – and his eyes . . . It made Joanna shiver. She loved Bill so consumingly that it unnerved her to think there could be more than one of him, or even someone who looked a bit like him. Sometimes George had a look of Bill about the eyes . . . Nature, eh? Full of little tricks to make you catch your breath.

'Besides,' said Mr Slider, 'you never know who might turn up. Always good to have a bit extra, in case. Angels unawares.'

He must have been psychic, because hardly had the lamb gone in the oven when Atherton phoned.

Joanna answered it. 'Hullo! What's up?'

'Why should something be up?'

'You usually phone to wrench my husband from my side.'

'Oh, would t'were that it were! But this is not that. Emily's back. I've fetched her from the airport, but the fridge is empty. I was going to go out to the Seven-Eleven to buy a tragic frozen lasagne, when I had a sudden vivid conviction that you wanted to invite us to lunch.'

'Just came over you, did it?'

'It was amazing. Such a strong feeling. Do you think I could be psychic?'

'Psychotic, possibly.'

'I expect you're having a proper Sunday lunch? Roast beef and Yorkshire—'

'Lamb.'

'—roast potatoes, all the veg, proper gravy—'

'Get off your knees, Atherton!' Joanna commanded sternly. 'You can't drive in that semi-recumbent posture.'

'I love a woman who can quote Wilde,' he chuckled. And then, faintly alarmed. 'When you said "drive", you did mean—'

'Here, not the Seven-Eleven. I'll set two more places.'

He brought two bottles of wine. 'Claret, with lamb,' he instructed. And then: 'Oh, blimey, you can't drink, can you? I'm an insensitive clod. Look, I'll abstain with you. Solidarity.'

Just for a moment he was serious. Joanna looked into his eyes and felt a little cold finger on the back of her neck. There had been a time, when she and Bill were having a rough time and it looked as though they wouldn't make it, when she had thought that perhaps . . . She had always liked Jim, had even been attracted to him. He was handsome, intelligent, everything a girl could want, and he liked her. A lot. But he was not Bill. She had never loved anyone before Bill, and would never love anyone else like that. It was the absolute, no-questions-to-be-asked, nothing-to-be-done-about-it, that's-it-for-your-lifetime love. He was her right place, her home. And having seen Jim through a number of relationships, she didn't think he had ever felt that. He and Emily seemed happy together, and she hoped they would stay a couple, but she didn't think he felt about Emily as she felt about Bill. It was sad.

She touched his hand briefly and said, 'You can drink. I've actually gone off the whole idea of wine, so it's no hardship. Must be hormones, I suppose.' Then she turned to Emily. 'How was Washington?'

'Fascinating,' she said. She had the bare-eyed look of someone from another time zone. 'You're looking well.'

'I look like a traffic hazard,' Joanna corrected. 'Glad to be back?'

'Mostly,' she said. 'The cats were glad to see me.'

'I am too,' said Atherton.

'They show it more.'

'Well, Siamese are highly strung. Did you know domestic pets get the same mental health issues as humans?'

'Seems reasonable,' said Joanna cautiously.

'Emily was telling me. Some animal psychologists at Stanford did a study. They asked a representative sample of dogs how their mental health had been recently, and ninety-eight per cent replied "Rough".'

When they all sat down, Lydia produced a small tissue-wrapped gift for Joanna: a baby cardigan she had knitted herself. 'I did it in yellow, so it will be all right whichever you have.'

'You've really held off from knowing the sex?' Emily said. 'How disciplined of you.'

'She never wants to know what I'm getting her for Christmas, either,' said Slider.

'But how will you choose a name?' Emily asked. 'I've always thought that must be the most fun part of pregnancy.'

'I've always felt you can't really choose a name until you see it,' said Joanna. 'I mean, what if you decide you're going to call it, say, Archie, and when it comes out it just *isn't* an Archie?'

'Certainly wouldn't be if it was a girl,' said Atherton.

'You could have alternatives, a girl's name and a boy's name,' said Emily.

'And a yellow name, in case it isn't either,' said Atherton.

'I don't care about all that pink and blue stuff anyway,' said Joanna. 'Babies don't know the difference.'

'Did you know,' Atherton said pouring wine, 'that at the turn of the last century, it was blue for a girl and pink for a boy? Nobody knows how it switched round.'

'I believe it,' Joanna said. 'Before the war, horse-show rosettes were blue for first and red for second. Now it's the other way round.'

'That makes sense,' said Emily. 'We talk about things being "blue-ribbon" when they're the best.'

'And these potatoes,' said Mr Slider, passing the dish of roasties, 'used to be called baked potatoes when I was a lad. A roast potato was the jacket sort you cook in the embers.'

'I remember that,' Slider said. 'Mum always called this sort baked potatoes when I was a boy.'

George, mouth open and brow furrowed, was following the conversation with intense interest. 'You're talking about babies, aren't you?' he said. 'When you say potatoes you mean babies.'

'He's onto us,' Atherton said with a wink.

George was pleased. 'I know about babies,' he boasted.

'What do you know?' Mr Slider asked.

George thought furiously. 'Jayden says, when a baby's borned, you get a present so you won't be jealous,' he recalled.

'We have *got* to get him some new friends,' Joanna said to Slider.

He looked round the table at the faces, and thought, *Family! It's everything.* And he thought of Erik Lingoss, who had none. *Damn, I don't want to think about Lingoss.* So he thought, as a counter-irritant, about Matthew and Kate, and felt the therapeutic sting of guilt that he had not managed to hold *their* family together. Irene had left him because the demands of the Job had made him a neglectful husband. Joanna was fine with it because she had a career of her own. But George was already wistfully longing for a father who was there every Saturday. He must do better. And the new baby . . .

'Are you all right?' Joanna said. 'You looked as though you had a pain.'

He cleared his thoughts and smiled. 'Trying not to think about work.' He turned to Emily. 'Tell us about the build-up to the Primaries. Who's going to be the next president of the United States?'

'What's "primaries"?' George asked suspiciously.

'He means babies,' Atherton stage-whispered.

THIRTEEN
Sunt Lacrimae Rerum

McLaren had left his card with the proprietors of the shops along Russell Close, and Kadan at the heel bar rang him on Monday morning. 'He's just arrived, the guy from K D Electronics. He's opened the shop,' he said. 'You said you wanted to know if he turned up.'

'Yeah, right. Thanks a lot,' said McLaren, and got over there as fast as possible, in case he closed up again.

The shop was a narrow slice – in fact, a half-shop, the heel bar being the other half. It had a counter along the right side with packed shelves behind, and seemed to deal in, at least, mobile phones and accessories, tablets, burglar alarms, baby monitors, security cameras and motion-sensitive lights. The only furniture was a beat-up red plastic chair for the customer who felt faint in the presence of so much technology.

The proprietor was a short, burly young man who counteracted the lack of heating in the shop with a donkey jacket and beanie cap. His name, he said, was Kachela Darain, originally from Birmingham, 'But everybody calls me KD.' His swarthy face was decorated with various bits of beard, moustache and cheek tufts, like the victim of a palsied barber, and he wore a couple of silver rings in one eyebrow. But he had a bright, welcoming smile, and greeted McLaren with friendly enthusiasm, even *after* he learned that he was police.

'Yeah, I missed all the fun, dint I?' he said. 'What a week to take off! But there's only me, see, so I have to close up when I go anywhere.'

'Where did you go?' McLaren asked.

'Birmingham. There was this thing on at the BCEC – big electronics show. Gotta go to that! And then I went to see my mum for a few days. She lives in Selly Oak. My sister's getting married and she's in a right old tizzy, my mum. So what's with this bloke in the flats? Did he really get murdered?'

'Did you know him?'

'Nah,' he said with genuine regret. 'It would've been a bit of excitement, innit? So what can I do for you, mate?'

McLaren explained, and KD's face brightened. 'Yeah, I got two cameras. One's at the back, covering the shop, in case of break-ins. The other's trained on the street.' He drew McLaren's attention to it: fixed at the top of the window, it poked its lens out between two slats of the blind. 'I use it for demonstrations for customers. You know, when they come in first time for security and don't know what they want. It's top of the line, this one. Fabulous definition, infrared night vision, all the extras. Blummin' brilliant. Course, they generally want something cheaper, but sometimes I can talk 'em up.' He grinned.

'And would you still have the recordings for last Tuesday?'

'Tuesday? You're just in time. It's a seven-day recorder, automatically tapes over itself after that. I'll show you what there is on the monitor over here. If you want anything, I can download it onto a firestick for you.'

Porson encountered Slider in the corridor on his way back from the gents. 'The march is going ahead,' he said. 'I can't keep your firm out of it unless you've got something serious to follow up. Where are you?'

Slider was assembling his magnificent body of negatives for parade when McLaren came out and said, 'Got something, guv!'

'I hope it's good,' said Slider.

'Might be,' said McLaren.

He led them to his monitor while Slider explained to Porson about K D Electronics.

'The camera's pointing straight out at the street,' McLaren went on, 'so it's not actually covering the entrance to the flats. But I've logged this motor' – he cued up the tape – 'going in at nine thirty-six p.m., and coming out again at nine fifty-nine.' He looked at Slider. 'Just the times we want?'

Slider nodded. 'I know that's not all you've got to tell me. You've identified the car?'

'Got the index. It's a top camera, this one. Clear as day. The motor's a three-year-old Mazda3. You can't see the colour cos it's on night vision, but it's Soul Red Metallic – flashy little bugger. And the registered owner is Gilda Steenkamp.'

Slider felt a thump of excitement in his gut, which had undertones of regret. He never liked it when it was a woman.

Porson groaned. 'Not another celebrity! What is it with you? The last thing we need is to go stirring up another hermit's nest!'

'She flatly denied seeing him on Tuesday,' Slider said. 'Denied even having an appointment with him. Wait a minute! Norma – have we got her phone number?'

'On it, boss,' said Swilley, pulling out various sheets. 'Here we are. From the client list in the black book. Mobile and house.'

'Check them against his phone log, incoming, for the last day.' He looked at Porson. 'She denied having an appointment, but maybe it was a last-minute thing.'

A breathless silence while Swilley ran her finger down the list. 'Got it,' she said at last. 'The mobile. Nine twenty-five – twenty-two seconds.'

'But she must've already been on the way by then,' McLaren said. 'So she's not making a new appointment.'

Swilley looked up. 'Yes, and what could she say to him in twenty-two seconds?'

'Maybe just checking he was at home,' Slider said. '"It's me. Where are you?" "At home." "Are you alone?" "Yes." "Good. I'm on my way." Then she rings off before he can object.'

'You'd think she'd check he was in before setting out,' McLaren objected.

'Maybe she was upset. Just lit out to see him without thinking he might be out,' said Swilley. 'Or they could've made the arrangement last time they met. Maybe what she said was, "Shall I get some chips on the way?"'

Porson was pondering, his shaggy brows leaning together like two tired yaks. 'It's enough. Bring her in,' he concluded. But he sighed. Celebs, like children, might come trailing clouds of glory, but they also came trailing clouds of lawyers and trouble. Upsetting them caused unhappiness among the top brass. And unhappy top brass liked to spread the misery as widely as possible, with generous provision for those beneath. But you had to do what you had to do. 'She's got some questions to answer, and doing it here'll concentrate her mind.'

'Yes sir.'

'But do it gently.' Porson backpedalled a bit.

'Of course, sir. And if we request her phone record, it'll show where she was when the call was made. We can trace her journey.'

'Then she can't deny she was there,' said Swilley with satisfaction.

'Do it,' said Porson. 'Make it priority. Get your ducks in a row.'

Slider nodded and turned to McLaren. 'Meanwhile . . .'

'I know, guv,' he said resignedly. 'Trace the Mazda, both ways.'

There were interview rooms downstairs behind the front office where they took arrested villains for questioning: stark, bare rooms smelling of feet and guilt and lies and despair. Upstairs, there was the soft room, which had carpet, an upholstered sofa and chairs, and prints on the walls, where they took witnesses and the bereaved. Or celebrities, and others who needed careful handling. Atherton thought that being subjected to such ghastly fabrics and pictures was punishment verging on the cruel and unusual, but voicing the opinion drew retorts from his colleagues like 'pretentious', 'ponce', and other epithets beginning with 'p'.

Gilda Steenkamp, tall, elegant, stately of gait, looked as out of place in the cop shop as a giraffe in a chicken run. After some thought, Slider had asked her to come in voluntarily rather than arresting her – he could always go that way if she refused – and slightly to his surprise she had agreed, and slightly more surprisingly had turned up alone. No solicitor. He couldn't decide whether that was evidence of innocence or sheer chutzpah. She looked around the soft room as she was led in with an expression more of surprise than horror, as if wondering that such places could be.

She sat, refused a beverage, and fixed the large, tired, bleak eyes on Slider. 'I knew you wouldn't leave it at that,' she said. 'I'd have been surprised if you hadn't come back.'

'You didn't tell me the truth,' he said mildly.

'My private life is my own affair. I felt no obligation to talk to you about it.' He waited that one out. 'Besides, I was at home,' she said. 'One must be careful what one says at home.' She seemed to be appealing to him to understand the logic of it.

'Your husband might have come in, or overheard,' he said.

'I didn't mean that.'

'Really?'

'Not entirely.'

'But he didn't know about you and Erik.' She was silent, looking at her hands, which was admission enough. 'All the same, you must understand that lying to the police is not only pointless, but lays you open to serious charges, with penalties up to and including imprisonment. So now let's have the truth, please.' He had understood her reply of 'not entirely', and added, 'In this neutral place, you can talk frankly.'

'To you, perhaps.' She looked at Atherton. 'But we're not alone.'

'That is not possible,' Slider said. 'Regulations, I'm afraid. But what I know, my colleague knows. For these purposes we are one person. However, if you'd prefer a female officer to be present . . .?'

She wrinkled her nose. 'No, thank you. I suspect . . .' She didn't finish that thought. Her shoulders went down in surrender. 'Very well. What do you want to know?'

'Let's start with your relationship with Erik Lingoss. How did you meet him?'

'My sister told me about him. She heard of him from a friend who'd been training with him at a gym.'

'Shapes in Kensington High Street?'

'Yes. Myrna was a member there. I went with her once, but I don't like gyms. They're too noisy and – oh, this will sound precious, but you never know who may be photographing you, and when you're famous . . . You don't want pictures of you in unattractive positions getting onto the internet.'

'I understand.'

She nodded. 'I've always tried to keep fit, exercising at home – I have my own exercise room set up – but it's hard to keep motivated. And one never knows if one's doing the right things. So a personal trainer at home seemed the perfect solution. And my sister recommended Erik.'

'Did she train with him?'

'She had a couple of lessons, but then gave it up. She's not a great sticker at things, my sister. And she's never cared as much about staying fit. She's not in the public gaze like me.'

He nodded. Obviously the sisters didn't tell each other everything. And it seemed Erik Lingoss really was discreet.

'Tell me about Erik,' he invited.

'We clicked from the first moment. He seemed to know at once just how to motivate me, exactly what my body needed, exactly how far and how fast he could push me. He was an excellent trainer.'

'But it was more than that.'

She sighed. 'We understood each other. Sometimes there are people like that – don't you find? The moment you meet, you connect with them on a deeper level, as if you've always known each other. From the first meeting we spoke to each other without reserve. He was like a dear friend.' She paused.

'How soon did it become a physical relationship?' Slider prompted.

'It was always physical,' she said, sounding surprised. 'He was my trainer. My body was his responsibility.'

'I mean, how soon did it become sexual?'

She hesitated, then said, 'It was always sexual. There was a spark between us from the first moment.' She looked closely at him, then at Atherton, then Slider again. 'You are thinking a woman of my age has no right to a man of Erik's age. If it was the other way round, if he was an older man having an affair with a younger woman, you'd slap him on the back and tell him what a fine fellow he was.'

'I wasn't thinking that at all,' said Slider stoically. 'Please, just tell me what happened between you.'

'He was beautiful,' she said. 'You've no idea. Some trainers are *too* muscled, all lumps and bumps, but his body was perfectly in proportion – everything the human frame should be and rarely is. He was like a glorious, sleek, lithe cat. I loved looking at him. Watching him move. And he loved my body, too. As an artist loves his creation. We worked together to make something beautiful.'

Atherton didn't say anything, but Slider, who knew him very well, felt him cringe at the language. Well, she was a writer, he thought resignedly. It was her business to see more than was there. To get her to talk, he must encourage her to use her own words.

'So it was natural for you to drift into a sexual relationship,' he prompted, in as un-policemanlike manner as possible.

'After training, he would give me a massage,' she said, almost dreamily. She was staring into the past now. 'And then we would make love. He brought me back to life after a long sleep. My husband – suffice to say, we lead separate lives. Erik made me feel beautiful, young again.' She looked at him sharply as though he had demurred. 'You're a man – you can't understand what that's like. Women become invisible when they pass forty. They're not supposed even to *want* to be touched any more. But inside, we are still the same age as we always were. We don't want it any less than a man – but we're not allowed to have it. But Erik – to him, I wasn't old and invisible. I was just me.'

Slider felt Atherton stir in embarrassment, and knew he was thinking *what a deluded idiot*, or words to that effect. She was still staring at memory and didn't notice. Slider had to force himself to burst her bubble.

'Did you pay him for the extra attentions?'

She looked as though he had slapped her, but she was right back to the present. Her mouth turned down. 'It's not the way you think. Yes, I paid him extra, but it wasn't paying for sex, as though he was a . . . a rent boy.'

'You gave him presents,' Slider suggested.

'Yes,' she said. 'He was saving up to start his own business. I have plenty of money, more than I can spend. What I gave him meant nothing to me, but it was important to him. There was nothing sordid about it. I'd have given him more, enough for the whole start-up, but he wouldn't take it. He was honourable, you see. He said he had to earn it himself. He had a lot of pride. He'd come up the hard way, and he wanted to be independent, and to prove he had it in him to succeed without help. I respected that. It was one of the things I loved about him, his honesty.'

'You paid him in cash?'

'It was easier that way.'

'You mean, it didn't leave any trace?'

'I beg your pardon?'

'You left no evidence lying around – cheque book stumps, credit card statements. So your husband didn't know that you and Erik were lovers.'

'Of course he didn't,' she said, irritated. 'We were absolutely discreet. It would have been—'

'Yes?'

She frowned. 'Brian and I don't have a sexual relationship, haven't for years. But he's still my husband. It would have been insulting to him to flaunt a lover in his face. I wouldn't do it. I have more respect for him than that. And for myself.'

'But he might have suspected anyway?'

She shook her head firmly. 'I'm quite sure he didn't. Like most men, he thinks a woman of my age is past it. It would never cross his mind that I might be interested in a handsome young man. Or that a handsome young man could possibly be interested in me.'

Yes, there was a touch of bitterness there. She might appreciate Seagram's loyalty, but resented the part that was pity-loyalty.

'It sounds like a perfect arrangement,' said Slider. 'So what went wrong?'

She frowned. 'Why should you think something went wrong?'

'You found out that Erik was having sex with someone else as well as you,' said Slider. It was a guess, but she reddened slightly.

'I don't know what you mean.'

'I think you do.' He stared at her steadily. She held it. 'You discovered you were not exclusive.' Her lips trembled. 'And to make it worse, she was younger than you.' Kelly-Ann, Ivanka and Lucy were all younger. Erik's other clients might not all have been – her sister was older – but it was still a good spread bet.

The 'younger' bit stung her. 'I didn't care about that,' she said. 'I'm not that insecure. The age difference didn't matter with Erik and me – I've told you that already. And it wasn't sexual jealousy either. I was surprised, yes, but he was young and virile with tremendous energy, and realistically, there was bound to be some overspill. When a man's tempted, it's more or less automatic, isn't it? I was hurt at first, I admit it, but when I thought about it, I realized it didn't mean anything to him. It didn't touch what we had.'

'Which was what?' Atherton couldn't help asking.

She looked at him. 'Love,' she said starkly. Her eyes were too shiny. For a moment it seemed as though they might run over, but she tightened her lips. 'We loved each other. I see what you're thinking, you with your youth and your assurance and your *arrogance*, but you can't take that from me. You can believe what you like, but you don't know, because you weren't there. It was love.'

Atherton had no follow-up question. Slider took it back.

'You say you didn't mind him having sex with someone else. So what *did* you mind?'

She hesitated. 'It was too close to home,' she said at last. 'My husband mentioned one day in passing that his assistant, Lucy, was going out with Erik.' She made a slight face at the words 'going out'.

'He knew Erik?'

'He knew he was my trainer, that's all. He knew the name. He just mentioned in passing that Lucy had said she had been seeing him. And it was obvious from the way he said it that he didn't know there was anything more between Erik and me.'

'And what did you do?'

'I told Erik it must stop. I told him he must break up with her.'

'When was this?'

'I don't know. A few weeks ago.'

'And what did Erik say?'

'He was fine about it. Said he understood. Apologized if I'd been upset. Said she didn't matter to him, and he wouldn't see her again.'

'And you believed him?'

'Of course I did.' She was impatient. 'You don't understand – things between us were at a much deeper level than that. He could no more have deceived me than I could deceive myself.'

The words hung on the air, and she looked quickly from one man to the other as if to catch any exchanged glance of ridicule. The temptation was, of course, to believe she was hopelessly self-deluding about what a young man could want from a rich older woman – and she was intelligent enough to know that. But from Slider's point of view it hardly mattered whether it had been true love or a true facsimile. He left a pause for her to relax off her guard, then said quietly, 'So what happened to make you want to kill him?'

Her scalp shifted backwards and she seemed to pale. 'Nothing! I didn't! What are you talking about?'

'You arranged to see him on Tuesday night, at a time when your husband would think you were safely in your room working. A time when you knew no one would ever disturb you, so you could slip out and back unseen, and never be suspected.'

'This is madness!' she said.

'You lied to us. We know you had an appointment with him. We know you went there, to his flat. You went to his flat, and you killed him. What happened? Did you have a quarrel? Did you lash out in a temper?'

'I don't know what you're talking about!'

'It will be better for you to admit it now. Telling more lies will count against you. If you struck him in hot blood, without meaning to kill him, that will be taken into consideration.' There were the finishing-off blows, but he wouldn't go into that now. Get the admission first.

But her face had gone cold and hard. 'I didn't kill him. How could you even think it? And I didn't go to his flat that night. I've already told you, I was at home working. My husband bears witness to that. And now I've done talking to you. If you want to speak to me again, you will have to go through my solicitor. I've nothing more to say.'

He nodded calmly. 'That's as you wish. But I have to tell you, the evidence against you is sufficient to warrant further investigation. We will have to search your premises and examine your bank and credit card accounts and telephone log.'

'Absolutely not!' she said hotly.

'You have no choice in the matter. I'm sorry,' he said, and he meant it.

But he remembered Erik Lingoss lying like discarded clothing with his head bashed in. That was the bottom line.

'She's a cool one,' Atherton said as they went back to the office afterwards. 'Took her a while to get lawyered up.' He looked at his boss. 'You're not going to say you don't think her capable of violence like that?'

'I wouldn't say that about anyone.'

'There's quite a lot of violence in her books. Interestingly, in the last one, *Blood River*, an older woman kills her unfaithful lover. OK, he was a double agent putting her network in peril, but still . . .'

'A jury would enjoy that,' said Slider. 'All the same, the fact that she went to his flat doesn't mean she killed him.'

'It would be a bit of coincidence if someone else came along, just after her perfectly innocent visit, and murdered him,' said Atherton. 'Especially as she wasn't in the habit of *going* to his flat.'

'It's a pity that camera didn't cover the door.'

'You think she just drove there to sit in her car to sing "The Street Where You Live" under his window?'

'No, I mean we need our evidence to be watertight. She's a very rich woman who'll get the very best legal representation. If they can get the tip of a crowbar of doubt into any crack . . .'

'Oh. Well, we can log and trace every other car that passed. And every pedestrian. And I'm betting none of them will have any connection with Lingoss. People don't tend to have multiple suspicious visitors on the night they get murdered.'

'Unless they're drug dealers.'

'True. But he wasn't. So, we get a warrant to search her flat?'

'Yes, though I don't suppose we'll find bloodstained clothing or a handy diary entry saying "I done it".'

'We'll have to pin our hopes on cameras and her mobile logging the entire journey. Something she can't wriggle out of. Oh, and what about Lingoss's missing phone?'

'I think her flat is out of the area where it was turned off. But of course it doesn't mean it didn't go on there afterwards. If she's got it, we'll find it.'

'We've got the motive, anyway. She was really in love with him, and thought he was in love with her. Pathetic!'

'She's only fifty, and very attractive. Young men do fall in love with mature women.'

'And vice versa. But I can't help thinking of the money – bundles of lovely fifties in a shoe box. A man with good active hormones doesn't have to try very hard to simulate love. We know he could be charming. And we *know* he was doing other people. She might have been in love with him, but I doubt it was reciprocal.'

'Yet he broke it off with Lucy for her sake,' Slider said. 'He didn't have to.'

'If he hadn't, Steenkamp would have found out about it, wouldn't she, from blabby hubby? And then – leave this house and never darken my door again. Bye-bye lovely cash.'

'You're such a cynic,' said Slider. 'I don't know how Emily stands it.'

'She's a journalist,' said Atherton. 'When it comes to cynicism, she's the guv'nor: I'm the merest tyro.'

FOURTEEN

When You Vacuum, Everyone Can Hear You Scream

I n the age of the computer and Online Everything, the information was all there to be accessed. It only required a bit of high-powered leaning to get it released. Detective Superintendent Porson had leaned with the best in his time, and with the threat of the march looming over him, he gave it his all. The mobile data was promised for the afternoon, the bank's for the next morning. Meanwhile, every available hand was set to examining traffic camera and ANPC logs.

Slider had just finished a belated lunch of a cheese-and-tomato sandwich at his desk, when he received a telephone call from a solicitor, Michael Friedman, to say that any further contact with his client, Ms Steenkamp, must be channelled through him. He said it with steely politeness, and in a voice so upper-class and armour-piercing it could have brought down jet fighters.

'Friedman,' Atherton said when Slider told him afterwards. 'Solicitor to the stars.'

'I thought the name sounded familiar.'

'He's one of the ninety-nine per cent of lawyers who give the rest a bad name. He was the brief who got Foxy Fairbairn off that groping charge. Well, he *got* off, so one surmises it was Friedman.'

'"One surmises"?' said Hart, passing at that moment. 'Gawd, you don't even talk like a copper.'

'I take that as a compliment,' said Atherton; then frowned and called after her, 'What do you mean, "even"?'

Later on that afternoon, Hart was back, and spread out the pages of the mobile log while the others gathered round to breathe over her shoulder. The network log first, which showed the position of the device as its signal was passed from cell mast to cell mast – though with a journey as short as from Campden Hill Square to Russell Close there were not many masts involved. But the log showed the device stationary all day within the area containing Campden Hill Square, then moving through a second, covering Kensington High Street (with a short pause, which could have been traffic lights), and becoming stationary in a third, which covered Russell Close. It remained stationary for twenty-three minutes before moving again.

'A solicitor would say none of that proves anything,' Gascoyne said somewhat wistfully.

'Yeah, but a jury can use common sense, and common sense says where else would she be going,' said Hart. 'And at that particular time.'

'But this is interesting,' said Atherton. 'The return journey.'

Instead of travelling straight back to the first zone, the device remained stationary for almost half an hour in the second zone.

'She made a stop on the way.'

'Ken High Street,' said LaSalle. 'Where her old man's antique shop is. And the gym – Shapes.'

'And a lot else besides,' Gascoyne pointed out. 'The shop would have been shut at that time of night. And why would she go to the gym?'

'I'm just saying,' said LaSalle.

'You're missing the point,' Atherton interrupted. 'Zone two, if we can call it that, is the area we've already identified as where Lingoss's mobile was when it was turned off.'

'Which covers Allen Street, where Jack Gallo's local pub is. And Marloes Road, where Jack Gallo's flat is,' said LaSalle.

Hart twisted her head round to stare at him. 'Are you tryna say she was in league wiv Gallo to off Lingoss? Maybe you think he paid her to do it – hired assassin?'

'Settle down,' Slider said. 'There's a hundred thousand places within zone two and a hundred thousand reasons she might have stopped off. She might just have parked somewhere because her hands were shaking too much to drive.'

'She might have stopped for a drink or a cup of coffee to settle her nerves before going home,' Gascoyne said.

Hart gave him a look and groaned. 'If we've got to check every pub and coffee shop in the area . . .?'

'If it comes to it, we'll have to do it,' said Slider stoically. 'But for now we need more information. To begin with – Hart, co-ordinate the location data of Steenkamp's device with that of Lingoss's, see if they were in the same places at the same times. If we can show they were travelling together, it makes our case stronger.'

'Yeah, how else could she get his phone, if she hadn't just killed him,' Hart agreed.

'I'm not sure why she'd take it in the first place,' Atherton said, 'but still . . .'

They checked the call log of Steenkamp's mobile. There were a number of calls in and out during the day up until around eight forty-five. 'I'll have to check 'em all, but I can see Lingoss's number's not there,' Hart said.

'Probably normal traffic,' said Atherton. 'She did have a life.'

'Then there's two missed incoming calls between eight fifty-nine and nine fifteen.' Hart looked up. 'Missed calls could mean the phone was switched off.'

'She said she turned it off when she was working,' said Slider.

'Right boss. Then there's the outgoing call we know about, at nine twenty-five to Lingoss's mobile.' She went on down. 'And one more outgoing, at ten oh five. That's after the Mazda leaves Russell Close. Don't recognize this number.'

'Find out who it's registered to,' Slider said. 'It must have been important, if she had to make the call right then.'

'It would have to be someone who was involved, wouldn't it?' Gascoyne said. 'Because all her friends and close contacts would know she was always out of touch during the working hours. If she'd phoned one of them, they'd want to know why.'

'Good point,' said Slider. 'But if someone else was involved, we're into a whole different game – and one I don't like at all.'

'Jack Gallo,' said LaSalle stubbornly.

'I notice that you've started calling her Steenkamp instead of Gilda Steenkamp,' said Atherton. 'So she's just a suspect now, not the famous author.'

Slider looked up from shuffling papers together on his desk. 'Your point being?'

'It's taking me a bit longer to process it. I suppose because I've read her books. It'll be a tragedy if the author of *Bitter Mountain* and *Blood River* goes to jail – she is a genius.'

'I expect Erik Lingoss would think it was a tragedy to get killed,' said Slider.

'Right. But do you really think she could have done it?'

'I don't think anything. I'm just assembling evidence.' He gave Atherton a curious look. 'It was you who said there was a lot of violence in her books. You called her a cool one.'

'I'm just thinking of the loss to literature.'

'You're not.'

'Wouldn't you sooner it was a man? Jack Gallo, for instance.'

'Go home,' Slider instructed. 'You're getting sentimental.'

Atherton drew himself up. 'There's no need to be insulting,' he said.

Joanna looked more tired than she had on Saturday.

'I thought you'd have been all rested and relaxed,' Slider said, kissing her, and stooping to stroke Jumper, who was headbutting his legs. 'Staying at home with nothing to do all day.'

'Nothing to do?' she said derisively. 'You plainly haven't noticed the pristine state of the house. Carpets don't hoover themselves, y'know. Kitchen floors aren't self-washing. And staying at home is also popularly known as "cooped up".'

'Kitchen floors do not a prison make, nor ironing a cage,' Slider offered.

She scowled melodramatically. 'Men have been slapped for saying less than that.'

'You don't need to scrub and slave for my benefit. I'm not made of sugar – I can stand a bit of dirt and disorder.'

'I needed to keep busy. Doing nothing leaves too much time to think.'

'You're missing work?'

'Actually, not, just at the moment. But doing nothing makes you realize how many bits are hurting.'

'Anything I should know about?'

'Settle down. Nothing like that. Just general strain on the bod. I'm fine, really. How's the case coming along?'

He told her the day's developments while she made him a gin and tonic.

'Well, that's pretty conclusive, isn't it?' she said.

'A good lawyer would pull it to pieces,' he said, 'and she's got a good lawyer.'

'I should hope so, with her millions.'

'Michael Friedman, brief to the stars, according to Atherton.'

'I know that name,' she said. 'He's been in the news a couple of times. Didn't he get that TV presenter off – the one with the silly name?'

'Foxy Fairbairn?'

'So you do know.'

'Atherton told me. He reads the papers. Anyway, Friedman would say that her mobile travelling through those zones means nothing, that she could have been going anywhere. We've got to get visual evidence of the car, pin it down to actual roads, if possible. And that's a laborious business.'

'Gilda Steenkamp,' she marvelled. 'Best-selling author. You really think she did it?'

'The evidence seems to be heading that way,' he said.

'That's not what I asked. I know you – you won't want it to be her. You have a soft spot for women.'

'I have a soft spot for one woman,' he said, putting a hand on her neck, which he liked to nuzzle in more relaxed moments.

She ignored it for the moment, pursuing her thoughts. 'What would make a woman in such a public spotlight do something like that?'

'Couldn't be money. Emotion of some sort, I suppose.'

'Jealousy? Because he was sleeping with other women?'

'Possibly. Who knows what goes on between lovers, except the lovers themselves? Passion is at the bottom of so many violent acts.'

'And enjoyable acts, too,' she said, turning her face to kiss his stroking hand.

He eyed her hopefully. 'Are you having a hormone surge?'

'I wish.' She gestured to her embonpoint. 'NB my uncooperative shape.'

'Here's something interesting, boss,' Swilley said, coming in with the bank print-out.

Banks were usually the slowest to provide information, but

Porson had called in a favour from a very senior director whose son had got into trouble a year ago; heads had been banged together and stops had been pulled out.

'Most of this activity looks routine – I haven't had time to examine it all in detail, but she was in the habit of drawing out quite large sums of cash, which is slightly unusual these days. I'm guessing some of it found its way into Lingoss's pocket. And, here's the interesting bit – there's a withdrawal on Tuesday night from a cashpoint in Ken High Street at nine twenty-three.'

'That's just before she makes the phone call to Lingoss.'

'Right, boss. And we know there was a brief stop on the way. She must have a premier account, because the amount she draws out is seven hundred pounds.' She looked at him hard to make sure he got the point.

'The same amount as was under his pillow,' Slider said obediently.

'I know what you're thinking. It's not proof it's the same money. But, boss, who takes out seven hundred? It's such a specific amount. People usually take out two, two-fifty, three. Five, even. But seven—'

'That's a good point. It is unusual. And it certainly strengthens our case.'

Hart was the next in. 'That phone call she made after the murder at ten oh five – the number she called is a mobile belonging to someone called Leon Greyling, with an address in Adam and Eve Mews. Which is in our zone two, where Lingoss's phone ended up.'

'Leon Greyling?'

'Yeah, boss, I've not come across him either. He's not in her phone contacts, and as far back as I've gone, she's never phoned him before. Or, not on the mobile. I haven't got house phone records yet. And he's not in Lingoss's contacts either – I checked just in case.'

'Interesting. Better see what you can find out about him.'

'Maybe she was lining up another trainer, now she'd offed the one she'd got,' said Hart, and was not entirely joking.

'You might as well find out if anyone else knows him – Gallo or anyone at any of the gyms. Everyone in this case seems to be connected in some way.'

'Will do. It's weird, though, innit? Can't just be a random call, not when Lingoss is still warm.'

He went to see Porson. 'I need every man I can get to trace the car from Russell Close to – wherever it went in between – and back to Campden Hill Gardens. It's easier, obviously, to verify a suspected route than discover one starting from nothing, but even so, there are a lot of cameras – shops, traffic, Transport for London. It's labour intensive.'

In a rare reaction, Porson beamed, from ear to ear and for some distance beyond on either side. 'That's what I want to hear,' he said. 'Work to be done, lots and lots of it. Can't possibly spare anyone from the department.'

'Thank you, sir.'

'On the subject of which, I had a bell from Mr Carpenter. Apparently he's had his elbow jolted by Michael Friedman, the solicitor to the stars.'

'That was quick,' Slider commented. 'But not unexpected.'

Porson rolled his eyes slightly. 'Apparently he was kicking up a pavlova about "my client this" and "my client that". Professional ear-bending. I told Mr Carpenter we're putting everything we've got into it. Nose to the grindstone, eckcetera.'

'Celebrity is a two-edged sword, sir,' said Slider. Steenkamp's fame meant that they could keep their warm bodies, but it also meant Head Office would be watching, so they couldn't make any mistakes.

'Right,' said Porson. 'So you'd better get me a result.'

Hart came in, flopped into the visitor's chair, interlaced her fingers and stretched them backwards until they cracked. Interesting dumbshow, Slider thought, designed to show him how hard she'd been working. Probably wasn't even aware she was doing it.

'Leon Greyling,' she said.

'Yes?'

'Age twenty-five. Criminal record: busted twice for possession of cocaine. First time, four years ago, let off with a warning. Second time, May last year, caught in the act of snorting up in the gents' loo at the motor show and got six weeks' suspended.'

'Motor show?' Slider queried. 'What was he doing there?'

Hart shrugged. 'Everybody's got to be somewhere.'

'Fair enough.'

'No, actually, he was doing demo work, apparently.'

'I thought they usually draped female models across the bonnet of the new Ferrari.'

'That was the bad old days. Equal opportunities now, innit. Anyway' – she consulted her notes – 'born in Hertfordshire. Private school. His dad's a solicitor and lives in a house called The Old Rectory, so he must be rich. Studied at the London School of Dance and Drama. Done some modelling and demo work, as noted. And three months in the chorus line of a chorus line.'

'Come again?'

'The musical called *A Chorus Line*. It was on at the Palladium. And he was in one episode of *Lockhart* – you know, that telly series about the dodgy antiques dealer.'

'I remember. Lovable rogue syndrome. Was it a big part?'

'No, walk-on. Anyway, apart from that, I can't find that he's ever done anything, dance-and-drama-wise so I don't know what he's living on. Maybe his folks stake him. Or he's a waiter or a barman. He's got a LinkedIn, touting for business, says he can act, sing, dance – tap, modern and ballet – and play piano and clarinet. And I've found some photos. He looks the goods, all right.'

She passed one over – a willowy youth, fair, with crinkly hair and large pale eyes, posing in the close-fitting vest and tights combination that trapeze artists call skins. He seemed to be wearing make-up – at least, it didn't seem natural for someone so fair to have such dark eyelashes – and the pouty, stunned-fish expression that was the required look for models.

A second picture Hart passed him was a straightforward actor's black-and-white, in dinner jacket and black tie, three-quarter face and smiling urbanely: the sort of picture you see on the walls in theatre corridors.

Slider handed them back. 'But what's his connection to Gilda Steenkamp?'

Hart spread her hands. 'That's the really interesting bit. I can't find any.'

'You call that interesting?'

'Interesting, but stupid,' she modified. 'OK, she rung him that night, but maybe it was a wrong number. We could check if she's got a contact with a similar number. Or maybe . . .'

'Yes?'

'Maybe he was on the game, sidelining while he "rested", and she saw his advert somewhere.' She read his expression and added, 'Well, she'd got a taste for it by then.'

'On the way home from murdering her lover? Isn't that a bit cold and ruthless, even for an author?'

'The female of the species is deadlier than the male,' Hart reminded him.

Slider looked pained. Not that old chestnut again. 'Do you like Kipling, Sergeant Hart?' he asked discouragingly.

'Dunno, boss. I've never kippled,' she said.

When you were to search a suspect's home, it was important to move fast, before they had a chance to clean up – although clumsy attempts at cleaning could be useful in pointing, screamingly, at the things you should be looking at. But Slider couldn't imagine Gilda Steenkamp doing anything clumsy. In her case, the fear was that she would get rid of some piece of evidence entirely. Of course, she would have to do it without her husband's knowing – unless, intriguing extra possibility, he was in on it. Not the original murder, obviously, but by now he must know that she was under suspicion, and it would not be the first time a husband, even a deceived husband, had rallied to the defence of a guilty wife. My woman, right or wrong. *Mine.* Or old-fashioned, damson-in-distress chivalry. Brian Seagram looked the sort to suffer from that.

At all events, the warrant was hurried through, and the team went in just before six in the evening. Slider went to the flat to see the work begun, and to field any questions from Steenkamp or Seagram. He was met at the door by Michael Friedman, who had a look of combined satisfaction and anticipation, like a lion resting beside a half-eaten wildebeest. He almost licked his lips as he said, 'You have made a very grave error. My client is entirely incapable of the sort of actions you are imputing to her. I've reviewed your evidence, and it is pitifully circumstantial. You have no direct evidence against her, none at all.'

Slider merely nodded politely. 'I shall have to ask you to stay out of the way. Please do exactly as Detective Constable Swilley asks you.'

'I shall wait with my client,' Friedman began, but was bustled out of the way by Seagram, who came, red-faced, to protest in less measured tones.

'This is an outrage! An outrage, I tell you! My wife is an internationally acclaimed writer! She cannot and must not be harassed and troubled in this way. Your ridiculous and unfounded suspicions are affecting her creativity! She is in the middle of a book – millions of readers worldwide are waiting for it! And you have absolutely no right to subject her to this sort of thing. I've *told* you she was at home with me all evening on the night in question. Do you think I'm lying?' He said it indignantly, as though such a possibility was literally beyond question.

Slider said gently, 'No, sir. But you admitted yourself that you did not actually *see* her at all after nine p.m.'

Seagram opened his mouth, shut it abruptly, opened it again, and could find nothing to say. Was it possible, Slider wondered, that Mr Doubt had finally paid a long-promised visit? Out of the corner of his eye, Slider saw Friedman about to intervene, but at that moment, Swilley, who was to co-ordinate the search, came in for a word and he was able to turn aside.

'There's been a clean-up,' she said in a low voice. 'Fresh Hoover tracks everywhere. And no dust.'

Slider turned to Seagram. 'Do you have a cleaner, Mr Seagram?'

'Yes. She comes in once a week. She came this morning, as a matter of fact,' said Seagram.

It was a nuisance. But blood leaves a hidden presence even after it's been washed away, and forensic tests could find the least traces, on clothes, on carpets and upholstery – even in the waste pipe of the sink.

Having seen that the occupants of the house – Steenkamp, Seagram and Friedman – were safely corralled in the drawing room, under the watchful but soothing gaze of PC D'Arblay, Slider prepared to leave. Seagram was still steaming and muttering, but Steenkamp, Slider noted, had shut down. Her face was stony and closed and she sat rigidly upright, staring at nothing. It seemed a good moment to jolt her out of it.

'Ms Steenkamp, what exactly was your relationship with Leon Greyling?'

Both Friedman and Seagram looked at him sharply, but Steenkamp's expression didn't change, and she looked up only slowly, and didn't seem about to answer. 'Leon Greyling,' he prompted her firmly.

'I don't know that name,' she said faintly. 'I don't know him.'

'Really? Yet you rang him on Tuesday evening, on your way back from Erik Lingoss's flat. It must have been something important, to ring him at such a time.'

She stared at him so miserably, he almost felt sorry. 'I've told you, I was here all evening.' Tears began to gather in her eyes, but she looked more exhausted than grief-stricken. 'Why can't you leave me alone?'

'Inspector,' Friedman said warningly, and then, to Steenkamp, 'you don't need to answer. You are not under arrest.'

Slider ignored him. 'Just to be clear, you say that you don't know the man Leon Greyling, who you called from your phone last Tuesday evening?'

Seagram jumped up. 'She said she doesn't know him! I won't have her badgered! This whole business is a farce, and I shall have something to say to the commissioner about your behaviour.'

In America they said, 'I'll have your badge.' It was fewer words, but it meant the same.

FIFTEEN
Breakfast, with Stiffer Knees

'Mysteries,' said Atherton. 'Why did she take out seven hundred pounds on her way to kill Lingoss?' He sat on Slider's windowsill, blocking out the light – not that there was much, this being both November and overcast. And Shepherd's Bush, despite its sylvan name, tended towards the dark and dreary end of the Arcadian spectrum.

Hart had done the breakfast run to Mike's stall on her way in, but Slider was a slow eater, and was still finishing the last of his sausage sandwich. He was aware that Atherton was watching him with fascinated horror. Atherton was not above a bacon sandwich, in the way that the sea is not above the sky, but a sausage sandwich, on white, with tomato sauce, broke several of his taboos.

'I don't think she planned to kill him,' Slider said.

Swilley agreed. 'If she was that upset over him seeing Lucy Gallo she'd have acted sooner. Not waited a month to whack him.'

'Unless she'd been brooding, and it all came to a head,' said Lœssop, leaning against the door jamb.

'But if she'd gone over there deliberately to kill him, she wouldn't have taken the cash with her,' Swilley pointed out. 'She stopped at the cashpoint after leaving home and took the money out, and we found it under his pillow, so it must have been meant for him. She must have gone over there for sex, and the killing was an act of impulse. Something was said, they quarrelled, and she hit him.'

'All right as far as it goes,' said Atherton, arms folded, magisterial, 'but the mystery is, why seven hundred?'

McLaren appeared at Lœssop's shoulder eating a hot sausage roll (his breakfast ran to two courses), and Lœssop stepped aside nimbly to avoid the dandruff shower of pastry flakes. 'Maybe it was five hundred for him, and the other two was for her, her walking-about money,' McLaren suggested.

'But the whole seven ended up under his pillow,' said Atherton.
'She changed her mind. She came over all generous. He performed better than expected. Or maybe he just needed exactly seven hundred more for his grand plan. Why is it important?'

'Anything mysterious is important,' Atherton said. 'If we can't explain it, a jury won't buy it.'

'If you're talking about mysteries,' Swilley said, 'why wouldn't an intelligent woman like her arrange a better alibi for herself?'

'She thought she had one,' said Atherton. 'She works from nine to midnight every evening and mustn't be disturbed. No phone calls, no tender enquiries from hubby, no cups of tea. *Noli me tangere.* The perfect cover.'

'You lost me with the tangerines,' said Swilley.

He carried on regardless. 'Obviously, she never expected any connection to be made between her and Lingoss's death. Why should it be? She couldn't know about the camera in K D Electronics' window. As long as she kept saying she was at home all evening, no one could prove any different. Or so she thought.'

'But she's still sticking to it now, when we know she was out,' Swilley said. 'Why doesn't she make something up to cover herself?'

'She's frozen,' Atherton said. 'Gone tharn. Can't think. All she can do is cling to her story and hope for the best.'

'So her protestations of innocence are all lies?' Slider asked him.

Atherton gave him a curious look. 'Point a, we know they are. And point b – what do you think she does for a living? She tells lies professionally – writes about things that never happened to people who never existed.'

'So the line between truth and fiction necessarily becomes blurred?' Slider asked.

'I didn't say that. Only that she must be good at making things up, and doing it with a straight face.'

'That's my point,' Swilley said doggedly. 'Why doesn't she make something up now?'

'It wouldn't look good to change her story, would it?' said Atherton.

'It'd look better than having no answer to the whole car and cash question,' Loessop pointed out.

'Moving on,' Atherton said. 'Second mystery – why did she take his mobile phone away?'

'Because she knew her call to him would be logged,' said Swilley. 'She was trying to leave no evidence.'

'But why didn't she destroy it straight away? Or at least turn it off?'

McLaren sucked the last crumbs off his fingers. 'I still reckon she picked it up by accident. Natalie's always doing that at home. We've got the same model, she just picks up whichever one she sees. And Steenkamp and Lingoss's phones are the same model. She was on her way out the door, saw it lying there, picked it up without even knowing she'd done it.'

'Even though she still had her own phone in her handbag or pocket or whatever?' Swilley objected.

'Automatic reaction,' said McLaren.

'But then what would she have done with it?' Atherton said. 'People do behave automatically with their phones, I agree. She'd have put it wherever she usually put it. Not in her pocket – she'd have found the other one there straight away.'

'In her handbag?' Lœssop suggested.

'All right. But when she felt for it later, to ring Greyling, wouldn't she have found she had two?'

'Women's handbags are strange, trans-dimensional spaces,' said Slider. 'Things put in them defy the laws of nature.'

'That's true,' said Swilley. 'Doesn't matter where you put your keys, they're always right down at the bottom where you can't reach them.'

'So there are two phones in her bag and it's a matter of chance which one she fishes out when she wants to make that call?' said Atherton.

'Seems likely to me,' said Swilley. 'That's why I never put my phone in my bag. And I always put it on the seat next to me when I drive.'

'All right,' said Atherton. 'But I still maintain it's more likely she took it for a reason.'

Slider moved it on again. 'Why did she ring Leon Greyling? It could hardly be a pocket-dial when he wasn't in her contacts list.'

'Nobody's ever said Lingoss was the only geezer she was doing,' said McLaren. 'If she was into young blokes, why stick at one?'

'You're making an unusual amount of sense this morning, Maurice,' said Swilley.

He shrugged off the insult and stumped away, back to the eternal verities of his cameras. McLaren might be annoying in many ways, Slider thought, but he had a work ethic that would shame a bee.

'But she says she didn't know Greyling,' Slider said, going back to the argument. 'And it seems she had never rung him before.'

'Well, she must have,' said Atherton. 'Maybe he had another number. Or she had another mobile for her secret trysts.'

'You're reaching too far,' said Slider. 'And we've got enough phones flying around for now, thank you. I admit there are mysteries, but for the moment we have to concentrate on firming up our evidence, then we can have another crack at our famous authoress and see if we can get her to break.'

'On a point of order,' Atherton said, levering his elegant length upright, 'the word "author" refers to the relationship between an artefact and its originator, and cannot therefore be gender specific.'

'You what?' Swilley said impatiently.

'It's analogous with the word "maker". You don't talk about a "makeress", do you?'

'There's a word that springs to my mind,' said Swilley coldly, 'very like "maker", only it starts with a "w" and it's got an "n" in it.'

'You know where to hit a chap, don't you? Right in the philology.'

'Phil who?' said Swilley vaguely. 'You mean Gascoyne?'

'Go away and find evidence,' Slider dismissed them all.

He surfaced some time later from re-reading everything from the beginning, feeling stiff of body and stuffy of head. He stood up, and his knees made a noise like a goat chewing on aluminium foil. He thought of all those Lingosses and Gallos tirelessly treading and lifting and pulling and pressing, tending their bodies as though they were exotic plants, searching for perfection. Were they in some way closer to God, or was it just an extreme form of vanity? He had some respect for Gilda Steenkamp, who was older than him and probably rose both seamlessly and silently from a chair. Policemen were supposed to maintain a certain level of fitness, but the reading-heavy life of a detective chief inspector did not conduce to lissomness. Cautiously he tried a few stretches, then swung his arms about to relieve the tension in his neck and shoulders.

Of course, someone chose that moment to come into his office. It was Hart.

'Doing karate, boss?' she asked with interest.

'Is that what it looked like?' Slider said hopefully.

'Nah. More like you'd just walked into a spider's web.'

'Is there something you wanted, detective sergeant?' he asked sternly.

'Yeah,' she said, grinning. 'I got something good for you.'

She had been co-ordinating the two mobile phone logs, Steenkamp's and Lingoss's, and presented him with a single sheet on which were two columns of times.

'Lucky they were both on the same server, so the same phone masts registered them. And there we are. Both start from zone three at the same moment, pass into zone two, both stationary for the same time, then Steenkamp's goes back to zone one and Lingoss's goes off. Beautiful, innit?'

'Very satisfying,' he said sadly. The noose was closing round that elegant neck. 'Now, if we could just find the phone itself . . .'

'It's gotta be this Greyling geezer, hasn't it?' Hart said. 'He's the loose marble in the toybox. She rung him and he lives in zone two.'

'So do a lot of other people,' Slider reminded her. 'We need to find out exactly where the car went. She says she didn't know Greyling . . .'

'But maybe Gallo did. He lives in zone two. Maybe he gave her Greyling's number.'

'But for what purpose?' Slider said. 'You're suggesting the killing was planned? But if she did it, what did she need either Gallo or Greyling for?'

'I dunno,' Hart said. 'Haven't thought that bit out yet.'

He made it up to the canteen this time, and was thoughtfully ingesting liver, bacon, mash and cabbage when Atherton appeared, and predictably wrinkled his nose.

'Liver is brain food,' Slider informed him. 'Rich in choline, vitamin A and zinc.'

'I didn't say anything.'

'You looked.'

'The look was to accompany the news that Norma's back from Steenkamp's flat, and they didn't find anything.'

'I wasn't hopeful,' said Slider. 'It is over a week since the event, plenty of time to get rid of anything incriminating.'

'And she's intelligent enough – and rich enough – to throw away stained clothing rather than trying to wash it,' said Atherton. 'The search does seem to have calmed Seagram down, though. Norma says he'd got very quiet and thoughtful before they left. Apparently, he buttonholed her while Steenkamp was in confab with her brief, and asked if she really thought his wife had anything to do with it.'

Slider's eyebrows shot up. 'He said that?'

'Quite humble and anxious, Norma says. It didn't last long – she gave him a professional answer, and he bounced straight back into how dare you suspect my saintly wife mode. But it's interesting that we seem to have sowed a seed of doubt.'

'Interesting,' Slider repeated thoughtfully.

'Of course,' Atherton went on, 'if she did her writing on a computer like normal people, it would have been time-logged and we'd have been able to prove she wasn't working that evening. But she says she was writing by hand that night. Tiresome of her. What with that and the self-isolation, you'd almost think she'd planned years ago to murder someone.'

Slider looked up sharply. 'What did you say?'

'I thought liver was brain food. Or did you not hear?'

'I heard. And I was thinking.'

'Do tell.'

'Not yet. The thought isn't fully formed.'

'And you never show your work until it's finished? You have a lot in common with a novelist, you know.'

'But I wouldn't have to make it up.' He stood up, abandoning lunch. 'I wonder how McLaren's getting on.'

McLaren was looking tired but triumphant, like a woman who had just given birth. Fathom, at his shoulder, provided the rumpled and sweaty bit – but actually he always looked like that. It was after six, and the borrowed uniforms had packed up, rubbing their

eyes, and gone home. McLaren had been collating the results of
the team's labours, and presented them in the CID room with full
and impressive detail. Slider would have let him have his moment,
aware of what a soul-sapping job tracing a car from camera to
camera was, but Porson had sidled in at the back, as inconspicuous
as Stonehenge, and was soon starting to fidget. He'd had his
patience tested once. It turned out negative.

In essence, through a variety of cameras, they had managed to
piece together the red Mazda's journey from Russell Close.
'Course, it was easier knowing what time we were looking for,'
McLaren acknowledged. 'And what motor we were dealing with.'
After leaving Russell Close at nine fifty-nine and turning into
Holland Road, it must have swung round the one-way system of
Addison Crescent and Addison Road, because it appeared on the
camera at the traffic lights where Addison Road met Kensington
High Street. Two cameras marked its progress along the High
Street, but it had taken a lot of trawling before they found that a
bus camera in an eastbound number nine had caught it turning
into Adam and Eve Mews.

'After that, we lost it for a bit,' McLaren said regretfully. 'You'd
think there'd be a lot of cameras, place like that, but there's only
two, and they're both pointing down at their own front doors. The
mews isn't a cul-de-sac – you can get out onto Allen Street. So
we had a big area to check. But we didn't get a ping on it anywhere,
until a westbound number twenty-seven bus catches it trying to
turn right out of the mews at ten thirty-seven, and an eastbound
number forty-nine at the same time shows it turning left into
Campden Hill Road. On its way home.'

Porson broke the digestive silence. 'So it's missing for half an
hour.'

McLaren looked apologetic. 'It goes into Adam and Eve Mews,
sir, and it comes out of there. It's fair to assume that's where it
was for the half hour.'

'Assuming's not proving,' Porson grunted.

'It's very suggestive. She rang Greyling, and went to see him,'
said Atherton.

'A man who she'd never contacted before,' Slider said,
troubled.

LaSalle spoke up. 'Gallo lives two minutes away in Marloes

Road. And he drinks in Allen Street. There's *got* to be a connection.'

'Maybe,' said Slider. 'Or maybe it's just geography. Everything's happening within a small area, but not everybody in that area knows everybody else.'

Porson gave him a look so old-fashioned it had mutton chop whiskers. 'Maybe's not good enough! Can't arrest a celebrity on maybe. That Friedman type's going to scrupulize everything with a magnifying glass. Slightest crack in our case and he'll be through it. It's got to be watertight as a duck's back.'

'I know, sir,' said Slider. 'We've still got work to do.'

Jack Gallo's flat was the top floor of a typical three-storeys-plus-basement mid-Victorian terraced house, which had been converted the cheap way, by sticking up plasterboard partitions wherever needed, without regard to aesthetics. LaSalle was not architecture-sensitive like the boss, and like many Londoners judged the desirability of a dwelling solely on its proximity to a Tube station. But even he thought Gallo's pad was a bit dismal. Mostly, this was because Gallo was so big and the place was so small. Effectively it was one decent-sized room that had been divided up into three inadequate ones – a bed-sitting room, a sliver of bath-room and a galley kitchen – linked by a narrow passage from the front door. The fact that it was on the top floor so the ceilings were low didn't help. LaSalle had to force himself not to stoop. He was impressed that Gallo walked so freely in the upright pos-ition, given that he had only about an inch clearance. And he did have to bob under the doorways.

He accepted LaSalle's visit resignedly and led him without question through to the tiny living room. There was a sofa bed, which was still in the out position and took up most of the room. There was a small table, occupied by a computer screen and keyboard, in one corner, and in the other a jumble of CD and DVD equipment and speakers, topped with a portable TV. It was a typical guy room, LaSalle thought: the bedding was dark grey with a dull red stripe and was strewn with clothes, there was no carpet on the wood-effect floor or curtains at the window, no possessions or aids to comfort anywhere. In passing he had noticed a mountain bike in the bathroom – the only place to put it, but you'd have to move it into the passage to use the loo. Small as it was, this flat would still carry a hefty rental because of its Kensington address. Gallo owned a successful gym and ought to have been making a decent amount – most people, once they were established, moved further out for more room. Perhaps, LaSalle supposed, he had lived here since before his success, and cared too little about his living arrangements to bother to move.

LaSalle was still sure Gallo was the man they should be concentrating on. Despite the compelling Mazda-and-mobile evidence against Steenkamp, he felt in his gut that Gallo was at the bottom of it; Gallo with his missing alibi, his undeclared meeting with Wilson on Murder Night, his geographical proximity to all the action. And he was the one with the steaming-hot motive. LaSalle knew these Italian families and their fierce loyalties, and particularly the protectiveness of brothers towards sisters, especially younger sisters. It made a lot more sense to him that Gallo should have killed Lingoss for dissing his sister than that a mature and sophisticated woman like Steenkamp should be driven by jealousy to kill her toy boy, when she must have known he would stray eventually and would have to be replaced.

So instead of going home, he had sought out Gallo. There were two upright chairs at the table, and Gallo pulled them out, waved LaSalle to one and took the other himself. Their knees were almost touching, but there was nowhere else to sit, apart from the bed. LaSalle supposed that when it was folded up into a sofa, you could sit and watch TV from it, but for a man living alone, the temptation to leave it out, when you were only going to want it again that night, would be nigh-on irresistible. He didn't suppose Gallo spent much time here anyway.

Gallo was in grey track bottoms and a tight sleeveless pale blue T-shirt that left his impressive biceps to be admired. When he moved his arms, the muscles shifted under the skin like boulders trying to pass each other in an earthquake. He looked as though he could have snapped skinny LaSalle in two like a twig, but Rang, as his friends called him, had a rare psychological condition, useful in a copper, of being incapable of fear. He was just never at home to Mr Coldfeet.

So he sat for a while studying Gallo and hoping to get him shifting nervously in his seat. And eventually it was Gallo who broke the silence. 'So what is it you want? I suppose you've come to ask me more questions. I don't know what else I can tell you.'

'You and Erik Lingoss,' LaSalle said.

Gallo sighed. 'Look – I've told you lot till I'm blue in the face—'

'You were pretty angry with him over your sister.'

'Yeah, I was. I've admitted it. I mean, I'd introduced him to my family, we treated him like one of us. I'd always felt a bit sorry for him, tell the truth, because his mum and dad were shit to him and he didn't have any brothers or sisters. I mean, that sucked. When you come from a big family . . . So we took him in. We were like the family he never had. And then . . . But it was just Erik, all right? It was just how he was. I should've known better'n to let him get anywhere near my sister. Yeah, I wanted to break his neck. Doesn't mean I'd ever do it.' He met LaSalle's eyes somewhat wearily. 'Look, people say all the time, "I could kill you!" You don't take it literally.'

'Except when the person actually does get killed.'

Gallo muttered, 'Oh for God's sake!' but said no more.

'You knew he was having sex with his clients at the same time as he was seeing your sister,' LaSalle said. Gallo shrugged. 'One in particular. The one he dumped her for. That was getting a bit close to home, wasn't it?'

'What are you talking about?'

'How well do you know Gilda Steenkamp?'

'Who?'

'You heard me. Lucy's boss's wife. How did you meet her?'

'I don't know what you're talking about. Lucy's boss is called Seagram, not . . . what you said.'

'Did you meet her in the shop, was that it?'

'What, Lucy's shop? The antiques shop? I've never even been in there.' He was getting irritated now.

'Or did Leon Greyling introduce you to her?'

'I tell you, I don't know her.' He surged to his feet.

LaSalle rose simultaneously. 'I haven't finished with you yet. Sit down, please.'

For a moment, Gallo stood scowling, his hands clenching and unclenching, before he subsided. 'Look, I've had a long day, I'm tired, I haven't showered, I haven't eaten since lunchtime. So will you stop asking me about people I don't know and leave me alone?' he growled.

LaSalle produced the photo of Greyling in his skins. 'You know Leon Greyling,' he said. Actually, he had started to think Gallo was telling the truth about not knowing Steenkamp – he had sounded genuine – and if he didn't know her, there was no reason to suppose he knew Greyling. If Gallo had killed Lingoss, the whole Steenkamp-Greyling thread was redundant anyway; maybe she had gone over to Lingoss for sex and left him alive, and Gallo had gone in afterwards.

But to his surprise, Gallo took the photo impatiently, paused, and then said, 'I do know this bloke. I've seen him a few times at Shapes. Last year, I think it was – he trained there for a bit. Don't think I knew his name though. What did you say it was?'

'Leon Greyling.'

'Yeah, it sounds familiar. He was an actor, or he said he was. Erik seemed quite friendly with him.'

'Erik Lingoss knew Leon Greyling?'

'Well, Erik had this private client that was an actor – he got him in shape for a telly part. It paid really well, so he'd've liked more work like that. I think he was a bit star-struck, actually – kept talking about "my client on telly" and the special requirements he'd had. So I suppose this Greyling being an actor made him more interesting. They seemed to have things to talk about, anyway.'

'So did Greyling take him on as a trainer?'

'I suppose that's what he hoped for, but I don't think anything came of it. I think he'd have told me if it did.'

'So Leon Greyling – are you telling me you haven't seen him recently?'

'Not as far as I know.'

'Despite the fact that he lives just round the corner from you.'

'I didn't know he did,' Gallo said.

'In Adam and Eve Mews – halfway between your local pub and your flat.'

Gallo scowled. 'A lot of people live in Kensington. Are you saying I'm supposed to know them all?'

'Seems a bit of a coincidence, doesn't it?'

'And that's all it is. If you've got nothing else, can you go, please? I want a shower, and my supper.'

LaSalle got up. 'If you remember anything else about Leon Greyling, or anything about him and Erik, you'll let me know, won't you?'

Jack Gallo snorted, which wasn't saying he would and wasn't saying he wouldn't.

SIXTEEN
Only Connect

As soon as LaSalle arrived in the morning, Slider called him in, with the tautness of one who came in to work early towards one who is not *technically* late and therefore cannot be castigated.

'I've just had a phone call from Jack Gallo.'

'Yeah, guv, I went to see him last night. I was just about to write it up.'

'Give me the gist,' said Slider.

LaSalle looked a bit rumpled first thing in the morning, but he was a good copper and his mind was freshly ironed and neatly folded. 'So what did chummy want?' he asked when he'd concluded his report.

'He said he'd just remembered that Lingoss told him Leon Greyling had the same agent as his actor client. He didn't know if it was important but you'd told him if he remembered anything else to let you know. He rang on the way to work and you weren't here.'

LaSalle managed not to look guilty. 'Lingoss's actor client – that was that Gavin Spalding bloke that Funky went to interview,' he said. 'It was in his report, apparently Spalding said it was this agent that found him Lingoss when he needed a trainer.'

'So now we have a connection between Lingoss and Greyling,' said Slider, 'but still not between Steenkamp and Greyling.'

'Well, guv, Lingoss is a link between them.'

'But where is that taking us?' LaSalle was silent. 'What's the agent's name? Gallo didn't know it, only that Lingoss had said it was the same person.'

'It's in the report. Wait a minute, I'll remember.' He screwed up his face in thought. 'Heinz, that was it. Like the beans. Marjorie Heinz.'

'Look her up,' Slider said. 'I suppose it's not out of the

question that Steenkamp knew her. Two of her books were made into TV, so she might have bumped into a theatrical agent at some point.'

The area of London called Soho had first been converted from farmland into a hunting park by Henry VIII, but had been sold off piecemeal for building in the seventeenth century. So while the façades lining its streets were largely Georgian and Victorian, many of the buildings behind them were much older, and some still retained the small rooms, heavy panelling and dark, narrow stairs that added so much to romance and so little to utility. As Jerome K. Jerome noted, oak panelling might be thrilling to the tourist, but can be somewhat depressing to live with, which accounted for how often it got boarded over and wallpapered.

Perhaps a theatrical agent had to take a more historic view, for having conquered the north face of the steep and narrow staircase, Slider and Atherton emerged into an unapologetically oak-panelled room, and were directed by the secretary working there into another beyond. Its low ceiling sported elaborate decorative plasterwork, and the scene was dominated by a fabulously carved fireplace that would have had an architectural salvage merchant drooling. The grate sported only a single-bar electric fire, but it glowed welcomingly in the overall ligneous gloom.

The agent, who rose from her massively cluttered desk to greet them, also glowed, her face being almost unnaturally white and surrounded by a wild frizz of hair dyed a shade of ginger that was almost orange.

'Marjorie Heinz?' Slider enquired courteously.

'Marjie, please. From childhood I hated my name. If people call me Marjorie I think they're about to tell me off. So it's Marjie, OK?'

Standing up, she was not much higher off the ground than she had been when sitting. She was about five feet two, and almost as broad as she was high, and was dressed in layers of floaty, silky garments swirlingly patterned in shades of green. From her sleeves and a rattle of bracelets her wrists and hands emerged slim and dainty; her face was round and white with red painted lips, and green eyeshadow and mascara surrounding hazel eyes as bright as a cat's, and as watchful. The whole eccentric appearance, Slider judged, was her *mise en scene.* You would notice, you would remember. Underneath the flamboyance, she would be – indeed, if successful must be – a hard businesswoman.

'My secretary said you wanted to talk to me about Leon Greyling,' she said when Slider had performed the introductions. 'What's the silly boy got up to now? It's not coke again, is it? I can't believe the full might of the law would be deployed for the sake of a little bit of victimless charlie. I've told him to knock it off, but there's a lot of temptation in their world, and I can't be with him all the time.'

'It's nothing like that,' Slider said. 'We want some information about him, that's all.'

'He must have done something,' she said, the bright eyes steady. 'A chief inspector *and* a sergeant?'

Atherton gave her one of his rueful, conspiratorial and still somehow flirtatious smiles. 'Our lives are so dull. The chance of taking a glimpse inside the magical world of theatre – having a little of the fairy dust brush off on us—'

'If you're auditioning, I can get you something for next Tuesday,' she said sharply; but her expression had softened. She looked at Atherton now, not Slider, and Slider was content to leave it that way.

'Have I got a chance?' Atherton asked winsomely.

'As much of a chance as most of the poor saps I see. What d'you want to know about Leon? He's a pretty boy, moves well, nice voice. Potentially he's got talent, but he's lazy. Won't put the work in. He's not hungry enough, is my evaluation. I told him last time, come back and see me when the arse is hanging out of your pants.'

'Why did you take him on?' Atherton asked.

'As a favour to his mother. We were at drama school together. We both wanted to go on the stage, but it never happened. Well, I went into agenting, and that's a much better living, I can promise you. Geraldine was a photographic model. Used to model cosmetics, mainly – you never saw such skin! It was a crime to put make-up on it. Then marriage got in the way. So she sublimated.'

'Worked out her ambitions on her son?' Atherton suggested.

'You're quick,' she said approvingly. 'Yes, Leon had to be the star she never was. Not happening yet.'

'You also agent Gavin Spalding.'

'Yes, he's a treasure. A real trouper. I could do with twenty like him on my books. I've just got him a very nice little gig on *Walking With the Dead IV*, and he deserves it. Character actors – they don't call them that any more, but they're what keeps the whole business going. OK, everyone wants to be Daniel Craig, but he'd be one lonely boy on the set without the half dozen Gavins to bounce off.'

'You look after your people well,' Atherton said.

'It's what I'm here for,' she said, but sensed a line being taken and there was a wariness in her now.

'You got Gavin Spalding a personal trainer when he needed to bulk up for a part.'

'Where are you going with this? I wouldn't go to that much trouble for everyone, but like I said, Gavin's a treasure. He did the work, he hit that part right out of the park. What's wrong with that?'

Slider took over. 'Nothing at all. The personal trainer – Erik Lingoss, wasn't it? How did you find him?' She looked at him suspiciously. 'Was it Leon Greyling who introduced him to you, by any chance?'

'Yes, it was,' she said, 'but that was for me, not for Gavin. I was having a lot of neck and shoulder pain, it was getting me down, I was complaining about it one time when Leon was hanging around the office. He said he knew this guy who did proper sports massage, genius fingers he said he had. Well, he was right.' She looked at Slider, and then at Atherton, as if daring them to contradict. 'Two sessions and he had the whole thing released. He really knew his stuff.'

'You didn't go on seeing him then – Erik Lingoss?' Atherton asked. 'It was just the massage?'

She reddened slightly. 'What are you suggesting?'

'I wondered if you used him for personal training as well, that's all.'

'Are you making fun of me, sonny?' She spread her hands, indicating her general shape. 'Do I *look* as if I do training?'

Slider took it back. The line of question was irritating her, which suggested she knew more about Erik's proclivities than she was letting on. 'He impressed you enough with his professionalism for you to recommend him to Gavin Spalding, at any rate.'

'Yes, and he did a boffo job with Gavin. I wouldn't hesitate to recommend him again if the situation arose. But I thought you were here to ask me about Leon, not Erik.'

'Am I right in thinking Leon doesn't get a lot of work?'

She shrugged. 'I keep him on my books more as a favour to Geraldine. I've got him the odd bit of modelling and demo work.'

'You did get him a part in *Lockhart* – that's big stuff, isn't it?'

'He must have been thrilled about it,' Atherton said. 'How did it happen?'

'I'm a bloody good agent – that's how it happened,' she said, giving him a stare that could have taken barnacles off a hull. He stared right back, and finally she relented. 'Tony McNally – the producer? – is an old friend of mine.'

'You asked for a favour?' Slider said sympathetically. 'I'm guessing you didn't like doing that.'

She gave a bark of laughter. 'You got that wrong! I'm an agent. I'd ask Old Nick a favour if I was likely to get it. Anyway, it was quid pro quo. I did Tony a solid, he did me one back. He needed a particular location for this episode of *Lockhart*. Most of it's shot in the studio, but there was one sequence that needed an actual antique shop in a town location, certain other requirements as well – corner site, wide pavements, access and so on. Leon was in my room when I was talking on the phone with Tony about it, and he suggested this particular shop he knew. It turned out to be perfect. Tony was grateful – his researcher would have found somewhere sooner or later, but time was tight. So Leon, cheeky boy, asked me to ask Tony for a part in the episode in return. Always with the shortcuts! Always looking for the easy way, you see.'

'But he got the part,' said Slider.

'Tony gave him a walk-on. Chances like that don't come every day. Leon could have made something of it. He knew Tony would be looking at him, it could have been his breakthrough. But like I said, he's lazy. He did just enough to get by. Tony wasn't impressed. So I told him, no more favours.'

'The antique shop concerned – was it in Kensington High Street, by any chance? Heneage and Seagram?'

'That's the one. You know it?'

'How did Leon know about it?'

'He said it was right opposite the gym he went to.'

'Did Erik ever mention it to you?'

She frowned. 'Erik? Why would he?'

'He worked at that gym. Isn't that where he met Leon?'

She shook her head indifferently. 'I suppose it probably was. But the subject didn't come up on the two occasions I had massage from him. Why are we back on Erik again?'

Slider glanced at Atherton, and let him be the one to say, 'He's dead, Marjie. Somebody killed him.'

She turned her head away, and the colour came briefly to her cheeks again. She said, 'What . . .?' But that was all.

Slider said gently, 'Did he offer you more than massage?' No answer. 'Did he make a pass at you?' Now she looked at him, her eyes over-bright. She was holding her lips tight until she was sure she was in control. He said, 'You refused him. Were you angry?' Still no answer. 'He overstepped the mark. It was sleazy. But then, why did you recommend him to Spalding when he'd—'

'It wasn't sleazy,' she said. It burst out of her. She swallowed, and then spoke calmly, but without quite meeting Slider's eyes. 'I thought he was making fun of me, you see. Just at first. At the end of the massage, he kissed the back of my neck, and said I had beautiful skin. Then he kissed my ear, and asked if I'd like to make love. Then I knew it was no joke – he meant it. And I was tempted. When you're relaxed like that, after a really good massage – and the pain was gone, you don't know what that's like, the pain gone after months of putting up with it. All your endorphins are released – you're in the mood.'

'I understand. But you still refused.'

Now she met his gaze, and gave a rueful, downturned quirk of the mouth. 'One of my more heroic moments. Should have been a medal in it. He was *gorgeous*, you know? But I knew I mustn't. You have to learn to recognize things you'll regret afterwards. Still . . .' She shook herself. 'Why would anyone kill him? Who did it?' Her eyebrows shot up. 'You don't think *Leon* . . .?'

'We're just gathering evidence,' Slider said.

'Leon's too lazy to kill anyone,' she said, but he could see her mind working. When it came to it, a person with sufficient motive – a person in a rage – a person under the influence . . .

'When did you last see Leon, or speak to him?' Atherton asked.

'Not for weeks. He rang me some time in September – my secretary could find the date for you. Everything is logged. Asking if I had anything. He didn't sound too bothered about it, though. That's when I told him to come back when he was hungry enough. Last time I got him an audition he didn't bother to turn up. That makes me look bad. So I wasn't going to put him up for anything without a change in his attitude. And there was no sign of that.'

'Do you know what he's living on?'

She shook her head. 'Bar work, maybe. Or his parents might be giving him money – that could be the problem, of course. They've got plenty – and Geraldine's a doting mother. But she ought to know, if anyone does, that you have to push yourself to get on. You can't buy your way into this business.'

Slider had one last question. 'Do you know Gilda Steenkamp?'

She frowned. 'The novelist? Never met her. I'm not a literary agent.'

'You've heard of her?'

'Of course. The Ridley novels. *Bitter Mountain* and *Blood River*. Benny Macrillo made the TV serials, and there's talk of a third. *Savage Rock*, is that the title? Benedict Cumberbatch was asked for Ridley – did you know that? – but he couldn't fit it in with other commitments, that's why they got Sam Wroughton instead. His big break. Made a good fist of it, I thought. Darcy Raymond agents him. I got one of my boys, Sedley Parkes, lines in *Blood River*. Benny's a sweetheart. Never forgets an old friend. Why do you ask?'

'No reason,' Slider said. 'Just making random connections in my mind.'

'Bafta-winning producer/director Benvenuto Macrillo, and she calls him Benny,' Atherton marvelled. 'I love that. OK, I know they all do it – calling Madonna "Madge" and so on – but in her case I get the feeling it's genuine. He really is an old friend.'

'Shush!' said Swilley. 'I'm trying to watch.'

They had found the appropriate episode of *Lockhart* archived on line, and were watching it on Hart's monitor.

'Then presumably you believe her when she says she doesn't know Gilda Steenkamp?' Slider said.

'Why would she lie?' said Atherton. 'We didn't expect her to. We only wanted to know about the Greyling/Lingoss connection.'

'But as a bonus we've now got a Greyling/Steenkamp's-husband's-shop connection,' said Hart. 'For what that's worth.'

'He might have met her during the filming,' said Atherton. 'If she dropped by to watch – who wouldn't?'

'Will you *shush*!' said Swilley.

'It's hokey,' Atherton said. 'Run it on.'

Hart ran it on. 'There's the shop!' several people exclaimed. They watched the scene in real time. It didn't mean anything to anyone out of context, but all eyes were peeled for anyone they knew. But neither Seagram nor Lucy Gallo was in the shop, which was presumably manned by actors for the shot; Greyling was merely in the background, a browsing shopper who looked alarmed and hurried out when Lockhart and the shop's proprietor started arguing.

'Well,' said Atherton, 'I'm impressed. I've never seen a better nervous glance.'

'Don't be so snarky,' Swilley rebuked him automatically. 'What are you – Laurence Olivier?'

'What now, boss?' Hart asked, ignoring them. 'Everything seems interconnected, except nothing is.'

'Chaos is just a pattern you don't recognize,' Atherton said.

'Who said that?' Hart demanded.

'Einstein,' said Atherton. 'Or it could be Alan Turing.'

'One should never mistake pattern for meaning,' said Gascoyne. 'Iain Banks.'

'Bollocks. Gordon Ramsay,' said Fathom.

'But the only evidence is against Steenkamp,' said McLaren impatiently, tipping the last Maltesers out of a fun bag into his mouth. 'We know about her. I dunno why we're watching this crap.'

'Because she rang Greyling, genius,' Hart said. 'He's gotta be involved somehow.'

Slider shook his head. 'Something doesn't feel right. We're missing something.'

Hart gave his mighty cogitations a respectful silence of a full 1.4 seconds, then asked, 'So what are we going to do next?'

'Go and talk to Leon Greyling,' Slider said.

Adam and Eve Mews was a narrow, cobbled turning off Kensington High Street, but like other London mews hadn't seen a horse in seventy years. In the fifties and early sixties they'd been inconvenient and rackety semi-slums, but when the tidal wave of Fashion crashed over the capital at the end of the sixties, it had suddenly become cute and funky to live in a converted hayloft above a stable. Girls in knee-length white plastic boots and Biba dresses could be seen tripping (sometimes literally, on the cobbles) from their gaily-painted front doors; red, white and blue Minis could be found parked outside, between tubs of geraniums; and film-makers invested mews-dwelling with the aspirational glamour of swinging parties and Michael Caine draped with multiple starfish-eyed dollies.

It had all calmed down now, and with the rise in property prices – combined with the fact that mews were always located in highly desirable areas – nobody could afford to be funky in them. Now they were very expensive homes for the privileged few.

'And the adorable name can't hurt,' Atherton remarked as they turned in.

'There was a pub called the Adam and Eve on the corner,' Slider told him. 'It closed in 1973. Paxman says it was a bit grim. Mind you, most places were in 1973.'

'Still, it makes for a cute address.'

'They're all bijou residences now,' Slider remarked. 'You can tell from the pristine paintwork. And the burglar alarms.'

'As McLaren said, you'd think there'd be more security cameras.' He braked. 'This is it.'

With the rise in property values, the early simple conversions of the sixties and seventies had been swept away, and little remained of the original structures but the façades, which were protected features. Behind them lurked modern-built luxury urban cottages with every convenience electronics could provide.

'How the hell does a resting actor afford to live here?' Atherton said, stepping back after ringing the doorbell to stare up at the perfectly-laundered brick and exquisite paint job. 'You couldn't do it on bar work.'

'Rich father, doting mother?' said Slider.

Atherton gave a tight smile. 'Or are you thinking, old guv of mine, that blackmail might provide a suitably large income for a work-shy mama's boy?'

'The thought hadn't begun to cross my mind,' said Slider. 'And we don't know that he's a work-shy mama's boy. He might just be nice but dim.'

The door opened. 'Sorry, I was in the bog.' A very slender figure, in cashmere joggers and a silk shirt hanging open, was topped by a rumpled shock of blonde hair and a blonde-stubbled face; blue eyes in rather sleep-deprived sockets, and very expensive teeth spread out in a welcoming smile.

'I think you could be right, guv,' Atherton murmured. And then, aloud, 'Leon Greyling? We're police officers. Could we have a word with you?'

SEVENTEEN
The Stars Look Down, a Bit

The eyes and the smile, interestingly, had been all for Slider. Now he looked at Atherton and the eyes narrowed. 'What about?'

'We can't talk about it here on the doorstep,' Slider said. 'May we come in?'

He said 'may', but he used a tone that brooked no dissent. Greyling obviously responded to the smack of firm government, because he made big eyes and a pout but stepped back to let them in, saying, 'Ooh, well, if you're going to be like that about it . . .'

Inside, the ground floor area, which had been the stable and coach house, was now an achingly modern kitchen with, even at a quick glance, every contrivance known to twenty-first-century man, and included a dining area and a huge sofa facing a wall-mounted sixty-five-inch TV. The disadvantage to mews-living was the lack of windows on the ground floor, which made it cosy but a touch claustrophobic, so the main sitting room tended to be on the first floor where the hayloft and groom's living quarters would have been. Straight ahead was an open-tread light oak staircase, from the top of which came the sound of shrill and monotonous barking. But Greyling led them into the kitchen area, leaned himself against the central island counter, folded his arms defensively across his chest, and said, 'Well, what d'you want?'

Slider could do it standing up as well as the next man. 'We want to talk to you about Erik Lingoss.'

'Don't know him,' Greyling said promptly.

'Yes, you do,' Slider threw back. 'You were both members of Shapes Gym, and were seen talking together on several occasions.'

'You talk to a lot of people at a gym. It's just "hi, how's it going?" stuff. I don't *know him* know him.'

'You introduced him to your agent, Marjorie Heinz,' Slider said relentlessly.

He pouted. 'Oh, if you've been talking to *Marjie* . . . I just told her he did a good massage, which people at the gym had told me – and by the way, I don't go there any more. Haven't been for ages. Anyway, she's a bit cross with me these days, you don't want to believe everything she tells you. She said a lot of things to my mother, which weren't true. Well, hardly any of them. And she won't get me any work. Just because that beast Jon Sanford said I stood in his light on set. They're such bitches, all those stars, you've no idea. Soon as they get the top billing and their own dressing room they think they're better than the rest of us. He was *nothing* before *Lockhart*. I remember Marjie told me he—'

Slider, well aware that this sort of rattling monologue was a smokescreen, interrupted him. 'Mr Greyling, I don't think you realize how serious this is.'

'*Mr* Greyling? Well if you're going to get all humourless about it.' He shrugged, looking away.

'Erik Lingoss is dead,' Slider said. 'He was murdered. And please don't pretend you didn't know.'

At the last moment, Greyling aborted the shocked expression, and said sulkily, 'It's all over social media. You'd have to be a monk not to know. Or old. So he's dead. I'm sorry. He seemed an all-right bloke, but I hardly knew him. What's it got to do with me?'

'You know perfectly well what it's got to do with you,' Atherton came in sternly. 'Where were you on the evening of Tuesday the fourth?'

His face shut down. Stony eyes and tight lips. 'How on earth am I supposed to remember that? That's over a week ago.'

But Slider, watching him closely, thought there was a flicker of something underneath it. Perhaps not quite alarm, but certainly caution.

'You *will* remember,' Atherton said. 'Either here, or at the station.'

'You can't threaten me,' Greyling said. 'I haven't done anything. Even if I remember, I don't have to tell you. And I *don't* remember.'

'Let me help you out,' Slider said kindly. 'That was the evening Gilda Steenkamp came to see you.'

'I don't know anyone called Gilda Steenkamp,' he said, in a tone that finished the sentence: 'so there!'.

'She rang you to say she was on the way,' Slider said. 'The telephone call from her number to yours is a matter of record. It's pointless to deny it.'

'I don't know her, and I'm not answering any more of your questions,' he said, becoming a little shrill. The barking upstairs, which had ceased, started up again. 'Will you please leave.'

Slider gave him a long look, and said in an avuncular tone, 'You really would do well to co-operate now, you know. If we have to come back later, you'll have missed your chance, and things will be a lot stickier for you.'

'I'm not talking to you,' Greyling said, but his eyes lingered on Slider's like those of a schoolboy who wants to oblige, but daren't peach.

At the door, Atherton said, conversationally, 'It's a gorgeous pad you've got here. How do you afford it, when you haven't had any work for ages?'

Greyling had liked the compliment, and almost answered. 'I've got . . .' he began, but then shut down again, looking cross. 'It's none of your business,' he said, and folded his lips into a zipped line until both his tormentors were outside, whereupon he snapped the door shut as well.

'An innocent man,' Atherton said. 'Well, I'm convinced, aren't you?'

'I hoped he might be,' Slider said. 'If we could have eliminated his thread from the tangle . . . He's not in the contacts folder on Lingoss's phone, remember. So he might be telling the truth that he hardly knew him.'

'You notice he didn't query when we altered the line of questioning from Lingoss to Steenkamp. He should have said, "What's that got to do with Erik?" Proving that he knows there's a link.'

'But what is it?' Slider said in frustration. He reflected for a moment. 'He knows something – and he wants to tell. The question, is how to get it out of him.'

'But I don't see him as First Murderer, do you? He struck me as weak and petulant.'

'I don't know what part he played,' Slider said. 'There's a kind of little dog who'll nip round the back and bite while the big dog

keeps the victim occupied. If he had a spite against Lingoss, and
he could do it without danger to himself . . .'

'Hit him while someone else held his arms, you mean?'

'Except that that's not what happened. No defence wounds.
Lingoss wasn't restrained in any way. And in any case, what about
Gilda Steenkamp?'

'Yes, what indeed,' said Atherton. 'As McLaren said, in a rare
access of lucidity, the only evidence we've got is against her. And
yet . . .'

'You don't want it to be her. Because you admire her writing.'

'It isn't that, it's just that at her level of celebrity – I don't
know, you wouldn't think she'd even think of it.'

'You saw the murder scene. I don't suppose thought came into
it much.'

They had reached the car, and Atherton stopped. 'While we're
here, shall I go and have another talk to Lucy Gallo?'

'Good idea,' Slider said. 'I've got to get back to the factory.
Can you find your own way back?'

'Of course.'

'See if you can firm up the link between Greyling and
Steenkamp, via the TV episode.'

'That was my idea. Everything connects, except that nothing
does. "Only connect, and the beast and the monk will die."'

'The who and the who?'

'E.M. Forster. *Howards End.* The beast was Lingoss, presumably, and he's dead. The monk is the cool-headed killer who's
hidden himself so far. But when we make the connect, he'll die
too.'

'No capital punishment any more,' Slider pointed out.

'Don't be so literal,' Atherton said.

Lucy Gallo was alone in the shop, working at the desk. She
buzzed him in, and came halfway to meet him, looking worn
and tired.

'Boss not here?' Atherton asked cheerfully, to relax her.

'He's staying at home with Mrs Steenkamp,' she said. 'To keep
her spirits up. And protect her from the media.'

'The media?'

'Well, they haven't turned up yet, but they could at any time.'

'Why should the media make any connection between Gilda Steenkamp and Erik Lingoss?'

'Sooner or later someone will spill the beans. People always find out, and they love to point the finger if it's someone successful. It's *awful* that she's even suspected!' she said, giving him a look that told him how disappointed she was in him. *You've let the school down, you've let your parents down, and you've let yourself down.* On a female her age, it was actually cute. 'Mr Seagram is absolutely devastated. He's devoted to her.'

'He is?'

A little frown creased her brows. 'Of course he is. Just the Saturday before all this happened, he took her out for a special celebration for their wedding anniversary.'

'It was their anniversary?'

'Well, the actual anniversary was back in October, but she'd been too busy. He took her to dinner at the Ritz, booked a chauffeured car so she wouldn't have to drive—'

'Why would she have to drive?'

'Well, he won't drive her car – says it's too small, gives him backache. And his Bentley's got something wrong with it, an electrical fault, so it's in the repair shop. Anyway, it's nicer to be driven, and it meant he could have a glass of wine as well. *And* he bought her roses – which must have cost a bit, in November – and a pair of diamond earrings. Had them brought to the table with the champagne, and arranged for the harpist to play "Oh How We Danced on the Night We Were Wed". So romantic!' She sighed.

'It sounds it,' he said, mentally sticking a finger down his throat. Did women *really* like that sort of thing? Of course he knew some did, but surely the magnificently intellectual Gilda Steenkamp was above all that? More interestingly, was she at that point already planning to kill Erik Lingoss just three days later? The thought that she might have sat through a glutinous wedding-anniversary celebration with that on her mind intrigued him. Or had the killing been a moment of madness?

In either case, what was Greyling's connection with it all? He should remember why he was here.

'It was you I wanted to talk to, anyway,' he said. 'Do you remember when this shop was used for an episode of *Lockhart*?'

'Yes, of course,' she said. 'It was a big bit of excitement in our lives. Or, well, we thought it would be. It didn't turn out quite as exciting as we expected, because they wouldn't let us near while they were filming. I sort of hoped we might be in it – you know, in the background, just for local colour – but they shut the shop for two days and I had to stay outside with the general public. Still, there it was, our shop on TV, and Mr Seagram said it was really good publicity.'

'So you didn't get to meet the stars?' Atherton said in a voice of sympathy.

'Only in passing. Mr Seagram gave me the days off, so I stood outside for a lot of the time to watch, and I saw them going in and out. And the first day, one of the production assistants asked me where the nearest Starbucks was, so I said I'd go for her, and she let me. I got the coffees for everyone, and Jon Sanford said thank you to me in person and gave me such a lovely smile.'

'And where was Mr Seagram all this time?'

'He was in the back office most of the time. He wanted to make sure nothing got damaged. And the producer asked him to stay on hand in case they needed to consult about anything. Of course, they'd got their own experts, but they used some of our furniture for the set – paid Mr Seagram rental for it too. There was one particular table – a lovely marquetry console – and in the story one of the characters was trying to buy it.'

'Do you remember one of the actors, man called Leon Greyling?'

She shook her head quite naturally. 'No, that name doesn't mean anything to me. But like I said, I only saw them going in and out.' He produced the picture of Greyling, and she looked at it, but slowly shook her head. 'I don't recognize him. He wasn't one of the stars, anyway. But there were a lot of other people there, crew and extras and so on. I didn't really notice them all.'

Poor Greyling, so forgettable, Atherton thought. 'Did Erik ever mention Leon Greyling to you?'

'No, not that I remember.' Her eyes widened. 'Are you saying Erik knew him? What's he got to do with anything?'

'Probably nothing,' Atherton said soothingly. 'We have to follow up every possible connection. Did Mrs Steenkamp come down to the shop while the filming was going on?'

'I don't think so. Not that I knew of, anyway. Unless she came in the back way to see Mr Seagram. But he never mentioned to me that she did – though of course there's no reason he should.'

'There's a back way?'

She gestured behind her. 'There's a door from the back office into the yard, where the dustbins are. But if she did come to have a look, she'd be more likely to come in the front way and demand a guided tour. She's quite famous you know. And she knows her way around – she visited the set of both her books that were made into TV. I bet the producer would have known who she was and bent over backwards for her. People always do, somehow.'

Atherton was silent a moment, thinking again of the difference between the bright sun of Steenkamp's international celebrity and Erik Lingoss's little local gleam, more warmth than light. But creatures who got too close to flames often got burnt. The more he thought about it, the more he liked the idea of blackmail. It was, after all, the thing that could most easily be imagined bridging that gap between the nobody and the somebody. But if Lingoss and Greyling had blackmailed her together, why had she killed Erik and not Leon?

Lucy was looking at him curiously. 'You haven't found out who killed Erik, then? Do you think this Greyling person had something to do with it?'

'We're working on it,' he said. 'We're working very hard, I promise you.' She nodded, and blinked away the momentary brightness of her eyes. 'You still care for him?'

'I knew him a long time,' she said, by way of answer.

'When he broke up with you, and he said he was seeing someone else – you had no idea who it was?' She shook her head. 'You still have no idea? Do you think your brother knew who it was?'

'No. Why would he?'

'Erik might have told him. They were friends. And Jack *was* very angry about it.'

'He was angry because I was upset. I'm sure Erik wouldn't have told him. He'd never kiss and tell.'

Men like Erik *always* kiss and tell, Atherton thought; that's part of the thrill. But he didn't say it. There was something about being surrounded by lovingly cared-for antiques that booted up the old-fashioned chivalry. Even in a hound like him.

*   *   *

Slider got home in reasonable time for once, but no less tired for it. Feeling your way forward through a fog was exhausting. There was no adrenaline rush to it. He'd had a long talk with Mr Porson, who agreed with him that they couldn't yet make a case the CPS would run with, and that arresting Gilda Steenkamp at this point would attract nothing but unwelcome publicity, which could go either way. The fickleness of fandom might turn against her, or might vilify the police for daring to suspect her.

As Porson had put it, 'She might end up a social piranha, or it might all resound on us.' There was nothing to do but keep buggering on and hope, Micawber-like, that something turned up.

He found his father pottering in the kitchen, and a savoury smell on the air. 'Got hold of a bit of venison,' Mr Slider said, his bright blue eyes considering his son thoughtfully. 'Knocked up a bit of a stew for you.' He still had difficulty calling stew 'casserole'. 'Reckoned you wouldn't want to be cooking when you got back.'

'Venison?'

'Present. Old friend of mine from back home popped in for a visit.' In Dad's world, you didn't pay a visit without taking something. You mustn't leave the house poorer than before you arrived. 'You remember, Doug Forrest? Doing a bit o' culling on the estate where he works. Nice shoulder, he brought me. I've cut us off a bit, left it marinading, done the rest for you.'

'It smells wonderful. Where's Joanna?'

'I made her go upstairs and lie down.'

Slider felt a twist of his stomach. Back home, on the farm, Dad had always somehow known when a cow was going to calve, even though he wasn't a cowman. He had a sixth sense about it. 'She's not . . .?'

'No, no. Just tired. It's too much for her, taking care of little George.'

'She was looking forward to spending more time with him.'

'Ah, but he's a lively lad, and she's carrying a lot around with her. Just getting up and down's an effort. I've had him most of the afternoon, give her a break. Done some drawing together. He did one for you, I promised to give it you.'

He handed it over. There was a house, of the sort children drew, a box with a triangular roof, four windows and a door. Next to it was a stick man in a top hat, and a thing that, best guess, he thought must be a giant mutant space-centipede about to eat all before it. A circle with sticks coming out all round was the sun shining relentlessly down on the unfolding disaster.

'I suppose that's our house,' Slider said, 'and that's me.' For some reason, George always drew him wearing a top hat. Slider didn't know how he even knew what a top hat was. 'But what's this? Is it a story?'

Mr Slider chuckled. 'He's a one, that lad. I was telling him about when you were a boy, and how in those days we didn't have computers and Nintendos and all that sort of thing. So he says, "Were you poor people, Grandad, like Mary and Joseph?"'

'Christmas again,' said Slider. 'Well, at least it wasn't the Three Kings and the gifts.'

'S'right. So I says to him, what does he think poor people had in their houses instead of central heating and dishwashers and such-like. And he has a long think, and he says, "a lion". So I ask him, why would they have a lion, and he says, "cos they'd have room".'

Slider laughed. 'Logical!' He looked at the drawing again. 'Is this supposed to be our old house, then?'

'That's our house on the farm, and that's you as a lad.'

'Complete with top hat. And the centipede?'

'He wanted to draw the lion, but I couldn't find a picture of one for him to copy, but I did find a cow.'

Slider studied it. 'It's got eight legs.'

'Four of them's the udder. I had a lot of trouble explaining the udder. I said he could leave it out and let it be a boy cow, but he insisted.'

'I hope the udder doesn't come back to haunt us,' Slider said, looking for a place to prop up the drawing. The artist would expect proper appreciation in the morning.

'I didn't go into a lot of detail,' said Mr Slider. 'But you got to face up to udders sooner or later.'

Slider shuddered. 'Especially with a new baby coming.'

Mr Slider nodded. 'Well, now you're back, I'll pop off back home. Get our supper started. Your . . . Lydia'll be waiting.'

'You almost said, "your mother", didn't you?' said Slider.

'Slip of the tongue.' Mr Slider examined him for a moment, and said, 'I don't interfere.'

'I know you don't. You could if you wanted. We wouldn't mind.'

'She's very tired. It takes a lot out of a woman at her age.'

'I wouldn't say "at her age" when she can hear you.'

Mr Slider wouldn't be joked out of what he wanted to say. 'Nature expects women to be mothers in their teens. Can't be doing with that sort of thing now, of course. But – us men, we've got the easy part.'

'I know,' Slider said humbly.

'She might say things to me she wouldn't say to you,' said Mr Slider. 'Looking after a kiddie, let alone two – it's harder work than playing the violin. I don't think she'd want another one. You should think about having the snip.'

'Da-ad!' Slider protested, resisting the urge to cross his legs. This wasn't a conversation you wanted to have with (a) your father or (b) anyone.

Mr Slider remained steady. 'A man ought to take responsibility. Contraception's hard for women. All sorts of problems, it causes. And it's not a hundred per cent. A man wouldn't put all that worry onto the woman he loves. If you don't want any more, you should be the one to do something about it. That's all I'm saying.'

And he gave a brisk nod, and left Slider to it.

In the bedroom he found Joanna on the bed, under the counterpane, with Jumper curled up against her. They both gave him a squinty look.

'I was just going to get up,' Joanna said.

'No hurry.' He sat on the edge of the bed and leaned over the cat to kiss her. 'Supper's in the oven.'

'Your dad's a marvel. I thought I heard voices?'

'Yes, he was still here. I think he was waiting to have a stern word with me.'

'About?'

'You.'

'Oh. I'm all right. Just tired.'

He took hold of her hand. 'I was thinking – maybe two is enough.'

'I thought one was enough. This wasn't planned, if you remember.' She searched his face. 'But I'm happy about it now. Honestly. I really do want it.'

'I know. But no more after this?'

'That's what you said the last time,' she grinned. 'You don't know your own strength, Bill Slider.'

'Prize stud, that's me,' he said modestly. 'But I shall take responsibility after this, so don't you worry about it.'

'What's that supposed to mean? It sounds alarming.'

Before he could answer, a small figure appeared at the open bedroom door, a small plaintive voice said, 'Daddy?'

'You're supposed to be asleep,' Slider said, getting up.

'Can I have a drink of water?'

Joanna stirred. 'I'll get it.'

'No, I'll see to it,' said Slider. He scooped his son up onto his hip, managing to scrape the pyjama pants into place in the same movement. 'One drink of water coming up.'

'Can I have a biscuit, too?' asked George. 'And a story?'

'That's blatant opportunism. You should have been a cat,' said Slider.

'If you could be a animal, Daddy, what animal would you be? I'd be a tyrannosaurus rex.'

'Predictable choice. Why not a lion?'

'A tyrannosaurus could fight a lion. Daddy, if King Kong fought a tyrannosaurus, which one would win?'

Debating matters of cosmic import, Slider took his son back to bed.

By the time he got back downstairs, Joanna had got the table laid, and the potatoes Dad had left peeled, quartered and covered in water in the pot were boiling.

She directed him to the table. 'I had the dinosaurs earlier. Could an elephant fight an allosaurus? Could a golden eagle fight a pterodactyl? Could a hairy mammoth fight a crocodile? I'm in need of adult conversation. Sit down and tell me about your day. Unless there are prehistoric animals in it, I'll listen to anything.'

He sat, and she brought him a glass of St Joseph. 'I should be waiting on you,' he protested.

'It's easier to stand than sit, and easier walking about than standing. Your day, please. Begin at the beginning and go on till you come to the end, then stop.'

He was sharp enough after a day with Atherton to recognize a quotation. 'Sartre?'

'*Alice in Wonderland*. It's so easy to get those two mixed up.'

'Wasn't it Sartre who said, "I am what I am"?'

'No, that was Popeye the Sailor Man.'

Slider sighed happily. 'It's lovely talking nonsense with you. Atherton was quoting E.M. Forster today.'

'Then I gather you haven't solved the case yet.'

He told her about the day's events. 'Why did she ring Greyling?' he concluded. '*Why?* If it was to say she was on her way, why did she visit him? If she didn't visit him, where did she go?'

Joanna pondered as she strained the potatoes. 'Do you think he's another lover? She'd had one toy boy, why not two?' He shook his head – a 'don't know' shake, not a negative. 'It would make her a cold, predatory woman, wouldn't it?' He looked up. 'Oh, not the having two lovers,' she said impatiently. 'Anyone can have two lovers—'

'You'd better not.'

'—but going to see number two when she'd just killed number one.'

'That *would* be ruthless.'

She got in amongst the potatoes with the masher, pretty ruthless herself. 'But why did she kill number one?'

'Why is often the least of it,' Slider said, 'though of course the jury likes to have a good, solid motive.'

'And her alibi's no good?'

'It ought to be golden. It is a fact that she routinely works from nine to midnight and won't allow anyone to disturb her in that time. But of course, that makes the time slot the perfect choice for someone bent on slipping out for a spot of murdering. And despite his loyal support of her, her husband can't deny that he didn't actually see her during that time.'

'If he didn't know she was there, she didn't know he was there either.' She was serving now. Green beans and broccoli, a mound of mash and a lake of Dad's fragrant venison. 'I can smell the juniper berries,' Joanna said. 'I'm always impressed your dad uses exotic flavourings, herbs and so on. I'd love to know where he learned to cook. Though I suppose juniper with venison's fairly standard. Did he consult cookery books when you were young? After your mum died, I mean?'

She turned with a plate in each hand, and saw the congested

look on her husband's face. 'Either you're awaiting a bowel movement, or you've had an idea,' she suggested.

'I think you may have just said something important,' Slider said.

'Everything I say is important. And juniper berries grow wild on English trees, don't they, so they're not terribly exotic.'

'I wonder,' Slider said, but wouldn't go any further. And knowing that his mind worked best on the subconscious level, she placed the plates, sat down, and changed the subject.

EIGHTEEN

One Giant Creep for Mankind

He went into his office in the morning by way of the CID room, and stopped at McLaren's desk.

'Can you go back over the Mazda camera shots, and see if you can see who's actually driving it?'

McLaren looked up from his Breakfast Burrito – the McDonald's on the green had just started doing them, and McLaren had never met a chilli he didn't like – and gave Slider a look that blended hurt pride with compassion. 'I already did that, guv. I always check if you can see the driver, but you can't. Can't even see how many people's in the motor.'

LaSalle, lurking nearby, said, 'You think someone else was driving her car? But it was her mobile as well.'

Slider mentioned the important thing Joanna had said.

'They were in it together, Steenkamp and her old man?' said McLaren. 'The alibi works both ways, for both of them.'

'If they were in it together, surely they'd have said they actually *saw* each other during that time,' Hart said impatiently. 'The way it is, it's not an alibi for either of them.'

'We've never considered before that Seagram even needed an alibi,' said Swilley, looking keenly at Slider.

Slider, thinking, had been looking at nothing. It was Hart's eye he finally caught. 'We need to find a connection between Seagram and Greyling.'

'He could have met him during the filming at the shop,' she said.

'Could have's not enough,' he said. Then, restlessly: 'There's got to be *some* reason for that damn phone call.'

'It's a pity we can't look at *his* mobile log,' said Swilley.

'We'd have to have reasonable grounds,' he said.

'But, boss, anyway, why Seagram? We've got no reason to suspect him.'

'I don't know,' Slider admitted in frustration. 'We're getting nowhere with this case. And there he is, right in the middle. You could draw circles centred on his shop and cover all the other places.'

'*Steenkamp*'s in the middle,' Swilley corrected him in a motherly way, like Joanna telling George it wasn't *cargidan*, it was *car-di-gan*. 'She and Lingoss were lovers. Seagram only knew him by name. All the evidence is against her. We just need to find some connection between her and Greyling and we're home.'

Slider looked back stubbornly. 'I've got a feeling,' he said shortly. 'Humour me.'

She shrugged. 'Oh, well, if you've got a hunch . . . You should have said.'

Now they think I'm irrational, he thought, going back to his office. But he was the boss, so they could damn well do as he said.

And it was Swilley who came back to him first. Swilley was a good copper, and she trusted Slider. He'd never need to say 'I told you so' to Swilley. 'Boss, when we got Greyling's address from the mobile number, we didn't check it any further. And now you've seen the place he lives—'

'It's a lot too expensive for a resting actor,' Slider finished for her.

'That's what Jim said. Of course, he could be getting an allowance from his parents.'

'You checked with them?' He was surprised.

'No, boss. I could do. I'd have to find them first. I suppose that'd be easy enough, given his mum's an old friend of his agent's. She could give us the name and address. But what I *did* do was have a look at the property. Greyling's on the electoral register as the sole occupant—'

'Well, that's a relief,' said Slider. 'The last thing we need is for a spouse or housemate to clog up the works.'

'Right, boss. He's the sole occupant, but he doesn't own the place. Maybe he pays rent, we can't tell without looking at his bank records, but I looked it up on the land registry, and the owner is Brian Seagram.'

Slider almost put his hands over his face. 'Oh, thank God,' he said.

Swilley gave him a curious look. 'I don't know why you suspected him. But *there's* the connection between them, loud and clear.'

'When did he actually buy the property?' Slider asked.

'July last year. Sixteen months ago. And three weeks after the date of the TV filming at his shop – that could be significant. I don't know where Greyling lived before that – I've tried cross-checking his name with the land register, but as you'd expect he wasn't a property owner. If he was renting, it'll be hard to find out where – I'd have to try the electoral roll, or the last census. Anyway, you have to ask, why did Seagram want the house at all? If you buy a property as an investment, you either sell it again, or you rent it out. Even if he put Greyling in as a caretaker, to stop it being vandalized, there's still no return on his capital – if we're assuming Greyling couldn't pay a commercial rent.'

Slider nodded. 'Let's assume that. So you're thinking there was a more personal relationship?'

'Maybe Greyling was the son he never had.' It was plain she meant it ironically. 'On the other hand, Jim did say Greyling was as gay as a row of tents.'

'I wouldn't go as far as that. But even if it's true, it poses as many questions as it answers,' said Slider. For one thing, as he didn't need to say, there was no suggestion Seagram was gay.

'I know, boss. It gives us a connection between Seagram and Greyling, all right, but it's still a fact that Steenkamp had never rung Greyling before that night, and she said she didn't know him. If he was her husband's tenant or even caretaker, surely his name would have come up somewhere, some time? And if he'd kept him secret from her for some reason, why would she suddenly phone him?'

'All good questions,' said Slider.

'Of course, if Steenkamp and Seagram were in it together, and Greyling was just his tenant, she might know about him but never have had reason to ring him. Before that night. And then she'd deny she knew him because he was involved in the plot – somehow. But how?' Her tone betrayed her frustration with the half-ideas. 'If it weren't for that phone call, we'd never even be looking at Greyling, and he may be nothing to do with it anyway. I *hate* that phone call!'

'All we can do is keep pushing on, find things out, ask the questions. And keep in mind the end we're working towards, to find out who killed Lingoss.'

'I hate Lingoss, too,' Swilley said irritably. 'He was a slime-ball. Why have men always got to be so disgusting? Makes you wonder why you even bother.'

'Let's never forget he was the victim here. It's not just an intellectual puzzle.'

'Yes, boss.' It was dutiful rather than convinced.

'For now, try and find out where Greyling lived before Adam and Eve Mews. You might be able to find friends of his online and pick their brains. And – Atherton! In here.'

Atherton had been passing the door, and looked in enquiringly.

'The other thing that's been sticking in my mind is Seagram's car. Have a look into it. Why was it out of commission, just so conveniently at the time of the murder?'

'Conveniently? How was that convenient?'

Slider gave an impatient sigh. 'I'm feeling my way here. I don't know why I'm asking the questions I'm asking, you'll just have to go with me. Bentleys hardly ever go wrong, but here's this one out of order on Saturday, and still out of order on Tuesday. Where there's an anomaly, you have to look at it.'

Swilley said, 'Have you got an idea which way you're going with this, boss? I'm just asking.'

'I've got my eyes shut, flying blind, using the Force,' he said. 'Try to keep up.'

'There is no try, only do,' said Atherton.

'Go!' he told them. 'Find things out!'

If you were a very rich Londoner and wanted a very rich sort of car, you probably never thought further than P.F. Barclay, the old-established firm that had started with Rolls-Royces and Bentleys and gone on in modern times to Bugattis, Ferraris, Maseratis, and anything else that turned heads as it roared its way through London's more expensive boroughs. There was a prestigious show-room in Mayfair – where else? – but the headquarters were in South Kensington, just round the corner from the main service department.

When you deal with mega-rich people, discretion has to be a

prime characteristic, and the service manager, Poole, was reluctant to admit anything, even after Atherton had shown his brief. He barely even acknowledged there was any such person as Brian Seagram. Atherton had to quote address, telephone number, model and registration index and get just a little impatient before Poole would allow him to penetrate the workshop and speak to the mechanic.

The mechanic, Haslett, by contrast, was chatty and forthcoming, a youngish enthusiast with wiry fair hair, healthy outdoor complexion and frank blue eyes. In a previous age, Atherton could have imagined him as the cheery young groom who looked after his lordship's favourite hack. 'Oh, the Bentley,' he said. 'Yes, that was a bit of a mystery.' He was wearing blue overalls, but they were pristine, and he didn't even need to wipe his hands on a grubby rag before conducting Atherton into his glass cubby. Tightening things with a spanner and, as a last resort, giving them a clout with the heavy end, no longer featured much in car repairs.

'He rung me late on the Friday,' said Haslett. 'Said he got an intermittent fault, an error message on the display screen, and could he bring it in. Well, everything's supposed to go through Mr Poole, but he said he was sure it was nothing and he wanted the motor for something special on the Saturday, so I said pop it round and I'd have a look. Well, of course, once he'd got it here, the fault never showed up.'

'Isn't it always the way?' Atherton said sympathetically.

'Yeah, intermittent faults are a bugger. So I said what did he want to do, and he said, better check it in and get it seen to.'

'Was it something that could affect the performance of the car?'

'Not from what he said,' said Haslett. 'And she was running lovely when I tried her. But of course, it's all electronics these days, and to get her on the diagnostic computer I'd have to have her at least for the Saturday. And I said, as he'd got something special on, like he told me, would he prefer to keep her over the weekend and I'd have her picked up on Monday. He said, no, he'd leave her with me, I could get her booked in, and keep her for as long as it takes.'

'That's what he said?'

'As long as it takes.' Haslett nodded.

'So he thought it was going to be a long job?'

Haslett shrugged. 'Shouldn't have been. These Bentleys are lovely bits of kit, they never go wrong, an electrical glitch like that should've showed up on the computer right away. Anyway, I said I'd check her in for him, but he'd have to speak to Mr Poole about a replacement motor.' Haslett gave Atherton a look. 'And he says don't bother, he'll manage without.'

'But he'd said he had something special on.'

'Well, that's what I said. But he said it was only in London and he'd manage all right. I couldn't see him using public transport, but I suppose he could've got a taxi. Anyway, the long and the short of it is, he left his motor with us and he didn't want a replacement.'

'And did you find the fault?'

'No, I never did. I got her on the computer the Saturday and ran everything, but nothing showed up. And I took her out a couple of times and never saw this fault he'd mentioned. So Monday morning I rung him up and said there didn't seem to be anything wrong with her, and would he like her back. I said maybe it was just one of those gremlins and it'd never happen again. But he said no, I must keep it and find out what the fault was. And he still didn't want a replacement. Well, I run her through the computer again, and took her out I don't know how many times, but I couldn't find a thing wrong. I talked to Mr Poole about it, and he said to his mind Mr Seagram had imagined it, but we had to do what the customer wanted.'

'Yours not to reason why?' Atherton suggested in a friendly way.

Haslett warmed. 'Yes, sir, and to be fair, we charge them plenty for our time, so if that's what they want . . .' He shrugged. 'We're not losing by it. Though it's frustrating when you could be doing other things.'

'And you never saw this error message?'

'No, I didn't. Then, the Wednesday morning, Mr Seagram rings me and says how's the motor, and I say I can't find anything wrong with it, and he says in that case he might as well have it back. So I dropped it back to him that morning – or Phil did, my lad. And that was the end of that. He never come back to say the fault had showed up again, so it must've cleared itself, or maybe Mr Poole was right, and he'd imagined it.' He gave a straight look that said rich people were different from normal folk, but there was no real harm in them. You just had to get on with it.

'It's quite a new car, isn't it?' Atherton asked.

'Yes, it's the 2018 Flying Spur, the all-new model they unveiled at the motor show last year. Mr Seagram saw it there and fancied it, put his order in right away, and we got it for him the beginning of June. He had a Continental before that – we did a part exchange. He likes Bentleys – says they're comfortable.' He smiled. 'His wife's got a little Mazda, and he says he can't stand it, nearly cripples him any time he has to get in it. Course, he's not a Mazda sort of person, Mr Seagram. Bentley's much more his style.'

'And if you remember,' Atherton said, perched on Slider's windowsill, 'the motor show in May last year was where Greyling was working as a demonstrator when he got busted for snorting charlie. So we know he was there, and now we know Seagram was there, so although it's not proof, they could have met there. And he bought the mews house two months later.'

'Reasons why Greyling recommended the antique shop for the TV episode,' said Swilley, leaning on the door jamb. 'Not just because he'd seen it opposite when he came out of the gym, but to do a favour for his . . . what? Friend?'

'Benefactor. Patron,' Slider suggested.

'Sugar daddy,' Atherton countered. He intercepted their looks. 'What? You think that house is the sort of gift you give a random chap who's a decent sort and happens to need a place to sleep?'

'He didn't *give* it to him,' Swilley said fairly.

Slider said, 'There's another thing to ponder – how does Seagram afford new model Bentleys and mews houses in Kensington? Does the antique business bring that much in? Or is he independently wealthy? Norma, you're our financial guru. Can you find out?'

'I can certainly look at the business accounts,' she said, and heaved herself upright. 'He bought her diamond earrings for their anniversary, too,' she remembered.

'She's rich enough to buy her own diamonds,' Atherton said. 'Must be. He doesn't actually need a flourishing antiques business – he could live off her.'

'I hope he's rich in his own right,' Swilley said. 'It'd be a bummer if he bought her earrings with her own money.' She left.

Atherton got up too. 'Norma says you didn't pick up on Greyling being gay.'

'I saw what you saw, but I think you should be cautious about jumping to conclusions. Many actors are camp, without being gay.'

'True, oh king, but one's gaydar is calibrated to allow for that.'

Slider stared at the wall. 'I wonder . . .'

'What?' Atherton asked. But Slider didn't answer, so he left him alone.

Slider went alone to Gillespie's, driving slowly, grinding his thoughts. Deedee Donnelly, the manager, greeted him kindly, and sent him to the GLicious cafeteria, saying she'd find Ivanka and send her up to him.

He went past the gym with its brain-bleed music, felt the thump coming up through his soles, looked in at the people running on treadmills, their faces blankly serene, and had a sudden strange urge to be one of them. It seemed a blessed thing to pound away, the mind empty, remote, untouchable. To run and run, your feet flashing away down there in a relentless rhythm, your heart thumping steadily in your chest, your lungs sucking air in and out, the hypnotism of the ever-reeling road taking you far, far away from your worries and responsibilities and fears and failures.

Except that if you looked down, you would see those worries and responsibilities and fears and failures racing alongside, keeping pace effortlessly; like a pack of zombie dogs, tongues lolling, eyes bright with the knowledge that you would eventually tire and slow, but they never would; that when you finally stopped . . .

He shook himself and went up to the cafeteria. Shortly afterwards, Ivanka came in, in a pale lilac leotard and leggings, a towel round her neck, her horsetail of pale bright hair swinging as she moved, her skin sleek and shiny with decent honest exercise. She sat down opposite him and looked at him expectantly; and did not speak when he failed to say anything. It was a rare person who could walk into a silence and leave it intact.

At last he said, 'I need to know something about Erik. You were his best friend, I think. He probably told you things he wouldn't tell other people.'

Her lovely eyes did not waver. 'Maybe,' she admitted, waiting for the question.

'Among his private clients, the ones he did extra services for, was there a special one?'

'How you mean, special?' The eyes were watchful.

He shook his head, feeling for the words. 'You said it was all about the money – he wanted lots of money for when he couldn't do the work any more.'

'Money, yes,' she agreed. 'Rich clients. But he enjoyed his work, too.' She was helping him.

'Perhaps sometimes it was more than just enjoyment? Did he ever speak to you of being *emotionally* involved with a client?'

She tilted her head very slightly. 'That what you mean by "special"? You mean – *lo-o-ove*.' She elongated the word mockingly. He nodded. 'Those like Erik and me, we cannot afford *lo-o-ove*. We are workers. Clients don't see us as people. We give service, they pay, we say bye-bye.' She waved her fingers as one does to a baby.

'But sometimes,' Slider prompted.

'Sometimes?' And she sighed. 'When you get very close, one body to another, touching, looking, week after week – it can seem like love. Then there can be trouble. They want more than you can give. Then they get angry. You pretend for a bit, because they pay, but that makes it worse when they find out.'

'Did Erik tell you about some trouble of that sort that he'd had?'

'Never tell me. But I think – maybe. Last time I see him before – you know.'

'Three weeks before his death.'

She nodded. 'We meet, have a drink, go back to his flat. He very quiet – not talk much. I think he has something on mind.'

'Was he unhappy? Worried? Afraid?'

'Not *sad* quiet. *Thinking* quiet. When we have sex, he not watching in mirror like usual. He smiling. But not at me.'

'His mind was elsewhere?'

'Elsewhere.' She seemed to savour the word. 'He thinking about sex, but not sex with Ivanka. So I wonder to myself, Erik, you big fool, you falling for someone? Is dangerous. Those like you and me, we can't afford to fall in love.'

'You wondered – but did you ask him?'

She shrugged. 'Not my business.'

'Did he mention a name – speak about anyone in particular?'
Shake of the head. 'Have you *any* idea who it might have been?'

'Maybe nobody. Maybe nothing. Maybe I big idiot – imagine
things.'

'But you don't think you imagined it.'

She shrugged again. 'Who can say. But if there was someone,
it was rich person. You can believe that. Erik would never fall
where there was no money. Maybe big fool – not big idiot.' She
made a getting-up, this-is-over sort of movement.

He held up a hand to stop her. 'Did Erik ever mention someone
called Leon Greyling?'

She thought a moment, then said certainly, 'No.'

'One more question – was he bisexual?'

'No,' she said without hesitation.

'So he never had sex with a male client?'

She made an impatient sound. 'Erik not *gay*. But he do what
client wants, for good money.'

'So, let me get this clear – if a male client wanted to have sex
with Erik, he would go along with it?'

'Not have sex. But do many things. Like we say at home, ox
or donkey, pulls the cart the same. Do you know who killed
Erik?'

The sudden question took him by surprise, but he answered
evenly. 'Not yet. But I'm getting closer.'

And she nodded and said, 'British Bulldog.' He couldn't tell if
she meant it approvingly or scathingly.

When he got back to the station, McLaren was waiting for him
with an air of suppressed excitement.

'You've found who was driving the car?' Slider guessed. 'A
different camera you hadn't looked at before?'

'No, guv, I told you, I'd already looked for that. I always do
– it's SOP.'

'Then . . .?'

'You know cash machines mostly have cameras in them?'

'Mostly? I thought they all did.'

'The bank ones do. Some of the independent ones don't. The
cash drawn out of Steenkamp's account came from an
independent.'

'Are you doing this deliberately? Winding me up then letting me down?'

McLaren looked frustrated. 'I'm trying to tell you, guv. It was the first machine in the High Street after turning out of Campden Hill Road, and it's in the wall between the travel shop and the Tesco Metro. It doesn't have a camera in the machine, but it's covered by a camera mounted above it. I looked at it before, for the Mazda, but the angle's not wide enough to cover the road, so I put it aside. But I've just had another look at it.'

'And?'

'I've matched the camera time to the time of the withdrawal that we got from Steenkamp's bank statement. It's Seagram that draws the money out. He's wearing a hat, but you can see his profile as he turns away, and it's definitely him. He used her card to draw the money out. This is the best print-out I could get.'

He handed Slider a print – a little grainy, but, yes, you could see that it was definitely Brian Seagram.

'Oh glory be!' said Slider.

NINETEEN
Artist's Impression

Greyling opened the door to them looking much less composed. He had been fashionably rumpled before, but now the informality was more dishevelled than cute. His face tautened at the sight of them. He had been doing some thinking since their last visit, Slider concluded.

'Oh,' said Greyling flatly. 'You again.'

'I didn't ask you the right questions last time,' Slider said. 'I asked you about Gilda Steenkamp. I should have asked you about Brian Seagram. I know you wanted to tell the truth . . .'

'I did tell the truth,' he said indignantly.

'But not all the truth.'

Greyling thought for a beat, and then said, a touch wearily, 'You'd better come in.'

This time he led them up the open staircase, towards the shrill, monotonous barking that was coming from above.

'That's Floss,' he said over his shoulder. 'Her name's Florence – you know, *The Magic Roundabout*? – but when she's naughty I call her Flossie.'

'Retro chic,' Slider heard Atherton murmur from behind him.

Florence turned out to be a miniature poodle, waiting at the top of the stairs in the perfect position from which to launch herself at the face of someone coming up. Fortunately Greyling was in the lead; he got the dog in the chest and saved his visitors inconvenient punctures. Cradled in his arms as he turned at the top, the dog relinquished barking in favour of a slow warning snarl. 'Shut up, Floss! She's such a naughty girl!' Greyling said. 'Don't you love dogs? Poodles especially. They're so clever. She has me wound round her little claw.'

Slider, who did love dogs, gained the level floor, stood up straight, and gave the dog a look in which manliness mingled with understanding. Greyling had had the beast dyed pale blue, and he thought there was a touch of shame-facedness in its defiance. Florence stopped snarling to smell him, and gave an ingratiating wiggle of her rear end.

'She likes you!' Greyling said. 'Do you like the colour? It's called Innocent Blue. I'm going to try Pattypaws Pink next time. She *is* a girl, after all. You can get lots of lovely colours. It's all organic, perfectly safe for doggies. It washes out over ten washes. But you have to be careful of their precious eyes.'

Atherton had now left the staircase, and Greyling put the dog down and led the way further in. Flossie shook herself vigorously, sniffed Slider's shoe with a connoisseur's air, and trotted after him, ignoring Atherton – which suited Atherton just fine. In his book, there were dogs and dogs.

The whole first floor was an open-plan living area, with polished wood floors, off-white walls and downlighting. There were abstract paintings on the walls, and modern art pieces scattered around – giant ceramics, stone and glass sculptures, an enormous beaten copper salver, a vast piece of what looked like driftwood mounted on a block, and among them one or two rather lovely bronzes. There was a huge and squashy sofa upholstered in black, purple and blue Paisley-pattern, into a corner of which Greyling curled himself. The dog followed him, climbed onto his stomach and settled down, and Greyling waved Slider and Atherton to two matching huge and squashy armchairs.

The chatter, the informal pose, the studied air of insouciance, were blinds, Slider understood, meant to convince them of his innocence. Or perhaps Greyling himself needed convincing. His mouth was nervous, and his eyes moved unsteadily from one intruder to the other. He crammed a finger into his mouth and gnawed at the nail, then remembered and pulled it away. Slider left him a challenging silence, into which Greyling finally launched himself with an unconvincing laugh. 'Am I supposed to offer you refreshments? I don't know what the protocol is with the boys in blue.'

'This is not your first dealing with the police,' Slider reminded him. 'You've been arrested twice.'

Greyling looked suddenly drawn and frightened. 'But I haven't *done* anything this time! I *really* haven't! You're not going to arrest me?' He gripped the dog inadvertently tightly and it let out a yip.

'I don't *want* to arrest you,' Slider said. 'If you co-operate fully, answer my questions—'

'Oh, I will, I will!'

'Then begin by telling me what your relationship with Brian Seagram is.'

'He's a lovely man. Ever so kind,' said Greyling nervously, as if he didn't quite know what question he was answering.

Slider realized he would have to be more specific. And as there was a shine of sweat under Greyling's eyes, he might need to be soothed and led up to the difficult bit by easy stages.

'When did you first meet him?' he asked.

'About eighteen months ago, it was.' He seemed relieved by the question, and grew expansive. 'At the motor show – I was doing demo jobs while I was resting between parts. It's pretty dire, but it pays the bills. He was there looking for a new car – he loves his wheels! Well, we got talking, and he asked me out to dinner – said I looked half-starved, which I took as a compliment, I can tell you! – but as it happened I wasn't able to make it.'

'You were arrested for tooting up in the gents,' Atherton supplied.

Greyling gave him a hurt look, and continued to narrate to Slider. 'But I bumped into him again on the last day – I'd left a sweater in the office and I went back to try and get it – and he took me out for lunch. Well, we got talking again – he was ever so easy to talk to – and it went on from there. We've been friends ever since.'

'Very special friends,' Atherton suggested, 'for him to buy you a house.'

'He didn't buy it for me, he bought it for himself,' Greyling said indignantly. 'I just live here.'

'I bet you don't pay any rent.'

'I look after his things.' He waved a hand around the room. 'The paintings, the artworks. There's a lot of valuable pieces here.'

'But why would he need to buy a house for them, when he's got a large flat already?' said Slider.

'Because his home's full of antiques. And it's not really his – it's his wife's. Well, it's in both their names, but she calls the shots. And Brian *hates* antiques – all that awful brown furniture and dingy old oil paintings! He likes clean, modern lines and

vibrant contemporary art. Colour! Movement!' He waved his arms
again, and the dog, which had been dozing off, jerked its head up
and gave him a warning look.

'You say he hates antiques—' Slider began, and Greyling interrupted eagerly.

'I know what you're going to say – why is he in the antiques
business? But he inherited it from his father, you see, and it's all
he knows. He makes his living from it, but it doesn't mean he has
to like it. I *totally* understand. You don't choose your parents, so
why should you be expected to like the same things they do? My
father's a solicitor, he wanted me to go into the law like him. I
said I'd sooner stick pins in my eyes.' He gave an artificial shudder.

'It can't have gone down well with him when you got busted
for drugs,' Atherton suggested.

He looked sulky. 'You keep bringing that up! I was just unlucky.
Everybody in our business does blow, to keep their weight down.
And to keep going on long shoots. It's a stressful job. Hours and
hours on your feet, and you have to stay sharp.'

'But it would reflect badly on your father's business to have a
son—'

'Yes, all right, he cut me off!' Greyling snapped. 'That's why I
was living in a grotty bedsit in Ladbroke Grove. That's why Brian
moved me into this house – well, you couldn't expect him to visit
me there. It wasn't a nice area.'

They had come to the point. Slider decided the question must
be asked. 'Are you lovers?'

Surprisingly, Greyling blushed. 'Of course, you *would* jump to
that conclusion! But it's nothing like that.'

'It must be *something* like that,' Atherton said mildly. 'He buys
you a house in a very ritzy area. He gives you money. He must
be getting *something* in return.'

'I told you, I look after his collection. He gives me house-
keeping money, and a bit of walking-about money, that's all. So
I can stay here and take care of things. You talk as if I was some
kind of—'

'There's no judgement here,' Slider intervened soothingly. 'I
just want to understand what your relationship is. And I would
advise you to be completely honest with me. You've already
impeded my investigation on a previous occasion. The last thing

you want is to face jail time. Now, there must be something more
between you and Brian Seagram than just friendship. There must
be something physical.'

The blush intensified, and he looked away. 'Look, it's not what
you think. I'm not gay. All right, I camp it up a bit, but that's just
an act. I started doing it to annoy my father at first, and it sort of
got to be a habit. And it's kind of funny, you know, the Palare. A
lot of people in the business talk like that.' He seemed to sit up
a bit straighter, and his manner became noticeably less camp from
then on. 'I was desperate when Brian offered me a place to live,
and I did think I might have to . . . you know, do something. Older
guys – sometimes they want spanking or wanking or something
. . . But it wasn't that. He likes to look at me. Nude.'

The last word seemed forced out of him. It hit the air and
hovered there like a fart in a teashop. In the silence that followed,
Slider could hear the dog snore – teeny *Magic Roundabout* whis-
tles. A car went past outside, mumbling on the cobbles. Greyling
found a new courage and now met Slider's eyes. 'He pretended
at first that he wanted to sketch me – you know, for me to be his
artist's model, sort of thing – but he's a crap drawer.' A short,
faint smile. 'I could draw better than him, and I'd make a mess
of paint-by-numbers. But he was embarrassed at first about asking
me to strip off. It was a long time before he stopped pretending
to draw me. It's . . . if you want to know, it is a *bit* weird. He
gets me to take up different poses and he stares at me, sometimes
he walks round to get different angles. But in the end, it's not
hurting me, is it? And he's a decent sort of bloke, he's very kind.
He bought me Florence for my Christmas present. He knew I'd
always wanted a dog – my father would never let me have one,
he hates dogs. OK, so he's got a weird sort of fetish, if that's what
it is, but there's a lot worse out there, and he's not doing anyone
any harm, is he?'

'Is there any touching involved?' Slider asked, because he could
hear Atherton's disbelief coming out of his pores.

'A bit, sometimes. But not . . . you know, sex stuff. He'll stroke
my arm, or my back, rearrange me, turn my head a different way.
It's the *look* of my body he likes, the lines, the way the muscles
move. It's an artistic thing, not a sex thing,' he concluded earnestly.
'He says the only part of the antiques business he likes is the

Greek statues, because the Greeks understood the beauty of the male form. He says the male body is the pinnacle of creation.'

'And he's never asked you to touch him?'

Now Greyling scowled. 'No! Can't you get your minds out of the gutter, try to have a *bit* of imagination? I know you're policemen but not everything in life's grubby and nasty. Brian thinks I'm beautiful and he loves beautiful things. It's not even every time that I have to strip. Sometimes he just comes round to sit and look at his pictures and things. He'll take up a bronze, for instance, and turn it over and over in his hands for ages, appreciating it.'

'How often does he come round?'

'Well, it used to be three or four times a week. In the early days, he'd even take me on buying trips with him. But lately – for the last few months – it's been more like once a week, even once a fortnight.' He shrugged. 'And when he does come round, often we just have a drink and watch a film together. He loves all those old black and white ones. He says they're true art, not like modern films. He's—'

'Yes?'

'I hope he's not cooling off me,' he admitted anxiously. 'He's been a bit distant the last few months. Maybe he's taken up with someone else. I don't know what I'd do if he asked me to go.'

'Tell me about the phone call you got on Tuesday the fourth.'

The question threw him. His eyes widened and breathing quickened. 'I didn't do anything, I swear! I didn't *know* anything. About anything.'

'The phone call,' Slider insisted.

'It was from a number I didn't know. My phone didn't recognize it. I was surprised when I answered and it was Brian. He said are you alone, and I said yes, and he said he was on his way, he'd be there in two minutes. Then he rang off.'

'Was he in the habit of dropping in on you like that?'

'No, never. He isn't a dropping-in sort of person. He always makes a date in advance. So naturally I was surprised – and a bit worried.'

'How did he seem when he arrived?'

'Well, all right, I suppose,' Greyling said warily. 'A bit . . . *tense*, maybe.'

'Tense how? Nervous? Afraid? Worried?'

'No, more . . . I don't know. Excited, I'd say. Wound up – but in a pleased way. Well, he was pleased, anyway, when he talked about the divorce.'

'Divorce?' Atherton said, with interest. This was a new line.

Greyling looked at him warily. He didn't like Atherton. 'He wanted a divorce from his wife because he said their marriage was long dead, but she wouldn't agree to one. She said it would be bad publicity for her. She said they each went their own way as it was, so why would they need one. But he wanted to be free.'

'Divorce is automatic after five years of separation,' Atherton said. 'If he left her she couldn't stop it.'

He squirmed a little. 'But then he wouldn't get any money from her. He said she could afford the best solicitors and she'd cut him off.' He seemed aware this placed his benefactor in a less than flattering light. 'When a person gets used to a certain standard of living . . .' he began weakly.

'Quite,' Slider said, not wanting to alienate him – or not yet. 'So why was he happy about the divorce that evening. Had something changed?'

'He said, "I've got her now. I'll give her bad publicity!"'

'What did he mean by that?'

'I don't know,' Greyling said, giving him an appealing look. 'He didn't tell me, and I didn't ask. I didn't want to get mixed up in anything like that, because, to be honest, he sounded a bit nutty when he said it – you know, over-excited. I made him a drink, I thought it'd calm him down. Then he asked me to take care of something for him. Said it was very important. And he gave me a mobile phone.'

Slider sighed with relief, but nothing showed on the outside.

'I thought it was his at first, because his was a Galaxy as well. He gave it to me and said, "Keep this safe, it's my insurance."'

'What did he mean by that?'

'I don't like to say.'

'Come on, you've told us the worst already – how bad can it be?'

'All right, he said the police were stupid, but even they ought to be able to follow a trail of breadcrumbs. But if they were so dim they somehow missed it, the phone might have to be found. "By accident," he said. "Or by an anonymous well-wisher."' He looked from one to the other, nervously. 'I didn't like it when he mentioned the police. I said, "What have you done?" and he said there was nothing to worry about. He said, "You won't be involved, I promise you. Just look after the phone until I ask for it, and don't talk about it to anyone." And that's all I did! It really and truly is! I didn't know anything about anything. But when you turned up, asking about Erik Lingoss – I'd seen on the internet that he'd been murdered but *of course* I didn't make any connection, not until you came asking me about him. And then . . . well, I didn't know what to do.' He looked an appeal at them. 'I mean, I hardly knew him really, Erik.'

'How well does Brian know him?' Slider asked.

'Not at all, or I didn't think so. I introduced him back in June when we did the filming at Brian's shop?'

'For *Lockhart*. Yes, we know about that.'

'Well, while we were hanging around outside – there's always a lot of hanging around when you're filming – Erik came over from the gym across the road, to see what was going on, I suppose, and remembered me from before, and we got chatting. And I suddenly thought – Erik's a super masseur, he fixed Marjie's neck, and Brian complains about his back a lot, why not do everyone a favour? So I took Erik round the back and introduced him to Brian. I haven't seen Erik since, and Brian's never mentioned him, so I thought nothing had come of it, and I never thought about it again until you came knocking on the door. But I still didn't . . . I mean it *can't* be anything to do with Brian, can it? He wouldn't . . . he would never—'

'Did you not know,' Slider said, 'that Erik Lingoss was Brian's wife's personal trainer?'

His mouth dropped. 'No. I had no idea. Brian never said anything. But – what does that mean?'

Slider didn't answer that. 'When Brian gave you the phone, it was still switched on, wasn't it?'

'I don't know,' he said. And then: 'Oh, well, yes, I remember now, he switched it off before he handed it to me. He told me to put it away safely and not tell anyone about it, because it was his insurance. So, are you saying it's Erik's phone? Are you saying . . .' He swallowed, his Adam's apple bobbing visibly in his neck. 'You're not saying he killed him, are you?'

Slider didn't answer that, either. 'Have you spoken to Brian since, or seen him?'

'No,' he said eagerly. 'Because after you came round asking about the visit last Tuesday, I was worried and I wondered what was going on, so I tried to ring him, but he was never there and even though I left messages, he never rang back.' He looked at his hands. 'I haven't got his mobile number, you see. He rings me from the shop, and though he's said I can ring him there in an emergency, he doesn't really like me to, in case his girl picks up.'

'He's keeping you a secret?'

'I suppose – he doesn't want people to know about the nude modelling thing. In case they get the wrong idea.'

As they certainly would, Slider thought.

Greyling must have read it in his face, because he said resentfully, 'Well, that's the conclusion *you* jumped to. And what gets me is that here I am being interviewed by the police, and I haven't *done* anything. He promised I wouldn't be involved. I didn't ask him to bring the phone to me. I wish I'd got rid of the bloody thing now.'

'You didn't, though,' Slider said, almost holding his breath.

'No. I suppose you want it? It's in the drawer in the bedroom.' He gestured with his head to the second staircase in the corner, leading up to the next floor. 'D'you want me to . . .?'

'No,' said Slider, and nodded to Atherton to go.

'The top left-hand drawer of the chest,' Greyling said. 'It's wrapped in a handkerchief.'

Atherton departed. The dog woke with the movement. Its eyes tracked him, and it gave a low, muttering growl. Greyling stroked it absently. He was looking at Slider in a troubled way.

'If you tell Brian I told . . .' he began.

Slider gave him a kindly look. 'It's a great deal more serious than that. I'm sure you must realize that by now.'

'But surely you're not saying Brian killed Erik? That's crazy! He barely knew him. Why would he do that? *Why?*' He didn't wait for an answer. 'I had nothing to do with it, you do believe me?'

'All you can do is tell the truth,' Slider said. 'That's your best defence. I understand your loyalty to Mr Seagram but I'm afraid it would not be in your best interests any more.'

He looked miserable. 'I'll get turfed out of this place, I suppose. I'll have nowhere to live and no money.'

'You might have to make peace with your parents,' Slider suggested.

'Mummy would have me back, I suppose, but my father? After this?'

Atherton came back down the stairs, and the dog's muttering growl went up a notch.

'Shush, Flossie. Quiet. It's nothing.'

Atherton held up an evidence bag, in which the phone was snuggling with a white cotton hanky. 'Is this your handkerchief?' he asked.

'No. I don't use them. Mummy says it's a disgusting habit, blowing your nose on fine cotton then wrapping it up and carrying it around as if it's something precious. I always use tissues.'

'So whose handkerchief is it?'

'Brian's, of course. He left it behind, so I put it with the phone so I'd remember to give him both when he came.'

'Sensible,' Slider said. 'You said Mr Seagram was excited when he arrived. Did you notice anything unusual about his appearance? His clothing?'

'I don't think so,' said Greyling, seeming genuinely puzzled.

'I imagine he was always quite properly dressed, quite formal and smart?'

'Yes, always a suit and tie. I used to tease him about it – told him he should loosen up, said I'd like to see what he looked like in jeans. He was horrified.' There was a smile, a bit tremulous, but the relief of having confessed was working on him.

'So, was he at all rumpled or untidy that evening?' Slider didn't want to lead him, but he was hoping for blood. 'Any marks or bruises that you noticed?'

The eyebrows went up. 'You mean – he'd been in a *fight*? No, he looked just the same as usual.' He stopped abruptly, and closed his lips tight.

'You've remembered something. Come on, you know you have to tell me. Tell the truth – remember?'

'The truth shall set you free,' he murmured in a distant voice. 'That was the school motto, at the school I went to.'

'What did you notice that evening, that you've just remembered?' Slider said implacably.

'I made him a drink, a whisky and soda – I hate whisky, I only keep it for him. He was sitting in that chair.' He nodded towards Slider. 'When I bent over to put the drink on the table beside him, I noticed there was something on his face. I said, "There's blood or something on your cheek," and he pulled his handkerchief out of his breast pocket and wiped it. He was talking all the time and I don't think he was even aware he'd done it.'

'He wiped it off on his handkerchief?' Slider asked. Greyling nodded. He had the big eyes of the victim now. 'The same one – this one?'

'I don't know. Maybe he had more than one,' he said pathetically. 'You see, when he'd wiped his face, he sort of crumpled it up and stuffed it into his jacket pocket, the side one, but he must have missed, or not pushed it in far enough and it fell out, because after he'd gone, I found it down the side of the chair. So I put it in with the phone.'

Slider stood up. 'I'd like you to come back to the station with us now and make a full statement, of everything you've just told me.'

'Am I under arrest?' he asked in a small voice. He looked very young and frightened now.

'No, you're just helping with our enquiries. And we will have to get a forensic team to go over the house.' If there had been blood on Seagram's cheek, there might have been blood on his hands or his clothes, which could have been transferred onto furniture or fittings.

'It's not my house,' Greyling said pathetically. 'You'd have to ask Brian's permission.'

'I don't think we'll be doing that,' said Slider.

Sometimes, when Porson *really* listened, he stopped pacing and stood still.

Atherton was downstairs, supervising the taking of the statement – a long process. Slider told his boss the story alone.

He stirred when Slider got to the naked staring part, but said it was weird enough to be true.

'That's what I thought, sir,' Slider said. 'It's not the sort of thing someone would make up.'

'Obviously Greyling wants to make himself out a parable of virtue. But he's already taking the money, so copping to a bit of slap and tickle wouldn't make much difference. It's probably true.'

'But if Seagram wasn't doing Greyling and he and his wife were off hooks, he must have been getting his jollies somewhere else,' Slider said.

'Some people can live without jollies,' Porson said. 'Some people have to.'

Slider continued and Porson went still again, until he got to the bit about the blood.

'And?' he barked.

'There does appear to be a smear that could be blood on the handkerchief. We've sent it to be analysed. Greyling thinks he wasn't aware he'd done it.'

'Nobody can remember everything,' Porson said approvingly. It was the crack through which they wriggled after criminals every day. 'So, why was the phone his insurance? What's on it? I suppose it *is* Lingoss's?'

'Yes, sir. We checked that before we gave it to forensics to be dusted. We should be getting it back any minute.'

'Let me know as soon as you get it,' Porson said. He met Slider's eyes. 'What? You think I'd miss the big reveal? We don't get a lot of excitement in this job.'

Slider smiled. 'And there I was, thinking it was wrong of me to be excited over something like this.'

'You're only human,' Porson said. 'We're all tarred with the same brooch.'

TWENTY
Cynical Studies

S willey was waiting for him when he got back to his own room.

'Heneage and Seagram, boss?'

'You've had a look at the accounts?'

'There's a lot more detail I can go into if you need it, but a basic overview says it's no more than breaking even. And I had a word with Crafty Harris.'

Colin Harris was a former fence of stolen antiques, now turned legitimate and an outlier for SCD6, the Art and Antiques Crime unit. He got his nickname from his haunting of craft fairs in his previous life.

'He says the antiques business is going through a rough patch. Houses and flats are smaller, and everyone wants open-plan spaces and light modern furniture. There's still money to be made at the top end, for people who've made it big and bought a country mansion, but even then, if they're not brought up to it, they're often just as happy with repro. And the top end of the genuine antiques market is crowded with experts all trying to make a living.'

'I see. So when you say "just breaking even", is Seagram drawing any money from it?'

'Hard to say, boss. There is an item for wages on the balance sheet of forty thousand pounds. He can't be paying Lucy Gallo that much – I doubt she gets more than eighteen, tops – but we don't know if he has any other employees. If not, the rest is probably a salary he pays himself.'

'So at best he's getting around twenty thousand a year? That's not enough for his lifestyle.'

'Right boss. Cue large cash injection from mega-rich wifey.'

'We don't know that,' Slider said.

'Well, somewhere, anyway. The phone's on its way back. Fingermarks from at least two, possibly three people, all overlaying each other. They're trying to separate them but they don't think they'll get more than a partial, if that. Are we arresting Seagram? The report on the handkerchief's not back yet.'

'Mr Porson says that with or without the blood, we've got enough to bring him in, assuming Greyling's story holds up. But I would like to wait and see what's on the phone before I talk to him.'

'If Greyling was going to lie,' said Swilley, 'surely he'd lie the other way, to protect Seagram. I mean, why would he lie to drop him in it?'

'I agree. I think he's only coughed now to save his own hide – he was plainly rattled when we turned up again. But of course there's always the possibility that Seagram was lying to *him*.'

Swilley looked puzzled. 'But about what, boss? The phone *is* Lingoss's. He couldn't have got hold of it any other way, surely? He must have killed him.' She thought. 'Unless he and Steenkamp are in it together? Or she killed Lingoss and he's protecting her? But' – she shook her head – 'it would be a funny way to protect her. And then there's all that about a divorce. I can't see why he'd want to divorce her when she's the paymaster. Unless he was only talking about divorce to impress Greyling – maybe Greyling had been making a play for him, trying to pressure him into marriage.'

'But Greyling says he isn't gay.'

Swilley gave him a sceptical look. 'He *says* he isn't. Do you buy all that celibate gazing malarky?'

'Don't you?'

'I say, if you don't want the watch, don't breathe on the works.'

'BILL! My old firecracker! How goes it? Has the lovely Mrs Bill sprogged down yet? I'm guessing not, or you'd have phoned your faithful friend with the news as a matter of priority?'

Slider, who had winced and recoiled at the first explosion, cautiously approached his face to the phone again. Tufnell Arceneaux, the forensic haematologist – the bodily fluids man, as he generally characterized himself – was large of life, larger of appetites, and largest still of voice.

'Nothing doing yet, Tufty,' he reported. 'It's supposed to be another two weeks.'

'Tell that to the babeling, old banana! They've got no sense of timing. Or rather, they have, but in a totally perverse manner. Just wait till you're doing something vital that you absolutely can't leave, and *that's* the moment it'll choose to poke its little head out. Take Uncle Tufty's word for it. I've forgotten – is it a girl or a boy?'

'We decided not to ask.'

'My God! Your self-control fills me with awe. And astonishment. *Why?* Never put off till tomorrow a pleasure you could have today, that's my motto.'

'I was taught as a child to save my pudding until last.'

'Crackers! Eat it first, while you've got room. Before the fire alarm goes off. Or war is declared. Well, let me be the first to hear the good news, won't you? You owe me that, as your oldest friend. And, by the way, there was a trace of blood and what appears to be brain matter on the handkerchief.'

'I thought this was purely a social call?'

'You should thank God you have me, because anyone less devoted to you would have gone home and given you the good news tomorrow.'

'I am in awe of your devotion to duty. It's definitely blood?'

'You can take that to the bank. Human blood. It's amazing what we can do with a smear these days. Back in the old days, we needed an eggcupful to be sure.'

'Who keeps blood in eggcups?'

'Deeply weird people, don't ask.'

'Now we just need to know that it's the victim's.'

'Ah, that will take a bit longer. We have deceased's DNA profile on record, of course, so as soon as the sequencing's done I'll let you know if it's a match.'

'I hope it is. Chummy' – there was something oddly satisfying in describing the terribly posh Mr Seagram as 'chummy' – 'wiped it off his face.'

'Filthy beast! Well, then, I shall trawl for the inevitable skin cell he will have wiped off his phizzog at the same time. Just one cell will do it – I'm that good!'

'As soon as I arrest him I'll get a buccal swab over to you for comparison.'

'Good man! We'll get him – if he's the one. Love to Joanna. Toodle-oo!'

*   *   *

Atherton came up, looking weary. 'Got it,' he said. 'God, I hate taking statements. If the ability to speak is a God-given gift, why are most people so inarticulate?'

'Has he changed anything?'

'No, it's come out the same. You obviously impressed him with that "truth shall set you free" speech. He's clinging to it like a drowning man to a glass of water.'

'Steady lad. You *are* tired. Go and get a cup of coffee. Tufty Arceneaux says there was blood on the handkerchief. And as soon as we've had a look at the phone, we'll go and reel Seagram in.'

Everyone gathered for the unveiling of the mobile. Slider felt like making a speech. Atherton steepled his fingers and twiddled them in mock excitement. 'Hurry up, I can't wait! What can it be that was Seagram's insurance?'

'We know from the phone log that there was a call from Steenkamp to Lingoss at half past nine,' said LaSalle.

'Accuracy, please,' said Atherton. 'From Steenkamp's phone.'

'All right, but if he's that clever he'd know we could find that out from the log, we wouldn't need the phone for it. It can't be that.'

'We don't know what he knew, or how clever he is,' Swilley said. 'We don't even know it was him that made the call on her phone.'

'It was him that drew out the cash,' LaSalle said. 'If he had her card, he had her phone as well.'

'She could have been in the car with him,' said Swilley. 'It could have been a joint enterprise.'

'But *why?*' said Hart in frustration. 'Why does either of them want to kill Lingoss?'

'Perhaps we shall find out,' Slider said mildly, waiting for the phone to boot up.

'Blimey, this show's a bit lacking in oomph, isn't it?' came Porson's voice from the back. 'Glad I didn't put my dickey on. Stop all the bunny and get on with it!'

'Sorry, sir.'

As many heads as possible were crammed into the space around Slider's, till he felt he might pass out from a lack of oxygen.

'D'you want me to do it, guv?' McLaren offered kindly. 'There might be stuff on there you don't recognize – there's new apps coming out every day, y'know.'

'Give over, Maurice – he's not a geriatric,' Hart said, shoving herself in front of McLaren. 'Let me do it, boss. I've got quicker thumbs.'

'It might be something on the dark web,' said Gascoyne anxiously. 'You'd need his passwords.'

'You'd need a Tor browser,' said Lœssop.

'Stop talking or I'll send you all back to your desks,' said Slider.

'Yerss, stand back and let the dog see the rabbit,' said Porson, taking the role of dog himself as he inserted his considerable person into the space at Slider's left elbow. It was not that he was fat – quite the opposite – but he did seem to take up a lot of room.

And in the end it wasn't anything hidden or encrypted or even password protected. It was right there in Gallery. Photographs of Gilda Steenkamp.

Atherton, in the favoured position on the other side, whistled soundlessly. 'She wouldn't want *them* to get out onto her fansite.'

'Very tasteful,' said Porson.

'Blimey, she's got a fantastic body for her age,' said McLaren, who had climbed onto the desk behind so he could see over Slider's head.

Slider felt bad suddenly about everybody ogling her, and handed the phone to Swilley, who was at least a woman. The photos were, as Porson had said, tasteful – not porno shots. Steenkamp stretched out on her side on a bed like the Rokeby Venus, head propped on one elbow; sitting backwards on a hard chair staring contemplatively out of the window; kneeling on the bed, arms folded across her breasts; a rear view, kneeling again, looking over her shoulder and laughing; and so on. Ten in all, and you would have called them art photos if you hadn't known who took them. They could have been publicity shots, if she hadn't been naked. She was smiling or laughing in several of them, and there had obviously been no coercion or deception. And the thing that made Slider saddest was the perception that they had been taken with love. Steenkamp did have an amazing body, for which he supposed Lingoss took some credit, and he had shown her in the best light. Perhaps all those hours studying himself in the mirror while making love had given him an eye for it; perhaps he had a natural artistic streak. But he had immortalized in digital form a woman he cared enough about to make her look her best – and a woman who was looking at the camera, and therefore at the photographer, with eyes of love.

She had said it was love between them, and as a cynical policeman who had seen everything his first instinct was to dismiss that as a sad fantasy. But there had been love, at least on her side. And on his side? Love of a sort, anyway.

The photographs were dynamite. Enough to blackmail a celebrity, who would *not* want them falling into the wrong hands.

But Seagram had not talked about blackmail as such, only that it was his 'insurance'. If Seagram thought they would make a divorce case for him, he was out of touch. Adultery was no longer the be all and end all, and though it would work as his grounds for demanding it against her will, it would not necessarily secure him a large slice of her money. But then, if Greyling was remembering accurately, he had spoken of the insurance in terms of the police, if they were too stupid to follow a trail of breadcrumbs.

Breadcrumbs – i.e. the evidence, which as McLaren had said, was all against Steenkamp.

And still, *why*? Why would Seagram – why would either of them – want to kill Lingoss? Steenkamp loved him. Seagram wanted a divorce anyway.

Porson, who had been watching Slider's face, said, 'Time to wheel him in.'

There was no answer at the door for so long, he thought it would not be answered. But in the end it was Gilda Steenkamp who opened it. It was a very different woman from when he had last seen her. Then she had been as elegant and poised as any polished celebrity. Now she looked worn, in loose slacks and a baggy sweater, her un-made-up face was pale, her eyes puffy. Her mouth made a downward bow which he knew, all too well, from the faces of tragedy he had confronted over a long career. The mothers of dead children, the wives of dead husbands, the survivors of dead lovers – the mouth of one who had finally realized the absoluteness of loss.

'I can't talk to you without my solicitor,' she said, but it sounded automatic, as if she didn't really care any more.

'It's your husband we've come to speak to,' Slider said.

'He's not here. He's gone.'

Damn! thought Slider. *Skipped?* He wouldn't get far, but there was a world of weary work involved in tracking down a fugitive. 'He's left?'

She took a moment to register the import of the question, and then said, 'Not left me. He's gone to Northampton, to see a lady with a pair of wine coolers.'

Atherton, behind him, made a slight sound, and Slider knew quite clearly what he was thinking. *Cor, look at the wine coolers on that!*

Gilda Steenkamp flicked a glance at him, then said to Slider, 'Regency wine coolers, *with* their liners. One would be rare enough, but a pair – and in fine condition. It's the sort of thing you could sell ten times over. Not to be missed.'

'You know a lot about antiques.'

'I've had to learn, over the years.'

'When will he be back?'

'I don't know. He didn't say. Tonight some time. He left after lunch, so it could be any time, unless he has dinner somewhere.'

'May we come in and wait?' Slider said. 'I'd like to talk to you.'

She made an escaping movement of her head. 'I'll have to call Michael. I can't talk to you without him present.'

Slider lifted a hand slightly, the gesture you make to a nervous animal. 'This isn't that, I promise you. I just want some information. There's no harm to you here.'

She let them in, walked before them to the drawing room, sat, looked at them passively. She hadn't asked him why he wanted to speak to her husband. *She knows*, he thought, and compassion tightened his chest.

'What do you want to ask me?' she said. 'I can't promise to answer.'

Slider paused, working out the best route. 'Have you and your husband ever talked about divorce?'

She looked at him consideringly, as though trying to work out if answering the question was safe. 'I suppose all couples do at some point.'

'Have you?' She didn't answer. 'I have evidence that he asked you for a divorce and that you refused.'

She looked sour. 'If you know, why ask me?'

'Everything has to be confirmed. And I'd like your side of the story.'

She pushed her hands down between her knees, clasped together. It was almost a girlish pose, except that it came from extreme stress – the knuckles, before they disappeared, were white. 'Yes. He said he wanted a divorce. The first time, oh, about two years ago. I don't remember exactly. Then again more recently – a few months ago, perhaps. I said no. I don't want the publicity. And I couldn't handle the disruption to my writing schedule. Anyway, what would be the point? I never ask him where he is. He's free to come and go. The subject has not been mentioned again. I don't think he was really serious about it. It was just a whim. He's a very attentive husband. Affectionate, even – well, you've seen for yourself how he defends me. He's very loyal.'

'Did he say why he wanted it?'

'He just talked about freedom. I think it was metaphysical rather than specific.'

'Did you think he'd found someone else?'

She wrinkled her nose. 'What a *quaint* phrase. No.'

'Has he ever been unfaithful to you?'

'Not that I know of. Brian is not a very sexual being. That phase of our marriage only lasted a few months. Since then, we've pottered along quite happily as housemates. Despite what you read in the papers, sex is not at the bottom of everything, and not everyone is thinking about it all the time.'

Slider begged to differ, but only internally. 'Until recently. Until you met Erik Lingoss.'

Her eyes immediately reddened, and she bit her lip to control it. 'Must you be so brutal?' she said in a half-voice.

'I'm sorry. I didn't mean to be. Did your husband know about Erik?'

'No. I've told you that already. He had no idea – and he wouldn't have cared if he did know.'

'If that's true, why did you take pains to keep it secret?'

'Because . . . because . . . oh, it was *mine*! Can't you understand? You don't seem stupid. When something is as precious as that, you don't want other people trampling all over it, making comments, *belittling* it. Brian wouldn't have cared – but he might have *laughed.*'

The last word was full of pain. 'I understand,' Slider said.

'You should go,' she said. 'You shouldn't be asking me questions.'

'One more. I'm not trying to trap you or incriminate you. I'm just trying to understand.'

'Just leave me alone.'

'I will go, but please, one last question. Did you pay your husband an allowance?'

She looked surprised. 'What a strange thing to ask.'

'Not so strange. You are, forgive me, very wealthy, and his business is only just breaking even. He has expensive tastes. You have an amicable marriage. It's natural to infer that you must have been supporting him in some way.'

'I give him money, yes,' she said with a faint tautness of anger, 'but not an allowance. That would be humiliating. I transfer a hundred thousand into his bank every January. If he wants more, he only has to ask.'

'The house in Adam and Eve Mews – he couldn't have bought that within that budget.'

She didn't immediately answer, and Atherton said, 'You did know about the mews house?'

'Of course I did,' she snapped. 'That was an investment. They don't come up for sale very often, and when they do, they're worth snapping up, because they keep going up in price. My accountant approved of it. One has to invest somewhere.'

'I presume there's a tenant installed?' Atherton asked casually.

'I suppose there is,' she said indifferently. 'Brian deals with all that. He has a portfolio. There's a house in Radlett and a flat in Ramsgate as well. It's an interest of his. I encourage it. He bought a racehorse once – that was just money thrown away. I don't like waste. We weren't poor when I was a child, but there wasn't a lot to spare, and I was brought up to look carefully at what I spend.'

A portfolio? Slider wondered if there were other little birds in those nests – beautiful boys to be gazed at. Or plump little

mistresses to satisfy his carnal urges. Or, as they were known to
a beleaguered policeman, More Complications.

Atherton, picking up Slider's preoccupation, asked the next
question. 'The Bentley – I suppose he would need extra money
for that, as well?'

'Large purchases like that, he has the bill sent to my accountant.
I've never questioned anything he wanted – even the racehorse.'

'Was it a good buy, the Bentley? Has it been reliable?'

'What an odd question. I have no idea. I believe Bentleys are
reliable. That's why people buy them, isn't it?'

'But it went wrong recently?'

'It didn't break down, if that's what you mean. There was some
sort of electronic glitch. It didn't affect it, as far as driving it was
concerned. But Brian likes his cars to be perfect, so he had it taken
in.' She looked suddenly worn out. 'I think you're just asking
anything that comes into your heads. Will you go now, please. I
really have had enough of this.'

Slider stood, and said, 'You've been very patient. Thank you.
And will you—'

The sound of a key turning in a lock stopped him dead. He
walked to the doorway, looking down the hall towards the front
door. He turned quickly back to Gilda Steenkamp. 'Your handbag,'
he said in a low, urgent voice. 'Do you always leave it on the
hallstand like that?'

She looked puzzled, but said, 'Yes, why?'

There was no more time. The door had opened and Brian
Seagram had come in, in a tailored charcoal wool overcoat and
an old-fashioned trilby, both beaded with rain. He took the hat off
and shook it before he looked up and saw Slider. His head snapped
up, his scalp shifted backwards in shock, and for one sensational
moment Slider thought he was going to bolt. But then, slowly, his
shoulders came down, and he assumed a patient, inquiring look.

'My goodness, you again,' he said. 'Is Michael here, Michael
Friedman? I hope you haven't been bothering my wife without
her solicitor present?'

'It's you I've come to see, Mr Seagram,' said Slider.

TWENTY-ONE
Witness of the Persecution

S lider had got as far as, 'Anything you do say may be given in evidence,' before either spoke.

Then it was Gilda Steenkamp. 'You?' she breathed, in horror. 'It was *you*?'

Seagram's head snapped round to her. 'Shut your mouth,' he said, in a voice unlike any Slider had heard him use before. Then, to Slider, with a sad, headmastery smile: 'You are making a very silly mistake, and I'm afraid you are going to regret it. I shan't say a word to you until I've seen my solicitor, so don't bother asking me any questions.'

'That is your right, sir,' Slider said stolidly. He was more interested in the shock and pain crossing Gilda Steenkamp's face like fast-driven clouds. No, she hadn't exactly *known*, but at some subconscious level she had *suspected*. And now the confirmation was like a second blow on an already wounded place. She put both hands over her mouth, but he could still see her eyes, and he wished he couldn't.

While they waited for Michael Friedman to arrive, Slider got in a quick cup of tea and phoned home.

'We've made an arrest,' he told her. 'Brian Seagram. It's going to be a late session. Maybe an all-nighter. Will you be all right?'

'Of course I will,' she said. 'Your dad and Lydia are in; if I need company I can ask them to come up. But I thought I might do a bit of practice.'

'The p-word? I thought you didn't *do* the p-word.'

'Got to keep the fingers flexible. You never know when they might be needed.'

'You're missing it already. I'm sorry,' he said, feeling the familiar guilt creeping up.

'Pregnancy was a joint enterprise,' she said, banishing it. 'I was there when the dastardly deed was done. Speaking of which – it was the husband? Well, you'll be glad it wasn't her, anyway,' she said from long experience of his sensibilities.

'I can't really talk about it,' he said distractedly. 'I'll tell you everything when I see you.'

But from those same sensibilities, he was almost wishing it had been Steenkamp, because now she would have to live not only with the pain of losing her lover, but of knowing the man closest to her, whom she had trusted, had deliberately caused her that pain.

A solicitor in a five-thousand-pound Jermyn Street suit could never look less than polished, but when it came to lawyers, a lowly copper had to take comfort where he could, and Slider believed that Michael Friedman was the tiniest fraction less impenetrable than before. OK, so a barnacle would have skidded straight off him with a cry of despair, but there were many scathing things he could have said and didn't. Slider took that as encouragement. And when they all faced each other across the table in the interview room, Friedman was the one who looked as though he wished he wasn't there.

Seagram looked – not quite amused, but close to smug. 'Michael's assured me I don't have to answer any of your questions,' he said, 'so you can say what you like. It's your own time you'll be wasting. I shan't say a thing.'

Slider nodded. 'If that's the way you want it. I'll tell you what happened on the evening of the fourth of November, and you can correct me if I go wrong, all right?'

Seagram shrugged, folded his arms, and said nothing.

'It was a good plan,' Slider went on in approving tones. 'If slightly over-engineered in some parts. To begin with, your wife, as both you and she confirmed, was accustomed to working in her study from nine p.m. until at least midnight, and during that time was never to be disturbed. She never came out and you never went in. But you made a point of showing me your "snug", where you watched television that evening, to demonstrate to me that you could not have seen or heard if she had decided to slip out of the house during that time.'

Seagram's face tightened slightly. 'I *told* you—'

Friedman coughed, and Seagram shut his mouth.

'Yes, you *told* me you were sure she was there. You were playing the part of the loyal husband, while subtly warning me that she really had no alibi at all. I get it now. It was very clever. But it means, alas, that you have no alibi either.'

'*I* don't need an alibi.' It seemed he'd forgotten the bit about not saying a thing. That was all to the good from Slider's point of view.

'To continue: when you were sure she was settled, you slipped out, taking her keys, mobile and debit card from her handbag, which she always left on the hall table. You took her car, the red Mazda you despised so much, and drove over to Erik Lingoss's flat.'

Seagram stirred, and Slider could tell he wanted to say, 'Preposterous!' It was a word tailor-made for him. But Friedman was looking at him hard, and he said nothing.

'On the way you stopped at a cashpoint in Kensington High Street and used her debit card to withdraw seven hundred pounds. An odd amount. One that sticks in the mind – not two-fifty, not five, but seven. The reason for that we will come to. You also made a telephone call from your wife's phone to Erik Lingoss, presumably saying that you were on your way. I think you must have made the appointment with him at some earlier stage, or you couldn't have been sure he would be at home. Am I right?'

Seagram made a little huffing noise, shook his head slightly, in a pitying way, and folded his arms tighter.

'At Erik's house, you went into the bedroom with him – where his training equipment was laid out. You picked up one of his weights, and hit him with it, knocking him unconscious. I think you thought you had killed him outright. You put the seven hundred pounds under his pillow, where it would be found, the unusual amount noted and a certain inference would be bound to be drawn. Then you went into the other room. There you put your wife's initials in his appointments diary for that day – G.S. nine thirty p.m. I suppose that on a previous visit you had seen the way he recorded his professional appointments – perhaps he'd answered the phone while you were present. I think you probably also examined his client address book to make sure your name didn't appear in it.'

'Why should it? I wasn't one of his clients.'

'Brian, it would be better if you didn't say anything,' Friedman warned him. Then, to Slider: 'This is all pure supposition. You haven't produced the slightest shred of evidence.'

Slider ignored him and continued with the narrative. 'Probably at this point you heard a sound from the other room, and went back to discover that Lingoss was not dead after all. He was stirring, perhaps moaning. How hard could it be to kill the man? You grabbed the barbell again in a fury and beat his head to a pulp.' Seagram's face was pale, but hard; Friedman was maintaining a professional blank, but Slider liked to think his eyes were worried. 'Then you picked up his phone and left, drove away in the Mazda, knowing that once the police had worked out that G.S. in the appointments book was Gilda Steenkamp, they would be able to trace the movement of her car between your home and Erik's flat. They would check her phone and find she had rung him just before the appointment. And they would check her bank statement and find that she had drawn out seven hundred pounds – the same amount as was stashed under his pillow. It's what you called "a trail of breadcrumbs".'

When he said those words, Seagram's eyes, which had been fixed on the wall behind Slider's head, flicked for an instant to his face. Slider wondered whether he remembered saying them to Greyling, or if he thought his mind had been read. But he was not thrown yet. He carved his features into a pitying smile and said, 'What you seem to be laying out is evidence of my wife's guilt, and while I am shocked beyond measure that you should suspect her, I don't see what this has to do with me.'

Friedman rallied. 'I think you must present some evidence of these allegations, inspector, or immediately release my client. Otherwise we may have to consider an action for wrongful arrest.'

'I shall certainly present evidence,' Slider told him. 'There are fingermarks on the cover of both the address book and the diary. Paper is very poor at taking fingermarks, but Moleskine is better. They're not absolutely distinct, but we might get a partial. Then there's the seven hundred pounds drawn out of her account.'

'How could I draw that out of her account without her PIN number?' Seagram said triumphantly.

'Well, married couples often do know each other's PINs. Where there is trust between them – and I'm sure there was trust between you and your wife.'

'But you can't *prove* that I knew it,' Seagram crowed.

'You must have known it, because you did draw out the money.' Slider's eyes were fixed unwaveringly on Seagram. 'Did you not know that cashpoint machines have cameras in them these days?'

'*Bank* ATMs do,' Seagram said contemptuously, 'but that one's not a bank machine.'

'How do you know which machine I am referring to?'

Seagram looked confused.

Friedman closed his eyes for an instant. 'I told you, you don't have to say *anything*,' he said.

Slider went on. 'You are right, that particular machine is *not* a bank ATM. It's a private one. And it doesn't have an integral camera. It does, however, have a camera mounted on the building above it, which you've probably never noticed. If you'd like to look at the monitor.' He nodded to Atherton, who cued the tape. Friedman was back in full professional stoneface mode, and did not react, but he would know it was a body blow; Seagram glared at the screen as if to say, *right, machine, you're going to regret this.*

'We've correlated the time of withdrawal with the time of this camera shot. Would you like to explain why you withdrew seven hundred pounds cash from your wife's account?'

'I can think of a dozen reasons why I might, but I'm not saying anything,' said Seagram. 'I don't have to offer explanations.'

Atherton scribbled something and pushed it in front of Slider. *Fatally gabby*, it said. Both Friedman and Seagram watched the bit of business. Slider nodded to Atherton. Like the adulterer who deep down wanted to get caught, the cleverer they thought they had been, the more they subconsciously longed to tell about it. What was the point of stunningly fooling the police if the police never knew how they had been fooled? Seagram *would* talk – it was a question of leading him the right way so that it all came out.

Slider continued, 'You don't have to explain, of course, but may I remind you that it may harm your defence if you do not mention during questioning something you later rely on in court?'

Seagram looked at Friedman. 'I think we should go now. Our

friend here seems to be on a fishing expedition – or else he's in
the grip of a strange fantasy. Either way—'

'We have Erik's mobile phone,' Slider said calmly. First blow,
to the chin. 'We spoke to Leon Greyling.' Second blow, to the
solar plexus.

Seagram's face twisted instantly, shockingly with rage. There
was temper under there, rarely allowed out. 'That little swine!
What's he been telling you? He's a pathological liar. Don't
believe anything he says!'

Atherton had laid the mobile, in its evidence bag, on the table.
He said, 'There are quite a number of fingermarks on it, and not
all of them are Erik's. You didn't think it necessary to use gloves?
I suppose you meant to wipe it clean when – or if – it was necessary to "find" it.' He made the inverted commas around *find* clear.
'Perhaps when you tragically, accidentally, stumbled across it in
your wife's handbag or underwear drawer: the final proof that she
must have killed him. You took it away from Lingoss's flat, and
left it with Leon Greyling for safekeeping.'

'Not proof,' Seagram said. He sounded short of breath. He
looked at Friedman. 'None of this is proof, is it?' Friedman looked
back gravely but said nothing.

Slider put in the final upper-cut. 'We also have your
handkerchief.'

'What handkerchief?' His eyes snapped back to Slider. Slider
saw that he had forgotten it. Atherton laid it, in its bag, on the
table.

'You wiped your face with it. Meant to shove it into your pocket
but it fell out, and in the excitement of the moment you didn't
notice. There was blood on it, Mr Seagram. Blood and brain matter.
When you bend over a prone man and beat his head with a heavy
object, there is always splatter. Perhaps you didn't know that? And
when you wipe it off your face with your handkerchief, it's advis-
able to make sure you don't mislay the handkerchief afterwards.'

For once Seagram didn't speak. His eyes moved and he gripped
the edge of the table as his brain scrabbled for a way out.

Friedman was the one who spoke. 'I would like a private word
with my client, if you don't mind,' he said.

'Of course,' said Slider.

*   *   *

In the corridor, Atherton rubbed his hands and said, 'The game's afoot. And he's on the wrong one. D'you think he'll cough?'

'Friedman will be trying to persuade him to as we speak, I imagine. Plead mitigation.'

Atherton scoffed. 'As in "something come over me, guv"? The old red mist plea?'

'He hasn't got much else,' Slider said.

'You almost have to feel sorry for him, don't you?'

'Seagram?' Slider was surprised.

'Friedman. I bet he's only doing Seagram as a favour to Gilda Steenkamp, the one with all the money. He must have been a bit puzzled as to why we fastened on her husband. Well, he knows now.'

'We're not home and dry. As long as Tufty comes up with a match, we're safe. The rest of it . . . well, I'm sure a glossy barrister of the sort Friedman would know could explain it away. And we still don't know *why*. Without a *why*, the jury won't like it.'

'*You* won't like it,' Atherton corrected shrewdly.

'I like to understand things.'

'Understatement of the decade,' said Atherton.

'My client has agreed to talk to you,' Friedman announced, making it sound magnanimous and noble. Seagram no longer looked smug; he looked angry and defiant. If he folded his arms any more tightly he'd crack his own ribs.

Slider considered him for a long moment, wondering how best to begin. It would all come out, if he could get him going. First, he needed to relax him, with an off-topic question.

'How come you own an antiques business when you don't like antiques?'

Seagram looked surprised, as Slider had wanted him to be. His arm-clench relaxed slightly. He didn't question how Slider knew he didn't like antiques, but said, 'It was the family business. My grandfather started it. My father built it up. He made such a success of it, he was able to take over Heneage's, and they were the biggest name in the field in those days. He made Seagram an even bigger name. It was natural that I should be expected to go into the business and carry it on.'

'Couldn't you have said no?'

He laughed, a short, humourless bark. 'You didn't say no to my father.'

'He was a hard man?'

'He was . . .' Seagram seemed to be searching for a word sufficiently laudatory. But then his mouth twisted suddenly. 'He was a sadistic brute.'

'Did he hurt you?'

'He believed boys ought to be thrashed regularly for their own good. Spare the rod and all that sort of thing. Make a man of your son. It was the waiting that was the worst part. "Go to your room!" And then you'd wait ten minutes, fifteen, twenty, knowing what was coming. That was the sadistic part. I believe he loved it, the old ogre. He never left it too long, so you'd start believing he'd forgotten. Just long enough to have you wetting your pants in fear.'

'What about your mother?'

'She was a concert pianist – Myra Solomons?'

He said it as if Slider ought to have heard of her, so he nodded appreciatively. 'I mean, couldn't she have defended you against your father?'

He looked away for a moment. 'She didn't care for me. I had lessons from the age of seven, but I had no talent. I tried, for her sake, but she couldn't understand that music really meant nothing to me. I didn't hear it the way she heard it. My sister Lainie – Elaine – was brilliant. She was beautiful, clever, and talented. They both adored her. She was going to follow in my mother's footsteps. I was a disappointment to both of them. They had no time for me.' He paused, watching some internal home movie. Slider waited. Seagram was absorbed by his story now; he would talk without prompting. 'She was drowned in a boating accident when she was seventeen. It was the most awful tragedy. My mother never really got over it. My father threw himself into the business. I couldn't refuse to be part of it, could I?'

'Were you jealous of your sister?'

'I loved her,' he said, as if surprised by the question. 'She was . . . supremely loveable.' He paused a moment. 'She was older than me. Sometimes she tried to distract my father when he got in one of his rages, and sometimes it worked. She saved me some thrashings. But not all. After she died his temper got worse. I wasn't sorry when he died. He had a stroke while he was bawling

out a warehouseman who'd scratched a walnut loo table. I know
it was wrong of me, but I was glad he'd gone.'

'It's understandable,' Slider said.

'I thought, when he was gone, my mother would . . . But she
still had no time for me. Music was her world, and I was tone-
deaf. I had nothing to say to her.'

'It must have been a relief to you when you got married and
moved away.'

'Gilda reminded me a bit of Lainie. She was slim and dark and
vivacious too. I thought . . .' He paused, still staring at the past.
His mouth made a sneer. 'Turns out I was a disappointment to
her, too.'

'Why was that?' Slider asked. But Seagram didn't answer. Slider
remembered what Gilda Steenkamp had said about their physical
relationship not lasting long. Perhaps that was it.

'When did you first know you were attracted to men?' he asked
quietly, hoping to slip the question in without startling the quarry
to flight.

Seagram was a long time answering, and Slider held his breath.

'Michelangelo's *David*,' he began at last. 'My father had a scale
copy of it that he acquired for a client. It was in the shop for a
couple of weeks before they could take delivery. It was the first
time I'd appreciated the absolute beauty of the male body. It was
the curve of his neck that struck me first. I wanted to stroke it.
When it had gone, I looked for more examples, in paintings, in
art books – photographs of statues. Then one day I came across
a magazine in a shop in Monmouth Street, a newsagents. It was
. . . I suppose it was published as pornography, but there
was nothing gross about it, just photographs of nude, or near-nude
men posing. But my father found me looking at it, and he thrashed
me. The worst thrashing of my life. So after that, I was careful
not to be seen looking.'

'Did you have experiences with real men?'

He didn't seem to resent the question. 'No,' he said. 'That
wasn't possible. I made do with photographs. And museums. Thank
God for the B M.' A silence. 'Then I got married, and for a while
it was all right. I had enough new experiences, and the business
to run. And company. I thought Gilda . . . would be a friend, I
suppose. I'd never had a friend, since Lainie. But antiques bore

me, the business bores me, and then Gilda started to be successful and had less and less time for me until . . .' He paused. 'I was at a loss. I thought, is this all there is in life for me? Is this it? And then one day I got a ticket for a pre-viewing of modern art for auction at Spink. And I saw that it didn't all have to be brown furniture and oils. There was life and colour and . . . it was like being reborn. And there was a young man.'

He stopped. Slider waited. Just as he felt a little reboot might be needed, Seagram came back online and said, 'His name was Desmond. He had skin like milk. For one lovely summer, we went everywhere together, looked at the world with one pair of eyes. But he was a student working for the vacation, and when October came he went back to Ireland. I didn't want anyone else after that. I found my outlet in collecting contemporary art. And cars – beautiful cars. My search for perfection.'

'Was that why you bought the racehorse?'

'Horses are beautiful,' he agreed, 'in the same way. Sadly, they are expected to produce money, and mine didn't. Gilda was angry. She didn't understand that the money wasn't important. She thought it should be an investment. She has a pedestrian soul. She writes, but essentially she is not an artist – the souk and the bazaar are in her blood. They are what drives her. So I didn't buy another.'

'You bought property instead.'

'That *is* an investment,' he said absently. 'Nothing perfect about houses. Though they can have little elements of beauty. A line here, a moulding there. But they're not organic.'

'And then there was Leon Greyling,' Slider said.

'Yes, beautiful Leon. I found him at the same time as my new car. The car, I fear, will last longer. His body is lovely, but his mind is prosaic. He too often jars me by the things he says. But he's been useful as a caretaker of my collection. Gilda didn't like my pieces so I had to keep them in a storage facility and visit them when I could. I don't know why I didn't think of buying a house for them before.'

'She doesn't mind that the house doesn't bring in rent?'

'She doesn't know. She never bothers with the details of such things.'

'It's not really an investment, is it, if there's no return on it?'

He shrugged. 'The capital value will always increase.'

'So she doesn't know that you installed Leon in the mews house?'

'No, why should she?'

'She's never met Leon?'

'Of course not.'

'She doesn't know about your relationship with him?'

Now he scowled, irritated at being dragged back from the benign past to the fractious present. 'My relationship with Leon is entirely innocent. I don't know what he's told you—'

'He said your relationship with him was innocent.'

'Oh.' The scowl cleared. He looked disconcerted.

'He said you like to look at him.'

'He was the best I'd found, since Desmond.'

'Until you met Erik.'

His face took on a stalled look, as if he'd just remembered what he was doing here.

'Tell me about Erik,' Slider said.

TWENTY-TWO
Un Po' Per Non Morire

It was not often you saw a solicitor looking uncomfortable. Slider took a beat to enjoy it before he continued.

'Shall we begin at the beginning? How did you first meet Erik Lingoss?' For a moment Seagram looked as though he was going to deny knowing him, so Slider prompted, 'Was it during the TV filming at the shop?'

'*Lockhart*,' said Seagram, almost absently. 'Pure trash.'

'That was in June this year?'

'Leon had a small part in it. He brought Erik in to watch. I didn't know they knew each other. Apparently, they had both used the same gym for a short time.'

'He brought Erik in?'

'Not into the shop, of course – no one was allowed in while they were filming. The back office. They'd set up a monitor there. I was watching from there to keep an eye on the stock. And in case they wanted anything moving. Leon brought him in and . . .' He drew a breath, even at the memory. 'He was like a young god,' he said softly. 'He was David, made flesh.' He lapsed into a brooding silence.

Slider gave him his space. He guessed this was going to be difficult for him. Finally, he prompted him. 'What happened?'

Seagram came back, more slowly this time, like a tired swimmer breaking the surface. 'I knew, as soon as I saw him. And I knew he felt the same. It was as if we didn't need words. We communicated on another level.'

'How did the relationship develop?'

'We chatted for a bit until Leon left. When we were alone I said that I knew he was my wife's trainer, and asked if he would be mine as well. But I said, not at home. I said I didn't want my wife to know. He didn't ask why. He understood. He just smiled. And he said he could take me to his own flat, and that he promised absolute discretion. We made an appointment. When I went there the first time I was nervous. I thought it would be difficult – embarrassing – that I would have to explain that I wasn't really interested in keep-fit. But he seemed to understand without words. It was as if . . . our minds were on the same plane. I never had to explain anything to him. He always understood exactly what I meant, what I was thinking – what I wanted.'

'Were you lovers?' Slider asked.

He didn't want to answer that. He looked away, at the ceiling, at his hands. Slider intuited that he was afraid of being laughed at, mocked, rather than afraid of incriminating himself. He was, after all, in an environment not only alien to him, but brutally masculine in the most old-fashioned way. Sweat and feet and testosterone and suppressed violence. No, you couldn't imagine him at a gym, even a posh one like Shapes. Inside the large, well-fed, well-dressed body there was something as tender as a pea shoot that he had to protect.

'Not in the way you mean,' he said at last. 'You wouldn't understand.'

Slider tried different words. 'You loved him?'

Then he looked up, on the defensive, afraid of ridicule, hostility. 'I love beautiful things. So do many people – it's how I make my living, appreciating beautiful things, helping others to acquire them. Artefacts, wrought by the most skilled in society, in a futile quest to replicate the beauty that is in nature. But the beauty in nature is tragically short-lived. Perhaps that's why Michelangelo made his statue – because he knew his boy would grow up. Grow old.'

It wasn't an answer of course – except that it was, in a way. 'Did he love you?' Slider asked.

'*Yes.*' He said it vehemently, as if expecting challenge. Then a bleakness seeped in. 'I believed he did. I believed him. Now . . . I don't know. He must have. How could anybody act a part that convincingly? And yet – what he did . . .'

Time for provocation. 'He betrayed you.'

Seagram didn't answer, staring broodingly at his memories.

'How did you know about the photographs?' Slider asked.

He came back. 'You've seen them?'

'Of course,' said Slider. 'You left a trail all the way to Adam and Eve Mews and Leon Greyling. Why did you take the phone to him, by the way?'

'I needed a safe place to leave it.'

'But by telephoning him from your wife's phone, you led us to him. Why did you do that?'

He rubbed a hand over his forehead. 'It was a mistake. I thought it was my phone. I didn't notice – didn't realize—'

'It's not so surprising. You had a lot of phones to juggle with,' Slider said kindly. 'Yours, hers, Erik's. And you had a lot on your mind. You *had* just killed a man.'

'No!' Seagram cried, and it sounded like genuine pain.

'It's too late to deny it. We have the evidence,' Slider said, mostly for Friedman's sake. 'But I want to understand *why*. I want *your* side of the story.' Those, like Seagram, who had never felt understood, would fall for that one every time. But with Slider it was always true. He really did want to know. 'How did you know about the photos?'

Yes, now he was looking at Slider, urging his comprehension. 'It was about a week before. I was going to see a client in Salisbury. I was supposed to be out all day. But when I got to the motorway, he rang and cancelled, so I turned round and went home. When I let myself in, I heard a murmur of voices, and I remembered that she was having one of her training sessions. I didn't want to see Erik with her, so I was going to leave again. But then I heard Gilda laugh. It was the sort of laugh . . . A low chuckle . . . I hadn't heard her laugh like that since when we were first married. It made the hair stand up on my scalp. So I had to see. I had to know how he could make her laugh like that. I tiptoed down the passage. The voices were coming from her bedroom, not the spare room she uses as a gym. The door was half open. I could see through without getting right up to it. I saw her, naked, striking a pose, kneeling on the bed, with her hands behind her head, making her breasts stand up.' He shuddered. 'And then – Erik must have been moving about, trying different angles. He passed across between her and the door, photographing with his phone. He was naked too. His back was to me, but there wasn't an inch of his body I didn't know.' His face screwed up in pain. 'For six months, I had loved him. And he was betraying me – *with my own wife!*'

Plainly he saw no irony in the statement.

'Why didn't you confront them?' Slider asked.

'Confront them? No! God, no.' His voice was shaky. 'I couldn't, not then. It was all too much. I felt as if I'd got a javelin through the chest. I could hardly breathe. I couldn't think. I had to get away from there. I had to get away.'

'What did you do?'

'I slipped out of the house again, got in my car and drove. I had no idea where. I just drove. I finally stopped in a layby somewhere out west of London. Somewhere near Marlborough. I must have been on the motorway at some point to have got so far but I don't remember anything about it.' There was a long pause, and when he resumed he was composed again, his face expressionless. 'Then I went home. And that was that.'

'And that's when you started plotting your revenge?' Slider said.

'You don't have to answer that,' Friedman intervened.

Seagram looked at him blankly, as though he had forgotten who he was. He looked at Slider again. 'Revenge? It wasn't revenge. When I thought about it, when I realized what he'd done, how he'd betrayed – not just me, but *us*, and the beauty . . . There had been perfection, and now it was . . . trammelled. I knew he had to die. It wasn't revenge, it was . . . euthanasia. I couldn't leave him like that, a broken thing. I had to take responsibility. That's what a man does – a real man.'

Slider said, 'I can see that – but your wife? Didn't she deserve to die too?'

'You don't have to answer that,' said Friedman again, but Seagram didn't seem even to hear him. His eyes were fixed on Slider, *willing* him to understand.

'I thought of it,' he said. 'If I'd gone in right away, when I saw them, perhaps. But afterwards, when I thought about it, I realized she was the real guilty party. I didn't want him to suffer, I wanted him to die cleanly, but that was too good for her. She *should* suffer for what she did. Then I saw a way that she could be made to pay. She'd killed him, the best bit of him, his beauty and his innocence, so why shouldn't she be blamed for his murder? There's no death sentence now, but perhaps twenty years in a prison cell thinking about it was better. She'd suffer more that way. And it might bring her to a proper frame of mind.'

'And you,' Slider said approvingly, 'would get the divorce you'd been asking for, and which she was blocking. What better grounds could there be than her being found guilty of murder? And there's not a divorce judge in the land that wouldn't give the husband of a convicted murderess a generous settlement.'

'This is quite improper,' said Friedman. 'You are badgering my client, provoking him. This must stop at once.'

Slider lifted a hand in acknowledgement. He had done enough, anyway. Seagram would speak unprompted now. He had gone beyond reason. He panted with anger.

'Why shouldn't I have the money? I've supported her emotionally all these years, for little reward. She couldn't have written her best-selling novels without me to take care of her, keep everyone away, make a stable home for her, wait on her hand and foot, *cherish* her. And what thanks have I ever had? Nothing but disparagement and indifference – "Oh, not now, Brian, I'm writing." Writing! Yes, that was the only important thing in the world!' He glared at Slider as though he might be one of those wretches who sided with his wife. 'But what about *my* wants, *my* needs? She never cared a jot about them. And when I finally asked her for a divorce, she waved it away, dismissed it, because it might adversely affect her *career*. Her precious career! Her sacred bloody talent!' He was grinding his teeth now, his fists clenched on the table. 'She had everything, and I got nothing out of it, and when I found one thing for myself, one little piece of beauty that was mine, she took that away too. I wish I had killed her now. I should have run in there and smashed them both right there and then, smashed them and smashed them and killed them! They both deserved to die!'

'That man,' said Atherton as they walked away, 'is not playing with a full keyboard. If Friedman's thinking of entering an insanity plea, he's got plenty to choose from. Mummy issues, father issues, dead sister issues. Sexual inadequacy, sado-masochism, paranoia, megalomania, schizophrenia. He's a walking text book of neuroses.'

'That's probably why he allowed him to talk,' said Slider.

'Emasculation by his father. Emasculation by his more successful wife. Trying to replace his idealized sister with a pure love of boys. Steenkamp reminded him of her, he said – but she had gross sexual requirements. Not pure enough. Greyling was pure, but not very bright. And then there was Lingoss. Hmm.'

'And so much anger,' Slider said. 'Repressed, of course. Hit by his father, can't hit back, squash it all down until one day it just erupts. How many times have we seen that?'

'Well, it keeps us in a job,' said Atherton.

'We've got one of the soundest cases we've ever had, with the car trace, the mobile trace, the ATM camera, Greyling's testimony, fingermarks on the books and the phone – even if they're only partials – and the DNA from the handkerchief. And now a top-notch motive.'

'"Jealousy is cruel as the grave",' Atherton quoted. 'But, you were going to say, it takes the shine off it when the perpetrator is as nutty as a fruitcake?'

'I don't think,' said Slider slowly, 'I have ever come across a more lonely man.' It made him shiver to think about it.

They took the stairs. 'All these people,' Atherton marvelled, 'in love with Lingoss and thinking he was in love with them. He must have had something. But what? We thought at first he was a shallow narcissist.'

'Perhaps he was just hollow enough for people to fill him with their own fantasies,' Slider said.

'All things to all men? Well, I suppose that's possible.'

'He took people's colour and gave it back to them enhanced. He wasn't a Narcissus, he was a chameleon. And perhaps he was happy to be the person of their dreams, as long as it contributed to his.'

'Money.'

'Financial freedom.' Slider frowned. 'He seems to me to be the victim in all this.'

'He *was* the victim, guv,' Atherton pointed out kindly.

'You know what I mean. Everybody wanted a piece of him. He was being pecked to death, one beakful at a time.'

'I wonder if *he* loved any of *them*?'

'He cared enough for Gilda Steenkamp to break it off with Lucy just for the asking. Maybe he really did love her.'

'Oh, come on!'

'Why did he take pictures of her, and keep them, if it wasn't love?'

'You're a romantic at heart, really, aren't you? Gilda Steenkamp was the wealthiest of all his wealthy clients.'

'Doesn't mean he didn't care for her,' Slider said. 'Rich people need loving as much as poor people.'

'If you say, "or perhaps more" I shall walk away. Does it not occur to you he had future blackmail in mind?'

Slider shook his head dismissively. 'You have to think,' he said, 'what a person needs most. And what Lingoss was most missing in his life, it seems to me, was a proper mother.'

Atherton grimaced. 'One he could boff? Straight to Oedipus.'

'Don't be crass,' said Slider. 'You know what I mean.'

'I do. Don't have to agree with you, though.' Atherton stretched. 'It's going to be a long night.'

'I must have tea before we start again,' Slider said. 'About a bucketful.'

'We'd better have something to eat as well,' Atherton said. 'I'll send someone out for sandwiches. What did you mean, by the way, about the plot being over-engineered?'

'Eh? Oh, putting the car in for repair. And the anniversary celebration. Showing he was a loving husband. I don't think those were really necessary.'

'I suppose once you start plotting something like this it's hard to leave it alone. You keep elaborating. You keep trying to second-guess what might come back to trip you up.' They turned the corner. 'I'm glad it wasn't Steenkamp in the end, though. She's still got more books in her.'

'She could write in prison,' Slider said. 'Jeffrey Archer did, didn't he?'

'You're thinking of Oscar Wilde.'

'I rarely if ever think of Oscar Wilde.'

'You will, guv'nor, you will.'

He had turned off his mobile, of course, while he took the inter-view, and reaching his office was about to turn it back on when Lawrence came in from the CID room and said, 'There's a couple of messages for you, sir, to ring home. I hope it's nothing serious.' She gave him a sympathetic and yet hungry look. We're all drama junkies these days, he thought.

Lydia answered, which made his heart jump with alarm. But

she said at once, 'You're not to worry, it's not bad news. Joanna
went into labour about seven o'clock. She didn't want you to be
bothered, knowing you'd be doing an important interview. And
she thought there was enough time. But it started to go quickly.
It's like that sometimes with second babies. Your dad took her
in, and I stayed to look after little George.' She always called
him that because Slider's father's name was also George. 'I
offered to be the one to go with her, but she thought I'd be better
with the boy if it was a long time, not knowing when you'd be
able to get away. You know I'm happy to stay on. I'll feed him
and put him to bed, and if necessary I can bed down in the spare
room.'

'You're wonderful. Thank you. Is she all right?'

'Last bulletin from your dad she was fine, but I haven't heard
anything for a while now. But she'll be all right,' Lydia said
comfortably. 'She's healthy as a horse.'

Yes, but horses could get ill and be hurt, couldn't they, and this
was childbirth, the big lottery, all hunky-dory and straightforward
until it wasn't.

'Go,' said Porson. 'Go straight to the hospital. You don't want to
miss all the fun.'

Fun? Slider thought. 'I think I've missed it already,' he said.

'Never mind. There's hours of work here, and Seagram's not
going anywhere. I can do anything you'd be doing.' As Slider
hesitated, Porson's eyebrows shot up. 'What? You think I can't do
the basics? You think I live in some ivory towel, cut off from the
world? I was a copper when you were in short pants, laddie.'

He wasn't that much older than Slider, of course, but it's the
thought that counts.

And then there was the traffic, the bloody, bloody traffic, and what
with bus lanes and bike lanes cramming everyone else into single
file it was never going to be any better. When you're stuck in a
car crawling along there's nothing to take your mind off various
scenarios which your subconscious, the bad fairy of whimsy, likes
to spread out for your amusement. He put the spinner on to go
round Hammersmith Broadway, which was all right as far as it
went, but London red buses have a dispensation from God and

don't have to heed the police or indeed anything else. He always thought the famous wartime photograph of the number 77 to King's Cross stuck in a bomb crater was mostly evidence of the bus driver's belief in his own immortality.

Then there was finding somewhere to park, and finding the way in. All the doors seemed to be locked or have No Entry signs on them. Are hospitals like that to keep people out, or keep the one's they've caught in? Finding someone to admit there was such a person as Joanna in the system. Finding the ward. Then finding anyone who *worked* on the ward. A large West Indian cleaner shrieked with laughter when he applied to her for information and said, 'Don't ask me, darlin', I only work here.' Amusing, yes, but not helpful.

Finally, it was Dad who found him. 'I thought I heard your voice,' he said. Slider scanned his father's face, and saw no doom or horror in it. 'She's in a private room, round here. Room G.'

'Wh—?'

'They ran out of beds on the ward, that's all. It's not costing anything.'

He hadn't been thinking of cost. He'd been thinking they put people in private rooms who are too sick for the ward.

Mr Slider read it in his face. 'She's fine. It was really quick.'

'She's had it?'

'All done and dusted. I'm not sure, I think she'd been having pains at home for a while and not told us. I think she was hoping you'd get back in time to go with her. Almost left it too late – once she started the second stage it was over like lightning. But it's all right now. Go on, you daft devil, don't just stand there – go in. She's waiting for you.'

When he was a boy, and came home from school to seek out his mother in the kitchen, sometimes the surge of love and joy at seeing her again was quite simply too much. Had to be deferred, deflected, or he might die of it. So instead of rushing to her and flinging his arms around her waist, he would pour out extravagant caresses on the smooth black head of Ben, their collie, while Ben, willing proxy, had wriggled his rear end and licked Slider's face. His mother had understood. She would look round from the stove (he always remembered her standing at the stove) and smile, and remark to the unseen audience, 'He kisses the dog!'

Joanna understood, too. When he stepped into the room he

couldn't look at her, and heard himself say, idiotically, 'This is a nice room. Lots of light.'

And she said, 'I'm glad you like it. I picked out the wallpaper myself.' *He kisses the dog.*

But then it was all right, and he could look at her, and bear the terrible stretching pain of his love for her that sometimes seemed as though it would split him in two. She was propped up on pillows in the high, white bed, and to one who had got used to her big belly she looked unexpectedly flat, like a cartoon of the unpopular schoolteacher run over by a steamroller. She looked tired, but no more than at the end of a long day at work; only her flattened, sweat-darkened hair gave the game away. Normally her hair stood up and out like the petals of a chrysanthemum. It took a lot to wilt it.

He crossed to the bed and took her hand; plugged himself in; life started up again. 'Are you all right?'

'Piece of cake,' she said boastfully.

He smiled, and saw it reflected in her eyes. 'I like cake.'

'Everybody likes cake.'

His eyes were avoiding the other significant piece of furniture in the room, the hospital-issue cot, with something doll-sized and tightly wrapped under the cover, a small red face between hospital-issue cotton shawl and ludicrous stockinet hat. Too newly born to have its own clothes from home yet. And he had the feeling again, that he would die if he looked properly too soon.

'Considering how big you were,' he said, 'it looks like a very small cake.'

'Next time, you can bake it in *your* oven. It didn't feel all that small on the way out.' Now her smile was quizzical. 'Don't you want to know what we got? I made your dad promise not to tell you. And I made him make Lydia promise as well.'

'He didn't. He was as good as his word,' said Slider. Then he looked.

'What do you think we should call her?' Joanna asked.